W9-AXT-037

She was the only
woman as wickedly
sensual as he was . . .
and nothing
would stop him
from taking her
for his own.

"I want every man in London to know you're mine."

"I belong to no man, Lord Erith."

"You'll belong to me."

Before she could move, he bent across the table and grasped her chin.

His implacable hold stifled struggle or protest. Panting like a trapped fledgling, she waited for his mouth to meet hers. Her heart beat so fast, she thought it would burst from her chest. For one moment, she felt like a virgin trapped in a rake's net.

Those firm, almost cruel lips captured hers. A moment's clinging pressure. Hot like fire. Hard like steel.

He let her go and stepped away with a bow. "Until this evening."

Before she could summon an adequate reply, he turned on his heel and strode from the room.

Dazed and shaking, she clenched and unclenched her fists in her lap. His taste lingered. Rich. Tantalizing. Evocative.

"Damn you, Erith," she whispered to the empty room. "Damn you to hell."

By Anna Campbell

TEMPT THE DEVIL
UNTOUCHED
CLAIMING THE COURTESAN

Anna Campbell

TEMPT THE DEVIL

AVON

An Imprint of HarperCollinsPublishers

AVON BOOKS
An Imprint of HarperCollins*Publishers*
10 East 53rd Street
New York, New York 10022-5299

*I'd like to dedicate this book
to a remarkable woman
who was a huge influence on me
as I grew up.
Aunty Joan, I still miss you.*

Acknowledgments

Thanks to everyone at Avon Books. You're the greatest people to work with and I'm eternally grateful I'm an Avon author. Thanks especially to my editors, Lucia Macro and May Chen, to the fabulously talented folk in the Art Department, and to the team in Marketing, who always do a wonderful job of letting the world know that another Anna Campbell book is about to be unleashed. I'd also like to thank Linda Funnell and her team at Avon Australia, who have been unfailingly supportive to a new Aussie romance author. I'd also like to express my deep appreciation for the sterling efforts of my agents, Paige Wheeler and Nancy Yost.

As always, I would like to offer heartfelt thanks to my critique partner and dear friend, Annie West. Annie, what would I do without you? I'd also like to express my sincerest gratitude to Christine Wells, Vanessa Barneveld, and Sharon Arkell, for their help and friendship. And a big thank-you to all my Bandita buddies on the Romance Bandits blog. You girls never fail to give me a smile and remind me why being a writer is the greatest job in the world. I'd also like to thank my friend Susan Parisi, whose fascinating conversations about the darker side of life launched me on my current writing career.

Above all, my warmest gratitude goes to all those readers who contacted me to say how much they enjoyed my previous books. Your pleasure in my stories is my greatest reward.

Chapter 1

London
April 1826

$\mathscr{A}$cross the packed, noisy salon, Julian Southwood, Earl of Erith, studied the notorious strumpet who would become his next mistress.

He was in the middle of Mayfair on a fine spring afternoon. Yet the reek of sex for sale was as pungent as in the slave markets of Marrakesh or Constantinople.

The crowd was mostly male, although a few provocatively dressed women mingled in the throng. Nobody paid them the slightest attention. Just as nobody but Erith seemed to notice the startling and realistically detailed frescoes of rampant Zeus seizing swooning Ganymede.

From a corner dais a pianist and violinist doggedly plowed through a Mozart sonata. The music came from a different world, a cleaner, purer world untainted by animal carnality.

A world the Earl of Erith would never again inhabit.

Erith shook off the bleak self-reflection and turned to the man beside him. "Introduce me, Carrington."

"Shall do, old chap."

Carrington didn't ask the object of Erith's interest. Why would he? Every man here, including his companion, focused on the slender woman reclining with studied nonchalance upon the chaise longue.

Without being told, Erith knew she'd deliberately chosen her setting in front of the tall west-facing windows. Late afternoon sun flooded her in soft gold and played across her loosely bound tumble of tawny hair. In the clear light, her vivid red dress was like a sudden flame. The effect was worthy of the Theatre Royal.

Even he, familiar to ennui with courtesans' tricks, had felt the breath catch in his throat at first sight of her. One glance and the blood in his veins hummed a deep, dark song of desire, and his skin prickled with the compulsion to make her his.

And she achieved this remarkable effect from half a room away.

Of course, this was no ordinary courtesan.

If she were, he wouldn't be here. The Earl of Erith only bought the best. The best tailoring. The best horses. The best women.

Even by his exacting standards, this particular cyprian was a prime article.

Two extraordinary women had set London on its ear in the last ten years. One, Soraya, cool, dark, mysterious as moonlight, had recently married the Duke of Kylemore, igniting the scandal of the decade. The other, radiant sun to Soraya's moon, arrayed herself now before Erith like a spectacular jewel.

He assessed her as closely as he'd contemplate an addition to his stables.

Lord, but she was a long Meg. A sheath of crimson velvet displayed her lean body to dramatic advantage. She'd fit his tall frame to perfection, even if his taste usually ran to plumper, more voluptuous bedmates. His memory filled pleasantly with the fleshy blond charms of Gretchen, the mistress he'd left in Vienna a month ago.

Gretchen couldn't contrast more strongly with the jade before him. Where the Tyrolean beauty offered soft, yielding curves, this woman was all spare elegance. The bosom under her gown's low neckline wasn't generous, and her waist was long and supple. He guessed the narrow skirt hid legs as graceful and elongated as a thoroughbred's.

Gretchen had been dewy with youth. This woman must verge on thirty. By that age, most bits of muslin frayed at the edges. But this bird of paradise continued her unchallenged reign over the male half of the ton. Her longevity as the most sought-after courtesan in London made her yet more intriguing.

His gaze slid up to her face. Like her body, it was unexpected. After the rhapsodies he'd heard in the clubs, he'd imagined less subtle attractions. The unmistakable greed he'd heard in her admirers' voices had led him to imagine a brassier, more overtly available bawd.

Her jaw was square, almost masculine. Her nose was a trifle too long, her cheekbones too high. From where he stood in the gilt-framed doorway, it was impossible to tell the color of her eyes, but they were large and brilliant and set at a slant.

Cat's eyes. Tiger's eyes.

Her mouth . . .

Her mouth perhaps explained what he'd heard about her preternatural allure. It might be too large. But who would complain? No man could look at those succulent lips without wanting them on his body. Erith's groin tightened at the decadent pictures rocketing through his mind.

Undoubtedly, she had . . . *something.*

She wasn't a great beauty. She was well past first youth. Nor did she flaunt her charms like tawdry trinkets on a fairground stall. If he'd encountered her at a respectable gathering rather than this louche brouhaha, he'd almost believe she belonged to his own class.

Almost.

After the hubbub, all this was surprising. Disappointing.

But even as he dismissed the wench's heralded charms, his eyes gravitated back to that spare, strangely aristocratic face. To that sin of a mouth. To the luxuriant hair. To that long, graceful body curved in complete relaxation upon her couch while men eddied around her in an endless whirlpool of fascination.

She was the most powerful figure in the room. Even at the distance, he felt the sexual energy sizzling around her.

She swept the room with a contemptuous glance. The raised angle of her chin and the irony that teased the corners of her mouth indicated defiance, courage, challenge.

He tried to deny the sensual pull she exerted. While his reckless heart kicked into the emphatic rhythm of a drum beating an army into battle.

No, she wasn't what he'd expected, but he didn't fool himself into believing she was anything less than quality.

She lifted her head and smiled at something the effete fellow standing at her elbow said. The lazy curve of those lush red lips shot another jolt of lava-hot arousal through Erith. That smile spoke of knowledge and sharp intelligence, and a sexual confidence he'd never encountered in a woman. Never, even though he'd dealt with the fallen sisterhood for the last sixteen years. Every drop of moisture dried from his mouth, and his interest, wearied through playing this game too long, engaged with an intensity that astonished him. The covetous buzz in his blood notched up a degree.

Oh, yes, she was going to be his.

Not just because she was the elite of London's courtesans and his prestige would accept nothing less as his *chère amie*. But because he wanted her.

More than he'd wanted anything in a long, long time.

* * *

"Miss Raines, I am happy to see you. I hope I find you well."

Olivia looked up from the wild Roman orgy painted on her silk fan. Lord Carrington stood before her. He'd vied for years to win her favors. For his sake, she'd never consented. He was a good, decent man and deserved better than her. Still, because he was a good, decent man, she made herself smile and extend her hand in its long crimson glove.

"Lord Carrington. I'm very well. And you?"

The old social dance. She was so sick of it. Almost as sick of it as she was of her current life.

Doggedly she fought back the dragging, persistent ennui. She was here because it was past time she selected a new lover. She couldn't stay with Perry indefinitely, although he made no secret that he was happy to have her in residence. Even now he hovered over her like an anxious duenna.

Olivia just wished to heaven she could summon a scrap of interest in who shared her bed next. She needed to choose someone. Her hard-earned reputation for eternal dominion over the male sex depended upon it.

How tired she was of her reputation too.

"Tip-top, thank you." Carrington bent briefly over her hand. "May I present the Earl of Erith, recently returned from abroad and in London for the season?"

Without interest—after all, whoever he was, he was just another man—she withdrew her hand from Carrington's and glanced at the tall figure beside him.

A *very* tall figure. Her glance paused, became a stare. Slowly her gaze traveled up a lean, muscular body clad in the height of fashion to meet deep-set eyes the color of steel. Or perhaps that impression came from the frost glittering in the gray. If she'd been a fraction less self-possessed, she'd shiver under that chilly regard.

But she was Olivia Raines, London's most famous courtesan. She might wish her reputation to the Devil, but she knew to the inch how to use it both to lure and daunt a potential lover.

Her imperious expression didn't soften as she held her hand out. "My lord."

"Miss Raines."

As Lord Carrington had, the earl took her hand and bowed over it. His touch was cool, even through her satin gloves. For an odd moment the room's bustle receded. She was aware only of his strong fingers curling around hers and how his glossy dark head inclined toward her in a gesture that held more command than politeness. The fine hairs on the back of her neck prickled, and her heart kicked into a wayward race.

What on earth was wrong with her? Olivia blinked and forced herself back to reality.

The reality of deciding on her next protector.

Lord Erith, she already saw, offered definite possibilities. And she immediately recognized his interest.

He didn't hold her hand longer than manners decreed. He didn't leer down her bodice. No flash of unseemly desire or possessiveness. Not even the contempt she sometimes found in men's eyes. As if her freedom were despicable, whereas theirs was cause for celebration.

Nothing in that composed face indicated what the Earl of Erith thought or felt.

So why was she sure he determined to become her lover?

He was strikingly handsome, with a hard-angled jaw, a haughty blade of a nose, and thick black hair. How had she failed to notice him earlier? He was without question a man one noticed. His impressive height and his looks should have drawn her attention even without that indefinable air of authority he wore like armor.

Armor against what?

She stifled the fugitive curiosity. Why should she care? He was just another spoiled scion of the aristocracy. Another man for her to use then abandon. The pattern never changed.

With a languid gesture worthy of the queen of courtesans, she raised her fan and waved it gently before her face. She made sure the picture of two naked men servicing the nymph top and tail faced outward. A childish ploy, but something in Lord Erith made her itch to shake his composure.

Lord Carrington colored and looked away. Lord Erith's glance flickered down to the fan then up again. The silvery eyes under their heavy lids showed no reaction, although something told her the obvious gesture amused him.

"How do you find the capital, my lord?" she asked calmly.

"I discover it has unsuspected beauties," he said without inflection.

Aha. The game began.

"How kind," she said flatly, not pretending to misunderstand. False coyness had never been her stock in trade. "I hope you have opportunity to explore further."

"That is my dearest wish, Miss Raines. May I call upon you?"

"Olivia is very busy," Perry said sharply from her side. His hand came down hard on her shoulder, bare under the gown's wide square neck.

Startled, she looked up at her friend and host. He sounded positively hostile. In truth, she'd almost forgotten he was there, the silent duel with Lord Erith was so intense.

"I don't believe I've had the pleasure," the earl said in the same neutral tone, at last shifting his cold metallic stare from her.

"This is Lord Peregrine Montjoy," Carrington said quickly, glancing between the two men. "Lord Peregrine, the Earl of Erith."

"I know who he is," Perry snapped. His grip on Olivia's shoulder tightened.

What was wrong with Perry? He knew the purpose of this gathering. They'd even discussed possible candidates. Erith hadn't featured, but then, until a few minutes ago she hadn't known he existed.

"Lord Peregrine," Erith said with another bow. His voice remained soft and deep but those few words sounded like a warning in Olivia's ears.

She made a sudden decision. "I take tea here at four tomorrow."

"Tea." The earl's expression didn't change, but she knew she'd disconcerted him at last.

"Yes, tea."

Did he imagine she'd spread her legs just for the asking? If so, he truly had been away from England too long. She chose her bedmates, she set the rules, she finished the affairs. Her flagrant independence was notorious. That was why she was such a prize.

She sensed Lord Carrington's unspoken eagerness to be included in the invitation but ignored him. He wasn't for the likes of her. Erith, however, was another case entirely.

"Thank you. I shall be delighted." Not a hint of satisfaction in the bass murmur. How, then, did she know that triumph surged below his urbane exterior?

"Tomorrow, then."

"Tomorrow." He bowed over her hand again. Another fleeting brush of those long fingers. "Miss Raines."

"My lord."

He sliced his way through the throng with an ease that impressed her. This room brimmed with the cream of society, or at least the cream of the male half of society. Yet for the Earl of Erith, the rich and powerful stepped aside without hesitation.

"How can you even consider that blackguard?" Perry flung himself on her bed and stared in violet dressing-gowned glory at the ballet of plaster cupids on the ceiling.

"I haven't made my mind up yet." Olivia rested her heavy silver hairbrush on the dressing table and watched Perry in the mirror. She didn't need to ask who he meant. The Earl of Erith had been an invisible presence since her friend had stormed into her bedroom moments ago.

"He thinks he's got you." Perry sounded sulky and unhappy.

"What he thinks and what will happen aren't necessarily the same thing." Her gaze sharpened on the young man with the sultry good looks arrayed upon her sheets. He was like a painting by Caravaggio come to life. "Why don't you like Erith?"

"He's an arrogant ass."

"True. But so are most men in the ton. What do you know about him in particular?"

"I know he's a cocky sod. I know he's cut a swath through the petticoat brigade. He left England sixteen years ago to join the diplomatic service and has rarely been back since. Everywhere he goes, he sets up the most popular courtesan as his mistress then abandons her flat when he moves on."

"That hardly matters," she said tranquilly. "I'm not planning a lifetime of devotion to the fellow."

"He treats women as trophies." Perry scowled at her, clearly annoyed she didn't share his outrage. "Sops to his vanity. Now he's back for his daughter's wedding . . . "

"His daughter's wedding?" Her hand tightened on the engraved handle of the hairbrush. For some reason, she hadn't imagined a wife. Stupid. Lord Erith must be nearing forty, and most men that age were well and truly shackled. "He's married?"

Perhaps Lord Erith was beyond her touch after all. The one rule she kept was that her paramours were unmarried. In spite of many extravagant offers to compromise, she'd kept her vow never knowingly to break another woman's heart with what she did.

Perry's full rosy lips turned down. "No, he's not married, confound him." He knew her rules as well as she did. "He wed young and his wife died in a riding accident after she gave him two children, a boy and a girl. The girl's match is the talk of the season. You've kept to yourself these last months, I know, but surely you've heard Lady Roma Southwood is to marry Thomas Renton, old Wainfleet's heir."

"No, I hadn't heard." Her voice seemed to come from a long way away.

Olivia sucked in a deep breath. That couldn't be relief unfurling in her belly, could it? One man was the same as the next, although even she admitted that Erith was more interesting than the majority of his sex. But perhaps only because he was a stranger.

She met her troubled brown gaze in the glass. *Perhaps.*

She released the hairbrush and turned on the stool to face Perry. "You haven't told me if he's rich."

Perry's unhappy expression intensified, but to his credit he didn't lie. "As Croesus."

"He sounds perfect."

This afternoon Erith hadn't seemed perfect. This afternoon that arresting, tanned face with its deep-set gray eyes and cynical expression had disturbed her.

He looked like a man who had experienced everything and felt nothing.

Perry all but snarled. "He's anything but perfect. He's a rake without a scrap of kindness to offer a woman. He has a reputation for ruthlessness and hard dealing. He's fought duels on the Continent and killed three men I know of. If he weren't so cursed brilliant at what he does, the Foreign Office would have brought him home long ago. He's a disgrace to his country and to his name. Good God, Olivia, he foisted his own children on his sister before his wife was cold in the grave and he's barely seen them since. He's interested in his own selfish pleasure, and Devil take anyone who gets in the way. Does this sound like a man you wish to entrust with your person?"

Perry's vitriol surprised her. "Why the indignation? You're hardly a pattern card for conventional morality yourself."

His mouth tightened. "I look after my own, at least. You used to have a greater sense of self-preservation. Give yourself to Carrington if you must give yourself to anyone. He's always been mad for you and he's damned plump in the pocket. Or stay here."

"I can't be your pensioner, Perry." This was an old argument. Her occasional sojourns in his opulent town house served both of them, but she didn't want to become a permanent fixture. She began to plait her hair ready for bed. "I'd break Carrington's heart. I suspect Erith has no heart to break. I can handle him."

"He's clever and merciless and self-centered, Olivia. He'll end up hurting you."

Her busy hands stilled. "He's violent?" She wouldn't have thought so, but Perry kept up with gossip much better than she.

"No," he said reluctantly. "I haven't heard that. But there are more ways to hurt a woman than hitting her."

Yes, wasn't she living proof of that? She spoke quickly before cruel memory sank its claws into her. "I can look after myself. You credit the earl with powers he doesn't possess."

The anger seeped from Perry's face, and she read the aching concern underlying his temper. She loved only two men in the world and he was one. It hurt her to distress him. But whom she took into her bed was always her choice alone.

"Anything I say falls on deaf ears. You've decided, haven't you?"

She rather thought she had. Although tomorrow's conversation over the tea table—she smiled to recall the earl's shock at being invited to share the harmless beverage—would lead to a final decision.

"Yes." She tied the end of her plait, rose and shucked off her robe. Underneath she wore the plain white nightdress she preferred when she wasn't working. "My next lover is the Earl of Erith."

"Then God help you. I'll say no more." Perry rolled off the bed and kissed her on the cheek. "Good night, my darling."

"Good night," she murmured, staring into the fire as Perry closed the door behind him.

God help her indeed, although instinct whispered that both she and Erith were beyond heavenly help.

She hadn't told Perry the real reason she'd selected the earl as her keeper.

When she looked into those cold, cold eyes, she'd seen a man without a soul. Who better for a woman who was herself without a soul to choose as lover?

Erith arrived at Lord Peregrine Montjoy's town house precisely at four. As he handed hat, gloves, and cane to the butler, he surveyed the gaudy decorations. Mirrors, gilded candelabra, ormolu, painted plasterwork, naked classical statues. All male and none sporting a concealing fig leaf over their exaggerated genitalia.

Had Lord Peregrine chosen the decor to advertise his houseguest's profession? Olivia Raines didn't need to resort to such blatant measures. Her air of conscious sensuality was apparent to any man with blood in his veins.

The house was gorgeous, although overdone. It could have been an expensive brothel, if not for the fact that everything was the highest quality and beyond the purse of even the most successful madam. Strangely, he'd imagine his prospective mistress would prefer more restrained surroundings. Perhaps that dramatically plain crimson gown yesterday was the aberration.

While he cooled his heels on a fiendishly uncomfortable chair in the hall—the wench certainly wasn't making a fuss of him to soothe his vanity—he puzzled over the fabulous Miss Raines.

What was she doing living here, openly under Lord Peregrine's protection? And if Montjoy was her long-term lover, why tout for trade elsewhere?

From what Erith had learned, she always returned to this house after a liaison ended. Did Montjoy operate as her benevolent pimp? What did Lord Peregrine have that brought her back? What did she seek that she inevitably left again?

Perhaps she was merely another faithless jade. Although gossip indicated that once she accepted a man's carte blanche, she remained loyal until she tired of him. So far he'd yet to hear of a man tiring of *her*.

He'd met a few lucky fellows who had shared her favors. Well, perhaps *lucky* wasn't the precise word. It was perfectly clear all would relinquish their hopes of heaven for a chance of one more night in Olivia Raines's bed. Her paramours had spoken of her with awe, almost as if she possessed supernatural powers. A more sentimental person than Erith would say she spoiled her lovers for other women.

One thing he'd noted was that not a one of them seemed quite *man* enough for her. So either her voracious passions sapped the poor beggars of their masculinity or she chose spineless samples of manhood in the first place.

If that was the case, she was due for a surprise when she took on the Earl of Erith. He glimpsed his dark face in a gold-framed mirror on the opposite wall and straightened from his slouch. Julian Southwood might be justifiably confident but he never *smirked*.

Still, his blood heated pleasurably as he contemplated the unspoken challenge she'd issued yesterday. Their encounter had sparked with edgy awareness and lightning shifts of power. Oh, yes, he'd enjoy himself mightily before he finished with Olivia Raines.

"This way, your lordship." The butler appeared and showed him upstairs to a small room quite as gaudy as yesterday's salon.

Erith caught the eye of one of the many rampant young men filling the room's murals. Naked and improbably endowed wrestlers in a classical setting surrounded him on three walls. The fourth wall was lined with windows facing an immaculate parterre garden.

"Lord Erith." Olivia Raines rose and curtseyed with a poise that wouldn't have discredited a princess.

He stepped forward and took her hand. No gloves today, he noticed with a ripple of pleasure. He bent and grazed his lips across her fingers. It was the first time he'd touched her flesh. Her skin was fine and cool and faintly perfumed. Soap perhaps. But beneath the flowery sweetness lurked a female essence that lured him to sin. He mightn't barter his place in heaven for a night in her arms, but she certainly smelled like paradise.

"Miss Raines. No Lord Peregrine?"

"I always hold these discussions alone," she said coolly, withdrawing her hand and gliding across to a laden tea table. Even the jaded Erith yearned after the delicious fragrance of her as she moved away. "Or do you require a chaperon, my lord?"

He bit back a snort of laughter. He'd been right about her yesterday. She was a forward baggage with no proper respect for his standing. His interest piqued, focused. This was quarry worth the hunting. The first in a long time.

"My reputation will survive half an hour in your company."

Half an hour now. Decadent days to come. Sensual anticipation swirled into turbulence at the thought.

"I'm pleased to hear it."

The voluptuous mouth that had haunted his dreams quirked into a wry smile. Good God, he couldn't remember the last time he'd dreamt of a woman. Or a living woman, at least.

With the grace that invested every movement, she gestured toward a chair opposite her. "Please sit down, my lord."

He took his place and, apart from answering how he preferred his tea and whether he wanted a sandwich or cake, watched her in silence. Yesterday he'd wondered if *tea* were a euphemism for something more interesting. Apparently not. He could already tell his chances of a quick tumble in this oppressively elaborate room were less than none.

It was like taking tea with his sister. If not for the blazing sexual awareness in the air.

She was less formally dressed than yesterday. The light green muslin set off her creamy skin and tawny hair to perfection. He'd been right about her height. When she stood to greet him, her head reached his chin. It was a rare woman who came that close to staring him eye-to-eye.

He'd already decided she *was* a rare woman.

"You know why I'm here," he said once he had her full attention. Most women who attracted the Earl of Erith's fancy worked hard to keep it. Olivia Raines was as calm as a deaf dowager at a charity musicale. "I want to be your lover."

A blunter approach than usual, but something in him insisted this woman wouldn't respond to a hypocritical wooing. He remembered her flaunting that ridiculous fan under his nose yesterday. She'd dared him to be shocked, the impudent wench.

He hadn't been shocked. But he'd most definitely been intrigued.

Another twitch of those lips, although she didn't smile. Today he noticed a small dark mole near the corner of her mouth. The need to taste that velvety spot then possess her mouth with his surged in on a tide of heat.

Devil take it. He hadn't got excited at the thought of a kiss since he was a boy lusting after the chambermaids.

And he was undoubtedly excited. Thank God the table hid quite how titillating he found her elegant detachment.

"Straight to the point, I see," she said musingly.

She lifted her cup to take a sip. It rankled that her hand was perfectly steady. He suspected she wasn't impressed with the great Earl of Erith. An unfamiliar situation. Particularly when he approached a member of the demimonde. His fortune, if nothing else, always gained him an eager hearing.

"Would you prefer something more indirect?"

He hated that his voice betrayed his annoyance. Who was

this flibbertigibbet of a female to needle him? Yet she did. More than he cared to admit.

"No. I find your frankness . . . refreshing." She replaced her teacup and regarded him with distant curiosity. He'd built a brilliant diplomatic career on his ability to read the most subtle signals. For the life of him, he couldn't read this woman. "How do you see this proceeding?"

He'd like to proceed with a long, hard fuck on the Aubusson. He shifted in the delicate mahogany chair to relieve his heavy erection. How the hell had she got him so stirred up? He'd barely touched her, and she'd said nothing overtly suggestive. Yet he was so randy, his cock was harder than an iron bar.

He swallowed and strove for his famous sangfroid. But his voice was husky as he spoke. "I'm in London until July, when I return to my diplomatic posting in Vienna. I'll lease you a house, arrange servants, an allowance, a carriage while I'm here."

"And in return I am at your disposal." Her tone held an irony he didn't fully understand.

"Exclusively." He didn't share. She needed to know that before they negotiated further.

What if she denied him this condition? Any other doxy, he'd shrug his shoulders and move on to the next candidate. With this woman, he didn't know.

Damn her. How did she do this? He suffered a moment's nostalgia for placid, willing Gretchen who had been as stupid as a sheep but never presented him with a moment's puzzlement or concern. He could already tell Olivia Raines was a million miles removed from his last mistress. From any previous mistress, he recognized with a sinking feeling of disaster. The sinking feeling a man got when he realized no amount of swimming would save him from the engulfing wave.

So why didn't he get up and leave? The fact that he couldn't answer quickly or easily was just one more irritation.

"I can't imagine you entered this house yesterday before priming yourself with the gossip," she said coolly. Her astonishing eyes, a clear and unusual light brown, revealed nothing of her thoughts. "You've heard I'm faithful to my lovers."

"Yes." Hell, he reacted like a callow boy, but the word "lovers" in that rich contralto made him break out in a sweat. He only just stopped himself from tugging at his neckcloth, which suddenly seemed uncomfortably tight.

"While the liaison lasts, of course." With an aplomb he both envied and resented, she surveyed him in a critical light.

Most definitely, the Earl of Erith's addresses didn't overwhelm this lightskirt. The topaz regard was perceptive, assessing, probing. It wasn't, by any stretch of the imagination, seductive.

Yet he was immediately seduced. More powerfully than he could remember. God help him if she deliberately set out to entwine him in her wiles.

She was still speaking as though they discussed a business transaction. He supposed for her they were. He wished to Hades he were half so uninvolved. "I'm sure you've also heard I claim complete freedom when I take a protector. I choose when the liaison starts. I choose when it finishes. My time is my own to dispose of. My one promise is that for the affair's duration, I pledge complete fidelity."

"It sounds, madam, as though I'm paying a lot of damned money to let you run wild," he said sardonically.

She shrugged. "Your choice, my lord. There are other women in London."

Yes, and none were Olivia Raines. Blast her, she knew that as well as he. The tight ache in his balls became unbearable. If only he could say her indifference didn't make him want her more.

She'd folded her hands in her lap. The pose could look demure if one ignored her smoldering sensuality. It was a long time—perhaps never—since a woman had challenged him so brazenly. This woman vibrated challenge from her perfectly coiffed hair to the delicate green silk slippers peeking out beneath her hem.

He hoped she didn't notice he fumbled as he reached into his coat's inner pocket. "I brought you a token of my esteem."

He extracted the slim velvet box and slid it across the table. Without any great show of interest, she opened the case and devoted a few silent moments to studying the contents.

Perhaps at last he'd impressed her. He'd spent two hours at Rundell and Bridge that morning choosing the bracelet. The moment he saw the magnificent row of ruby flowers linked on a diamond-encrusted trellis, he knew he'd found what he wanted.

The bracelet was as unusual and spectacular as Olivia Raines herself. Somewhere, his initial doubts about her attractions had disappeared. Now he believed she was the most beautiful woman he'd ever seen.

Her expression didn't change, but a cyprian of her experience must know to the penny what the glittering frippery had cost.

The bracelet's message was unmistakable. The Earl of Erith was rich, he was generous, and if she consented to his protection, he was willing to shower her with treasure.

Very carefully, she closed the box. Then she raised her topaz eyes and considered him with an unreadable expression. "Yes, Lord Erith, I'll be your mistress."

Chapter 2

*E*ven as Olivia spoke the words to place her in Lord Erith's bed, her instincts screamed to deny him. Her mind told her she risked no more than she'd risked with any other keeper. Her deepest self insisted the earl threatened everything she'd created since she'd accepted harlotry as her inevitable fate.

Unreasoning fear tightened every muscle.

Fear was her oldest, most insidious enemy. More powerful than any man.

I will not surrender to fear.

And why should she be frightened? Since reaching womanhood, she'd never met a male she couldn't dominate. Lord Erith was nothing special. She'd have great pleasure proving that. To the world. To him. To herself. Her reluctance now was just part of the odd humor that had gripped her since she ended her last affair, months ago.

A sharp ache in her wrists made her realize how hard she clutched her hands together. Deliberately, she relaxed her grip, although she already knew he'd noted the betraying gesture.

Something—satisfaction, triumph, possession?—gleamed from under his heavy eyelids.

"Good." He stood and stared down at her. She'd never been so conscious of his impressive height or the latent power in his body. "I'll see you tonight, Olivia."

It was the first time he'd used her Christian name. Given what they'd soon do to each other, the small intimacy shouldn't matter. Somehow it did. That deep voice saying "Olivia" shredded her protective formality and laid her bare as if she already stood naked before him.

I will not surrender to fear.

She tilted her chin and glared. "I don't entertain my lovers in this house," she said icily.

"I didn't imagine you would." His narrow, sensual mouth curled into a sardonic smile. "I want every man in London to know you're mine. I want to see you. It builds the . . . *anticipation.*"

How could he make such a harmless word sound more decadent than all the profanities she'd heard in a lifetime of whoring? The temperature of her voice sank another couple of degrees. "I belong to no man, Lord Erith."

"You'll belong to me," he said steadily.

Before she could move, he bent across the tea table and grasped her chin. She registered a chaotic mix of impressions. His fresh, clean smell. The warmth of his fingers on her skin. The almost feminine abundance of the lashes fringing his cold gray eyes. The flare of his nostrils as he inhaled her scent, like an animal before mating.

His implacable hold stifled struggle or protest. Panting like a trapped fledgling, she waited for his mouth to meet hers. Her heart beat so fast, she thought it would burst from her chest. For one blind, terrified moment she felt like a silly virgin trapped in a rake's net.

Those firm, almost cruel lips captured hers. A moment's clinging pressure. Hot like fire. Hard like steel.

Abruptly, the searing contact ended.

He let her go and stepped away with a bow. "Until this evening."

Before she could summon an adequate reply, any reply, he turned on his heel and strode from the room.

Dazed and shaking, she clenched and unclenched her fists in her lap. When she licked her lips, she nearly groaned. She'd kept her mouth shut during that importuning kiss. Even so, his taste lingered. Rich. Tantalizing. Evocative.

Fear surged up and overwhelmed her.

"Damn you, Erith," she whispered to the empty room. "Damn you to hell."

Erith paused at the entrance to the large salon where he'd first seen Olivia Raines. It was late, past midnight. The room was almost empty, and lit by only two candelabras, felt even more cavernous. Half a dozen men gathered around the fire, smoking and drinking brandy. He noticed the group's air of ease as they lounged on the pair of gilt couches or stood leaning against the mantel. He also noticed that ease evaporate at the sound of his name.

Where was Olivia? The sulky but undeniably picturesque Lord Peregrine turned toward the doorway. The four seated young men stood to greet him. They were strangers, although all were young and handsome. So handsome that any could have modeled for pouting naked Ganymede in the frescoes. Erith barely spared a glance for one gentleman lingering in the shadows.

Then that last member of the gathering stepped with languid grace into the light. Erith found himself staring into his mistress's slanted sherry-colored eyes.

The breath jammed in his throat while shock warred with astounded admiration. His hands curled at his sides as he physically restrained himself from reaching across the few feet separating them.

My God, she was magnificent.

Olivia was dressed like any buck of the ton. Biscuit trousers, close-fitting black superfine coat, white brocade waist-coat, elaborate neckcloth. Her long hair was bound tightly to her head, so he hadn't immediately realized he was looking at a woman. Why would he? Women of his acquaintance didn't dress as men.

The pure white neckcloth set off her fine-grained, slightly olive skin, and the stark tailoring shaped her lissome body with the closeness of a lover's hand. Erith felt a kick of arousal and his heart began to hammer wildly. His fists clenched harder. He wanted her under him. He wanted her naked and gasping her pleasure as he pounded into her.

You are mine. He nearly growled the words aloud.

"Lord Erith," she said calmly, and lifted her hand to take a long draw on a slender cigar. He bit back a groan as he watched her full lips close on the cigar. Decadent images of her taking his cock into her mouth seared every coherent thought to ashes.

Her eyes were brilliant with challenge as she stared back at him. She knew what she did to him.

Of course she did, the teasing baggage.

With difficulty, he fought back the covetous clamor in his blood and found his voice. "Miss Raines." He bowed. "Gentlemen."

Lord Peregrine looked even more hostile than he had yesterday. Clearly, Olivia had told him she'd accepted Erith's carte blanche. Yet again the puzzle of the decorative lordling's relationship with her teased Erith. He sensed closeness but no frisson of sexual attraction.

He studied the men, then glanced at the frescoes once more. No female forms graced the walls. No female forms anywhere in the house, if one discounted his mistress's lithe figure. A suspicion grew in his mind, a suspicion sheltered English minds mightn't entertain but that seemed increasingly plausible to a man who had traveled across Europe and Asia. If true, it explained a great deal.

"Fancy a brandy, Lord Erith?" Olivia drawled as if they'd

bumped into one another at his club. "Perry's broached a fine bottle tonight."

Her overtly theatrical behavior made him want to laugh. She dared him to explode into outrage, but she picked the wrong target. He could play games with the best of them. It was what made him a brilliant diplomat.

"Why not?" he said smoothly. "Lord Peregrine, I don't believe I've met your friends."

While Montjoy performed introductions, Erith watched Olivia pour him a drink from the decanter on the Boulle sideboard. Her attire was so severely masculine. Why did it make her seem more a woman? His eyes dwelt on her legs. His guess yesterday had been right—they were long and slender. He savored the prospect of those legs wrapped around him while he thrust into her.

He emerged from his brief daydream to find her passing him the glass. She very deliberately stroked her fingers across his. It was the first time she'd done anything overtly seductive, and his skin tingled under her touch.

He wanted her immediately. Since he'd met her, the delay had chafed. Now it became unbearable.

But for the moment, bear it he must.

She lifted her cigar again, drew on it, then exhaled so a drift of blue smoke wreathed her angular features. Features that merged to form a more compelling whole than conventional beauty ever could. No wonder she had every man in London in a flap.

"Lord Erith, this is Sir Percival Martineau," Lord Peregrine said with a distinct snap. Clearly he'd been speaking while Erith stared lost into his mistress's fathomless eyes.

"Sir Percival." God help him if he needed to remember anyone's name other than Olivia's. She'd bewitched him.

Bewitched?

Hell, what was wrong with him? She was just another female. He'd grab her, he'd take her, he'd discover there was nothing new between her legs or in her head. He'd had so many women since his wife died, and none had engaged his heart. However much they'd engaged his body. His body, which currently hummed as though a mountebank ran an electrical current through it. He couldn't remember a female stirring him up like this since his first season. When tender emotions of love and respect had tempered his male excitement.

Good God, how could he link this harlot with Joanna? This conniving witch would never touch his finer feelings. Although she was welcome to touch anything else she liked.

Oh, yes, please. Raw expectation scurried down his spine.

She gestured coolly to a sofa. "Would you like to sit down?"

"No, I want to talk to you. In private."

She shrugged, placed her glass on the mantel and stubbed out her cigar. "As you wish. This way."

He followed her through a corridor and into a library. Lamplight gleamed softly on richly colored leather covers and picked out gold lettering on rows of books.

Olivia moved forward and turned to face him, leaning with a grace that stopped his breath against the desk behind her. "What is it?

He realized he was smiling. "This room. It's the only one I've admired in this house."

Surprisingly, she smiled back. A real smile conveying a wealth of affection for the man who owned the library. A shaft of unpleasant emotion stabbed Erith. Not jealousy. He was never jealous. And why be jealous when his suspicions about her host had firmed into certainty?

"Perry doesn't read much. He hasn't redecorated in here yet."

"You like it," he said softly. It was the first room he'd seen her in that didn't jar with his instincts about her. He slouched against the doorjamb and studied her.

"Yes, I do."

She bent her head and light caught bronze strands in her thick hair. She really was an extraordinarily beautiful woman. More beautiful at this moment because her usual self-consciousness was absent.

"There's a library in the house I found." When he'd seen the neat book-lined room in York Street, he'd assumed his new mistress would find it of no interest. Now he wasn't so sure.

She raised her head and the wariness returned. The regret he felt surprised him. For a moment he'd felt real connection. Not the connection of sexual attraction. That never waned. But briefly the ghost of a different bond had hovered, one that in other circumstances could blossom into friendship. Should friendship be possible between two such well-armored creatures as they.

"You've found a house already?" She didn't sound pleased.

"Something became available." He didn't tell her he'd had an army combing London for a suitable residence nor that the hunt had started when he arrived home from seeing her the first time.

The place he'd rented was perfect. Small, luxurious, private, and close enough to Erith House for him to maintain a double life without flaunting his affair before his family. After leading a bachelor's life for so long, he wasn't used to practicing discretion. Alluring as she undoubtedly was, Olivia Raines offered merely a diversion. His real purpose in London was to reconcile with his children, and he could do nothing to risk that.

He wondered if he'd been prudent in his choice of *chère amie*. The news that he'd become Olivia Raines's protector was already the talk of London. Over port after dinner at Erith House, he'd responded to his cronies' envious comments while avoiding Carrington's reproachful glower. How long before the story reached more respectable ears?

Too late to change his mind. Even if he could summon the will to break free of the jade's damnable allure. He spoke into the silence. "I hope you'll move there tomorrow."

Given a choice, he'd sweep her away now, ensconce her in the pretty little house and exorcize her inconvenient fascination over him. But his men worked all night on minor alterations and the place wouldn't be ready until morning.

She looked startled. "Tomorrow?"

"You have some objection?"

"I hadn't expected such dispatch."

She spoke with the smooth cadences and ironical inflections of a Cambridge graduate. Had she risen from the streets? If she had, she'd done an extraordinary job teaching herself the ton's manners.

He shrugged, striving for an appearance of detachment that was far from reality. "I'm a man who makes his mind up quickly."

"Clearly." Her lips twitched in the familiar wry smile.

"In the morning, I'll send my carriage to convey you to the new house, then call in the evening to discuss arrangements. Perhaps a visit to Tattersalls the next day to choose your cattle. I thought two carriage horses and a hack. I've also ordered a curricle that I dare say will meet your approval."

"Very efficient, my lord," she said with unconcealed irony. "You will stay to dine tomorrow?"

They both knew she offered more than food. Heat blasted him, made him hard as oak. "Thank you. It would be my pleasure."

Oh, absolutely.

Why wait? So far, the tame liberties his notorious mistress had allowed wouldn't raise an eyebrow among the marriage-minded misses at Almack's. Well, perhaps not altogether true. She was a dab hand at double entendre. And that one burning kiss still haunted him.

One burning, possessive, damnably short kiss.

Too short.

When he kissed her, he'd tasted anger. And surprise. She hadn't wanted to kiss him, but that flaring instant incinerated every one of his doubts and dissatisfactions. Even the dull, constant ache of old grief and old guilt had briefly faded. Only with the greatest difficulty had he forced himself to stop after that one searing kiss.

By then her fate was sealed. He would have her. She alone could offer him surcease.

He wanted to kiss her again. Straightening, he prowled across the rich red and blue Turkish carpet. She tensed as though scenting a predator.

"My lord, I told you my rules about this house." Her fingers curled against the desk's wooden lip. How delightful that she was nowhere near as self-possessed as she wanted him to think. It made him feel less helpless against the inexorable pull of attraction.

His approach didn't slow. "I can wait until tomorrow night for . . . satisfaction." He almost purred the last word. "But perhaps a kiss on account?"

Her chin's defiant angle was unmistakable. "I should have outlined my requirements in a lover more fully this afternoon."

"I'm all ears, madam," he whispered. Very deliberately, he placed each hand on the desk next to each of hers. He wasn't touching her but his body created a cage around her. "You have my complete attention."

Without a hint of a blush, she glanced down to where his erection strained against his trousers. She was no innocent, his mistress. He liked that. He'd been innocent once, and the tragedy of it had left him broken and ruined.

She was on edge and unsure, and he liked that too. He fought the urge to press himself against her. This close, he smelled her skin's delicate perfume. Lilies. Roses. Honey. Something warm and female that came from her and not a glass vial. His nostrils flared as he drew that delicious fragrance deep into his lungs.

"I don't kiss, Lord Erith." Her voice lowered and the husky contralto vibrated in his bones. "At least not on the mouth."

He leaned forward to catch another wash of her scent. Oh, she was glorious, this woman. "You'll kiss me."

Her mouth formed a stubborn line. "No, I won't. This, my lord, is how I conduct my liaisons. My time is my own, I'm completely faithful and I don't kiss."

He was an inch from tasting the creamy skin of her neck. A tendril of hair had broken free of the severe hairstyle. He reached to brush the stray lock aside. She stiffened under his touch.

"So many rules, Olivia," he murmured. "Rules are made to be broken."

"Not mine." She strove to sound forbidding but her unsteady voice betrayed her. He was close enough for her breath to brush across his face. He caught a hint of rich brandy and tobacco. "If my requirements seem onerous, it's not too late to cancel our arrangement."

"Now, that would be a pity." He let his fingers drift to her nape. "When I've taken such trouble over you."

He bent and placed his mouth fleetingly on her neck. Her skin was so soft there, like living silk. The honey in her scent left a sweet flavor on his tongue. She was exquisite. He couldn't remember wanting a woman more. His heart kicked into a pounding gallop.

Just one taste. Although the desire raging in his blood urged him to devour her whole. He raised his head and looked into her guarded whisky-colored eyes. Her lips were slightly parted, hinting at hot darkness within, and he heard the faint puff of her breath. His cock jerked and pressed against the front fall of his trousers. His fingers tightened in the soft hair at the base of her skull.

"I've never kissed a woman wearing trousers. The decadence is rather stimulating."

He watched that slender throat move as she swallowed. "You're not going to kiss a woman wearing trousers now. I told you, I don't kiss on the mouth. I can't believe you mistake my wishes."

"Ah, your wishes, Olivia. I look forward to hearing more about those." He smiled as his pleasure in her mounted along with his arousal. "I'll have you to myself tomorrow night. What harm a sample now so I wander home with sweet dreams?"

In her remarkable eyes he caught a flash of something that might have been fear. The thought nagged at the edges of his mind but not enough to stop him. Be damned to her rules. Somehow she'd hoodwinked every man in London into dancing to her tune. But he was the Earl of Erith. No woman snatched the lead from him as he waltzed her into his bed.

He pressed his mouth to hers. Her lips were sweet and soft. And firmly closed. It was like having the gates to heaven slammed in his face.

Well, there were more paths into paradise than the one through the front door.

Olivia remained taut and motionless beneath Lord Erith's kiss, while inside clawing panic shrieked to break free. A scream choked in her throat. It would be too humiliating to reveal how his kiss distressed her. She fought to stave off the blackness. She could survive this. She could survive anything. And with her pride intact.

This man would not defeat her.

Good God, she was a tall, strong woman, not a defenseless child. But his overwhelming height and heavily muscled body made her feel small and vulnerable in ways she hadn't experienced for years. The musky scent of aroused male sucked the air from the room. His kiss tormented her, frightened her, reminded her of events she'd tried desperately to forget.

The horrible black suffocation only lasted a moment. Her mind recognized that. Her soul cringed and cowered and felt it had plunged back into endless nightmare.

He wasn't even hurting her. His mouth wasn't brutal and the hand behind her head speared through her hair almost tenderly. For all its implacability, his grip was gentle. He didn't use his unquestionable power to flatten her onto the desk so he could rip at her trousers and push his way into her.

None of this mattered. What mattered was the sense of being overpowered, forced, compelled against her will. Her stubborn pride faltered, began to fracture. She was at the point of releasing the scream when abruptly the kiss changed.

The demanding pressure eased. He brushed her lips with a torrent of little kisses, seemingly innocent. Although innocence, she already knew, was a word foreign to this man.

No, these glancing nibbles and licks were the tactics of a hardened seducer. A man confident enough to know that if he took his time, lulled his prey into a false sense of security, he'd get what he wanted.

Well, he didn't know who he dealt with.

No man turned Olivia Raines into a helpless victim. On a surge of fortifying anger, she raised her hands and with all her strength, she shoved at his broad chest. She wrenched her mouth from his. "No!"

Her push didn't shift him. He brushed one last kiss across her mouth and stepped back, silently indicating the decision to release her was his alone. He breathed more quickly than normal and his eyes glittered like polished silver. For once they weren't cold at all. He was still heavily erect.

So he wanted her. Of course he did. That was why he paid a fortune to set her up as his mistress. Men always wanted her. They'd wanted her since she was a child. But she had the power. She made the choice.

"You had no right," she spat.

Her resentment didn't dent his arrogance. "What a fuss over nothing. You must know I intend to do more than kiss, Olivia. This coyness doesn't become you."

"It's not coyness," she said sharply. She sucked in a calming breath, although panic still frayed her composure. Deliberately, she lowered her tone so she sounded like Olivia Raines, queen of courtesans, not the frightened child she'd once been. "I don't kiss on the mouth. My lovers have no complaints about my generosity in other areas."

Her seductive response didn't fool Erith. She was paler than usual and her lush mouth, red from his kisses, settled into a strangely vulnerable line. That kiss had affected her. Although unfortunately not with overwhelming lust.

No, something else happened.

He just wished to hell he knew what it was.

Would she be similarly unresponsive when he got her into bed? Surely not. Her previous keepers had waxed lyrical on the pleasures of her body.

But she'd stood like a warm, fragrant statue under his lips. There had been no reaction, less even than he'd enticed from her this afternoon.

He leaned close to draw in another breath redolent of her, although he didn't touch her. He could wait. Even if his balls felt like they were on fire. "I'll see you tomorrow, Olivia."

He was close enough to see fleeting uncertainty cloud her gaze. "Lord Erith . . . "

She caught his arm. Even through layers of wool and cambric, he felt the burning heat of that touch. Before she could draw away, he placed his hand over hers. "Yes?"

"I was too hasty agreeing to your proposition."

Almost absently, his fingers stroked hers. "I thought you made of stauncher stuff, Miss Raines. Are you to falter at the first fence?"

The eyes she raised to his were dark and turbulent. Beneath her calm surface, wild storms raged.

"This isn't a hunt meeting on your estate, Lord Erith," she said with a hint of asperity. "You think to buy me much as you'd buy a horse or a new pair of boots. But more is at stake and you know it. You and I will not suit."

Ah, she came back to herself, thank God. He abhorred the idea that he might have scared her. Although with such a strong woman, fear seemed a puzzling reaction. Especially to something as ephemeral as a kiss. Even if the kiss at the time had felt anything but ephemeral.

"We'll suit very well," he said steadily.

"That's for me to say."

He reached out and tilted her chin to look into her eyes. He admired her courage in neither flinching away nor avoiding his gaze. "You're really not curious about how we'd be together?"

That ironic smile tugged at her lips. "A person in my profession loses her curiosity quickly, my lord."

"Then do it because you're woman enough to tame me. It's poor spirited to end our bout before we come to grips with one another."

Her smile deepened, and his glance fell again to that tiny, alluring mole near the corner of her lips. He was desperate to kiss her again. Only her frozen response to his last kiss stopped him. "This isn't a wrestling match either."

He laughed softly and let her go. The ghost of her warmth lingered on his fingers. "I intend wrestling to be involved."

"And fencing."

"Definitely. My blade is at the ready."

"Your blade is always at the ready."

"When I see an opponent worthy of my sword, it is. But my preferred opponent claims she's not up to my weight."

"Wrestling again?"

"Boxing, Olivia. I want to make you see stars."

"You don't waste time on false modesty, do you?"

"I don't waste time." He paused. "Will you come to me tomorrow or does London's most independent, capricious female admit she's met a man she can't bring to heel?"

She arched her eyebrows in perfect disdain. "You think to coax me with childish taunts?"

"I think to coax you. Any way I can. From what I've seen, you've terrified a bunch of milksops into bending to your will. Test your mettle on a hardier opponent. Why not bring the infamous Earl of Erith to his knees?"

She gave a huff of dismissive amusement. "You believe I have as much chance of achieving that as of flying to the moon."

"But I dearly look forward to watching you try, Olivia. Aren't you tired of easy conquests?"

"You think you know a lot about the men who've shared my bed."

"A good sportsman assesses his competition."

"If you tell me you're leaping into the saddle, I swear I'll slap you."

He laughed again. With every second, his appreciation of her grew. "I'd never be so crass, Miss Raines."

"No, you're a model of decorum," she said dryly.

"Not always. As I hope you'll allow me to demonstrate." He hesitated. The answer to his next question was more important than he'd have believed possible a day ago. An hour ago, even. "Tomorrow?"

When she looked at him, her face was vivid with challenge. "Tomorrow."

Chapter 3

*O*livia rounded the turn in the elaborately carved staircase and looked down into the hall. It was night and Lord Erith had just arrived at the lovely little house he'd taken for her near Regent's Park.

The earl stood below her, his feet planted square on the black and white tiles. He certainly was a handsome devil. Lamplight gleamed across his thick dark hair as he passed hat and cane to the butler.

He looked splendid in his evening dress. Black coat and trousers, a crisp white shirt, a high neckcloth. The scrolls of embroidery on his gray silk waistcoat shone in the soft light. When he glanced to where she hovered above him in the shadows, his eyes glittered silvery hunger.

"Olivia." The bass baritone rumble conveyed gloating satisfaction.

She read ownership in his stance. Ownership of the house. Ownership of her. Resentment made her raise her chin even as her belly churned with nerves.

Curse this uncertainty. She needed to remember who she was, who he was. Erith was only a man. Nothing would happen tonight that hadn't happened before. Once the old, banal dance started, surely she'd find her pattern, follow the steps that were second nature. Nevertheless, her hand tightened on the banister rail until her knuckles shone white.

The butler discreetly withdrew, leaving them alone. She fought to steady her voice. "My lord."

"I'm sorry I'm late. A family crisis."

The apology surprised her. After all, he paid her to await his convenience. "No matter."

She stood poised above him like Juliet speaking to her Romeo from the balcony. The fugitive thought left a sour taste in her mouth. Neither she nor Lord Erith was young or innocent or passionate.

Or in love.

Real love between a man and a woman was as unreal as Perry's randy painted gods. Years of servicing her patrons had taught her that.

His stare remained unwavering upon her. That hot gaze licked across her skin like living flame. He vibrated with unspoken desire. She was wrong to say he lacked passion. He could claim passion, or at least its earthiest variant. She'd seen that intent look on men's faces too often to mistake it.

Desperately, she sought the still, calm center that bolstered her when she entertained her lovers. She was appalled that it wasn't there. Instead, she was a roiling mass of fear and anxiety. Her palm became slick as it flattened on the polished mahogany.

Perhaps his unwelcome kisses had made her jumpy. They'd certainly inspired bad dreams last night from which she'd woken trembling and bathed in sweat.

Perhaps she was off-balance because she hadn't taken a lover for months. The intervals between her liaisons had steadily lengthened. The world interpreted her fastidiousness as an attempt to push up her price, but in reality it was nothing so calculated. As the years passed, she found having a man in her bed less and less palatable.

It might be time the great Olivia Raines relinquished her self-appointed crusade against the male sex. She had money, and Lord knew she was weary of this empty life. Weary to the bone.

But first she had to get through tonight, keeping her reputation for cold allure intact. Then the nights that followed, until she could discard Lord Erith on her own terms.

Retirement from this stale game might beckon, but by God, she'd end her career in triumph. She wouldn't sneak away like a whipped dog. She'd claim one last victory over a lover then vanish in a blaze of glory. Her pride would accept nothing else.

The silence, tinged with dark currents of craving and resistance, extended awkwardly. She made herself speak. "Would you like to come upstairs?"

"My pleasure."

She tried to ignore how he drew out the word "pleasure." He had such a deep voice. The soft but resonant sound set her heart to a frantic flutter.

With a swish of butterscotch yellow skirts, she turned and mounted the steps to the landing. Among Lord Erith's preparations for her arrival had been an elaborate wardrobe from her favorite modiste. He must have spent a fortune to have it ready so quickly.

Behind her, she heard him climb the stairs. Each booted footfall heavy and deliberate. She hid a shiver as she heard every inexorable step stake a claim to her.

She paused at the closed door and he loomed near enough for her to catch his scent, clean male and sandalwood. Cold sweat prickled her nape under her upswept hair. She kept her face averted for fear he'd see her vulnerability.

She must be going mad. She hadn't felt like this with a lover since she was a girl. Dear Lord, if she didn't seize control, she'd be completely defenseless. And she knew to her cost what men did to defenseless women.

She sucked in a ragged breath then cursed the betraying rattle of air in her lungs. Erith was too clever to miss any sign of weakness.

He was the enemy. As all men were the enemy.

Courage, Olivia.

She straightened her spine and faced him with a neutral expression. "The servants have laid out a fine supper."

His face was intent and he didn't smile. "Later."

His arrogance kindled her temper. At last, thank heaven, she sounded like the serene, worldly courtesan instead of the terrified child she once was. "We're not animals, my lord, who rut in a field without ceremony. A liaison is a work of art."

"You speak a lot of damned rot, Miss Raines."

This time her inhalation was pure annoyance. "This is how my affairs proceed, Lord Erith. We have supper, conversation, perhaps a little music, then I retire and prepare myself and you come to take your pleasure. More pleasure than any woman has ever given you."

"That's a big promise." He sounded unimpressed.

Curse him for a cynical devil. She deepened her voice to a seductive purr. "You'll discover ecstasy beyond your wildest dreams if you let me conduct this affair as I wish."

Hoping without great optimism that her extravagant promises convinced, she pushed the door. It opened silently on a room bright with candlelight. The air was heavy with the scent of hyacinths and freesias and cherry blossom. Vases of spring flowers whose heady perfume tugged on her senses and added an aura of innocence to an encounter that held no innocence at all. On a red lacquer Chinese sideboard, a lavish cold supper waited, along with a bottle of champagne cooling in ice.

Assuming an air of confidence, she stepped inside and waited for Lord Erith to follow. Ahead, the bedroom door stood ajar, revealing more flowers and the huge expanse of bed with sheets already turned down.

She stopped in the center of the room and turned to face him, her spine straight, her chin up, her gaze steady. He strode through the doorway and didn't stop. His jaw set with unmistakable determination and his eyes were alight with purpose.

She refused to retreat. He crowded her. Only when she thought he might trample her did she finally take a short step back.

When she recognized she made even that small concession, she stopped abruptly. Still he pressed onward. If she didn't move, he'd mow her down. With every unwilling step, the bedroom door behind her loomed closer and closer.

"What are you doing?" she asked sharply.

"That's a fool question, Olivia." His voice held a ruthless edge that made the hairs stand up on her skin. She'd seen hints of this side of Erith before, but tonight she was alone with him, and clearly he had plans that didn't require her consent.

Of course he didn't wait on her consent. He'd paid a fortune for her body and she'd accepted the bargain.

"My lord, I told you what I want." She strove for her usual authority. She tried to sidle from his path, but he stretched out one powerful arm to block her escape.

"Yes, you did."

She gritted her teeth, trepidation and anger a foul brew in her stomach. "I won't . . . " She tried to brush past him on the other side but he set his body before her like a barrier. "Blast you, my lord, I'm not a sheep! Stop herding me like one!"

The corners of his mouth kicked up in a faint smile. "If you insist."

She should have known a direct challenge was the last way to achieve her ends. For a shocked moment she registered the way his mouth firmed and his eyes narrowed. Then he grabbed her with implacable hands and swung her off her feet in a tumble of yellow silk.

Ever since she'd glimpsed him towering over the crowd in Perry's salon, she'd understood this was a man of more than usual physicality. But only now when he held her close did she register the thick, hard bands of muscle across his chest and arms.

And his heat. He was like a raging furnace.

"Put me down!" she choked through a throat tight with outrage.

"No." He bent and nipped where her neck met her shoulder.

"Ow," she protested, although he hadn't hurt her. It was galling that he remained so indisputably in charge without violence.

"I've waited for this from the first time I saw you." He marched across the floor to the bedroom's open doorway.

"That was only the day before yesterday," she bit out, straining away.

"An eternity." He adjusted his grip and jostled her closer to the bed. "Stop your damned wriggling. You know I won't hurt you."

"How can I know that? You're acting like a savage."

Olivia hooked her hand around his neck and tugged sharply on the dark hair that curled against the back of his high collar. She'd expected hair so thick and vital to feel coarse under her fingers. Instead it was soft, like rough silk.

"You cat! I'll put you down, all right." He stopped at the edge of the bed and dropped her unceremoniously. Gasping, she bounced on the fine linen sheets.

Furiously she tried to roll away, but Erith came down over her in a crouch, trapping her with his big body. She heard the fragile silk of her skirt rip as she made another futile attempt to escape.

Other men had tried to use physical superiority to control her. Her indifference, her strength, her obstinacy, always cowed them to her will. If a lover asked for more than she was willing to grant, she left. Her detachment lent her a power over her patrons few courtesans matched.

Yet here she was, seething and helpless under Lord Erith. How had he put her so completely at his mercy? And with such effortless ease?

She'd governed every lover she ever had, after her first. By heaven, she would govern the Earl of Erith.

"Stop this immediately," she said in a cold voice, lying stiff as a doll. "You will not treat me like some doxy you've picked up in Covent Garden for a few pence."

"I wouldn't dream of it," he said smoothly. "Just as you won't treat me like one of your lapdogs."

Olivia didn't bother to protest his insulting description of her previous keepers. He was right, confound him, although how he knew so much was a mystery.

He pressed a kiss to the place he'd bitten. She jerked away, although that fleeting contact echoed in her blood like distant music.

"Let me up, Lord Erith." Astonished, angry, edgy, she lay panting and trembling in the shadow of his body.

He still looked unimpressed. "Has anyone ever told you you're rather bossy, Miss Raines?"

"Not and survived with all their parts intact," she shot back.

He gave a startled bark of laughter. It was the first time she'd heard him laugh. The sound's unabashed freedom surprised her. She didn't know him well, she doubted she ever would. But she'd judged him as almost inhumanly contained. That sudden release of unfettered humor contradicted the conclusion.

"You're most welcome to touch my parts whenever you wish." He dipped his hips until his erection brushed her belly. Through his trousers and her dress, the heat burned like a brand.

He was a big man. Of course he was. He had too much swagger to suffer any lack of confidence about his manhood.

She placed both hands on the broad expanse of his chest.

She pushed, but it was like struggling to shift a huge slab of sun-warmed rock. His scent surrounded her. Soap. Clean skin. Arousal. Physically he was more overwhelming than any lover she'd ever known. It wasn't just Erith's size and power, but some deep source of energy that made the air around him buzz and swirl. Like he created his own weather wherever he went. Storm or sunshine.

She shoved harder and he made a scornful sound deep in his throat. "Give up, Olivia. I'm not going anywhere and neither are you. We're destined to end up in this bed. You don't need special techniques to seduce me. You seduced me the moment I saw you."

Desperately she studied his face, seeking some weakness. She saw only adamantine will and the burning regard of a man intent on having a woman. There was no help there. She was canny enough to realize she'd lost this particular battle.

"All right," she whispered, using the voice that gained her unfailing sway over simple male animals.

"All right?" He sounded suspicious. "As easy as that?"

A reminder that while he was definitely a male—she couldn't mistake that hard seeking organ in his trousers—he was more complex than most members of his sex. She trod such a fine line between overestimating his power and underestimating his cleverness, which she grimly recognized as prodigious. Managing Lord Erith was like crossing a river full of hungry crocodiles on a fraying rope bridge.

"Don't think too long and hard, my lord, or the offer may disappear," she said sourly.

"Long and hard sounds good," he murmured, brushing her belly again and sending searing heat shooting through her.

"Self-praise is no recommendation," she snapped. "Let me up from this ridiculous position and we'll begin."

Another huff of laughter and no attempt to obey. "You sound like a stiff-rumped governess. It's strangely arousing."

She studied Lord Erith's vivid features and reached a decision that had nibbled at the edge of her mind for a long time. He was the last man she'd sleep with for money. Given her contempt for all males, that meant he was the last man she slept with.

She'd play the old game to its end with Lord Erith then retreat to private life. Olivia Raines, queen of courtesans, would be no more.

Thank God.

But freedom must wait until pride was satisfied. Right now, she had to control a rampant and very large male.

Control. Her favorite word. Lord Erith's too, she'd wager.

"You'd like me to lie here while you do what you wish?" Sarcasm tinged her question. "It's a waste when you've paid a fortune for my skills. But I live to serve, my lord."

"I applaud your conscientiousness in making sure I get value for money."

His face was alight with reckless amusement as he bent to kiss the base of her throat where her pulse bucked and kicked like a maddened horse. His gesture delivered the message that he knew how nervous she was beneath her hard-won and completely artificial sangfroid.

He raised his head, his eyes still sparkling with laughter. "Are you always this cold-blooded with your lovers? Analyzing your actions, their actions, who has the upper hand?"

No, she wasn't. Usually her lovers were so dazzled at the prospect of bedding the legendary Olivia Raines that she merely expressed her slightest wish and it was done.

Lord Erith undoubtedly wanted her. But he was nowhere near dazzled, curse him. He went on without waiting for an answer. "Kissing you becomes more appealing by the minute."

Beneath her appearance of indifference, she suppressed a shudder. Nothing he'd done to her tonight compared to suffering his mouth on hers yesterday. "You can kiss me. Just not on the lips."

"Very generous." He rolled to the side and stood up. "Come here."

She sucked in her first full breath since he'd caught her up in his arms. "More orders?"

"Of course." He took her hand. She waited for him to haul her to her feet, but he drew her up very gently. When she reached for his neckcloth, he lifted a hand to still her busy fingers. "I want to undress you."

"We've only got until July," she said with asperity. "Perhaps you should begin."

"Your impatience is flattering."

His long narrow mouth curved in a full smile, carving deep grooves in his tanned cheeks. He was a handsome man when he was somber. Smiling, he was breathtaking. Her wayward heart abandoned its wild gallop for one lost moment and ceased beating altogether.

He raised his hand. She waited, with a breathless tension she was ashamed to admit, for him to paw at her bodice. Instead, he carefully slid a pin from her hair. One long tendril of shiny brown uncoiled to snake across the top of her bosom, revealed under the low neckline of her gown.

He lifted the lock and rubbed it between his fingers. "Pretty."

Fleetingly she was a child again, watching her father test wool shorn from his tenants' sheep. Sad nostalgia stifled the barbed retort that rose in her throat.

Slowly he pulled out another pin. Another tendril fell. And another. And another. Until the elaborate confection her maid had tortured her hair into was only a memory.

Lord Erith stroked the thick brown mass, smoothing tangles, straightening kinks. His eyes shone with fascination. He brought a handful of hair to his face.

"It smells like flowers." He dropped her hair and buried his face in the curve of her neck, where he'd bitten, then kissed her. "*You* smell like flowers."

"It's the bouquets."

"No, it's not."

His hands dropped to the hooks that ran up the back of her gown. In spite of all her experience, the dedicated attention he paid to undressing her had its own allure. With practiced ease he undid her gown and slid it off her shoulders. The room was warm with the candles and the fire in the grate. Still she shivered as air glanced over the bare skin of arms and shoulders.

Carefully, he drew her sleeves down over her hands so the bodice fell to her waist. She stood in her light corset and shift. Perhaps because tonight she didn't control the encounter, her near nakedness before a stranger gave her a frisson of discomfort. She raised her chin and swallowed to moisten a throat dry with nerves.

Her corset was delicately embroidered with ivy leaves and tulips. His attention fell to where her breasts mounded above the lace edging. His breathing wasn't as steady as it had been. When he raised his eyes, the gray was soft and deep like endless sea fog. Brittle excitement glowed like banked embers behind that gaze. The slightest spark would ignite his desire into an inferno.

"Turn around," he said gruffly. Definitely, his restraint wore thin.

Without a word, she presented her back and stretched to push aside her hair so he could unlace her corset. It sagged and she shrugged it away. She faced him, clad in her transparent shift. The silk was so fine that her light brown nipples were clearly visible. Her breasts were small but round. Even though she was over thirty, they'd hardly sagged. She wasn't ashamed of her body. It was as lean and spare as it had been in girlhood.

She wondered if Lord Erith preferred a fuller figure. Then wondered why she wondered. Current fashions didn't conceal her shape. He couldn't expect to discover a generous bosom under her clothing.

Her brief and uncharacteristic insecurity vanished as a

delighted smile crossed his face, making him look much younger. "Perfect," he said softly.

She lifted the hem of her shift, but again he reached out to stay her. "Let me."

She stood like a puppet, raising her arms as he pulled the shift over her head. Was he this careful with all his lovers? Even she, inured to any man's touch, found this slow unveiling piquant. One would almost imagine he cared about the woman he bedded as more than just a willing body.

A pity he wasted his concentrated attention on a woman who couldn't appreciate it.

Still, she didn't resist when he placed his hands on her bare shoulders and gently but firmly pushed her back onto the bed so she lay spread before him. He slid her shoes and stockings off then surveyed her with deceptively sleepy eyes. She wasn't fooled. He was about as sleepy as a starving leopard stalking a herd of antelope.

He shucked off his coat and flung it across the carved chair that backed against the elegant lemon and navy striped wallpaper. Then those deft hands lifted to his neckcloth. A few economical movements and he stood barefoot and bare-chested.

He was built like a wrestler. No, like a lithe young boxer, for all that he must be nearly forty. This was a man in the prime of life. His chest was heavy with muscle. Hair covered his pectorals then narrowed to disappear into his waistband. His shoulders were straight and wide, and his arms bulged with power.

He straddled her, his heat an enveloping blanket. The air felt thick as soup, heavy with the spice of his arousal and the sweetness of the flowers. Every breath clogged her lungs. As she braced for his possession, her fists clenched.

Still he delayed. He brushed his fingers along her body. Discovering the straight line of her shoulders. Tracing the hard collarbone. He shaped her flanks, running his hands down her ribs to the curve of her waist. Testing the gentle flare of hips, the firmness of thighs.

She shifted restlessly at last. This slow seduction disturbed her. Why didn't he touch her breasts, her sex? Why didn't he just push her legs apart and take her?

He cupped her breasts. The nipples had contracted into hard points, and he bent to kiss one whorled tip. His mouth was hot on her flesh, hotter when he took her into his mouth. Erith shifted his attention to her other breast, nuzzling and suckling as if she were some delicious piece of exotic fruit.

For a long time she lay unmoving beneath his ministrations. The sensation of his lips on her skin wasn't unpleasant. She'd certainly known men less skilled.

He drew away and stood, his hands going to his trousers. He removed the last of his clothing with another of those adept movements.

She should have been prepared for his nakedness. But even so experienced a courtesan as she felt the breath catch in her throat at the sight of Lord Erith wearing nothing but his skin.

He was superb in his masculinity.

There was nothing of the boy in him. Nothing unformed or undeveloped. Just confidence and virility and strength. Most men seemed diminished once they shed their clothing. Like snails without their shells. Lord Erith was only more vital. Slowly, her scrutiny traveled from his large feet, over his long powerful legs, to where his penis jutted, thick and large, from its nest of black curls.

The inevitable moment was upon her. When a man crushed her down on a bed and forced his swollen member inside her. The odd stasis that held her quiescent shattered. Her heart began to race and her muscles tightened with automatic resistance.

She'd had no chance to don the impenetrable mental armor of Olivia Raines, queen of the demimonde. She'd had no chance to convince Erith that no matter how he tried, he'd never possess her completely. Her ultimate unattainability always cowed her lovers into allowing her sway.

But tonight, with Lord Erith, everything was different. *Why? Why? Why?*

She resisted pulling the sheet up. Modesty was a luxury she hadn't enjoyed since she was fourteen. Real and unwelcome emotion vibrated through her and left her vulnerable.

Then she realized he no longer constrained her. At least she could make her most essential preparation for a lover. A preparation she usually took in private before she summoned her keeper. She rolled away and reached for a small ceramic pot on the bedside cabinet.

A powerful hand came down and circled her wrist. "What are you doing?"

"It's . . . it's an unguent that increases pleasure." She cursed the faint stammer. Good God! No man made her stutter. You'd think she hiked her skirts for her first customer.

"We won't need it." He angled her stiff body so she faced him. Naked, large, powerful, he knelt over her, leaving her nowhere to hide.

"The cream helps prevent conception," she said flatly. It wasn't true but it made a convincing argument.

Or should have.

"I'll withdraw," he said implacably. The gray eyes were burningly intense as they studied her. "I want to feel you and you alone the first time I fuck you."

She felt the blood drain from her cheeks. At his strong language and at the determination behind it. "My lord, I claim a certain freedom in my liaisons."

"So you've told me," he said with a trace of weariness.

"Sorry if I'm boring you," she snapped.

His lips took on a sardonic twist. "I expect you'll be interesting enough in a few moments."

She grabbed for the unguent but he was too quick, snatching it out of reach. "No, Olivia."

"You have no right to say that to me!"

"I claim the right." With an abrupt movement, he pitched the little jar against the wall, where it shattered, splattering her precious ointment across the wallpaper. A pungent herbal reek overpowered the perfume of the flowers.

"Lord Erith . . . " She was more shocked than angry.

"I claim you," he said, as though she hadn't spoken. As though he hadn't just acted like a barbarian. "Are you ready, Olivia?"

After his performance with the ceramic pot, she hadn't expected such consideration. Hiding her reluctance under an impassive facade, she slipped down to lie outstretched.

"Yes." Although she lied.

God give her strength and greater acting skills than she'd ever called upon before. She stared up at Lord Erith's saturnine face and lifted her arms in silent invitation.

Chapter 4

*E*rith stared down at a woman desirable beyond the dreams of earthly men. And wondered why, through his boiling need, instinct screamed to be suspicious. Very suspicious.

But God help him, he was only human. The clarion call of hunger smothered any doubt.

As he knelt between her legs, his heart thundered and sweat chilled his burning skin. He bent to nibble and lick the side of her neck, breathing deep so her sweet essence penetrated his lungs. Her warm fragrance was more intoxicating than wine.

She moaned, a soft breathy sound of need.

He trailed his hand across her thigh to the bronze curls on her mons. His palm moved in delicate circles while he took her pert, perfect breast in his mouth. A shaft of pleasure pierced him. She tasted like honey on his tongue. As he drew hard on the puckered crest, she released a smothered cry and hooked her hands around his shoulders. He slid his hand lower to test the slick evidence of desire.

She was dry.

Shocked disbelief juddered through him. His hand stilled at the junction of her thighs. He wrenched his head up and stared into her face.

The face of a woman ripped by talons of desire.

What the hell was going on?

Her head tilted back, her eyes fluttered closed, her lips parted in ecstasy. Her chest heaved as she fought for air. She moaned again. A rich, female, passionate sound. Her long slender legs framed his hips. She lay willing and open to his invasion.

"Take me," she pleaded in a guttural voice, her hands kneading his shoulders.

She wanted him. Everything she did told him she wanted him.

Was he going mad? Carefully he stroked her sex again.

Not a trace of feminine dew.

Another moan. She pressed herself into his hand in a paroxysm of need.

His fingers clenched as confusion rocked his mind. Damn it, what part of her was a lie?

She was a goddess in his arms, everything he wanted. But what did she want? She wasn't ready, whatever passion she pretended.

He fought the overwhelming impulse to plunge into her, although the delay nearly blew the top of his head off. He'd rushed her into this, his ravenous craving setting the pace. Did she need more preparation? He found the small fleshy protuberance and gently stimulated it.

"Yes, oh, yes," she hissed, grinding herself against his fingers in rapture.

Except rapture would make her moist and hot. Carefully, because dry as she was he could cause her discomfort, he pushed one finger into her. She surged up and bit him on the shoulder. The sharp nip of her teeth shot a blast of reaction through to his balls. He jerked and almost lost control.

All the time, his finger rasped in her dry passage.

Hell, he couldn't be mistaken. Damn it all to Hades and back. This woman showed no physical signs of sexual response. Although she did a marvelous job of counterfeiting passion.

"Stop it," he snarled, snatching his hand from her. She twisted as if she'd die unless he took her in the next second. The dishonesty of it all suddenly disgusted him. He ripped himself away and knelt over her, furious and naked and, Devil take her, nearly blind with unsatisfied lust. "I said stop it!"

As abruptly as if he'd tossed a bucket of icy water over her, the writhing siren vanished. When she opened her eyes, the topaz stare was clear and unglazed with passion.

Of course it was. That elaborate performance hadn't been real.

What was real, unfortunately, was the excruciating ache in his nuts and a cock as hard and hot as an iron brand. He set his jaw and struggled to hold onto what few shreds of control he retained.

He'd never had a lover who hadn't responded. It stung his vanity that Olivia was as cold in his arms as a tin automaton. And filled him with a regret that was the strongest emotion a woman had roused in years.

"What's wrong?" She drew herself up against the headboard and curled her legs under her. She looked annoyed and not at all frustrated. He, on the other hand, harbored enough frustration to fill an ocean.

He collapsed on his back and ground his teeth as he strove to master his need. He didn't touch her. If he touched her, he thought he'd explode. He wanted her with ferocious ardor. And he wanted her now. Hell, hunger was a raging fire that threatened to immolate him to a pile of smoking ash.

Lord save him, he'd have to stay hungry.

"You don't have to pretend," he said with difficulty, staring upward through unseeing eyes. His heart battered at his chest as if it fought to escape. His hands clenched and unclenched at his sides in time with each rasping breath.

"Pretend?" She sounded bewildered, lost. As though his behavior made no sense.

"Christ Jesus, Olivia!"

She stifled a gasp and flinched back against the bed head. Good God, he didn't intend to frighten her. He fisted his hands so hard, his arms ached. He sucked in a deep breath to beat back his unraveling temper.

So she could be in no doubt of his meaning, he turned to look at her and spoke slowly and clearly. "I'm awake to your game. You don't have to lie anymore."

The blood seeped from her face, leaving her pale as milk. The pretty little mole beside her mouth stood out like a black dot painted on a white canvas. "If I give you pleasure, that covers our contract."

Bitterness frayed his voice. "I paid for a lover, Olivia. Not a skilled actress with no real interest in the role."

He hadn't meant to be cruel but she winced nonetheless. Her chin lifted in quick resentment. "Surely I'm not the first woman who doesn't melt into the great Earl of Erith's arms," she said acidly.

"You're the first woman I've slept with who keeps a jar of ointment by the bed to ease a man's passage." He ignored her dismayed gasp and continued ruthlessly, "That's what the unguent is for, isn't it? It supplies the moisture your body doesn't."

As swiftly as a snake uncoiling, she straightened and dived for the edge of the mattress. He grabbed her arm, rolling so he loomed over her. "I haven't finished."

She arched her eyebrows and her damnably knowledgeable eyes dropped to where his staff rose so emphatically. "I can see that."

"Do you like women? Is that the problem?"

A scornful laugh escaped her. "It's simpler than that. I don't like you."

Her bluntness didn't anger him, just made him insatiably curious. Perhaps she didn't like him, but something told him the difficulty was more serious than antipathy for an uncongenial keeper. "Are you frigid?"

He felt her tiny start. "Does your conceit know no bounds?"

"I'm trying to understand."

"You're making this too complicated. Now, release me, if you please. I'll dress and return to Perry's."

"Don't go, Olivia," he said softly. "The game has just started."

Under his fingers, she trembled. Anger? Or fear? Her voice was brittle with sarcasm. "You haven't had your money's worth? My apologies. All isn't lost. At least some other woman you purchase can move into the house."

"I don't want another woman," he said calmly, disregarding her jibes. "I want you."

"Well, I don't want you."

"For now."

"The arrogance of the upper-class English male never fails to amaze me." She surveyed him with cold eyes. When she spoke, her voice was steady, almost prosaic. "You can have me before I go if you like."

His mind shattered into a thousand shards of excitement. All moisture evaporated from his mouth.

She was his for the taking. *His.*

"No, Olivia." His response was husky with sorrow. "I'm a large man and you're not ready. I'll hurt you."

She shrugged. He began to recognize it as a characteristic gesture. A slight hardness entered her face and her voice was expressionless. For a moment he'd touched the real woman inside the ravishing shell. Now she looked like the self-possessed courtesan he'd met in Montjoy's salon. "Then we'll have to see what else we can do for you."

She shook free but only because he let her go. He could tell that for the moment she wasn't going anywhere.

Departure would look too much like defeat, and if he'd learned anything about her, it was that his mistress had a pride to equal his own. He guessed at the effort and style and sheer courage she'd needed over the years to create the legend of irresistible, invincible Olivia Raines. She wouldn't sacrifice that hard-won reputation easily, no matter how much she wanted to flee his bed.

"Lie back," she said coolly.

He obeyed without question. His eyes didn't waver from her as he stretched out, itchy with a tormenting mixture of curiosity and lust. Breathlessly, he waited to see what she'd do next.

What she did next made his heart slam to a screaming halt.

She crawled between his legs and reached out. He jerked as her cool hand circled his burning flesh. His vision faded, every drop of blood in his body drained to his throbbing genitals.

She began a rhythmic stroking, tightening and releasing the pressure until he closed his eyes and saw exploding stars. She played his flesh like a great musician played an instrument. Racing scale passages. Thundering chords. Wild cadenzas. Thrilling trills. The world shrank to pure sensation. A choked groan emerged from his throat and he flung his head back. If she stopped touching him, he honestly thought he'd die.

Something silky and warm brushed his groin. A cloud of hair. The added sensation flung him closer to release. He barely stopped himself spurting into her hand. He opened dazed eyes to watch her tawny head lower with teasing hesitation.

A smile lifted the corner of her mouth. Mocking. Provoking. Triumphant. As though she knew that in this she had the advantage.

Of course she did. He wanted her and couldn't hide it.

Her expression became almost gloating as she leaned the final few inches. Then she paused. Every scraping breath he snatched seemed to catch in his lungs forever.

She waited.

Knowing each second's delay lasted a cruel hour. And each prolonged second drove him closer to insanity.

The gorgeous witch.

She bent so close, her breath glanced across the tip. His hungry, tumescent flesh yearned toward her lips.

She smiled again and inched back with deliberate slowness.

Oh, yes, she meant to torture him.

Her hand continued to squeeze and stroke, building his need to ragged desperation. Every touch blasted through him like a direct hit from a cannonade. But her hand alone was no longer enough.

Still she remained out of reach.

Dear God, Olivia, take me soon or I'll lose my damned mind.

"Hell," he grated, struggling against the urge to grab her head and press her down. Some last shred of intuition told him he'd never force her. That she intended his pleasure. But she also intended his torment.

And what measure of either pleasure or torment he experienced was completely in her power.

"No, not hell, my lord," she murmured, the words a taunting whisper across his searing heat. "Heaven."

Her head lowered the last fraction of an inch. If she teased him now, he'd lose himself. She'd driven him to the brink and he trembled as though in the grip of a fever.

She encircled the head of his cock with her lush, full-lipped mouth.

Glorious heat.

Moisture.

He closed his eyes and ceded himself to her seduction. It didn't matter anymore that she did this to prove a point.

Her hand and mouth set up a rapturous counterpoint. The breath jammed in his throat and his heart threatened to burst. "Olivia, you're killing me."

Blindly, he tangled his hands in her thick hair. The slippery silkiness perfectly complemented the hot, wet suction. He fell into velvety darkness where there was only her damnably skillful mouth and the soft sounds emerging from her throat.

His hands fisted in the tangled mane as she increased the pressure. He'd imagined her mouth on him like this since the first moment he saw her. But the actuality of those lips sucking him was beyond anything he'd ever known. He jerked toward her, wanting more.

Her fingers stilled. With a blazing slide, she moved upward. Surely she wasn't leaving him like this, shaking and frantic.

God, God, God. He couldn't endure it . . .

Cool air brushed unbearably over his swollen, oversensitized flesh. A deep groan forced its way out of a throat too tight for words.

Delicately, she licked the head. He shuddered at the calculated flick of her tongue. He was so close to coming. So close . . .

"Take me in your mouth." He didn't recognize the guttural voice as his.

She licked across the tip again. He surged up, fisting his hands in the sheets so he didn't grab her and make her do what he wanted. He couldn't risk stopping her now. It would destroy him.

"Take me, Olivia," he begged, and didn't care that his pride was dust. He only cared that she pushed this pleasure to its limit before she finished.

One last teasing foray with her tongue. Then abruptly she relented and surrounded him again with her sublime dark heat. He lost his last connection to any reality but her mouth and his blazing need.

With a broken cry he bowed up and gave himself to her.

For a long time he knew nothing but fiery release. She had him so desperate, so heavy, so ready, he flooded her mouth in an endless river.

On and on and on. Forever.

By the time he finished, he felt wrung out, empty, exhausted. She'd leeched away his last drop of vitality. Only a husk remained. He'd never had such a climax from a woman using her mouth.

He'd never had such a climax.

Inch by tormenting inch, she slid her lips off him, making him feel every clinging moment of withdrawal.

He sank back onto the mattress, gasping for air. Each tattered breath seemed more than his exhausted body could manage. His brain had ceased to function. There was only animal satiation.

Somewhere in those extraordinary seconds, he'd left the world far behind. He'd flown to a heaven of a thousand suns. He'd heard angels sing hallelujahs of unearthly praise.

No, perhaps not angels. There was too much of the Devil in her seduction. But the sin was glorious. He'd gladly face hellfire itself if she'd do it again.

When she looked up at him, a slow, victorious smile curved a mouth red and swollen from what she'd just done. She licked her lips as if savoring the last trace of his seed. A fierce need to have her take him again settled low in Erith's gut. An even fiercer need to possess her with his body.

She was his. From her tawny hair to her clever, hot mouth to her pale, elegant toes. He wasn't letting her go tonight. Or any time soon, damn it.

She shook her hair behind her shoulders in a movement that wordlessly conveyed her triumph.

Yes, she'd won the encounter.

So had he. She was still here.

The room was silent apart from the rattle of his breath. Outside a horse neighed as a carriage passed. Strange to think the real world continued on its way yet his life had totally changed.

New knowledge swam in the topaz eyes that studied him. As if having tasted him so completely, she'd claimed his soul.

For God's sake, Erith, stop this. Souls have no place in this transaction. And even if they have, you lost yours years ago.

"All right, you've impressed me," he drawled, although it nearly killed him to pretend nonchalance. Good Lord, it nearly killed him to find energy to speak.

"I've convinced you to allow me my sway?" With a grace that made his heart stutter, she crossed her legs and settled at the base of the mattress. She was brazen. Or would have been if her easy nakedness hadn't seemed so natural.

With a muttered curse, he lunged off the bed and picked up his shirt. "Here, put this on," he snapped, flinging it at her.

She caught the shirt then stared at him as if he were mad. He probably was. He'd certainly never started a liaison like this. He had a sudden nostalgia for sweet, uncomplicated Gretchen. Except he'd been bored with Gretchen long before he finished with her.

"Will you put on the bloody shirt?" His voice was strangled.

Her mouth quirked, drawing his attention to the mole near its corner. He resisted the urge to tell her to put that mouth on him again. Unbelievably, in spite of that titanic climax, his arousal stirred anew.

"You seem on edge, my lord."

She pulled the shirt over her head. His tempestuous state should calm now that she concealed her remarkable body. But something about the thoughtless grace with which she tugged the mass of hair away from the collar and shook it free to tumble down her back jolted him with electric awareness.

The movement wasn't designed to seduce. Yet seduced he was. Just as the flowery scent of her skin seduced him and the sound of her voice—even arguing, damn it—seduced him.

Her wide, sensual mouth glistened with moisture. With a

complete lack of self-consciousness, she raised her hand and wiped it across her lips.

That mouth had clasped him tighter than a new glove. He burned to discover how it felt to penetrate her body. Would her grip on him be as tight? Tighter? He swallowed to relieve the sudden constriction in his throat as he imagined thrusting into her.

"I don't want the game to end yet, if that's what you mean." His voice sounded rusty. He snatched up his trousers and tugged them carelessly over his long legs and hardening prick.

She looked troubled, and when she spoke, her tone was somber. The faintly teasing edge had gone. "My good sense tells me it's better to part, my lord."

His heart gave a great thud of denial. No. He couldn't let her go. Not now. Not after a glimpse of the pleasure she could give him. After what she'd just done, how could he endure the prospect of losing her?

His instincts homed in on something he'd already guessed. He kept his voice steady even as his heart broke into a panicked race that he might be wrong. "What will the world say if I toss you into the street after one night? The reputation of irresistible Olivia Raines will suffer a blow, perhaps a fatal one."

The voluptuous mouth flattened. "Perhaps the world will consider you inadequate."

"I'm renowned as a great lover, Miss Raines. I suspect gossip will favor me."

A frown creased her brow. "I don't care about gossip."

"Liar. Every male in the ton is at your feet and you love it."

She didn't bother denying his assertion. Her complete lack of coyness was one of many things he admired. "My charms don't bewitch you."

"Take me in your mouth again and you'll see how bewitched I am."

She gave a choked giggle. It made her seem suddenly younger, more real. She sat in radiant dishevelment, like an Arabian boy in front of a carpet stall. Except no Arabian street urchin had that luxuriant mass of tawny hair or those remarkable topaz eyes. No Arabian boy wore an expensive man's shirt, crumpled and open at the neck.

The hard points of her nipples pressed impudently against the fine white linen. He had to stop himself from leaning down and tasting her there even as hot blood began to pound in his ears.

He and Olivia played a subtle game of push and pull for sovereignty. He'd fallen prey to her dominion once tonight. Next time he planned to be the leader.

Surprisingly, a streak of color marked her slanted cheekbones. "What I did was a farewell gesture, Lord Erith."

He couldn't remember the last time a woman had walked away from him. Perhaps never. No wonder Olivia accused him of conceit.

He floundered for something to make her stay. Anything. Money wasn't the answer. A strange revelation when it came to a whore.

What did the witch want? His soul? She was welcome to it. It had never done him any good. Although surely such a canny jade wouldn't want anything as useless.

Not money. Not luxury. Not, blast her, sexual pleasure.

A shame. He could give her all three without a blink.

Ah, she was a complicated wench, his Olivia.

Well, he was the Earl of Erith, and he always held the whip hand. But she didn't have to know that. Instinct still told him her pride, and only her pride, would lead to her downfall. Her fall into his waiting arms, in any case.

His plan was sly. Manipulative. *Marvelous.* He almost laughed aloud in jubilation.

"Lord Erith?" Her tone was suspicious. "What are you up to?"

"I notice you like to ape the males of the ton."

"I sometimes find men's clothes convenient. How far I 'ape' my friends is open to argument."

"So you're up for a gentleman's wager?" He kept his voice casual and his expression merely interested. Thank God he'd always been a killer card player. If she knew just how desperate he was to keep her, she'd run a hundred miles.

Her eyes sharpened on his face and he almost heard her mind buzzing with questions. "Occasionally." A spark lit the topaz depths. "I work too hard to throw my money away."

He ignored the insult implicit in the *hard work* description. "Could I interest you in a small bet?"

She still sounded mistrustful. "I can't imagine I have anything you want."

He arched a disbelieving eyebrow and gave a scornful grunt. "You can't be that naive."

She snapped back, "What could you give me if I win?"

"You'd like my surrender," he said brusquely.

At last their jockeying for the upper hand emerged into the open. Olivia Raines liked to be in charge. Well, so did he. And he always won.

She didn't retreat. He knew she wouldn't. He was right. Pride was the key to her character. "You'd like mine."

He smiled with triumph. "Let's wager on who gives in first."

As she sucked in a lungful of air, he tried to ignore how her breasts slid against the fragile barrier of his shirt. Only the strongest exercise of willpower kept him from tumbling her back against the sheets. If he took her while he was so needy, victory would be irrefutably and eternally hers.

"Why should I care?" She did a fine job of pretending indifference. But a light in the tiger eyes indicated he'd caught her interest.

"Because if you conquer the world famous rake, the Earl of Erith, your reputation as Europe's greatest courtesan is assured."

She gave another smothered laugh. God, he was in a bad

way if the mere sound of her laughter made him edgy with arousal. "You don't hide your light under a bushel."

"Lights are for shining."

"Lord Erith, you mistake my level of involvement."

"If you leave now, the world will think I was too much man for you to master. What a pathetic debacle for the notorious, the superb, the all-conquering Olivia Raines I heard so much about when I arrived in London."

She still sounded like she didn't care, but he caught a glint of curiosity in her lustrous eyes as she looked up at him where he stood near the bed. "So what do you suggest instead, my lord?"

"Give me a month. If I can't bring you to pleasure in that time, I publicly go on my knees to you and proclaim you as the only woman who ever got the better of me."

She tilted one smooth eyebrow. "Got the better of you?"

"We can argue terms later. If you win, you can leave and keep any spoils that would have been yours if you'd stayed until July."

"And if *you* win?"

"You admit your defeat to me and stay as my willing lover until I leave for Vienna."

She smiled. A real smile like the one she'd given him in the library last night. Its warmth heated him like a stream of fire. "You don't believe there's the remotest chance you'll lose, do you?"

"Just as you're sure of your bastion, my lady. What point wagering on a sure thing?" He took a deep breath. His gut clenched as he recognized, for all his cunning, he might not have swayed her. "Do we have an agreement? Or does your courage fail?"

She laughed shortly. "You think I'm so easy to manipulate?"

"Are you?" he asked with a genuine interest he could no longer hide.

She took a deep breath and spoke with complete steadiness. "Absolutely. Lord Erith, you have a wager."

Chapter 5

$\mathscr{I}$n resigned silence, Olivia waited for Lord Erith to push her down and thrust into her. She hadn't missed his rising excitement.

But he didn't alter his relaxed stance near the bed. Instead, he stared at her as if he read her every thought.

Of course, he couldn't. No man could.

She hadn't sated him with her mouth. Although she'd employed every ounce of skill. Usually, she felt contempt at a lover's quaking surrender to her adroit lips. Her reaction when Lord Erith finally yielded himself to orgasm had been more ambiguous. One thing she recognized—he was the most virile man she'd taken into her bed. He'd come with a volcanic heat she'd never experienced.

Now a Devil's wager yoked them together for a month.

Curse him, he'd given her no choice. Or no choice her pride permitted. As little more than a girl, she'd set herself to dominate the despised sex that had destroyed her life. Every lover had fallen under her power.

Lord Erith would be her final protector. She was damned if he'd distinguish himself not just as her last lover but also as the only man to best her. She wouldn't countenance failure after so many years of brilliant success.

She'd been forced into this life but had created a work of art from degradation. Her pride insisted she left the demimonde as queen and not as beggar.

If she and Erith parted after one night, she knew that the glittering facade of her legend would disintegrate. The world that avidly reported her every action might look more closely. Might see an aging woman past her glory days. A woman offering sham promises of transcendent sexual pleasure. A woman who at heart was hollow.

No, nobody would ever know that.

Except Erith.

She hid a shudder as she recalled that fraught moment when he discovered her body held no more feeling than a lump of wood. She should have guessed he'd treat that lack in her as a challenge.

Now he set himself to coax a genuine response from his frigid mistress. Ha. He didn't know who he dealt with. She'd win this bet because she was dead to pleasure. All Lord Erith's self-assurance and sexual expertise would never change that.

But if he'd uncovered so much about her in one night, what other secrets would he reveal before their infernal bargain ended?

Chill unease trickled down her spine.

Erith sent her his lazy smile, his silver eyes glinting under heavy eyelids. She was immune to men, but even she admitted the earl was attractive, especially when the shell of cynicism fell away. Right now he looked at ease and rather pleased with himself. Of course he did. He thought he'd made a bet he couldn't lose.

"An extravagant supper waits in the next room." He stepped closer, towering over her where she sat on the end of the bed.

Physically, she found little to criticize about him. He was hard and muscular and generously endowed. And he knew his way around a woman's body. No wonder self-confidence cascaded from him.

Perry was right. Lord Erith was arrogant, if perhaps not an ass.

"Food, Olivia? Or would you rather ogle my manly charms?"

She emerged from distraction to realize he offered his hand. She shrugged, choosing to be frank. "You know you're a handsome fellow."

He looked startled, and she almost laughed. She accepted his hand and rose with the grace she'd been trained to exhibit. When she gained her victory, as she undoubtedly would, she wanted him not only to regret losing the wager. She also wanted him to recognize that he'd never breached the fortress of her real self.

She intended to keep the Earl of Erith in a perpetual lather of desire. He challenged her, not just with the wager but with his whole being. She couldn't say why, but the reality of that challenge was as solid as the mahogany dresser against the wall.

"I'm not blind, my lord."

"Neither am I," he growled, releasing her and striding through to the dressing room. He appeared within seconds holding something scarlet and shiny, which he threw in her direction. "For the sake of my sanity, put that on."

Olivia hid another smile as she shook out the garment to discover a Chinese dressing gown embroidered with fighting dragons. With a slowness she knew tormented, she pulled it on over his shirt. "You've paid a king's ransom to see me naked. It seems perverse to cover me up."

"You know why. Stop teasing me."

"Why?" She tied the robe loosely at her waist so it fell about her feet in a glorious shimmer. Yet again she appeared before him in men's clothing. This time the clothing was his. It added an interesting piquancy. "I enjoy teasing you."

His narrow mouth lifted in a wry smile. "Like a cat plays with a mouse. Be warned, I'm no mouse." He opened the door to the sitting room and waited for her to precede him. "Stop needling me and have something to eat."

He pulled out one of the elegant Sheraton chairs for her. Then he went to the sideboard to select from the delicacies supplied by the French chef. She was used to generous lovers—she chose no protector likely to keep her on short rations. But Lord Erith had spared no cost in furnishing and staffing his bower of love.

Including the woman who warmed his bed.

Strange, then, that he showed no great urgency now to get her into that bed. He'd retreated into a charming companion instead of a desperate lover. She wasn't sure it was what she wanted. If he was desperate, she could use it against him.

He slid her plate in front of her then served himself before opening the champagne. He poured two glasses and passed her one as he sat in bare-chested glory opposite her. On a purely aesthetic level, he was an impressive specimen.

"To us." His smile was faintly knowing as his toast drew her attention from his powerful torso.

"To victory," she said coolly, raising her glass in reply before sipping. The champagne fizzed pleasantly against her palate, combining with the lingering salty taste of Erith's seed.

He laughed shortly and tossed back a mouthful of champagne. Then he unfolded his napkin with a flourish. "I like that you don't give in easily."

She remembered his horrified shock when he realized her passion was false. Her lips stretched in a sardonic smile. "I suspect you'd like it better if I did give in."

They spoke as if she had a choice. Heaven help her if he learned how totally a victim she was.

With less drama, she laid her napkin across her red-silk-covered lap and took another sip of champagne. She liked champagne. The bubbles reminded her that her life held occasional pleasures for all its loneliness and dissipation.

"Do you want to try and see?" He watched her steadily, his gray eyes unwavering. She knew her face was expressionless. At an early age, she'd taught herself to be as mysterious as the sphinx.

"I didn't deny you, Lord Erith," she said calmly, beginning to eat. She was hungry. Surprisingly. After tonight's turbulent emotions, food should jam in her throat.

"You denied me what I want," he said with equal calmness, biting into a lobster patty with a snap of his strong white teeth.

He was an incredibly physical man. She imagined most women found him alluring. Even she couldn't ignore a certain excitement in the air when she was with him. And she'd never considered any man exciting. Frightening. Annoying. Boring. *Boorish*.

It was a sad reflection. But she could do nothing to change the way she was. Just as Lord Erith could do nothing to change her, for all his confidence.

"Do you always expect your mistresses to find pleasure?"

"Yes."

Thoughtfully he stared down at his champagne glass. His long fingers played idly with the crystal stem. The movement was unconsciously sensual. It reminded her of his hands on her naked skin. The breath caught in her throat and a strange shiver captured her. Perhaps she was cold, although a fire blazed in the hearth.

He looked directly at her. For once, cynicism didn't veil his gray eyes. "Unless my lover responds, the experience is barren."

The simple words sliced her defenses to shreds.

For her, the experience was always barren. Such an essential part of life stolen from her by male greed and carelessness and cruelty. A great lump of misery lodged in her throat and the room went fuzzy. For the first time in years she felt like crying.

She cried in front of no man. She strove for composure.

Still, her voice was husky when she answered. "You're not what I expected."

Brief amusement crossed his dark face. His stubble was a dark shadow across his jaw and his hair was ruffled. Soft firelight gilded the hard muscles of chest and arms. He was beautiful, she suddenly realized. Not as Perry and his friends were beautiful. But beautiful like a stallion or a raging storm or a rough sea. Beautiful like everything powerful and vital and dangerous.

"You're not what I expected either."

"Most men treat whores as commodities."

"Surely you consider yourself more than a whore."

She shrugged. "I barter my body for money. What else would I call myself? I'm not ashamed."

"No, and that's one of the attractive things about you. You select your lovers, you control the affairs. You have more in common with rakes I know than with those sad creatures who hawk their wares in Covent Garden."

Only the grace of God had saved her from becoming one of those creatures. And the obstinate determination that if she was destined to be a harlot, she'd become the apotheosis of harlots. "At heart, we are sisters."

"No." His voice was even and sure.

He took another sip of champagne and began to eat. Olivia stared at him in astonishment. She'd never met a man like him.

Apprehension chilled her as she wondered if his wager wasn't reckless at all. "I'm surprised you never married again, my lord. You're in the prime of life, and you'd find intimacy with a wife more readily than with a mistress."

His face hardened and his fist clenched on the damask tablecloth. He spoke with obvious difficulty. "Of course you know about my wife."

His unspoken grief was palpable, in spite of the many years since Lady Erith's death. But other currents swirled about him too. Unprecedented for sophisticated, detached

Olivia Raines, she found herself stumbling into clumsy apology.

"Forgive me, I had no right to mention your wife, Lord Erith. It's just when you . . . " Anger still shadowed his expression as she steeled herself to continue. "When you said you wanted to be more than a client to the women you bought, it struck me you wanted a wife, not a temporary mistress."

"I'll never marry again."

The words held such stark despair that she couldn't speak. The only sound was the flames crackling in the grate. Heavens, what lay behind his vehement reaction? Love? Hate? Indifference?

No, anything but indifference.

Who knew what he'd been like as a young man? Breathtakingly handsome, surely. She tried and failed to picture Lord Erith as an innocent. That saturnine face seemed too knowing for her to imagine him untouched by life. But perhaps once that face had held hope, trust . . . *love*.

Lord Erith liked to present himself as an unfeeling monolith. In that moment the already tottering image shattered, never to be restored. He might fool the world into believing him hard and cynical, but it was a thousand miles from the truth.

"I'm sorry I brought up unhappy memories," she said very quietly. "My only excuse is that this . . . this evening hasn't progressed the way I thought it would."

He shook his head. "Some memories hover too close to the surface, whether you talk about them or not."

"Yes." She looked down at her plate. She hadn't eaten much. Neither had he. She felt strangely awkward, she who hadn't been awkward with a man since she'd come to London. But when she spoke, her words emerged with an uncertain edge. "Do you want to go back to bed?"

He looked up with a smile that held as much self-derision as amusement. "No."

She was startled. "No?"

His hand relaxed from its tight fist. "Don't be a fool. You know how much I desire you. But you're not ready to give me what I want."

"This can't be the evening you planned when you gave me that spectacular ruby bracelet." Which she suddenly realized she should be wearing.

"Perhaps not. But it's been memorable."

Her lips twitched. Yes, he was right. Memorable indeed.

He rose and walked past her into the bedroom. He passed close enough for her to catch his scent, sandalwood and musk. It was as if she tasted him again. As she remembered how his engorged member had jerked under her lips, an odd sensation settled in her belly. Olivia drank more champagne to banish the memory. The wine settled sour and flat on her tongue and did nothing to stem her restlessness.

Erith emerged carrying a square velvet case, which he passed to her. "I meant to give you this earlier but my capacity for thought evaporated when I saw you on the stairs."

In his other hand he held a shirt, which he tugged over his head. A trace of real woman must lurk inside her, because she couldn't help regretting that he covered his superb physique.

"Open it," he urged.

In her concentration on Erith, she'd forgotten the jeweler's box.

Yet surely that was why she was here, for jewels and money and prestige. Not for the pleasure of watching a handsome man do something as banal as dress. Hot color rose. After all these years of balancing over her world like an acrobat on a tightrope, she risked tumbling to ruin just as she reached the chasm's other side.

After the bracelet, she'd expected another extravagant bauble. Still, her heart faltered as she opened the box, to reveal a collar of rubies and diamonds in the same trellis design as the bracelet. In all her time as a courtesan, she'd never seen anything as magnificent.

She stared dumbfounded at the necklace.

"Do you like it?" he prompted.

She raised troubled eyes. "It's beautiful."

His lips twisted in the already familiar wry smile. "Yes, but do you like it?"

"It's a collar."

"Yes," he said patiently.

"You want me to wear your badge of ownership."

He released a long satisfied sigh and leaned back in his chair, his hand still toying with his wineglass. He'd drunk surprisingly little.

Tonight the wildly debauched Lord Erith of Perry's unsympathetic description had lost himself neither in sex nor alcohol. The wildly debauched Lord Erith, she started to suspect, was a protective shell. Just like uncaring, wanton Olivia Raines.

He cocked one dark eyebrow in her direction and his lips tilted in a pleased smile. "There's something to be said for a clever woman."

The air between them charged with sexual awareness. How had he done it? She never responded physically to her lovers yet every hair on her body rose as if lightning must strike.

She stiffened in unstated resistance. "You have no claim on me. You fancy yourself a little too much, Lord Erith."

The smile deepened, lining his lean cheeks with interesting grooves. "I definitely fancy *you*. But you know that."

She shrugged. What was the point of arguing? Of course he fancied her. Men always did. She ignored the tiny voice that whispered if she were a different woman, a *normal* woman, she could easily fancy him.

"I haven't earned this," she said shortly.

Her ill temper didn't faze him. "You will before you're finished." He gave a short laugh. "Devil take it, you're the queerest jade. You're my spectacular and notorious mistress. I'm your keeper and the envy of every man in London. I'm supposed to shower you with jewels. It's part of the game."

She'd accepted largesse readily enough from her other protectors. Anything extra now would cushion her retirement. Nonetheless, something stronger than logic made her close the box and slide it across the table.

"I won't wear a collar as if I'm your dog."

"That rajah's ransom is a damned extravagant gesture for a hound, madam, even the swiftest," he said with a huff of amusement. "The rubies are the finest I've seen."

They were the finest she'd seen too. But the gift seemed wrong. "Not to my taste."

He lifted the case, opened it, considered the sparkling contents, and closed it again. He pushed it back to her. "Take the necklace, even if you don't wear it."

Unwillingly, she nodded, although she left the box sitting on the table. It remained an enigmatic statement between them, as so much tonight had been enigmatic.

"What is your pleasure, my lord?" she asked, as she'd asked so many paramours.

Why did the question this time hold such significance? Perhaps because for once she had no idea of a man's answer.

"My pleasure, Miss Raines, is to talk, if it is your pleasure also."

Shock left her mute. She struggled to muster her thoughts. *"Talk?"*

He laughed softly. He had a nice laugh, low and deep. It rumbled out of his chest and surrounded her with warmth. "You know, converse like civilized people."

Giving him access to thoughts and feelings was more threatening than allowing him unfettered use of her body. But as she watched him across the table, something surfaced that she'd stifled since her childhood. A sweet, desperate curiosity this man could satisfy.

She dragged in a deep breath. "When I asked Perry about you, he said you'd traveled."

The voice didn't sound like hers. It sounded like the girl

she'd been so long ago, before life had thrown her to the wolves.

"I'm a diplomat. I travel for a living." He sounded noncommittal, but a spark lit the gray eyes.

He couldn't break her simply by knowing she longed to roam the world, to experience a freedom granted to few women. In London, she'd carved out her own freedom within limits. That made it no freedom at all, much as she boasted her independence.

"What sights you must have seen." She leaned forward and extended her hand as if asking him to take it. She realized what she did and snatched her hand back, hiding its trembling in her lap.

"Where would you like to go most?"

"Everywhere."

He laughed again. She liked it when he laughed, and she didn't like that she liked it. "What shall I tell you about?"

She settled for the place she'd give her soul to visit. "Italy."

He leaned back and crossed his arms. "Italy it is."

Chapter 6

The next evening, Olivia sat at the piano, picking her way through a sonata. It was late, almost midnight, and her mind wasn't on the music but on the man she'd accepted as her lover and the bizarre wager they'd made.

And the even more bizarre way their first night together had concluded.

She struck a sour note and started the allegro again. Her fingers automatically found the right keys and she relaxed into the flow. Through all the turbulent years, music and books had been her solace. She remembered that odd, almost companionable moment in Perry's library with Lord Erith. He'd seemed to understand.

No, he understood nothing.

But he'd been surprisingly patient with her questions about Italy and left without forcing a parting kiss upon her. Or dragging her back to the bed where she'd brought him to shuddering climax with her mouth.

When she realized she licked her lips, her fingers stumbled into a tangle of wrong notes. What was wrong with her? She never enjoyed what she did to her protectors. Except as an exercise in power.

With a sigh, she turned back to the sonata's first page. Lord Erith would visit tonight, she was sure of it. He'd canceled their planned visit to Tattersalls that day, saying family business detained him. The note had been short and remarkably free of the usual compliments. He hadn't called her a goddess. He hadn't thrown himself, at least in words, at her feet in worship. Yet the few blunt words in a stark, flowing black hand had pleased her.

As she admitted, much of his behavior last night had pleased her.

Why wouldn't he please her? He was brilliant, witty, and well-traveled. And he treated her as if she had a brain.

She lifted her hands off the keys and crashed them down so notes jangled out like untuned bells.

"I don't think that's in Herr Haydn's manuscript."

She looked up to see Lord Erith in full evening dress, watching her from the door. He did that, she noticed. Paused before he went into a room, to check the lay of the land before stepping inside.

"Perhaps it should be," she snapped, too off guard to remember she was a practiced seductress who never revealed her true self to her lovers.

"That sounded more like Beethoven."

As had happened last night, she forgot Erith was her protector and she merely his temporary mistress. "You know Beethoven?"

"We've met. I wouldn't presume to say I know him."

"Will you tell me about him?"

She couldn't hide her eagerness. He'd made Italy sound so wonderful. She'd basked in descriptions of paintings and palazzos and piazzas. The hot summer sun. The dark blue Mediterranean Sea. The cold snows of the Dolomites.

Now he'd tell her about Vienna. She could hardly wait.

His lips slanted in the smile that was already so familiar it was part of her. How had he managed this in their few short meetings? Except last night, he'd stayed for hours, until nearly dawn, talking. She'd never before passed a night in a man's company without lying naked in his arms.

She'd been tired when Erith left. Jumpy and stimulated. Much more so than when she entertained a lover her usual way.

"You need to earn your traveler's tale, Olivia."

Abruptly, the small bubble inside her that might have been happiness burst.

Lord, what a ninnyhammer she was. How could she forget why he was here? Last night had been exceptional. In every sense of the word.

She fought to keep her expression neutral. With most men, she'd know she succeeded. With Lord Erith, she couldn't be sure. Nonetheless, she rose from the piano stool with the graceful, self-conscious languor her first lover had taught her. The man who, with her brother's conniving, had ruined her. She made her lips curve in the smile of the worldly courtesan who performed any act to please her keeper.

She would. All sullen reluctance had been beaten out of her when she was a girl. There was nothing she hadn't done. There was nothing she wouldn't do.

Lucky Lord Erith.

The bleak thought left a foul taste in her mouth. Where soon she'd taste Lord Erith.

"Would you like wine before we proceed, my lord?"

"No wine," he said softly.

Olivia cursed herself for a fool, because she thought she heard compassion in that deep voice.

Erith prowled after his mistress up the lamp-lit stairs to the bedroom. Her slender back was ruler straight and her hips swayed in a soft rhythm that made his heart accelerate with anticipation. Her rose evening gown indicated she'd expected him.

Of course she'd expected him. Something inexorable drew them together. He just wished to hell he knew what it was. Not sex. Although soon it might be.

Was she frigid?

He didn't believe that. But he also knew if he wanted more than a courtesan's tricks from her, he'd need every ounce of shrewdness and sensual expertise.

A worthy challenge for an infamous rake and seducer.

He'd stood listening long enough as she played to realize that whatever limits she placed on her physical response, there was passion in her. He heard that in the music, in spite of the odd fits and starts.

She played like a man, attacking the music as if she went into battle. She did other things like a man too. His blood heated as he remembered her in trousers, knocking back brandy like any society gentleman.

His wife had been the most feminine of women, except on horseback. She'd ridden like a demon. That recklessness had killed her, and left him a broken man at twenty-two.

Shocked, he paused at the top of the landing. Why think of his wife now? He couldn't imagine two more different women than Joanna and Olivia Raines. One was pure as an angel. The other sold her favors to any taker.

Except that wasn't fair.

Gossip indicated Olivia discriminated about who she took to her bed. A couple of lovers a year, fewer recently.

She reached the door and turned. "My lord?"

Two words in that husky contralto and his cock stood to attention like a damned soldier on parade. He'd had so many women. None of them, even his darling, dead wife, had affected him like this.

Primitive determination surged. He'd win Olivia Raines. He'd show her a world she'd never known. He'd make her his so irrevocably that she never forgot him.

He strode forward to join her in the doorway. In the confined space, they were mere inches apart, but neither moved to bridge the gap. He heard her breathing, soft and uneven. She wasn't as composed as she tried to appear.

Of course she wasn't. Last night he'd brought her to the brink of trusting him. Or as close as such a wary creature would venture. Now she thought he betrayed her by taking her to bed.

"I've bought some more unguent," she said bluntly.

"You won't need it."

She glanced down without a blush to where he rose rampant as a damned stallion. "It will be easier for me."

He reached out to touch her arm. Her skin was cool and smooth beneath his hand. He turned the touch into a caress, running his hand down to take hers. "I won't hurt you."

A cynical expression crossed her face. "Your pleasure will be greater if I have my way, my lord."

"Let me be the judge."

"What a typically male response." Disentangling herself with a skill he could only admire, she slipped into the room.

"I am a typical male." He followed her toward the bed.

She glanced over her shoulder with a slight smile. She didn't argue. "Shall I undress you?"

The rainbow shifts of power between them were familiar now. Inevitable. After last night, she thought she had his measure, but she wasn't going to gain the upper hand as easily as she imagined. He had a plan and it started now. "No, I'll undress you."

She shrugged as if the matter held no significance. "Be careful with the gown. I like it."

Erith laughed with reluctant delight. "Damn your impudence, Olivia. You treat me like a cursed ladies' maid."

Her lids lowered and she shot him back a look that was pure temptation. He had to remind himself it was nothing but an act. Or an act that covered a reality she wasn't aware of.

This damned game proved more a conundrum with every moment.

"How would you like me to treat you?" she purred, turning and running her hand down his jaw. "Mmm, freshly shaved."

"You've got such delicate skin. I don't want to mark you." He reached out and curled his hand around her neck. The fine hairs that escaped her upswept hairstyle tickled his fingers. He paused and dragged in a breath. "I have to kiss you."

Her expression froze and she jerked free. "No."

"We'll kiss before we're done, Olivia."

"We'll be done before we kiss. Should I let down my hair?"

"Let me." He felt like he was with a new lover. Of course, last night he hadn't been her lover. Nor, for all her sensual banter and his predatory desire, would he be tonight.

Unless he lost control.

The searing memory of how she'd sucked him dry turned his confidence to ash. How easy to surrender. Leave her in charge. Accept pleasure without her true participation. But the fruit of that tree was rotten at the core, in spite of the deceptive sheen on its skin.

No amount of logic could shake Erith's certainty that if he gained her genuine response, his every sin would be forgiven.

It was as stark, as important, and as unreasonable as that.

So he moved forward, hiding his inner turmoil, and pulled the first pin from her thick, shining hair. A tawny lock fell softly over her shoulder. He didn't know what color to call her hair. It combined every shade from blond to bronze to auburn. A hymn to autumn.

He returned to a question that niggled at him. "Do you like women?"

Of course she wasn't shocked. She hadn't risen to the position of London's most sought-after courtesan without encountering the less conventional variations on human passion. He imagined little was outside her experience. "As bed partners? No."

"You need fear no condemnation. I've seen so much in my travels, I call almost nothing unnatural anymore."

Olivia laughed softly and the sound curled around him like a warm fire. "Men and camels?"

He'd wanted her from the first moment he saw her. That was to be expected. He was a man of more than usually strong appetites and she was breathtakingly beautiful. Less expected was that the more time he spent with her, the more he *liked* her.

He laughed in return. "Perhaps not quite camels." His voice lowered into seriousness. "Some cyprians prefer their own sex because their history with my own is too cruel."

Because he stood so close, he heard her breath hitch. A clue. Although not one he wanted. Some bastard had mistreated her. It must have been long ago. The fellows he'd met who had shared her bed were so in awe of her, they wouldn't have the balls to abuse her.

Her jaw firmed. "My lack of response extends to men, women . . . and camels."

He knew she hated talking about this. Not from modesty but because it threatened some bastion inside. That was why he pursued it. She'd never surrender until he swept her barriers away.

"I've seen you with Lord Peregrine."

She stiffened and her expression became shuttered. "What about it?"

He shrugged, sliding another pin from her upswept hair. "I know what he is, Olivia."

She wrenched away, dislodging another serpentine lock of hair, and twisted her hands in front of her. "Perry is my friend."

Erith regarded her calmly. "He's also a man who desires his own sex."

She whitened further. For the first time, he noticed faint freckles sprinkled across her aristocratic nose. She'd have been a hoydenish tomboy as a girl, with her untamed hair and strong, wiry body. "You accuse him of a hanging offense."

He noticed she didn't deny what he said. "I accuse him of nothing. I just observe that if you find pleasure with women, your association with Lord Peregrine becomes understandable."

"I associate with Lord Peregrine because he's kind and he cares for me." She didn't add the obvious rider—*unlike present company.* "The details aren't your concern, my lord."

"I'm your acknowledged lover. Of course it's my concern."

"Acknowledged if not actual." She bristled. "Perhaps you take the most famous courtesan as your mistress in the cities you visit because you too hide something."

A bark of laughter escaped him. Nobody had dared to question his masculinity before. "Nice try, Olivia. You know as well as I do that I like women. One woman in particular, however prickly and difficult."

The tension didn't leach from her tall body, and her voice was urgent. "My lord, please promise you'll say nothing of your suspicions. I'll do anything to protect Perry. Anything."

The words sent a surge of resentment through him. "I'm not going to blackmail you into yielding, Olivia," he bit out. "I wouldn't even if I needed to—and I don't. Now come here."

"You won't say anything?"

Her voice was still strained as she stepped closer with obvious reluctance. Good God, what did she expect him to do? Threaten to expose her friend's illegal predilections unless she pretended to passion in his bed? She must know after last night she couldn't deceive him.

"His secret is safe." With ill grace, he returned his attention to her hair. "You have my word."

Mixed with his fading irritation was thundering relief. He had the answer he wanted. Olivia didn't hanker after her own

sex. And he'd been right about her relationship with Montjoy. No doubt she and Lord Peregrine lived in that overdecorated house like brother and sister. Idly, he wondered how
they'd formed the close, almost familial bond.

Her hair tumbled in shining profusion about her slender
shoulders. He shut his eyes and leaned in, breathing deeply
of her scent. When he opened his eyes, he was close enough
to see her pupils had dilated, almost swallowing the sherry-
colored irises. Her breath came faster through parted lips
and her cheeks were flushed.

She exhibited every sign of desire. Was it all false? Surely
not. She knew counterfeit arousal wouldn't fool him.

He bent forward. Fleetingly, he tasted her breath on his
lips. Fresh. Essence of Olivia. The air of heaven. She seemed
caught in the spell. Erith's heartbeat stalled in a strange suspended moment. Then she blinked and pulled out of reach.
His gut contracted with sharp regret.

*By God, she'd kiss him one day. Willingly. Endlessly. Pas-
sionately.*

It was a sin against nature that a woman this vibrant and
beautiful had never experienced full sexual pleasure. Any
sexual pleasure at all.

"I'm at your disposal, my lord." Her voice was husky.
"How would you like me to act?"

He moved behind her and brushed aside the heavy tumble
of silky hair. With practiced fingers he unfastened her dress.
"I don't want you to act at all."

"You know what I mean."

She lifted her hair out of his way. The scene was almost
domestic. His fingers began to work on the laces of her stays
then tugged at the tapes holding her petticoat. It fell to the
floor, revealing white stockings and pretty pink satin slippers with ribbons that tied around her trim ankles. The firm
pale globes of her bottom pressed against her transparent
shift. He resisted the impulse to shape that superb rounded
flesh.

He placed a kiss on her bare shoulder, revealed under the sagging gown. "Olivia, do what you feel."

"I feel nothing," she said in a flat voice unlike her usual musical contralto.

"Then do nothing."

Chapter 7

Do nothing? What breed of man was this?

Feeling at a complete loss, Olivia let Lord Erith draw her shift over her head. His hands were cool and sure as they brushed her skin. And pleasantly dry. She hated men with wet hands.

Lord Erith kissed the side of her neck. His hands curled around her body to cup her breasts, kneading gently. Slowly, luxuriously, he pressed her into his body. She felt as much as heard his sigh of pleasure when her naked back made contact with the wool and cambric that covered his broad chest.

He radiated heat. It was like leaning against a sun-warmed brick wall on a summer afternoon. She closed her eyes and drifted away as he played with her breasts.

He tugged gently on her distended nipples and rolled them between finger and thumb. She sensed the voluptuous enjoyment he took in her. Oddly, that gave enjoyment in return. Not the familiar enjoyment of knowing she'd mastered yet another lover. Instead, it was a new, gentler satisfaction.

"Aren't you undressing, my lord?" She was surprised she didn't have to pretend the throatiness of the question.

He gave a grunt of breathless laughter as he kissed her nape. The little glances of his mouth felt nice, like butterflies skimming her skin. "My plan involves working you into a frenzy of lust."

"And you staying uninvolved?"

"A shred of clear-headedness is my best hope. Clothes help."

He pressed his hot erection into her bare buttocks. Groaning softly into her ear, he rubbed against her and bit her shoulder. She gave a start although he didn't hurt her. Like the rest of him, his teeth were big and strong. There was something strikingly intimate about him using them on her. It made her think of a stallion mating with a mare. The breathtaking combination of power and sensitivity.

She turned in his arms to see his face. His eyes glittered silver, and hectic color marked his prominent cheekbones. Yet his hands didn't clutch at her and he allowed her to establish a small space between them. A space redolent of heat and the musk of excited male.

She took a deep breath before she spoke, and the spice of his arousal entered her lungs like rich tobacco. He smelled good. She'd noticed that the first time he touched her. Clean, masculine, without the cloying scents so many men used. She breathed in again, just for pure pleasure.

It felt odd to stand here naked while he remained dressed for society. Briefly she wondered at his life away from her. Probably the same as every other buck of the ton's. Drinking and gambling and chasing women. Although the same instinct that told her he wasn't the cad he acted told her he hadn't taken a woman tonight. Or yesterday either.

"This won't work. There's some . . . some lack in me." Obscurely it hurt her that he devoted this trouble to her when nothing but bitter failure awaited. She paused and licked her lips. She'd never had to explain her handicap to a lover. "You're a decent man."

He made a derisive sound in his throat. "That's more than most people think." He ran his hands down her arms and took her hands.

Because she mistrusted the fragile empathy building between them, she spoke harshly. "Far better to push me on my back and have your way. I know you're in pain."

"The pain will make the pleasure sweeter."

He brought her right hand to his groin. Under her fingers he was hard like steel. Alive. No doubting his desire. As she stroked him through his trousers, the huge member thickened. Erith closed his eyes and leaned in so his tumescent flesh pushed into her hand.

"God, Olivia," he groaned. "You'd try a saint."

"I suspect you're no saint." She increased the pressure, testing the shape and weight of him. She imagined taking him in her mouth again. Last night, having this virile male in her power had offered a special pleasure. She wanted to feel that pleasure again. It was the closest she'd ever come to enjoying the sexual act.

Past time she took charge of this encounter, cut the threads of tender intimacy he slowly twined around them. Tender intimacy wasn't for women like her.

"Lie back, my lord," she murmured in the voice she'd used with so many men.

She heard how he struggled to draw breath. "I'm not a dumb beast."

She raked her nails across his chest so his nipples tightened under his shirt. "You're putty in my hands."

His hips surged forward. "Putty isn't the word I'd use."

"You're big and hard. I've never felt a man bigger."

"Stop it," he growled even as he let her navigate him toward the bed.

"It's true." She laid her palms flat on his chest. One small shove and he fell against the mattress. "You're magnificent. When I took you in my mouth last night, you filled me completely. Do you remember?"

"I remember," he said hoarsely.

"I can do that again." She licked her lips and looked down at the man sprawled on the sheets. The front of his trousers tented and his face was stark with overwhelming hunger.

"I know you can." He frowned; more in regret than anger, she thought. "But what will it prove?"

She shrugged. "Why must it prove anything? Pleasure is its own reward."

"How would you know?"

She stiffened. He wasn't supposed to fight back. She shifted her focus from his superb body to his eyes. She already knew she wouldn't find what she sought—the blank sheen of unthinking desire.

He wanted her, all right. But he hadn't given in by a long shot.

As she'd expected, the gray eyes between the thick black lashes were steady. She hadn't won this particular battle yet. Perhaps she just needed to try harder. "That wasn't fair."

"You're playing pretty dirty yourself, Olivia."

"Just watch me."

"I can't do anything else. You're the most fascinating woman I've ever met." He didn't sound entirely pleased.

She placed one stocking-covered knee on the mattress beside his thighs and swung her other leg so she straddled him. "Shall I do what I did last night?"

"No."

"No?" She raised skeptical eyebrows and looked down into his face. How strong his features were. Her gaze dwelled on the high, straight brow, the arrogant prow of his nose, and the hard angles of his jaw. But his mouth was fuller than usual and his tanned skin was tight and flushed. "Didn't you like it?"

His lips twisted in a bitter line. "That's a fatuous question. Damn you, you flung me to heaven and back and you know it."

"Don't you want to take the ride again?"

"No."

Strangely, his resistance pleased her. She gave a mocking huff of laughter. "You've paid a fortune to refuse my attentions, Lord Erith. Such a waste. Like owning a Rubens and hiding it in the cellar."

He didn't smile. "You know what I want."

"And you know what I'll give you."

"To hell with this!"

His sudden anger startled her. As did his explosion into movement. The room reeled as he jackknifed up and grabbed her, tumbling her over onto her back. Automatically, she clutched his shoulders. He loomed above her, caught between her spread thighs.

"My lord!" she said breathlessly, more excited than angered. She stared up into those fierce silver eyes and silently willed him to surrender. Willed him to prove himself the same as the rest of his vile sex.

His trousers created a sensual friction against her legs. Just to torment him, she bent her knees and rubbed her thighs against his. His breath hitched and his grip on her ribs tightened.

"Siren. Witch. Circe," he groaned.

He began to move in the familiar rhythm of lovemaking. Except even hot as steel from the forge, he made no attempt to free himself from his clothing. The weight of his body on hers made something twist low in her belly. The odd sensation was like hearing the sound of distant thunder on a sunny day.

She arched up, wordlessly offering herself. "Calling me names won't make me stop."

He gave a ragged laugh and buried his face briefly in her bare shoulder. Strangely, the moist warmth of his breath and the uncertain movement of his shoulders as he laughed and fought for breath at the same time touched her. She strove to play the cold courtesan but he made it impossible. Her hands relaxed, shifted. Not the practiced touch of a whore inciting a lover to passion he'd paid for.

She caressed him as if she wanted to.

Dear heaven, what was happening to her?

He must have felt her sudden tension because he lifted his head and stared at her. "Am I too heavy?"

"No." He felt just right pressing her into the mattress. Although he'd feel even better if he removed his clothes.

He propped himself on his elbows. "Something's wrong."

She looked up into his face. His eyes glittered. His black hair was untidy and a wayward lock fell across his forehead. Nobody would ever mistake him for an untried youth, but he looked younger than usual. Her heart performed a strange flip.

Olivia, be careful.

The warning was sharp as a jab from a knife.

"I will prevail," she almost growled. The hands that had been almost tender tore at his clothes. She ripped off his neckcloth and threw it aside. His shirt sagged open and she rained feverish kisses across the broad plain of his chest.

"Can I kiss you?"

"No." Her usually adept fingers fumbled with his trousers.

"Pity. You need to be kissed."

"I need to be fucked." A word she rarely used. Some strictures of her upbringing lingered, however low she'd fallen in the world.

"When you get no pleasure from the act?" Curse him, she'd wanted to shock him. But he sounded imperturbable as ever. "I don't think so."

"What about your pleasure?" At last his trousers fell open and she forced her shaking hand inside.

"I can wait." The answer tangled in his throat. Betrayed how he fought himself as well as her.

"Why should you?" She traced his length. He groaned and thrust his hips forward. Teasing him, she touched the head of his member, oh, so lightly. He jerked again. She brushed the sensitive tip again, feeling the moist evidence of need.

"You're driving me mad, damn you."

He lurched up, tore his coat off then tugged his shirt carelessly over his head. His chest was as magnificent as she remembered, with its heavy arcs of muscle and thick pelt of black hair. She had a second to admire him while he shed his trousers. Then he lowered himself on top of her. Every tumescent inch of him pressed into the soft flesh of her stomach.

He resumed the rhythmic rubbing motion. It was strangely disturbing. Not unpleasant. She tried to angle up so he thrust into her. But he held her hard against the mattress.

"Surrender to me," she gasped.

"Never. Surrender to me."

"Never." She gave a breathless laugh. The duel thrilled her mind although her body remained as dead to sensation as ever.

He'd been aroused since he arrived. Surely that iron control must shatter. He was very close. But he'd confounded her before. He was the only man she'd ever met with a will to match her own.

"Do you feel anything?" he asked hoarsely, raising his head to see her face. He shook and his skin was damp with sweat. His chest heaved as he fought for air.

"You're heavy."

"You know what I mean. Do you want me?"

"Yes."

Roughly, he thrust his hand down between her legs. She was as dry as she'd been last night. Nothing he did could transform her into a real woman. What terrified was that for the first time, she wished she was a real woman.

For him, dear Lord help her.

Each moment she spent with Erith, she sank further into quicksand. And she didn't know how to save herself.

He clasped her chin so she met his eyes. Beneath the glaze of arousal, anger stirred. "You've lied to every other man you've slept with. Don't lie to me."

"What makes you special?" she said breathlessly.

"Yield and I'll show you." His lips stretched in a confident smile that sent that strange pang to her belly again.

"I can't be more available than I am right now," she said with asperity.

"You'd love Spain," he said in a dreamy voice. The rhythm of his strokes against her changed, became slower, more languid. "The cold fresh air on the ridges of the Pyrenees. The passionate Gypsy dances. The sound of guitars. When you walk beside the Mediterranean, you smell spice on the wind that blows from Africa."

More than his words, the tone of his deep voice as he crooned the evocative descriptions made her shiver with longing. She'd revealed too much last night. He was clever enough to see what nobody else ever had and ruthless enough to use his newfound knowledge against her. "Stop it."

"Would you like to come to Spain with me, Olivia? They appreciate a beautiful woman. I can see you in Spain, free and laughing."

"My lord . . . "

"I see you in the bright sunlight. All the colors in your hair shining. You'd dance to the wild music and drink rioja and eat fish caught from the sea at your doorstep. The sea where you'd swim, naked and beautiful. And you'd be mine."

His words hurt her. If she didn't stop him, he'd destroy her. "I'm not yours. I'll never be yours."

Unless she was careful, he'd break the heart she'd never thought in danger. She curved up and placed her mouth on his nipple, sucking hard.

He groaned and she felt him shudder.

Yes!

He gripped her arms and wrenched away.

He reared back and she spread her legs wider, preparing for invasion. He was such a large man, she wondered how she'd encompass him. She held her breath. He flung his head back and she caught the tormented expression that twisted his face.

She closed her eyes.

Oh, yes. She'd won.

Every muscle in her body tensed as he plunged down.

Then abruptly he rolled to the side.

"Christ," he gritted out, spending himself in mighty spasms upon the sheets.

Chapter 8

$\mathcal{L}$ord Erith sprawled at Olivia's side without speaking, his head buried in the pillow. She couldn't see his face but his black hair was limp with perspiration and the bare skin of his back glistened. His huge spread-eagled body vibrated tension.

Their ragged breathing was the only sound in the room. The atmosphere sparked with violent emotion. The air was sharp with sex and sweat.

A leaden weight settled in her belly. She'd never felt like this before. Edgy. Uncomfortable. Distressed. Regretful. Angry but without any target for her anger. Brimful of warring reactions that jostled to find outlet. *Dissatisfied.* Which was ridiculous, as satisfaction with a lover had never been a possibility.

She was tired and sad and absurdly heartsick. With no good reason. She should be rejoicing in her ascendancy over the arrogant Lord Erith.

Except she hadn't really won. He'd resisted all her sensual arts. At the last minute he'd wrenched back control. He hadn't taken her.

Just when she believed he couldn't withstand her, he stole a pyrrhic victory that left both of them lost in this cruel darkness. He found no relief in what had happened. She read no joy, no gloating, no triumph in the trembling, prone body next to hers.

She closed her eyes, but that just made her memory of the incendiary, devastating moment more vivid. His face had been tortured, and his harsh curse as he'd flung away had made her heart contract with despair. Something about the cheap, bitter encounter left her feeling used and alone in a way she hadn't experienced since her first keeper.

She heard the bedclothes rustle as he turned to observe her. "Is this what you wanted?" The grim question chimed exactly with the sour tenor of her thoughts.

"No." She opened her eyes and stared at the ceiling, willing the few acrid tears to evaporate. She needed her armor back in place before she met that probing gray gaze.

Another fraught silence. A log disintegrated in the grate, the sound as startling as a bullet fired from a gun. She drew a shuddering breath, raised herself against the pillows and at last looked at him.

"Why? Why, Erith?" The familiar name slipped out before she could stop it.

Even after what they'd been through tonight, he was too acute to miss it. "You've never called me that before."

"I shouldn't call you that now."

"My God, woman, you're lying naked beside me. Call me Erith. Call me Julian, if you like. I'd certainly like it. I don't expect my mistress to pull her forelock and curtsy before she services me."

"You don't expect your mistress to service you at all," she said acidly. "Or not this one. For pity's sake, why not just use me as you will? This noble act is insane."

His jaw set in a stubborn expression. "There can be more between us."

"No, there can't. I am the woman you pay to share your bed. You are the man I accepted as a client."

"Last night, you hung on every word I spoke."

Something that felt perilously like yearning pierced her. For a short space she'd forgotten she was cold, remote Olivia Raines with her available body and her clever hands and her willing mouth. For a short space she'd felt like he spread the whole world at her feet for her delectation.

Dangerous, dangerous illusion.

She wanted to snap at him that last night hadn't meant anything. But as she studied him, she noticed he looked weary, almost defeated. For once, he looked like a man approaching early middle age. Deep lines marked his eyes and dragged at the corners of his mouth. The crackling energy she'd believed unquenchable was absent.

Before she thought, she raised a hand and touched his stubbled cheek. The involuntary gesture conveyed more tenderness than anything else between them in this long, harrowing night.

"I'm sorry I'm not what you want," she said softly and with a genuine sorrow that would have surprised her two days ago.

Some of the bleakness fled his expression and one edge of his mouth kicked upward in a brief smile. He pressed his cheek into her hand and closed his eyes. "I never said that."

In spite of everything, she smiled back. She shouldn't touch him like this, but it was strangely sweet. She left her hand where it was. "Apart from the obvious."

He opened his eyes and looked direct into hers. "Which is very obvious. Devil take you, I've never had anyone affect me the way you do. When I'm with you, I hardly know who I am. When I'm away from you, I can't think of anything else. And believe me, there are things I should be thinking about."

She couldn't doubt his sincerity. The difficult confession—and she knew he spoke the words as reluctantly as she heard them—was probably the purest compliment any man had paid her.

She frowned and withdrew her hand. Her palm tingled with the warmth of his skin. "If you took me, you might find I'm less of an obsession."

He grimaced with a wry amusement she found charming, much as she wished she didn't. Passion was a weapon he used against her with no effect. Humor left her defenseless as a newly hatched chick facing a hungry fox.

"I've never met a woman who nags me to have sex with her as much as you do. Especially when she doesn't enjoy it." He rolled onto his back and pushed up into a sitting position. His voice deepened into sincerity. "I'm sorry, Olivia."

She didn't bother hiding her own sadness. "I'm sorry too."

He leaned over her slowly. For a moment she lay still and quiescent, waiting for him to touch her breast or her face or even her sex. It took a few fatal seconds to realize he meant to kiss her. By the time she flinched away, his mouth was almost on hers. His lips landed clumsily on her cheek.

"Don't," she whispered.

"Oh, Olivia. You're so frightened," he whispered back, and glanced a tiny kiss across each of her fluttering eyelids before he stood up. "Come, my beautiful mistress. Supper awaits."

He extended his hand and smiled. Fleetingly, something in Olivia's heart opened like a flower to the sun. Then she remembered what she was and what she'd done, and the flower shriveled into a parched brown husk.

Early the next morning, Erith rode toward York Street with a smile hovering around his lips. His gray thoroughbred danced along the cobbles, and the sharp, cheerful sound of hooves striking the road echoed his eager expectation.

Odd to be so blithe when he'd received even less satisfaction last night than he had the previous one. Those humiliating moments when he'd spilled himself onto the sheets had been wretched and angry.

But when he left Olivia, he was convinced he'd coax a genuine response from her. Odd that amidst all the regret and frustration and anguish, he'd found hope.

Last night he had glimpsed something beyond the gorgeous shell that protected Olivia Raines. He'd seen painful emotion. He'd seen vulnerability. Sweetest of all, he'd seen tenderness. The moment when she touched his cheek still rang pure as a silver bell in his heart.

His pride was obdurately engaged in the quest to discover the woman under the courtesan. No matter how Olivia lured him to abandon his intent, he wasn't going to surrender.

No lover had given her pleasure. Until him.

The glory of that prize made any hardship on the way worthwhile.

Today he intended to spend the day with her, stay into the night. His daughter was busy with fittings for her trousseau, and the troublesome females who plagued him at home danced attendance.

And tonight he would achieve splendid victory. Tonight, Olivia would cede him the sweet passion she'd never ceded to another.

He knew she had passion locked within her. He could smell it the way he could smell the morning air with its sour tang of coal dust and the river. He'd never been wrong about a woman, and he wasn't wrong about Olivia Raines. She was the essence of desire. It would be a crime against the world if she never discovered that for herself.

With every street closer to the house, his optimism rose. His horse whinnied and curveted as if to express Erith's extreme satisfaction with his world on this bright morning.

He'd come direct from a long canter in Hyde Park. He'd woken early. Ridiculous, given how little sleep he'd managed. He'd stayed late at Olivia's. *Talking.*

When was the last time he'd lost sleep through conversation with a woman? Probably the early days of his marriage. Certainly not since then.

He turned the corner near the house and jerked to a sudden halt. Shock kept him rigid in the saddle.

A fancy rig waited in front of the house. Four magnificent black horses that wouldn't disgrace his own stable stood in harness. Wooden panels obscured any arms on the closed carriage, and the coachman wore a smart and completely unmarked livery.

In one appalling instant, Erith's self-satisfaction evaporated. The day darkened even though the sun shone as brilliantly as it had a few seconds ago.

The jade had promised complete fidelity for the span of their liaison. She certainly hadn't said anything about choosing another lover last night.

Good God, he'd only left her a couple of hours ago.

He drew his mount into the shadow of the nearest building and watched, hoping something, anything, would prove his sickening suspicions false.

Why would she take another lover? She couldn't satisfy the one she had. Then he thought of her clever mouth on his straining cock and his heart slammed against his chest.

Oh, yes, she could satisfy a man. Especially a man not too fussy about his partner's enjoyment.

Most men.

The house's shiny black door opened and Olivia emerged, wearing a dress he hadn't bought her. He'd had enormous pleasure selecting her wardrobe from the best modiste in London. The modiste, incidentally, who currently measured his daughter for her wedding gown.

He'd found a primitive satisfaction in knowing this strong, independent woman wore only what he'd paid for, from underclothing out. But this dashing bottle green traveling ensemble, while infernally becoming, was unfamiliar.

He expected to see a parade of servants bearing baggage. If she abandoned him, he imagined she'd want her belongings. But nobody followed, not even a maid to offer a semblance of propriety.

Acrid fury stewing in his belly, Erith watched her step into the carriage and the footman close the door.

He tried to tell himself her outing could be innocent. A call on a female friend or a shopping expedition. If one discounted the presence of that incriminating, unmarked carriage. If one discounted his every screaming instinct.

The coachman flicked the reins and the vehicle rolled away. Erith's hands tightened, making his horse snort and dance in protest.

"Sorry, boy," he whispered, and leaned forward to pat the gelding's glossy gray neck. The horse quieted even as Erith's hand formed a hard fist against the gleaming hide.

Damn it, he should let her go. He should return to Erith House and send her a contemptuous note informing her their arrangement ended. She could keep whatever spoils she'd gained so far, but she'd never glean another penny from his pocket. He'd been a dupe but he was a dupe no longer.

He wished her unknown lover joy; she'd prove as faithless to him.

Let the jade rot. He didn't care. There were plenty more fish in the sea. Fish that were less trouble to catch and tasted just as sweet.

Confound the faithless slut.

He'd never chased a woman in his life. He had no intention of starting now.

He was the Earl of Erith. Good women, bad women, young women, old women vied to catch his eye. Dear God, he could hardly take a step outside his front door without tripping over strumpets fighting for the right to wriggle into his bed.

Her new lover was welcome to Olivia Raines. Let her . . .

"Oh, Devil take it," he muttered. He dug his heels into his horse's sides and pursued the elegant carriage as it disappeared around the corner.

* * *

With some difficulty, Erith trailed the coach through the heavy traffic. He'd assumed she went somewhere in town, so was surprised when she took the Dover road out of London.

Clearly, the lovers meant to enjoy a bucolic interlude amidst the apple blossoms and bluebells. Erith gritted his teeth against another blinding wave of rage.

Damn her, how had she fooled him? From the beginning he'd thought her an honest whore. Those steady sherry-colored eyes hadn't seemed to lie.

Yet lie they had.

Did she respond to her lover?

Did she offer him the bone-deep passion that Erith sensed in her but was yet to uncover?

Did she?

Strangely, in spite of the fortune he'd spent and the way she'd deceived him with false promises of fidelity, that was what settled in his gut with the weight of a huge stone. That she gave some other fellow, some *lucky* fellow, what she'd never given Erith.

With every mile, Olivia's treason ate deeper into the disturbingly fragile fabric of his sangfroid. He loathed feeling like this. Needy. Lost. Angry.

After his wife died, he'd banished such chaotic, difficult emotions. He'd thought himself forever immune from their onslaught. Mixed with his fury was dismayed surprise that he was clearly as much a dunderhead as any other man caught in a woman's coils.

How the hell had she whipped him into this state?

They'd headed far enough out of London for him to wonder if they would travel all the way to Dover—perhaps she was running away to the Continent—when the carriage turned down a dusty track marked with a faded signpost.

Erith didn't know this part of the country. His family properties were in Oxfordshire or the North. So when he read WOOD END on the signpost, it meant nothing.

As the roads emptied, he'd pulled back from his quarry. He didn't want his perfidious mistress to know he followed. Now he spurred his horse after the conveyance, noting the dust that covered its shiny black. He supposed he looked similarly travel-worn. What did it matter? He didn't intend to impress her with his sartorial splendor.

If truth be told, he wasn't sure what he intended. He never wrangled over females. Not for the first time, he wondered why in God's name he set out on this wild goose chase. If she betrayed him, the liaison finished.

He hoped Olivia would rue the loss of her generous protector and repent her faithlessness. Although he had a gloomy suspicion she'd just shrug, smile, and go back to Lord Peregrine Montjoy, where she'd soon choose another fat-headed booby to make a fool of.

Just as she'd made a fool of the Earl of Erith.

Nobody made a fool of the Earl of Erith.

For the sake of his reputation as a cold-hearted, ruthless rake, he should return to London and begin arrangements to turf the trollop onto the streets. Serve her right if she returned from her rural idyll to find herself out on her elegant rump.

He cursed under his breath, clicked his tongue to his mount and chased the carriage into a thick wood.

Erith waited concealed in the shade of the trees and observed the unpretentious stone house Olivia had disappeared into an hour ago. The boredom of standing out here holding his horse almost quenched the scorching heat of his anger. Almost.

It was a sultry day and he was parched and hungry. He'd planned to share a lavish breakfast in the charming downstairs parlor in York Street. Instead he'd come all this way without so much as a flask of water, and he'd wager he'd swallowed every speck of dust between here and London.

He stroked the gray's velvety nose. "Not much longer, Bey. A bucket of water and some oats for you—and for me, a tankard of ale to wash down sirloin and potatoes."

The horse's ears flickered. Erith hoped without optimism that he wasn't lying. When the coach had pulled up at this unimpressive dwelling, his every muscle had clenched as if he prepared for war. With violence coiling like an angry cobra in his gut, he'd waited to confront his rival.

But a woman in her forties and a man about ten years older had greeted Olivia with hugs and smiles and laughter. Even more surprising, the man was obviously a vicar. The significance of the church spire rising above the trees a short distance away had belatedly struck Erith

The knowledge that he acted like an utter blockhead left a nasty taste in his mouth. But still, stubbornly, he waited. Even though there had been no activity around the vicarage since Olivia and the couple went inside.

His horse's head drooped and Erith wasn't in much better state when the door to the house opened. Stiffening like a hound scenting a fox, he jerked into alertness. He inadvertently tugged on the reins twisted around one gloved hand. His mount snorted in protest, but the two people who left the vicarage were deep in conversation and didn't react to the noise.

At Olivia's side was a tall young man with black hair. Erith couldn't see the rapscallion's face because of the distance and the angle. But the youth wasn't dressed as a servant, and there was an obvious physical ease between him and his companion. She took his arm and laughed up at him, the delightful, traitorous sound drifting to where Erith seethed in the shadows.

Olivia carried the fiendishly complicated bonnet she'd worn leaving town, and she moved with a confidence that indicated complete relaxation. Even her walk was different. In London she sauntered with a self-conscious sway of the hips, as if she knew every man's eye was on her. Of course, every man's eye *was* on her, curse the jade's justified conceit.

Here she moved with the long easy stride of the born countrywoman. He'd always assumed she'd risen from London's gutters and gained her brilliant social polish on the way. Now he wondered if she originally came from a setting as rural as this. She wouldn't be the first country maiden brought to ruin amidst the whirl of the decadent capital. Somehow, though, it was hard to picture her as a foolish milkmaid or naive farmhand.

He dismissed the fleeting puzzle of her origins. What mattered was that she'd lied to the Earl of Erith, and he intended to exact recompense.

And try not to feel more of a bloody fool than he did already.

The woman and the youth walked around the side of the vicarage. Which was lucky because if either had looked up, they'd see Erith. He'd been too furious to consider concealing himself.

Without thinking what he'd do when he caught up with the lovers—for surely that's what they were—he surged in pursuit, tugging the horse after him.

The confounded rogue was noticeably younger than Olivia—perhaps she had a taste for fresher meat than her protectors. While the boy was as tall as a grown man, it was clear he had yet to develop into maturity. The shoulders were broad but the body was gangly, and his limbs had the awkward thinness of a half-grown stripling.

Perhaps she was this scoundrel's keeper, just as he himself was hers.

He ground his teeth as he watched that long back in its plain black coat move away. What was she doing with this damned blackguard? She needed a man to satisfy her, not a calfling. There was too much woman in Olivia for a mere boy to match.

His free hand clenched into a fist as he imagined beating the youth into a pulp. He didn't have the faintest desire to hit Olivia. Instead, he wanted to fling her down on the ground, shove up her elegant skirts, and show her what she missed by holding out on the Earl of Erith.

A low feral growl emerged from his throat as he watched her reach up and place a quick kiss on the boy's cheek. He would have given her every ruby in Burma for one tenth of the genuine affection she showed that milksop.

Blast her to hell and back.

For lying to him. And for making him feel this way.

There was a pond behind the house where a few ducks swam without enthusiasm. More ducks snoozed on the bank. The youth led Olivia toward a weatherworn wooden bench. Erith growled again. The setting's pastoral perfection only increased his fury.

He hadn't fought a duel in years, had never challenged another man even in duels he had fought. But something in him howled for this young man's blood. Because he stole Olivia, and Olivia belonged to Erith.

The savage possessive hunger he'd felt the first time he saw Olivia Raines blasted him anew and jammed the breath in his throat. Through a red haze, he watched them sit down. The couple held hands and the innocent sweetness made him want to puke.

One last vestige of reason urged him to leave, to delay this confrontation until he was sure of control.

His horse had other ideas. The smell of water was too much to resist. The animal snorted and tossed its head to escape the restraint of the reins.

"Hell," he muttered through his teeth as Olivia turned and caught him spying.

He felt like a beggar child outside a sweet shop. The pathetic image only stirred the roiling mixture of shame and anger in his gut. He sucked in a deep breath, which did nothing to calm his fury, and caught the troublesome nag's bridle, silently cursing the beast. With what he hoped was his usual assurance, he stepped forward.

"Olivia." The word was a snarl.

The sun was in his eyes so it took him a few moments to register that, as she rose, she looked pale and frightened.

"Lord Erith, what are you doing here?" Her voice shook and she twined her hands together at her waist with an open nervousness he'd never seen in her before.

She should be nervous, the baggage. Let her see how nervous she felt when he called out her youthful lover and put a bullet in his skinny chest.

"It seemed the perfect day for a ride in the country," he said silkily. He so obviously had the advantage, he could almost enjoy himself if not for the dogs of jealousy and disappointment howling inside him.

"You followed me."

Her glare accused him of betrayal. What right had she to look at him like that? Treacherous slut.

"Yes."

"You had no right."

"I claim the right." He moved closer to see the light in her lying eyes. He ignored his horse's stubborn yearning toward the pond.

"We had an arrangement."

"We certainly did," he snapped, looming over her. "Now if you please, we'll return to London and discuss the future of that . . . *arrangement*."

"It has no future, my lord." Her chill tone was more familiar than the husky, scared voice she'd used earlier.

Ah, she recovered her spirit. Good. He felt like a fight, and berating a woman who pretended fear offered no satisfaction. Now she faced him with her chin up and her backbone straight. Few men of his acquaintance would be so bold. She might be faithless, but she was undoubtedly brave. He quashed a twinge of reluctant approbation.

He grabbed her arm in its dark green, close-fitting sleeve. "We'll talk about that on our way back to London, madam."

"Sir, unhand Miss Raines!" The stripling lurched forward and snatched at Erith's hand, trying to tug it from Olivia. "You have no call to treat a lady in this fashion!"

"For your own sake, I'd step away, boy," Erith grated through clenched teeth.

"I'm no boy!" the youth retorted.

"Leo, stand back. This is between Lord Erith and myself," Olivia said urgently.

"No, Miss Raines. This man is no gentleman."

"No gentleman, hmm?" Without releasing Olivia, Erith turned his attention on the stripling. And found himself looking into a face that was a mirror image of Lord Peregrine Montjoy's.

Chapter 9

All Erith's certainties dissolved in a shocked instant. A taste bitter as aloes flooded his mouth while his mind screamed astounded denial.

For an absurd moment he stood paralyzed, one hand on Olivia, one gripping the horse's reins, and the boy clutching his arm. Then he snatched violently away. Breathing hurt, as though someone had punched him hard in the gut.

The boy was still bristling. He stared down his nose at the much taller earl. The haughty expression was so familiar, it made Erith's heart contract in his chest.

"I demand satisfaction, sir. You've behaved as a complete boor. You will name your seconds."

"Leo, no!" Olivia pushed herself in front of him, confirming what Erith already knew in his bones to be true. Her voice shook with urgency. "He doesn't mean it, Erith. He's only a child. You can't fight a child. I won't believe it of you. However angry you are, you won't do this. Not if you consider yourself a man of honor."

"I'm not a child, Miss Raines!" the stripling spluttered, his clear olive complexion turning a mottled red as his anger focused briefly on Olivia.

"No, of course you're not." Erith remembered with a pang how sensitive a boy's pride could be. And this boy with his courage and his bridling temper wasn't much younger than Erith had been when he married and had children of his own. "I hope you'll accept my unreserved apology."

"Erith . . . " Olivia's mouth dropped open with amazement.

He briefly resented that she was surprised when reason ruled him. But the crazy yen for violence had evaporated the moment he'd seen the lad's face. What remained was a desperate craving for answers.

The boy wasn't mollified. "The apology should not be for me but for this lady, sir. She's the one you offended."

"You're right," Erith said smoothly. He turned and bowed to Olivia. "Your pardon, Miss Raines. I spoke out of turn."

Gracious as a queen, she inclined her head. "I accept your apology, my lord."

"My lord?" The boy looked taken aback. He must have missed what Olivia said when she gasped Erith's name.

Displeasure tautened Olivia's face, but Erith had placed her in a position where introductions were unavoidable. He refused to help her. His curiosity burned like a brand.

She gave a sigh. "Lord Erith, may I present my godson, Leonidas Wentworth?"

"Mr. Wentworth," Erith said, even as his mind bounced the name around his acquaintance. He knew no Wentworths, but that hardly mattered. The boy's heritage was written in his features. No wonder Olivia kept him hidden in this backwater.

"Leo, this is a . . . a friend of mine, the Earl of Erith."

"My lord." Leonidas Wentworth performed a creditable if rather frosty bow. He was a graceful youth, Erith had already noticed. Of course with his parentage, he would be. "I've never met any of Miss Raines's London associates before. Apart from Lord Peregrine."

Erith approved of the stiffness in his manner. It spoke to the boy's principles being more important to him than the chance to toady to a rich nobleman.

But youthful hauteur cracked as Leo glanced past the earl to the horse nosing without much interest at the thick grass. Erith had no trouble interpreting the longing that glowed in his thickly lashed dark eyes. The same thickly lashed dark eyes that had surveyed him with abhorrence in Lord Peregrine's London town house.

"Would you care to water Bey? The poor beast hasn't had a drink since leaving London."

A smile lightened the boy's face. He truly was a beautiful youth. "I'd like nothing better, sir. Spanish, is he?"

Erith was impressed. The lad knew his horseflesh. "Yes. About ten years ago I imported a few Andalusians into my stud at Selden to strengthen the bloodlines. Bey's one of my first successes."

Anger forgotten, Wentworth accepted the reins. With palpable delight, he led the horse to the pond.

"You shouldn't have followed me," Olivia hissed under her breath as she stepped closer, although the boy was outside earshot of anything except the most vituperative shrieking. And Erith couldn't imagine his mistress descending to hysterics, however angry she was.

"No, I shouldn't," he admitted.

"What were you thinking?" She vibrated like a struck tuning fork.

He leveled a steely look on her. "You know what I was thinking. That you had a lover."

"I told you I was faithful."

"Women lie."

"I don't."

"Yes, you do."

For an electric moment the memory of the last two nights, difficult, painful, compelling, rose between them. With vivid bitterness he remembered spending himself on the sheets in great gasping spurts while she stretched, trembling and distraught, at his side.

Color flooded her cheeks much as it had flooded the boy's not so long ago. "You granted me complete independence of movement when I agreed to be your lover."

He shrugged. "What can I say? I was jealous."

Hell, he'd been mad with jealousy. The admission gnawed at him. Bewildered him. How had she brought him to such a peak of emotion when he discovered her leaving London, and even more when he caught her with Wentworth? She was merely a passing diversion during a brief sojourn in London. But when he thought she'd betrayed him, he had become a wild animal, ready to rend and claw and bite to keep what was his.

And he'd known her less than a week.

Would her fascination pall as familiarity grew? He had an ominous feeling that as time passed, he'd only become more entwined in the chains of attraction.

Just as quickly as Olivia's color had risen, it receded again. Clearly she recognized the shattering importance of what he'd just confessed. "I don't believe you."

"I have trouble believing it myself."

Her mouth flattened in an implacable line, and with an emphatic gesture, she brushed back a few loose strands of hair that came free around her cheeks. Even her hair was different here. Simpler. Looser. More becoming.

Her voice was still low. "Our affair can't continue, you realize? I will not be tracked or confined or spied upon." She paused, and he realized she resented having to come down off her high horse to ask a favor. "My lord, I rely on your honor never to speak of what you've seen in this place."

He gave a short, genuinely amused laugh. She really was used to leading a lover around by the nose. Sometimes he liked to oppose her just for the sake of watching her prickle. In this case, though, more was at stake than the seesawing game of dominance they played. "Oho, my lady, you're not getting out of things that easily."

"My lord—"

"You can 'my lord' me into the ground, Olivia. The formality changes nothing between us. It's too late to pretend we're little more than strangers."

"We *are* little more than strangers," she said sullenly.

"Intimate strangers, then." He glanced over to where Wentworth fussed over the gray horse. "I'll fetch Bey, if that boy gives him back. I have my doubts. It looked like love at first sight."

"What do you know of love?" she muttered, still simmering with hostility.

He reached out and touched her cheek briefly. "More than you'd think."

Her lips parted with surprise.

He laughed again. "I know you believe I was brought up by wolves and I've been living like a wolf ever since. Sorry to disappoint you. I'm as human as anyone else." Before she could muster any argument, he stepped past. "I'll go into the village. I assume there's one near the church and that it boasts an inn."

"Yes, Wood End is on the other side of the trees." Her voice took on a trace of satisfaction. "It's a sorry place. You won't like it."

His smile was grim. "I'm not expecting to like it. I want somewhere to wait while you finish your visit. I take it you don't want to introduce your mad, bad lover to the good vicar and his wife."

She became even paler. As before, he noticed that when her color fled, faint freckles formed a line across her cheekbones and nose. Like a ghost of the girl she'd once been. The girl he intended to discover, no matter how she tried to evade his questions.

"No. No, I don't want you to meet them."

"Bring the carriage by the village on your way and we'll travel back to London together."

"Wouldn't you rather ride?" she asked with a hint of desperation.

"No. I'd rather talk to you. There are things we need to discuss."

"I don't agree."

With another smile and a flourish of his blue coat, he sank down on the worn bench. He leaned back and folded his arms across his chest. "Well, we can talk now. I'm at leisure."

She cast him a killing look under her thick tawny lashes, but he knew that for once he had all the advantages. She'd want complete privacy for the coming interview, even if she intended to reveal nothing. His indiscreet questions could stir up trouble in this quiet retreat.

"I curse the day I met you," she said, with real feeling. Her mouth was tense with displeasure and the small mole on her cheek stood out on her white skin like a dark beacon.

He let his smile widen. "Don't think if you're nice to me you'll cajole me into letting you off the hook."

"I'm not a salmon, Erith," she said icily. "I'll see you in the village in an hour. If you're not outside the inn, I'll leave without you. And you and your threats can go to Hades."

With an irritated swish of her skirts, she stalked toward the rectory. Erith watched her go, as always admiring the subtle curves of her hips and the grace of her carriage. Annoyance added a swing to her gait. He liked it.

It was closer to an hour and a half later when the black coach pulled up outside the village's pathetic excuse for a hostelry. Olivia hadn't exaggerated when she'd called it a poor place. Erith had endured an awkward hour in the filthy taproom drinking watery beer while lumpen yokels stared at him in vacant wonder.

After the hour was up, he'd been pleased to go out and wait in the sunshine with Bey. Although the spectacular horse created even more stir among the locals than an earl had inside the dingy inn.

His discomfort wasn't purely a result of the unwelcome attention he received in the village. In this obscure corner of the kingdom, the smells and sights and sounds of rural England surrounded him. On the ride down he'd been too angry to notice the burgeoning green around him. He hadn't been in the English countryside for years, probably since the days of his marriage. He'd forgotten the sweet, blossoming poignancy of spring. He'd forgotten how lush the fields were. He'd forgotten the rich smell of English crops growing in English soil.

As a young man he'd wanted nothing more than to run his estates and grow old on the lands his father bequeathed to him. Then Joanna died and his life twisted away from its safe, comfortable shape.

Strange, he hadn't realized how much he'd missed the familiar countryside. And he had missed it, with a depth of painful longing he only now recognized.

Olivia's coachman climbed down and fought his way through the crowd of filthy urchins to take Bey's reins. "Shall I tie him to the back of the carriage, my lord?"

"Yes." Erith strode toward the vehicle. He'd thought he might have to trample the little ruffians, but they recognized his authority and swerved out of his way.

He swung the door open and climbed inside. As he'd expected, the conveyance was the latest word in luxury, from the ruby red Morocco leather seats to the tasseled silk cushions and gleaming wood fittings. He took his place with his back to the horses and looked speculatively across to where his mistress sat in mute elegance in the opposite corner.

After the bright sunlight outside, she was a creature of shadows. He felt her eyes on him as he settled, stretching his legs out across the well between the seats and resting his broad shoulders against the upholstery.

She was dressed for town again, in the fashionable bonnet and gloves. She seemed a subtly different woman from the virago who had confronted him beside the pond. But today he'd seen too much to believe that only the cold courtesan existed inside her.

For all Olivia's outward calm, he could smell the tension

under her sweet floral scent. She braced for his attack like a trapped antelope waiting for the lion to spring. The savage lurking inside him wanted nothing more than to seize her in his arms and kiss that stern mouth into softness. The enforced intimacy of the coach reminded him he was yet to lose himself in her spare, glorious body.

He tried to ignore the animal side of his nature. But it was difficult when she was so close.

"You're late," he said, as much to pierce the silence as to chastise her.

"Yes." Her voice was clipped. She was still angry. Perhaps even angrier than before, now that she didn't fear for Leonidas and there were no witnesses to their confrontation.

She didn't need to tell Erith that she'd deliberately delayed picking him up. Had she imagined if she was late, he'd go without her? What did the wench think? That his noble dignity wouldn't extend to waiting half an hour? She underestimated both his patience and his curiosity.

The carriage lurched into motion, and he watched her lift one slender arm to grip the leather strap for balance.

Aha, my lady, I'm going to put you off balance and keep you that way.

He spread his arms along the back of the seat, settling himself into the coach's rocking motion. His appearance of relaxation would rile her. His eyes had adjusted to the gloom, and he read the cool rejection in her striking features.

The air was thick with everything unspoken between them. He had no difficulty divining Olivia's strategy. She meant to freeze him into silence and keep him that way until they reached London and the announcement she would remove herself to Lord Peregrine's town house forthwith. With perhaps one final plea to keep what he'd discovered today to himself.

Unfortunately for her, his plans were different. And his plans would prevail. He drew a deep breath and launched his attack.

"Leonidas Wentworth is your son."

Chapter 10

$\mathcal{A}$s Erith flung the uncompromising words at her, Olivia flinched and her face turned pale as moonlight. She snatched her hand from the strap to press it trembling against her breast. Her shock and fear were unmistakable.

In the charged silence that followed his statement, he wondered if she meant to lie and deny what he'd said.

He should have known better.

He heard her draw in a shuddering breath. She raised her chin and spoke defiantly. "Yes."

Her expression was cold and closed. Her full lips took on a tense line and the gloved hand she held to her chest formed a fist. She bristled with hostility so powerful, it was almost tangible in the close confines of the carriage.

He sharply regretted that when he pried into her secrets, he hurt her. But while he waited in the village, he'd had time to ponder today's revelations. If he was to help her, he needed to know what had happened in her past and what he could do to gain long-delayed justice.

Ever since that jagged moment when he'd realized Leo was her son, a roiling mess of conflicting emotions had churned in Erith's gut. Amazement. Appalled outrage. Protectiveness. Sorrow. A voracious hunger for vengeance.

Curiosity that burned like acid.

"You must have been little more than a child when you bore him." His tone remained austere although he could hardly bear to imagine what she'd endured. He was afraid that if he loosened the ruthlessly tight rein on his rage and grief, he'd lash out and terrify her indeed. Even though none of his anger was directed at her. Good God, how could it be? "How old are you now? Thirty?"

"Thirty-one," she snapped.

Older than he'd thought. But in any just world, far too young to have a son of nearly adult age.

"And he's what? Sixteen? Seventeen?"

The boy's lanky height had originally fooled Erith into thinking him a few years older. Not surprising first impressions led him astray. Erith had observed the youth from yards away and through the distorting mirror of a virulent jealousy he still cringed to admit.

Leo didn't resemble his mother in much except for a slight lordliness to his manner. And that intense pride. The same pride he saw in Olivia now as she sat opposite him, spine ruler straight, eyes blazing, chin up.

"This is none of your concern, my lord." Her voice was as icy and cutting as sleet on a windy winter moor.

The frail intimacy they'd established in the last few days might never have existed. She built a high wall around herself, invisible but real as the leather-covered seat beneath him. Unluckily for her, he intended to lay siege to her defenses. Batter them down if need be.

"I make it my concern." Sighing, he ran one hand through his hair. He desperately hoped his motives weren't entirely selfish. He didn't think so. His voice softened. "I know you're stubborn, Olivia. After what I've learned today, I suspect you've had to be. But humor me in this."

Her lips thinned with resentment and her hands clenched hard on the green velvet reticule in her lap. "You've learned nothing."

Leaning his head back, he studied the rich interlaced pattern of red, blue, and gold on the carriage's brocade-covered roof. "Haven't I?"

He let the pause lengthen into awkwardness.

"Why should you care?" she snarled over the carriage's endless creaking. "I'm nothing to you. Just another woman to fill your bed. There were women before me and there will be women after me. Your questions are only prurient curiosity, and you have no license to ask them."

Undoubtedly there would be other women. But none would be like her.

He didn't understand his violent need to know the real Olivia under the spectacular facade. But in some obscure way, the challenge she presented seemed to him the last chance to save his soul. And he suspected, illogically, foolishly, obstinately, that in the process he might just save her soul too.

How had the stakes become so crucial? Why was this woman so important when others had just been warm bodies to fill the hollow coldness inside him?

It was a mystery. Perhaps one he'd only solve when he solved the mystery of Olivia herself. Olivia who clearly meant to fight him every step of the way.

He couldn't blame her. Already he guessed her history held harrowing secrets. Secrets it would pain her to revisit.

Why then did he push her? Did he do this for her or for himself? Were his instincts wrong when they decreed that only after she came to terms with her past would she break free of the cage of ice that trapped her?

He brought his eyes down to meet her turbulent topaz gaze. "What harm to tell me?"

"What harm if you don't know?"

"I can guess most of it."

"Or threaten to expose Leo's existence." Bitterness oozed from her words.

He knew he should swear that her secret was safe and that any battle between them was a private matter. He wished her and those she loved no ill. The opposite in fact.

But he said nothing. Add deception to his list of sins against her.

He kept his voice neutral. "How old is your son, Olivia?"

She avoided his eyes. Her hands in their tan kid gloves mangled the reticule completely out of shape. "Leo is seventeen in August."

"He doesn't know you're his mother."

"He must never know." Beneath the anger, he read lacerating sorrow. And something else he'd never thought to see in her.

Corrosive shame.

The realization plowed bloody furrows in his heart. Especially as if what he surmised was true, she had nothing to be ashamed of. He tightened the lid on his seething rage. He needed to find out more before he pursued recourse from those who had injured her.

He didn't bother asking himself why her causes were his. They just were.

He desperately longed to hold her, to offer her the comfort of human warmth, but he restrained himself. That was the last thing she wanted from him. And recognizing that grim fact cut him to the bone.

"He loves you."

"Yes." With an irritated gesture, she smoothed nonexistent wrinkles from her green skirts. "But in any real sense, his parents are Mary and Charles Wentworth."

Erith doubted that. The unspoken affinity between mother and son had struck him forcibly. He'd mistaken it for a sexual connection. But then with his mistress, his mind dwelled overlong on sex.

His belly tightened with the urge to hit something. Hard and repeatedly, smashing it to a pulp. He folded his arms across his chest to hide how his hands trembled with rage. "You were fifteen years old when he was born."

She'd already told him that in so many words, but he needed to say it. Needed to hear the vile truth spoken aloud.

The mongrel had fucked her when she was little more than a child. Disgust rose to choke him. Good God, how old was Olivia when she first learned the cruel truth of what men did?

"Yes." Still she refused to meet his probing stare.

Damn it, Olivia, you're not at fault here.

He paused to beat back the shrill demons of anger and violence battling for release. Even so, his voice was harsh. "Yet you feel affection for his contemptible father."

She frowned and at last looked at him. "His father?"

Her beautiful eyes were dark and cloudy as burned syrup with distress. Another pang of remorse stung him but he ignored it. He needed to know the truth, and, damn it, she needed to tell him.

"Lord Peregrine." He bit out the hated words like a curse.

He couldn't interpret the expression that crossed her face. Bleak amusement, perhaps. "You think Perry is Leo's father?" she asked.

"The resemblance is unmistakable."

"You told me Perry prefers the company of his own sex."

Why was she fencing with him? The boy's parentage was indelibly written in his handsome face. "Clearly I was wrong."

To his astonishment, she gave a scornful spurt of laughter. She sent him a derisive glance under her long eyelashes then stared out the window at an afternoon that rapidly clouded over.

"I'm sure you've never admitted that before."

"You'd be surprised."

"This inquisition stops now, Lord Erith." Her lips firmed and she spoke as though she loathed him. "I've told you all I intend to."

"Do you want me to ask Montjoy?" *And then kill him slowly and painfully.*

"You bastard," she whispered, obviously reading the unspoken threat. Her eyes flared temper as she glanced at him then away again. "Leave Perry alone."

He was so outraged and incredulous that she still protected the despicable miscreant, his words emerged like bullets shot from a gun. "How the hell can you bear the man who raped you when you were only a girl?"

"Perry didn't rape me." She pushed back the curtain so she could better see the view.

The gray light that flooded the window illuminated her remarkable face. She looked like a girl, too young to have a child Leonidas's age. She looked old enough to know the secrets of the millennia.

"Don't lie, Olivia," he growled. "The boy's the spitting image of his father."

"Yes, he is." This time when she leveled that perceptive, clear gaze on him, she seemed almost dispassionate. "But Perry isn't Leo's father. Perry is Leo's brother. Lord Farnsworth fathered my son."

For the second time that day Erith felt as though someone had knocked the air out of him with a single blow.

Her lover hadn't been the beautiful and kind Lord Peregrine, but his foul and notorious sire. Uncontrollable nausea made his belly cramp.

Oh, Olivia ...

Frederick Montjoy, Lord Farnsworth, had been a noxious roué with a taste for the exotic in his lovers. Women. Men. Even, near his death, a whisper about animals. Pain. Bondage. But if he'd liked children, he kept that fact hidden.

When Erith was a young man about town courting Joanna, he'd met Lord Farnsworth briefly. But his attention had been elsewhere and he'd found the raddled old man of no interest. He'd noted enough, though, to know he wouldn't entrust a stray dog to the villain, let alone a defenseless girl.

"You've found out enough, my lord. It's more than I've ever told anyone else." Her voice broke and he noticed that the hands she returned to torturing her reticule shook uncontrollably. "I never speak of those days to anyone. For pity's sake, please drop the subject."

Painful compassion paralyzed him. How could he put her through this? Her suffering was clear. And she'd already suffered too much.

Then he remembered the fear that shone in her beautiful eyes when she forgot to keep her barriers up. Perhaps this difficult confession would help her conquer the phantoms that pursued her.

"Tell me what happened," he said in a hard voice.

A flash of anger made her tawny eyes blaze, even in the dim light. "Will you give me no peace?"

"Tell me, Olivia."

She spat the answer at him as though she hated him. "My brother bartered me to Lord Farnsworth to pay his gambling debts when I was fourteen. Are you satisfied now?"

Dear God, her damned brother had sold her into prostitution. No wonder she had such contempt for men.

"I'm sorry." The words were hellishly inadequate.

She shrugged and turned to look out the window again. She tried to adopt the courtesan's impassive facade but he'd sheered too close to her essential vulnerability. Under the mask of composure, her face was pale and drawn, and her lush mouth tense with unhappiness. Guilt stabbed him in the gut.

They approached the outskirts of London. He'd been so intensely involved in what little she'd told him of her past that he hadn't noticed the passing miles.

"Where is your brother now?" His hands formed fists against the seat as he imagined squeezing the life out of the slimy blackguard's throat.

Her voice was flat. "He shot himself ten years ago when he couldn't pay his debts."

"And of course he didn't have another sister to sell."

She turned back to him and frowned. "Erith, I'm not some princess who needs rescuing."

He wasn't so sure. But how could he explain to her what was barely clear to him? He drew a deep breath to control his bile. But nothing could cleanse his mind of the foul images rocketing through it.

The thought of his daughter forced into Olivia's situation made him clench his hands around his elbows so tightly that they ached. Roma had a family, a father, a brother to protect her. Clearly the young Olivia had had nobody.

"I've got a daughter." It was the first time he'd mentioned his family to her. To any of his mistresses.

"Ah." The clear gaze she settled on him filled with understanding.

He waited for her to question him, but she merely looked out the window once more. The traffic thickened as they approached Town and the carriage wasn't moving forward with its former speed.

An uncomfortable silence descended. The only sounds were the vehicle's rhythmic creaking and the clatter of traffic on the street. As the miles passed, Erith's heart thundered a furious chant of vengeance.

Against a dead man. Two dead men.

Both her brother and Farnsworth were forever beyond his reach, God damn it.

Erith could never win justice for Olivia.

He looked blindly out the window at the passing London streets and tried to douse the futile anger that made every muscle clench. Frustration was a physical pain in his belly.

And now a more immediate problem than her past woes,

terrible as they'd been, raised its head. Devil take it, he had to work out how to hold onto her.

After a long time, he spoke. "Our arrangement isn't at an end."

Her head whipped around and she scowled at him. The brief cessation of hostilities when he mentioned his daughter was obviously over. "Of course it is. I laid out my rules and you've broken them."

"I won't let it be over," he said obstinately.

But what if she insisted on leaving? He had a reputation as a ruthless dog but even he balked at locking her in the house in York Street like a captive in a harem.

"You can't mean to use the secret of my son's whereabouts to force me, Erith." Desperation sharpened her features. "It's not just me you'd hurt, but Leo and my cousin and the good man she's married to. Surely your pride isn't worth that damage."

Her cousin? That was interesting. He remembered the kind-faced woman he'd glimpsed so briefly outside the vicarage. Perhaps Olivia came from a higher level of society than he'd imagined. If her brother had been born a gentleman in rank if not in honor, his crime against her was even more heinous.

"Erith?" She sounded genuinely scared now and her face was strained and pale.

He realized he hadn't answered her. "Contrary to public opinion, I still retain a shred of honor."

"What does that mean?"

"It means I won't betray you or Leo."

"How can I trust you?" Blistering anger invested the short question.

"I give you my word, Olivia. Your secret is safe."

Of course it was useless asking her to trust him. She didn't trust anyone. Particularly men.

She sent him a stormy look, clearly unconvinced. "Even if I leave you?"

How easy to use his knowledge to keep her. But he'd reached a point where lying to her, even by omission, left him feeling small and grubby.

"Even if you leave me." He paused then invoked the only hold he still had on her. "What about our wager? Do you admit I've won?"

She pursed her lips into a luscious bow as if dismissing the thought. "I don't consider a mutual agreement to part to be surrender."

"No, you wouldn't." He laughed shortly and leaned back, crossing one booted leg over the other. "But it's surrender all the same. You're running away and using the excuse of my execrable behavior today to justify your cowardice."

She arched her eyebrows with disdain. "You've tried this tactic before, Erith. It worked then but palls through familiarity."

He shrugged and kept his voice light. "Then stay for the challenge. Stay because you want to. Stay because I'll be gone after my daughter's wedding and you'll move on with memories of the one affair that didn't follow the pattern."

The carriage lurched to a complete halt and the coachman shouted abuse at someone. Inside, the silence crackled with tension.

She looked down at her hands then up at him. There was a troubled, turbulent light in her eyes.

"Don't pretend it's so simple, Erith." She made a furious gesture with her hand, slicing the air. "Already you know more about me than anyone apart from Perry. It gives you a power I can't accept. I've spent my life evading any man who tries to dominate me."

He let the implications of her admission sink in before he answered. It was clear that she felt the pull of attraction between them, but she fought it with all her might. With her history, he knew why.

"I don't want to know about you so I have power," he said quietly.

Her brows contracted as if she didn't understand. When she spoke, her voice was edged with new bitterness. "Men always have power over women."

"Except you."

"That hasn't always been true."

Tragically, after today, he believed her. "I'm not your enemy, Olivia."

A cynical expression hardened her face. Briefly he recalled the cold, manipulative courtesan he'd first met. He'd never think of her as that woman again. "Yes, you are."

Yes, he was the enemy.

The organ in his trousers made him her enemy. His powerful male passions made him her enemy. The fact that he wanted her more than he wanted to take his next breath made him her enemy.

The carriage swerved into motion again. He automatically adjusted to the movement. Heavy rain began to drum on the roof, underlining the dismal slide of his mood.

For once he had no idea how to win a woman. And the more he saw of her, the more he wanted her. The real her, not the beautiful, counterfeit shell.

He couldn't believe he'd reached this pitch of desperation. All he'd learned of her today just built his endless craving. He hardly recognized himself anymore.

But how could he regret following her? He'd never wish away what he now knew about her.

To think he'd been so blasé about choosing a mistress to adorn his weeks in London. A woman to entertain him while his attention focused on what was really important. His rapprochement with his children.

Olivia Raines had put him through more emotion in the last few days than he'd felt in the last sixteen years. Dangerous, painful emotion that he'd spent half a lifetime running away from.

So why the hell did the prospect of saying good-bye to her make him want to smash something?

Through the increasing gloom outside—the weather became a squall of the first magnitude—he noticed familiar house fronts. They weren't far from York Street.

"What are you going to do?" he asked. Then with more difficulty, "I want you to stay."

"Until July," she responded tartly.

"Olivia," he said with a hint of asperity. "Right now I'm trying to keep you into the next five minutes. It's premature to worry about what happens in a couple of months."

Her jaw set with a stubbornness he recognized. "Nevertheless, Erith—"

He interrupted before she could say the irrevocable words. "No."

He banged hard on the roof until the coachman slid the panel behind his head open. "Yes, madam? My lord?"

"Drive to the park," Erith snapped.

Chapter 11

"*W*hat on earth are you doing?" Olivia asked in bewilderment. "We're nearly back in York Street."

"I want to talk to you." Erith ignored the coachman, although he felt the man's avidly curious eyes boring into the back of his head.

An impatient frown crossed her face, bringing it back to vivid life. "You've talked all the way from Kent, for heaven's sake."

"I want to talk to you away from this damned black box that belongs to damned Peregrine Montjoy."

"But it's the middle of a rainstorm."

"I don't care."

"Madam?" The coachman sounded like he thought his betters had lost their minds. Olivia stared at Erith through the gloom as if she believed he'd gone mad too. He himself wasn't even sure of his sanity. What he was sure about was that he wasn't going to tamely watch her move out of his life.

He intended to fight for what he wanted. Probably for the first time ever.

No wonder he made such a god-almighty hash of it.

For a long silent moment she studied his face. The Devil knew what she saw there. But sudden decision entered her expression.

"Sherrin, his lordship wishes to promenade in the park." She glanced past him to the coachman. "So the park it is."

"Yes, madam." The coachman looked unhappy. Given the water cascading over his oilskins, Erith couldn't blame him for his lack of enthusiasm.

"Stop at the first folly."

"Very good, my lord." Sherrin slid the panel closed.

Olivia sent Erith a long-suffering look as the coach began to move again. "We'll both end up catching our death. Not to mention poor Sherrin. He's got a wife and six children."

"If I take you back to the house, you'll leave me," he said obstinately. He knew he made an utter fool of himself. He wished he could stop, but some demon possessed him.

"I can leave you from a park as well as from a drawing room."

Soon the carriage drew to a stop. Erith peered out the foggy window and saw the looming bulk of a Greek temple. The panel behind his head slid back again. "Here, your lordship?"

"Yes, Sherrin. Wait in the building until we summon you."

"Very good, my lord."

The carriage rocked as the man climbed down, and Erith watched him dash through the teeming rain and disappear into the temple. He turned back to Olivia. "Shall we walk?"

She sent him a disbelieving topaz glare. "It's a deluge out there."

"Just a soft spring shower." Roughly, he released the door catch and stepped into the storm, tugging her after him. "You won't melt."

"I honestly believe you belong in Bedlam." He expected her to struggle, but she didn't fight as she tumbled out of the carriage and into the weather.

"Probably." He'd only been outside seconds and already the lashing rain slicked his hair over his forehead. He blinked away the streaming water that obscured his vision. The wind blasted rain at them in cold needles. She was right. He did belong in an asylum. No person in their right mind would willingly go out into this storm.

He felt far from in his right mind.

Taking her arm, he headed doggedly toward a gray and soggy grove just off the path, his boots splashing through the puddles. She scurried to keep up. Her elaborate gown was a sodden mess and her bonnet collapsed into a lump of wet straw.

She removed it, observed it for a second, and tossed it to the side of the overflowing track. "Irredeemable, I'm afraid." She had to raise her voice above the rain.

"Like my character."

"Like mine."

"Then we suit each other."

"That doesn't mean we should remain together." She ducked her head as an eddy of wind gusted a torrent of cold water over them. "If I freeze to death, it won't matter whether I've decided to stay or not."

"Does that mean you're thinking about it?"

"Right now I'm thinking of a warm fire and dry clothes. And perhaps a brandy and a cigar."

At last they reached the copse. Erith dragged her under the shelter of the trees. He dropped his hold on her. Instinct told him if she'd come this far, she wasn't likely to run.

"You've got to stay with me, Olivia." He didn't have to shout here, thank God. "I'm the only man in Christendom who will tolerate your eccentric ways."

"That's the pot calling the kettle black. Who forced whom out into this tempest? Perry told me you had a reputation for

coolness and calculation. I've seen precious little evidence
of either. Couldn't we have this discussion in the carriage?"

She shivered. Her face was paper white. He should be
horsewhipped for making her stand in this downpour. Still,
stubbornly, superstitiously, he refused to return her to the
carriage that would take her away from him.

"You tried to keep me at a distance," he said with a trace
of sullenness he immediately resented.

"And drowning me will make you feel closer? If that's the
case, can't we do this when there's a warm bath handy?"

The idea of her long graceful limbs slick with soap and
hot water sent searing arousal through him that not even the
freezing weather could douse.

For a woman compelled into the middle of a tempest, she
didn't sound particularly angry. Irritated but not furious.
He wondered what went on in her complicated, fascinating,
brilliant brain. He wondered what went on in his to haul her
about like this.

She wiped her face. But it was useless. Water still poured
down. Her neat braided hairstyle, so different to the intricate
creations she usually sported, came apart under the flood,
and her hair, darkened to old bronze, clung to her face and
neck in long straggling rats' tails. She didn't look at all the
glamorous creature he was used to.

She looked more breathtakingly beautiful than any woman
he'd ever seen.

She fixed an uncompromising regard on him. "Say what
you have to and let me get back into the dry."

He moved nearer, partly to shield her from the weather,
partly because he needed to have her within the shelter of
his body. The scent of rain filled the turbulent air, but underneath he caught a hint of her delicate scent. He'd recognize
that fragrance from the other side of a room.

He stared hard at her. Raw, eviscerating emotion made
him shake. He felt lost, exposed, threatened. "Are you going
to leave?" he asked starkly.

Her face contracted with dismay. "Don't. I'm not worth it."

"Of course you are," he snarled with sudden anger. He caught her arm in a hard clasp. "Damn it, Olivia, I surrender. You can have your public avowal of power over me. If you'll stay."

"I don't care about the bet," she snapped. "Why is having me as your mistress so important?"

He answered with perfect, bewildered honesty. "I have no idea."

"Neither do I. You've had no pleasure."

His mind filled with his delight in her quick wit. His delight in her beauty. His delight in her spirit. His delight in . . . *her.*

"That's not true."

"Yes, it is. You won't take what I offer, and I can't give you what you ask for. Yet still you plague me." Her eyes were like washed gems between the wet fringe of lashes. Her face was white with cold and tension. *"What do you want, Erith?"*

The rain had eased as they argued. It provided a gentle pattering background to that one bleak question.

He could only speak the words engraved on his soul. The soul he thought had calcified into stone over the last sixteen years of grief and loneliness. "I want you."

He caught a flash of pain in those brilliant eyes. "But I don't want you."

"I can make you want me." His voice cracked with desperation. His chest heaved as he fought for breath.

"No, you can't."

She reached up and touched his cheek. The glove was smooth and wet against his skin. It was the same gesture she'd made last night. After all the strife, her sudden tenderness then had torn his heart. The simple touch still made the breath catch in his throat.

Closing his eyes, he let her warmth soak into his bones. She said she didn't want him, but that touch hinted she was far from indifferent.

He shouldn't do what he was about to. He knew it would destroy any chance of convincing her to stay. He opened his eyes and tightened his hold on her arm, not bruising but enough to stop her stepping away.

"Olivia," he whispered, just for the pleasure of hearing her name.

He saw awareness seep into the clear brown eyes, turn them the color of dark whisky. She trembled under his hand.

With cold? With fear? *With desire?*

He couldn't say. But she didn't recoil as he leaned closer.

"No, Erith." It was a mere thread of sound. Her breath brushed across his lips, heat to his chilled flesh.

"Yes," he said as softly. He cradled her jaw in his free hand and gently tilted her chin toward him.

For one suspended instant, the rain, the wind, the cold, receded to nothing. There was just the woman and the promise of the kiss to come.

She whimpered as his mouth touched hers. Unless he'd been so close, he would not have heard. Just for a moment, he lingered, tasting the coolness of her skin, the freshness of the rain. Then he pulled away a fraction so the ghost of the kiss hovered even after the kiss ended.

The rain fell in a curtain around them, adding a sweet edge of innocence to what they did. She parted her lips and sucked in a shaky breath. He waited for her to wrench away as she had when he kissed her before. But she remained completely still. Apart from the endless waves of trembling that combed through her tall, willowy body.

He must stop. That kiss meant more than anything she'd ever granted him. More than the contemptuous seduction of his body with her mouth their first night.

Right now he had her grudging consent. He had no right to demand more.

But he was only human and he'd wanted to kiss her since he first saw her. He bent forward and grazed his lips over the mole on her cheek. Then before she could protest, he sipped at her lips again. They were soft and smooth like damp satin.

He'd kissed her before, but he hadn't known what was at stake then. It was a game they played.

This tentative kiss was more important than life and death.

Delicately his tongue touched the seam, savoring a trace of the warmth inside. She made a soft humming sound deep in her throat and for a brief instant opened. Her breath touched his tongue and almost imperceptibly her lips moved against his.

He sighed and the hand cupping her jaw curved into a caress. Her tiny, hesitant, unpracticed response made him dizzy with arousal. Arousal tempered by an agonizing tenderness that made him want to cherish as much as ravish her.

He tasted her kiss for an endless moment, knowing to ask for more was to invite disaster.

But he couldn't stop himself increasing the pressure. Fleetingly her lips softened, parted, answered his.

Then she stiffened under his hands and pulled away. But slowly, as if she woke from a dream. She'd closed her eyes, and as her heavy lashes rose, he glimpsed the young girl she'd never had the chance to be.

Her dazed expression changed to horrified realization. "You kissed me."

"Yes," he said helplessly, wanting her so much, he thought he'd die of it.

"Take your hands off me." Her voice shook.

With an ironic gesture of apology, he released her arms. She struggled to erect barriers against him. But she was more vulnerable than he'd imagined.

Erith could be gracious in victory. For the present.

Now that he wasn't holding her, he became aware of his surroundings. The rain was cold. The wind rose again. The thunder in his heart found an echo in the crescendo of thunder in the sky. It was muddy and dank underneath the trees. An icy trickle of water ran down his face and disappeared into his sodden neckcloth.

"I'm going back to the house. Don't come with me."

"Let me escort you to the carriage." On such a foul day, the park was deserted, but nonetheless he didn't like the idea of her unprotected.

Her laugh sounded like a muffled sob. "I want to walk."

"Olivia, don't be absurd." He reached to catch her hand but she stepped away.

"Kindly allow me my way in this at least." She turned on her heel and twitched her saturated skirts, more black than green after their soaking. With her shoulders straight and her head high, she stepped out from under the trees.

He couldn't let her go like this. With nothing resolved. He snatched her arm and this time wouldn't let her rebuff him. "What are you going to do, Olivia?"

She cast him an unreadable topaz glance. "Change my clothes, for one thing."

She'd retreated into Olivia Raines, queen of courtesans. Although the queen of courtesans looked woefully bedraggled. It said something for the equally woeful state of Erith's emotions that he found her disheveled state endearing. More than endearing. Hugely alluring.

He let her go. And said words the notorious Earl of Erith would once never have believed himself capable of uttering. "Please don't leave me, Olivia."

For a fleeting instant her hauteur melted. He saw deep into the wild turmoil in her soul before she whirled around. With a choked curse, she picked up her skirts. He watched in despair as she ran across the muddy ground into the rain-swept afternoon.

Chapter 12

The door to the bedroom slammed open with a crash, rattling the windowpanes and setting the closed curtains, with their bright embroidered peonies and peacocks, to billowing.

The Earl of Erith loomed in the entrance. Potent. Intense. Vibrating with the same fierce desperation Olivia remembered from the park. He brought the storm inside with him.

With a shocked gasp, she sank lower into the cooling bathwater. She clutched her half full brandy glass in front of her like a shield. Her maid gave a shriek and dropped the pitcher she'd lifted to rinse Olivia's hair. The pottery vessel shattered and water flooded everywhere.

"Lawks, miss!" Amy gasped. Her panicked gaze settled on Erith and she bobbed a clumsy curtsy. "My lord."

"Get out," he told the girl without shifting from the doorway. Dripping black hair clung to his drawn face and his clothes were a soggy mess. His feverishly glittering gray eyes remained unwavering on Olivia.

Amy was too startled to take warning from his calm tone. She began flinging towels onto the puddle. "The carpet will spoil—"

"I said get out," he said even more quietly.

This time Amy heard the threat. She dropped the towels, performed another awkward curtsy, and dashed for the dressing room.

Olivia and the earl remained behind, sharing a charged silence.

For a fraught moment the memory of that wondrous kiss in the rain hovered between them. She tasted the spicy warmth of his mouth on hers. She felt his cold hands cradling her face. He'd held her as if he'd never touched anything so precious in his whole life. Her lips parted with trembling expectation, just as they'd parted under his gentle exploration.

That poignant kiss had sliced her soul in two.

She could hardly bear to recall it.

It was over an hour since she'd fled like a madwoman through the cloudburst. Blind with anguish after leaving Erith, she'd stumbled upon an empty hackney when she reached the rain-swept street. By the time she'd arrived home, she was chilled to the bone. She'd dashed out of the shabby hired carriage and into the house, intending to depart immediately, before he returned to confuse her with more demands and questions, and damnable tenderness that left her lost and defenseless and yearning.

Reason, self-preservation, experience screamed that she must end the affair. Now. This minute. Before the strange bond between them destroyed the powerful woman she'd created from the helpless, terrified, abused girl.

So why hadn't she left?

She met his wild silver eyes across the room and an electric jolt sizzled through her. Nerves? Fear? Resentment? Surely not excitement. Her fingers clenched on her heavy crystal glass and she couldn't look away.

Erith moved inside the room and shut the door with a studied care that indicated how close to the edge he was. "You're still here," he said softly, without coming closer.

"Yes."

He lifted one tanned hand to tug away his sodden neck-cloth. He dropped it to the floor. "Why?"

Dear heaven, she didn't want to answer. She wasn't sure she could. Or not in any way that made sense. Once, she might have said she stayed for the sake of her reputation as London's greatest courtesan. But that would now be a lie. Perhaps it had been a lie from the first. She could no longer deny Lord Erith had always drawn her like a magnet drew iron filings.

I'm here because you kissed me in the rain. You kissed me as if I broke your heart.

Ridiculous.

She sought to inject a practical note into the thickening atmosphere. "Erith, you'll catch your death in those wet clothes. Why not order a bath? I'll finish here and arrange supper if you're staying."

"Oh, I'm staying, all right." His sensual lips twisted in a grimace that wasn't quite a smile. "Why are you still here, Olivia?"

Confound him, he was as persistent as a mastiff with a bone. She decided to adopt the attacking position. Although how formidable could she be, crouching naked in lukewarm water with long strands of wet hair snaking around her?

She injected a sarcastic edge. "I gathered from your histrionics in the park that my presence was necessary for your continued sanity, if nothing else."

As she should have expected, her childish attempt to annoy failed. His voice remained steady and low, although she knew him well enough to guess the turbulent currents swirling beneath his composure. An ocean of titanic emotion seethed under his impassive facade. She remembered the desperation in his voice when he'd begged her not to leave him. Seeing this proud man brought to such a state had moved her to helpless tears.

"I thought I'd find you packing. Or gone." He shrugged out of his tight coat. With some difficulty, as it adhered soggily to his body. He threw it down next to the neckcloth.

Some devil made her say, "I have certain standards, my lord. I refuse to leave your protection looking like I've been dunked in the North Sea."

The bathwater had become uncomfortably cold. She told herself he'd seen her naked before. But absurdly, the day with its astonishing crevasses of emotion had left her shy.

How laughable. She hadn't been shy since her first lover.

"You're not going anywhere."

"Is that a threat?"

"No, it's an observation. An accurate one, as it happens."

As if to prove his confidence, he reached down to relieve her of the brandy glass. He took a substantial mouthful then placed it near the few remaining towels folded on top of the sideboard.

The shiver that shook her wasn't entirely from the cold bathwater. When he drank from the same glass, it felt like he set his claim upon her.

Oh, heavens, she couldn't sit in this bath much longer. She already looked like a prune. "Pass me a towel, Erith," she snapped. "If you can find a dry one."

He grabbed a towel from the pile on the sideboard. "Here."

She snatched at it and with humiliating clumsiness wrapped it around herself as she stepped from the tub. "Thank you."

He'd prowled closer when he took her glass. Only about a foot of saturated carpet now separated them. She tried to back away but her legs hit the side of the bath hard enough to hurt.

"Careful." He put his hand on her arm to steady her. Then he let go.

What was he up to? She knew men. Their impulses and weaknesses and contemptible thought processes that justified everything they did. But for the life of her, she couldn't read Erith.

"You don't understand me nearly as well as you think." Curse her sulkiness. She wanted to sound brave and defiant, not like a child denied a Sunday treat.

"You still haven't answered my question."

His long-fingered hands rose to the buttons on his waistcoat. She remembered it as pale pearl silk with silver swans embroidered across it. It had been beautiful, unusual, eye-catching. Now it was an expensive rag.

He slipped the waistcoat down his arms and let it fall behind him. His relentless undressing only increased her nervousness. She took an uncertain step to the side like a mare scenting a stallion.

"I'm here because . . . "

Her voice trailed away as she really looked at him for the first time since he'd burst in. His wet shirt clung, revealing smooth planes of muscle and bone, outlining ribs and broad shoulders. Her eyes traveled over that square jaw, that determined chin, the haughty nose, straight and commanding. Those heavy-lidded, deceptively slumberous eyes under the thick black brows.

Not a hint of prettiness or softness. Until one looked at the thick fringe of black lashes or the suddenly vulnerable line of his mouth.

He was the handsomest man she'd ever seen, wonderfully compelling. The bones were so strong, just as he was strong.

Perhaps even as strong as she.

What business did she have finding a man compelling? Men were beasts and brutes.

But she couldn't prod the old, familiar bitterness to life. Not when Erith stared at her as if his world began and ended with her. Every ounce of moisture in her mouth evaporated. She licked suddenly dry lips and thought she heard him muffle a groan. Her pulse pounded so loudly in her ears, she couldn't be sure.

"Damn you, Olivia," he gritted out, taking a step so she stood trembling within the shadow of his powerful body. "Touch me."

The hand clutching the damp towel tightened. The breath caught in her throat. Her vision shrank to encompass Erith alone while the rest of the room faded to nothing.

God help her, she craved the feel of his firm, muscled flesh beneath her hands. She yearned to touch a man for sheer curiosity. For pleasure. For need. She didn't recognize this woman at the mercy of her feral appetites.

But nor could she gainsay what she wanted.

She bit her lip, torn between sensible fear and crazy daring. Daring won by a whisker. As if she took the greatest risk of her life, she leaned forward to place her palm flat on the triangle of hair-roughened skin revealed under his open shirt. The shock of contact vibrated through her. He quivered under her hand but didn't make any attempt to take charge of her tentative incursion.

Slowly, luxuriantly, she pressed her bare skin against his, feeling heat, strength. The touch was more intimate than taking him in her mouth. Almost as intimate as that brief, tender kiss in the rain that counted as the sweetest sexual experience she'd ever known.

He sucked in a great breath. His chest rose beneath her hand, connecting her to the vitality that flowed through his veins. This chaste joining made her one with another person in a way a man invading her body never had.

He closed his eyes as if in pain. His prominent cheekbones flushed with color, and the usually cynical mouth relaxed into a beautiful soft fullness.

"You're so warm," she murmured.

After his walk in the rain, she'd expected his flesh to feel chilled, clammy. Without conscious thought, she edged closer. She'd been cold for so long that Lord Erith's radiant heat was irresistible.

"Let me warm you," he whispered, curving his hands around her bare, damp shoulders.

No pressure. No compulsion. Just more warmth. And a feeling of safety she couldn't recall feeling with a man before. How had he crossed the invisible line between being male, and therefore enemy, to becoming . . . *what?* Her lover? Her friend? Her ally? None of those words seemed adequate to convey the strange new landscape she entered.

He bent his head to kiss her. She stood trembling like a deer in the hunter's sights. Then something inside her flowered and she moved forward, not away. For the first time, she stretched up to accept a man's mouth on hers.

She waited for the old revulsion to surface, the vile feeling of suffocation. Instead there was just the same glorious sweetness she'd tasted when he kissed her in the storm. And a tempting trace on his lips of the rich brandy he'd stolen from her.

He didn't demand a response. He didn't press her up against him and his hands clasped her arms loosely. If she wanted, she could escape. Everything about his stance silently indicated that any decision about what happened now was hers.

The hesitant kiss was as chaste as the buss of a child's lips. But there was nothing childish about the burning passion in his gray gaze when he raised his head and stared down at her. How could she ever have thought those eyes cold?

This man was in so many ways a riddle. She had no real reason to trust him. Except that those intent, intelligent eyes seemed to pierce through all her deceptions and pretenses to her shivering, lonely, longing soul. And she was so tired of being the diamond-bright, diamond-hard jewel of the demi-monde.

But if she relinquished the courtesan, what was left?

"Do you want me to stop?" he asked softly.

An astounding question from a lover. And more astounding, she believed if she said yes, he'd step away. She'd never known a man like Erith. Still she hesitated. She'd learned in the hardest way to fear a man's power over a woman. "I don't know."

"Olivia, I swear I'll abide by what you want."

"I believe you." Although life had taught her all men lied.

He leaned down and brushed his lips across hers. One glowing moment of contact. Over before she had a chance to respond. The touch left a tingling, tantalizing desire for more.

She made a strangled, needy sound deep in her throat. Then she forced out words she'd never said to a man in all her years of dissipation. Words she never thought she'd say. "Kiss . . . kiss me again, Erith."

"Olivia . . . " he said on a long sigh. The murmur of her name in that deep voice soaked through her skin right to her bones. He sounded like an angel had pointed him toward a heaven he never thought he'd attain.

She watched his face change. The strain disappeared. The heavy eyelids lowered as his gaze narrowed on her mouth. She remained poised beneath his lips in quivering expectation. Something powerful held her captive, still, ready, like a sleeping maiden in a fairy tale, waiting for her magic prince to kiss her back to life.

Desperately she snatched at reality. *Angels? Maidens? Princes?* None of these belonged in her world. In her world, men paid her to service them, just as they paid their barbers to shave them or their grooms to feed their horses.

But that grim warning faded to a faint whisper at the back of her mind. It couldn't penetrate the mysterious enchantment that held her suspended between flight and surrender. A surrender she'd never offered any man, for all her wild and wanton history.

Erith's hands tightened, shifted their grip, drew her closer. The delicious heat of his clasp on the soft flesh of her upper arms made her tremble. "You smell like a garden in the rain. Flowers and fresh air."

He blew gently on the skin where her neck joined her shoulder. The sensation of his breath on wet flesh shot a wild shiver through her. Strange but not unpleasant. Not unpleasant at all.

"Do that again," she said in an unsteady murmur.

"This?"

He blew on her skin once more then leaned forward to nip her. A jagged thrill darted along her veins and goose bumps broke out all over. She gasped and pressed closer, fumbling at the slipping towel.

He began to nibble and suck at her neck, stirring up a storm of little shocks. Her blood beat thick and heavy. A weight settled low in her belly. She shifted to ease an unfamiliar heat between her legs.

Was this desire? How could she say? She had nothing to compare it to.

Her skin felt sensitive and too tight to contain her bones. She trembled like a reed in a gale and she couldn't control her breath. His teeth scraped her neck and a soft moan of delight escaped her parted lips. She stiffened in astonishment. That unpracticed sound couldn't have come from her.

"What's wrong?" he asked softly.

She was what was wrong, but she didn't want to say that. Although she suspected he was the one man in Creation who would understand what she meant.

"This . . . isn't what I'm used to." Her voice was stilted and her hand clutched her towel with nervous vigor.

"Nor I."

He drew back and studied her face. What did he see there? Erith's concentrated, endless attention on her slightest response made her uncomfortable. Scared her. She'd lived as an enigma for so long. Enigmas were safe.

She shifted awkwardly from one bare foot to the other, feeling the wet carpet squelch under her feet. Then, because his expression held no censure—only concern and a barely reined hunger—she forced herself to go on, however absurd she sounded. "You know what pleasure is."

"Yes. I do. But I've never had to show anyone before." A shadow of sadness darkened his face and his gaze turned opaque. She couldn't mistake the piercing sorrow that roughened his voice. "No, that's not true. Once. Once I had to show someone what pleasure was. It's one of my sweetest memories."

Her heart came to a shuddering, painful halt.

At last he opened the door of his soul to her.

She looked in.

And saw eternal love.

Who else but Joanna could he mean when he spoke about initiating someone into pleasure? The Earl of Erith had loved his wife. With a passion and a dedication that still, sixteen years after her death, turned his eyes the color of a stormy sea and made him speak of her with haunting reverence. Only the loss of real love could leave that aching, endless grief behind.

How willfully blind she'd been. How stupid. How insensitive. So much that had puzzled her about this man became clear, not least that his infamous debaucheries had been a futile attempt to assuage unendurable grief.

He'd told her he understood love, and she hadn't believed him. But she believed him now. Any fool would hear the love and unutterable yearning in his voice when he spoke of his wife. Any fool, apparently, but the canniest strumpet in London.

Olivia regarded him with the eyes of fresh understanding and gave up all hope of shielding herself from this attraction. Because she was attracted to Lord Erith. Unbearably so.

She could fight a man who used his masculine power against her. She couldn't fight a man whose weapon was his broken heart.

He'd end up hurting her profoundly. She knew that as she knew he was her last lover.

Her last lover would be the lover she'd never forget.

Chapter 13

Olivia couldn't hold herself separate from Erith any longer. Not after today. Not after the kiss in the rain. Not after realizing how deeply he'd loved his wife and that his wayward life since Joanna's death was an expression of inconsolable, unending grief.

"I'm yours, Erith," she whispered.

"Olivia . . . " Tenderly, he placed his arms around her and rained tiny kisses over her shoulders and cheeks and nose and eyelids. It was like he learned her through the touch of his mouth alone.

Tentatively, she moved closer. She'd had so many men, she should know what to do. But the feelings trembling to life inside her made her nervous as a virgin.

It would be safer to run. But if she left now, she'd lose something precious and irreplaceable.

Too late for second thoughts. Her decision was made.

A gentle tug on the back of the towel. "Let me see you."

Her deathly grip didn't relax. "You have seen me."

The towel seemed the last bastion. With other lovers, her body was merely a vehicle for earning a living. Her nakedness held no significance. Tonight with Erith, she felt completely different.

He pulled back and looked down at her, his face grave. "You still don't trust me, Olivia?"

Her breath caught at the somber beauty of his face. "Take your shirt off."

Pure delight curved his lips. "If you insist."

"I do."

He shifted a few inches away to tug the wet white linen over his head. He tossed it behind him without paying attention to where it fell. "Better?"

"Better." She stared up at him while unfamiliar anticipation thrummed in her blood. "Now the breeches."

His hands were shaking so badly, he fumbled as he ripped at the fastenings. His emotional extremity touched something deep inside her, made her feel less at the mercy of all-conquering chaos.

He paused in wrenching off his clothing, as if he just realized he still wore his boots. She tucked the end of the towel more firmly around her. "Sit on the bed and let me help you."

"I'm too muddy. Let me call a footman."

She shook her head. "No, I want to do it."

"If you wish." The look he cast her was perceptive. Perhaps he also believed this tremulous joy was too fragile to survive a stranger's interruption. He moved across to the bed. She hid a smile, but not fast enough.

"I hope you're not laughing at me, Miss Raines."

"No." A gurgle of amusement escaped her. He did look absurd, sitting there in his half-undone breeches with his boots still on. Absurd, and more appealing than any man she'd ever seen. "Yes."

"Just wait till I get my hands on you."

"Just wait." She dropped down before him, lifting one muscled calf across her knees.

Doing this for him made her feel like a wife. She'd never been married. Would never place herself permanently under one man's governance. Although she'd had offers aplenty. From men with no care for their standing in society. From men like Perry, with secrets to hide.

Heavens, why was she suddenly thinking about marriage? Was it because Lord Erith for all his rakish reputation struck her as someone who'd make a good husband?

Dear God, perish the thought. No decent man would have her. And she'd have no decent man. She'd be bored within a week.

With a sudden excess of energy, she tugged at Erith's boot. It was tight and took some pulling to remove. She was panting when she shifted her attention to the other boot. Her hair, already drying in the heat of the fire, flopped forward as she bent over his leg and wrenched with all her might. If her zeal stemmed from bitter regret that she wouldn't perform this humble task for Erith for the rest of her life, so be it.

He tilted her chin up. "Olivia, you don't have to do anything you don't want to."

His eyes were alight with concern and kindness. And hunger. She couldn't mistake the smoldering desire that turned the gray to molten silver.

She blinked to dispel the annoying mist clouding her vision. Damn Erith. How did he do this to her? Her voice was choked. "You're getting the worst of this bargain."

A lazy glint of amusement lit the gray. "A beautiful half-naked woman kneels at my feet and gazes at me adoringly. There's not a man in the world who wouldn't envy me."

"I'm not gazing at you adoringly." She straightened and drew in a shuddering breath. "I would never sink so low."

He leaned forward slowly and the fingers around her chin curved into a hold of such tenderness, she couldn't have pulled away if she'd wanted to. And for once in her life, she didn't want to.

"Keep throwing out challenges, Olivia." He pressed his lips to hers. Again, the least demanding of kisses. A mere touch then a kiss to each corner of her mouth, one to her chin and one to the tip of her nose.

He must want more than these sweet games. She *knew* he wanted more. He was hard and ready. His breathing came fast and shallow, and the unfastened breeches did nothing to hide his erection.

Erith brushed another teasing kiss across her lips. He lifted his head and looked at her, the spark in his eyes even more pronounced.

In spite of the playful kisses, she didn't deceive herself where this led. His musky arousal sharpened the air. She knew with bone-deep certainty he'd possess her tonight. For good or ill, they'd reached a pitch only sex would answer.

"I wish I could show you your face."

She frowned fleetingly. "What's wrong with it?"

"Nothing. If you don't mind a simper."

No man bantered with her like this. It was surprisingly arousing, even to a woman who hadn't known arousal. "I've never simpered in my life."

"Until now." He kissed her cheeks in another of those glancing, increasingly pleasurable touches and let her go. "Will you take the towel off?"

She hitched it higher. "Maybe. Will you take your breeches off?"

"Aha, you're curious."

She shrugged with a show of mocking indifference. "I've seen it all before."

"But you're yet to find out what I can do with what I've got."

"So vain."

"So good."

She laughed. "So misguided."

His face became intent. "Oh, no, madam. I know exactly where I'm aiming. And . . . " His voice dropped impossibly low, resonating in her marrow. " . . . I know what to do when I get there."

Ridiculously, she felt heat rise in her cheeks. He was the only man in Creation who could put her to the blush. The strange ache between her legs intensified. She shifted restlessly to ease the feeling then cursed the knowing arch of Erith's eyebrows.

The ache couldn't be arousal. She wasn't capable of arousal. But this was the closest she'd ever come. She wasn't sure she liked the sensation. It was . . . uncomfortable, disturbing.

She lurched to her feet to avoid his gaze. The towel parted and dropped into a crumpled heap.

"Oh, no," she gasped, scrabbling after it.

He surged forward and snatched her hand. His touch was hot as it encircled her wrist and his sandalwood scent made her dizzy with yearning. "Let it go."

She trembled in his hold, incapable of answering. Chill air brushed over her bare, damp flesh, contrasting sharply with Erith's heat. She fought the insane urge to cover herself with fluttering hands. He'd seen her before. He'd explored her body. He'd yielded his essence to her rapacious mouth. Yet tonight everything felt as though it started anew. Her pulse set up a frantic race and her lungs refused to release her breath.

With his free hand, he slid his breeches to the ground and kicked them aside. Her heart somersaulted at the sight of his nakedness.

Lord Erith was hard and strong. Like a huge tree. Or a god from an ancient legend. From his broad straight shoulders to his massive hair-roughened chest to his long legs with their firm horseman's thighs. Even his large feet proclaimed mastery of the ground upon which he stood.

She sucked in a shuddering breath and swallowed to

moisten a dry throat. Her gaze inevitably dropped to where his member sprang from the nest of black curls at the base of his flat belly.

"Yes, I want you. I'm not ashamed of how you make me feel." He paused and slid his hand down so his fingers twined in hers. "The question is what I make you feel."

Frightened. Nervous. Poised to run. Like a foolish girl instead of a woman in charge of her world.

She tilted her chin, pretending a courage her defenseless heart didn't feel. She'd long ago learned that counterfeit bravery could save her when real bravery was beyond her. Her voice was terse. "I'm ready."

A frown darkened his striking face and drew his marked black brows together. "Olivia, you don't have to defend yourself. I laid down my weapons today. I told you I surrendered, and I meant it. You're free."

She didn't feel free. With every second, attraction enmeshed her more tightly. Would the strands end up trapping her like a lark in the hunter's net, so she fluttered and fluttered until she failed with exhaustion?

As if he guessed her troubled thoughts, he very gently took her in his arms, bringing her into his body. It was like standing next to a huge stove on a cold winter's day. Satisfying. Comforting. Except she felt none of these safe emotions. Instead she felt restless and jumpy.

She rested her cheek against his chest, feeling the pleasant tickle of his hair, and curled her arms loosely around his waist. Few men were tall enough for her to lean against with this ease.

Beneath her ear his heartbeat thudded steadily. She felt him take a massive breath. And another. Slowly, almost hesitantly, he began to stroke her bare back. Small circular movements, alluring touches that drew the coiling tension from her muscles.

Gradually the movements widened, deepened, became long sweeping strokes from the slope of her buttocks to her shoulders. His hands were warm and slightly rough, nice. Dreamily, she stood quiescent and let him continue this silent, almost impersonal worship of her naked body.

How long they stood in a communion deeper than any sexual experience she'd ever known she couldn't say. The rain lashed the windows, the breeze rattled the casements, the fire crackled in the grate. Erith's breath matched hers. Slow. Deep. His hands roamed across her skin in a tender exploration sweeter than words could express.

In the end it was Olivia who broke the stasis.

By nature she wasn't a passive woman. While peace might beckon like the promise of heaven, she didn't belong in this honeyed stillness. Somewhere, her uncertainty had disappeared. Instead she was ready to embrace whatever the night brought.

She shifted closer, firmed her arms around his waist. At her slight movement, new tension entered his muscles. He was so aware of everything about her. His unwavering attention filled her with a heady mixture of nerves and excitement.

He was hard for her. It spoke to the preternatural strength of his will that he controlled his arousal. She wondered how long he'd allow her to set the pace. Erith wasn't a passive soul either. He reined himself in for her sake but volcanic passion roiled beneath his patience and must soon erupt.

Deliberately, she rubbed against him, her nipples tightening as they brushed his hairy chest. She slid eager hands down to clasp his tight buttocks. She pulled him closer, pressing his member into her belly. He throbbed against her soft flesh, hot, demanding, powerful.

"Kiss me, Erith," she whispered, lifting her head and staring into his avid eyes.

"If I kiss you, I mightn't stop," he returned equally softly.

"Then don't stop."

She stretched to touch her mouth to his, copying the glancing kisses he'd given her earlier. Before she broke the contact, his lips moved beneath hers and she tasted his need. In a sudden movement, he swept her across to the bed and tugged her down under him. He poised to take her.

This time he kissed her harder, with less careful finesse.

It wasn't fair to expect him to keep treating her as if she might shatter. But with his forcefulness, some of her dazed pleasure faded.

He raised his head, his face stark and pale. His jaw jutted with tension and his body vibrated with what it cost to hold himself back. "Olivia, I want you too much."

He began to withdraw but she grabbed him. His shoulders felt like warm rock under her hands. "Don't go."

"You know what will happen." He angled his hips forward so his penis rubbed against her cleft. Her belly clenched almost painfully as she imagined that heat and power thrusting into her.

"Yes." She dragged in a shaky breath and curled her fingers into the sinews of his shoulders. "Don't go."

"Oh, hell, Olivia," he groaned, and kissed each breast with fervent tenderness. Her nipples tightened, begging for more. His eyes darkened at her uncontrolled response.

He drew one pebbled peak into his mouth and flicked his tongue across it. An electric sensation made her jerk. She'd never felt anything like this before. Her belly clenched again, harder this time.

He raised his head. "Am I hurting you?

Perhaps there would be a miracle of life in the desert of her body after all. *Dear God, let it be so.* Her reaction when he kissed her breast was more than she'd ever felt with a man. "No."

A pleased smile tilted his mouth, full and sensual with arousal, and his eyes sparked with satisfaction. He bent to suckle one breast while his fingers toyed with the crest of the other. She tangled her hands in his thick hair and gave herself up to his unfettered exploration.

Her skin felt strange. Hot and oversensitive. Vibrantly

alive. After thirty-one years, how odd to discover she didn't know her body and its responses at all.

One hand slid down between her legs. "Open for me, Olivia."

The sound of his voice worked like a spell. Her thighs fell apart to his touch.

"Ah, that's it," he sighed into the soft plain of her belly.

Kissing extravagant patterns across her body, he began to stroke her. At first the sensation wasn't as vivid as when he'd kissed her breasts. He trailed his lips up again and took her nipple in his mouth. This time he wasn't so gentle. She started when she felt the scrape of teeth.

"Oh!" She tightened her hands in the silkiness of his hair.

He bit down gently at the same time as his hand pressed between her legs. She cried out and arched up toward him. She trembled and sweat broke out all over her body.

"That's right," he murmured into her overheated skin. "Give me more."

"I'm not a horse, Erith," she said on a sudden spurt of laughter that ended in a choked gasp as he pressed his hand down again.

He lifted his head and smiled with a knowing triumph that should have piqued her but instead made her shivery and hot. She framed his face between her hands and daringly placed a fervent kiss on his mouth.

He followed her back into the pillows. This time he slanted his open mouth across hers with a man's passion. His tongue outlined the crease between her lips. His weight pressed her deep into the mattress so she could only breathe in shallow snatches.

She tried to relax into the kiss, but for the first time tonight the old trapped feeling reared up, making her close her eyes and stiffen. Bitterness sharper than a honed razor sliced through her lost, yearning surrender and reminded her of the bleak truth at the center of her life.

She would never respond to a man.

She'd thought Erith too lost in his lust to notice her re-action but he raised his head. The agonized compassion that crossed his face made her want to cry. "Olivia, I forget myself."

Where was Olivia Raines with her practiced wanton arts? This woman was too raw, too easy to hurt. She didn't want to be this woman. She wanted to be the unfeeling courtesan. The woman who ruled. This woman couldn't even rule herself.

"Why do you stay?" she asked almost angrily.

"You know why."

"Why?" Her voice shook with furious anguish.

"Because I can't leave." With sudden ruthlessness, he hitched her knees higher around his hips and plunged forward.

He was large, and she braced for the discomfort she always felt, even with her unguent. But for once her body produced its own dew. He slid into her with perfect smooth-ness, stretching her with glorious ease that made her heart stutter with astonished wonder.

At last she was Erith's mistress in fact as well as name.

He groaned from the depths of his chest and buried his head in the curve of her shoulder. Automatically her arms curled around him. His skin was slick with sweat and he shook with the restraint he imposed upon himself.

He wasted his care. Physically she felt nothing more than she ever had. She wasn't even disappointed, although she knew he would be and that made her heart ache.

His breath rasped in her ear and his damp hair tickled her cheek. He filled her completely. Her interior passage gradu-ally adjusted to his size. He was hot against her. And silent except for the rattle of his breathing. She knew he fought the urge to plunge into her over and over.

If he were another man, she'd launch into her tired rou-tine. Moaning and thrashing as if caught in the throes of endless ecstasy. But Erith would know she lied.

With Erith, she didn't want to lie.

That was the most frightening admission of all.

She wriggled deeper into the mattress and felt his hardness shift with her. His heart thundered against her chest and his trembling became more violent. Instinctively she rubbed her hands up and down his back. She liked to touch him. Tentatively she explored the straight groove of his spine and the smooth heat of his skin and the hard bands of muscle around his waist. She felt him tense the moment before he moved inside her.

Her fingers tightened to anchor herself as he withdrew then thrust his way back in. And again. And again.

He tried to be gentle. She knew that. She accepted him with a naturalness she'd never felt before. But there was no pleasure. Not even the sparks he'd stirred when he touched her breasts or stroked between her legs.

Still, she angled to allow him greater access and her breath escaped in a broken moan. The sound released something untamed in him. He began to stroke deep inside, fast and hard. She felt as if a wild wind seized her and flung her up into a thundery sky. While she remained strangely unmoved at the tempest's center.

After what felt like a long time, he stiffened and shuddered. He flung his head back, his face white and set as he finally gave himself up. The tendons of his neck stood out and his nostrils flared to force air into his pumping lungs.

She felt a powerful flow into her dead womb. His climax seemed to last forever. Finally he gave a long, unsteady groan and fell against her. He was still trembling, not with strain now, but with absolute exhaustion.

She slid her arms around his back, cradling him against her bare breasts, not minding if he crushed her. She'd never enjoyed the aftermath before. But she enjoyed it now. Having him undeniably and completely hers offered a poignant pleasure that was new. The smell of sex was familiar but the glow inside her was not.

There was something unbearably moving about him lying utterly spent in her embrace. To know she'd given him full satisfaction, drained him of every drop of life force. She curled her arms more tightly about him in an involuntarily protective gesture.

She'd never felt like this before. As though she'd freely bestowed a gift upon a man.

Long silent minutes passed.

His breathing steadied and his heart no longer pounded like a drum against her breast. She turned her head and placed a soft, lingering kiss on his sweat-dampened dark hair.

Her throat tightened with regret when eventually he withdrew from her body and rolled over to lie at her side. He hadn't spoken. What could he say? What could she say? She hadn't responded and he'd know that. But she also hoped he knew his unfettered pleasure had granted her a pleasure beyond any she'd ever found in a man's arms.

His Adam's apple jerked as he swallowed. With a gesture that conveyed appalled disgust, he flung one arm across his eyes.

"Damn it all to hell, Olivia. I'd do anything to take back what just happened."

Chapter 14

"*Damn it all to hell?*" Olivia repeated in an ominous tone.

Through his pulverizing guilt, Erith felt immediate tension stiffen the body next to his. The body he'd just filled with every ounce of his passion. The body that had remained as unresponsive as stone while he'd thundered into her.

Self-hatred was bitter as bile. What a bloody unmitigated swine he was. He should be shot. After all his self-righteous posturing, he'd taken her and hadn't waited for her to find pleasure.

He'd broken his word. To himself and to her.

"Olivia . . . " he managed before she clouted him hard in the side.

"You pig!" She scrambled for the edge of the bed.

"What in God's name are you doing?" He snatched at her arm. His ribs ached like the Devil from her assault.

"Let me go," she snarled, trying without success to fling free of his hold.

"Stop it!" He rose on his knees and caught her around the waist. He tried to ignore how her bare breasts heaved with her fury. The peaked nipples were a rich dark brown. He burned to test their sweetness again. Her skin had tasted like warm honey on his lips.

His attention wavered a moment too long.

"Bastard!" she hissed, and punched him in the belly.

The blow winded him and left him choking. He struggled to speak. "Olivia . . . " He had to stop to get his breath. "Olivia, I know I'm a blackguard, but you really don't want to kill me."

"Yes, I do," she said stubbornly.

Yes, she did.

He saw it in the tense line of her angular jaw and the feral light in her whisky-colored eyes. Those eyes fell to the most vulnerable part of his body, and he realized he couldn't allow her tantrum to continue. Not if he didn't want to sing soprano at Covent Garden before she finished.

"Oh, no, you don't," he muttered, making a more determined effort to control her. She was strong but he was stronger. He only needed seconds to grab her arms and roll her under him, using his weight to keep her writhing body down.

"Let me go, you toad." She aimed a kick at his nuts. He only just managed to evade the lethal attack. Her naked body was graceful and lithe as a cobra's. And as slippery, with a tensile power he found wildly exciting. She bucked against his subduing weight, and his arousal mounted uncontrollably.

God help him, she was right. He was a toad. She wanted to kill him and all he wanted to do was fuck her.

Erith pressed her into the bed and wrenched her hands above her head so she lay completely helpless. And open to him if he was cad enough to take advantage of her position. He desperately tried to ignore the way her bare legs slid against him as she wriggled to escape.

Difficult to believe he'd only just lost himself in a volcanic climax that had left him utterly drained. He was rampant and ready for her again.

Holding her with no intention of taking it further was torture of the vilest sort. Agony. He closed his eyes and prayed for strength. She'd end up killing him before she was finished, with frustration if not with those hard and impressively effective fists.

He couldn't blame her for her outrage. He'd promised to control himself. Then, in the end, he'd proven himself a rank liar. "I'm sorry I took you—"

"I know you are, whoreson," she spat, at last lying in gasping stillness. He didn't fool himself that she'd given up the fight, though. "Well, you won't have to be sorry again."

"You didn't like it."

"Neither did you. 'Damn it all to hell,' I believe was your eloquent response."

She sucked in a shaking breath that made her enticing breasts rise. He bit back a groan. He wanted her again. Now. If he'd imagined sex would dilute his endless craving for her, every lacerating moment of this quarrel proved him deluded.

Her voice cracked. "How dare you say that after you've just been inside me? *How dare you?*"

Understanding struck him with the force of a bullet. Understanding and regret, virulent enough to overwhelm even his surging lust.

Good God, he was the world's greatest blockhead. Heaven forgive him. He'd hurt her twice. Once with his abominably selfish swiving. And more deeply with his insensitive reaction. She'd tragically misunderstood him, and he didn't know if he could make it right.

"I didn't give you pleasure," he said dully. His pride still revolted at the humiliating truth of what he'd done.

"No, but I wanted to give *you* pleasure. I'm sorry you found the experience so repellent." Her sarcasm didn't hide her coruscating hurt.

"You're mad. You made me come like a damned torrent," he said flatly. "For God's sake, Olivia, did you sleep through what just happened?"

Her face remained pale and furious. And unconvinced. "Then why did you sound so revolted? Why did you want to take back what we'd just done?"

He sighed with impatience. "Because you're right—I'm a swine. I lost control. I've wanted you too long, too much, and too desperately. I was a brute."

The resistance seeped from her long, slender body, and he gentled his clasp on her wrists. Under his fingers, her pulse hammered with crazy speed. Her breath still emerged in uneven gasps and her eyes glittered with fierce distress.

"I wanted to give you something, and you threw the gift back in my face. As if it was worth nothing." Her voice broke and tears began to pour down her white face.

Erith cursed himself for a bloody blundering idiot. He'd done this to her. He'd made her cry. Him and his masculine stupidity and his unending, unquenchable desire. Bitter remorse rose like nausea to choke him.

She'd abhor crying in front of him. He knew without being told that she rarely if ever cried. There had been too much control in the woman he'd met at Montjoy's for tears to be an easy outlet.

Generally he ran a mile from a crying woman. But the sight of Olivia overcome by misery hurt his soul in a way he didn't understand. All he knew was that her pain was his pain. He felt upset and terrified and guilty and helpless and confused. He'd happily slice off his right arm if only she'd smile again.

Waiting with sour certainty for a protest, he slid his arms around her. She remained silent apart from her harsh sobbing. He drew her into his body and pressed her wet face to his chest as gently as he'd picked up his children when they were babies. Before his life crashed into ruin and he couldn't bear tenderness any longer.

"It's all right, Olivia," he whispered. The same meaningless words of comfort he'd offered the infant Roma and William. "It's all right."

"It's not all right," she said in a thick voice, making a half-hearted attempt to break free.

Still holding her, he drew himself up until his back met the bed head. Ignoring her resistance, he tugged her onto his lap and wrapped his arms around her. He curved one hand across her bare back to support her and buried his other in her mane of hair. Murmuring reassurance, he tightened his grip.

"I'm acting like a fool," she choked out, her voice muffled against him.

"Everyone's a fool, Olivia," he said gently. "Sometime or other."

Her hands formed trembling fists against his chest. "I never cry."

"I can see that."

She gave a watery laugh then followed it with more tears. He was painfully aware of her nakedness. With every sob, her breasts grazed his chest. He spread his hands over her bare skin. Her long legs splayed across his. It would be so easy to tip her down and take her again.

He already knew she wouldn't say no.

And it would break his heart to thrust into that beautiful, passive body. Break his heart even as his animal self growled with ultimate pleasure.

He was indeed a swine.

He rested his chin on her disheveled mass of tawny hair. She fitted perfectly against him. She had fit perfectly lying under him too. Most women had trouble with his size but she'd taken him as if born for him. And she'd responded, at least before he'd pushed her onto her back. He couldn't be mistaken that for a fleeting moment, she'd been as lost to blind pleasure as he was.

Erith stared into the shadowy room and felt a tiny bud of

optimism shoot from his tumultuous regret. With patience and care he could make her respond again. He could feed that spark and turn it into a conflagration that would transform her world.

At first her lack of response had been a challenge. Now, awakening her sensual self had become an all-consuming quest. She'd lost so much in her life, and tragically, most of the damage was irreparable. But this was something he could restore to her. And perhaps in the process find his own salvation.

The fire in the grate had burned down from its welcoming blaze, and the guttering candles only provided dim light. He should get up and replenish the hearth. But he couldn't bear to relinquish his hold on her. She'd fallen quiet in his arms. No more difficult, heartbreaking tears. He sensed a weary peace in her now that the storm of weeping had passed.

And the problem that had nagged him since he'd taken her became paramount. He was grimly aware that what he said now would inevitably shatter this uneasy harmony between them.

"Olivia, I didn't withdraw."

He waited for a return of her anger. But her voice emerged toneless and scratchy with tears. "It's not important."

Puzzled, he angled his head to see her expression. Surely she knew what he meant. "I didn't use a sheath. You didn't use your unguent. Basically, I fucked you from here to Sunday. The consequences could be disastrous."

Except his heart didn't feel it was a disaster.

Good God, was he going mad? What did a man of nearly forty want with a pregnant mistress? He'd been a less than exemplary father to the children he had.

Her voice rang with bitter certainty. "Don't worry. I won't have a baby."

"You don't know that."

She frowned and ineffectually tried to pull away. "Yes, I do." Her voice firmed, became more familiar. But the tearstains on her cheeks belied her defiance. "I won't present you with a bastard in nine months. You can leave without a care."

Sadly, he already knew that would be far from the truth, whether she was pregnant or not.

Under her prickly response, he read a deep distress. A distress separate from any unhappiness he'd caused her tonight. A distress too deep for tears. "How can you be so sure?"

"I just am."

With a shock he realized something that should have been clear much earlier. He could only blame his slowness on the spin this woman had put him in. "Is Leo your only child?"

"No, I've got offspring littered from John O'Groats to Land's End," she said sarcastically. She tried again to move but he trapped her in an uncompromising grip.

"Tell me about Leo."

"Damn you, Erith!" Her eyes flared with temper.

"Tell me."

Her mouth settled in a line of displeasure and her jaw took on a square set. Odd how each feature was almost masculine yet the whole combined into something utterly womanly and beguiling.

She spoke quickly and with a grim edge that indicated she only answered under extreme sufferance. "I'm not built for childbearing."

With sharp force, she tugged away and slid off the bed. This time he made no attempt to stop her. Instead his mind processed the implications of that short, stark statement. She stalked across to the armoire, her hair tumbling down her back in untidy glory. She moved like a proud young horse. All long legs and straight back and easy elegant motion.

"There have been no more pregnancies?"

"You give me no peace!" With an angry flourish, she flung the armoire open. She ripped out the scarlet silk robe, which to his regret she flung around herself. With furious emphasis, she tied the belt at her narrow waist. She snatched out another robe and threw it in his direction. It hit the side of the bed and slithered to the floor.

His lips curved in a derisive smile as he pushed himself farther up against the heaped pillows. "Covering me up won't stop the questions."

She glared at him. Then her gaze flickered and fixed on his chest. Her inspection continued down to where his cock showed unmistakable signs of interest. She straightened abruptly as if awakening from a dream. "Stop flaunting yourself. You'll frighten the housemaids."

"Do you find my body attractive?" he asked in genuine astonishment. And with genuine interest.

"Lord, but you're a vain peacock, Erith." Surprisingly, her clear olive skin darkened with a blush, and for an instant she looked vulnerable and young. This was the Olivia who tugged at his heart. The woman who'd had all innocence and joy stolen from her yet summoned the courage to triumph.

He laughed softly. "Which means yes."

She cast him a dismissive glance, although her full mouth trembled on the brink of a smile. "You have no need to cadge for compliments."

"For your compliments, I do, Olivia." He bent down to snag the black silk robe and shrug it over his shoulders. He left it loose. He rather liked the idea of his bare skin tormenting her. After all, her bare skin tormented him.

"Then yes, on a visual level you appeal to me." She spoke as precisely as an apothecary measuring some dusty drug into a jar.

Erith gave a short bark of laughter. "Thank you." He took a risk that shouldn't have been a risk and extended his hand to her.

She glanced at his hand then into his face. Uncertainty danced in her topaz eyes. She made a fine show of overcoming the harrowing emotion that had reduced her to tears. But he knew that beneath her dry humor she was brittle as overheated glass.

Aching compassion rang in his voice as he said softly, "Come and sit with me."

As if unsure whether to stay or run, she accepted his hand and perched gingerly beside him. He wanted her more than he'd wanted any woman. But what made him tremble like a young boy with his first love was what he felt when he was with her.

He felt hope.

Tenderly he tucked her under his arm and drew her close into his body. To his surprised satisfaction, she didn't demur. She was warm curled up in his arms and smelled of sex and sleepy woman. The delicious scent seeped into his bones.

For a long time they maintained a strangely comfortable silence. The rain was a steady downpour, and the sound provided a pleasant backdrop to his sweet languor. His body was heavy with postcoital satisfaction. Whatever pangs his conscience suffered, his body had luxuriated in that explosive release.

"You looked ready to kill me when you thought I threatened your chick," he said eventually. She sprawled against him but he knew she wasn't asleep.

"Who's taller than I am and not far off going to Oxford."

He couldn't stem a twinge of jealousy. There was such love in her voice. He knew she smiled as she spoke. That lovely soft smile he'd only seen once or twice, and never for him. Damn it.

"I felt like that when I saw Roma and William for the first time after so many years. Roma's eighteen and marrying in June. William's nineteen and up at Oxford."

Their sons would soon move in the same milieu. Might even become friends. The idea was disturbing. As though his two worlds weren't as separate as he imagined. As though the barrier he'd always believed impassable was in fact as fragile as the ruby Venetian glass vase on the mahogany chest.

"Tell me what happened when you had Leo."

He felt rather than heard her sigh. "You won't leave this alone, will you?"

A faint smile stretched his lips. "No."

"I was too young and he was too big and I almost died." She spoke quickly, as though she could hardly bear to say the words. "I've never conceived since. Even if I did, I doubt I'd carry a child to term. If Lord Farnsworth hadn't paid for the best doctors, nothing would have saved me. I shouldn't have lived. Leo shouldn't have lived."

Her pain and bravery gashed his heart. "Oh, Olivia," he murmured, and held her closer.

"It's a blessing for a courtesan to be barren."

"No, it's not."

"No, it's not." She sounded tragically sad. When she looked up at him, anguish swam in her tawny eyes. "It's a convenience. But it's not a blessing."

He tried to imagine what her life had been like when she had Leo. So young, and with a baby to care for. "What happened then?"

"Lord Farnsworth had no further use for a child who'd turned into a mother." A world of weary rancor soured her tone.

"You can't have regretted that."

"I regretted losing the only home I had. I regretted leaving Perry and having to give up my child."

His hold tightened on her while the vain urge to kill her first keeper ran like acid through his veins. Too late, damn it. "Farnsworth didn't cast you out on the streets?"

"No, he sold me to one of his friends." Her voice was flat, almost unemotional.

How the hell had she borne it? How had she emerged as the wonderful woman he knew? A young girl, sold as a commodity by a gambling-crazed brother to a man whose name was a byword for vice. Then discarded like a worn-out shoe when she was no longer of interest to her vicious keeper.

Erith had trouble speaking past the horror that jammed his throat. If there was any justice, that bastard Farnsworth would roast in the hottest corner of hell for eternity. "Dear heaven, Olivia, that's barbarous."

"I survived." Her voice was flat.

He began to get an inkling of where her bone-deep pride originated. Pride was all she'd had to sustain her through the long nightmare.

"Farnsworth didn't want Leo?"

She gave a scornful laugh that held no genuine amusement. "Thank God, he didn't. Farnsworth abused his children as well as his lovers. He was crueler to Perry than he ever was to me. He thought torture would turn Perry into a *man*. I gave Leo to my cousin Mary. She and Charles had no family, and he took up a new living at the other end of the country. Nobody needed to know the baby wasn't theirs."

"Including Leo."

She lurched back on her knees, her eyes huge in her pale face. At that moment he had no difficulty picturing her as a vulnerable child forced to surrender her innocence to a foul old man. The repellent idea made his gorge rise.

"He can never know. Mary and Charles have loved him and educated him and brought him up to be a son I'm so proud of. Even if I'll never be a mother he can be proud of."

He spoke with utter sincerity. "You underestimate him. And yourself. You're a woman anyone would be privileged to claim."

Even a lost, hardened miscreant like the Earl of Erith.

Chapter 15

O livia flinched as if he'd struck her. "Stop it," she said sharply.

Erith frowned, not understanding. "Stop what?"

"This." Her left hand performed a chopping gesture as if cutting the intimacy that slowly, surely curled around them like a spider's silk around a trapped fly. "This . . . this attempt to understand. This attempt to get close."

He sighed and leaned back against the bed head. Under the temper, she was frightened. After the horrors she'd been through, fear must be a constant companion.

"I can't help it," he said with complete honesty. She fascinated him. Every moment he spent with her brought him more deeply under her spell. He'd never known a woman like her.

Where would his bewitchment lead? To disaster or joy? Already the idea of saying good-bye in July made his gut clench in anguished denial.

"Good God, Erith, I thought I was taking on the big, bad

terror of Vienna." She surged to her feet and glared down at him. "What about the infamous womanizer? The man who tupped half a dozen trollops before his breakfast eggs every morning?"

Her disgust was so vehement that he burst out laughing. "I hope for the sake of their enjoyment that it was a late breakfast!"

No glimmer of amusement lightened her expression. Her brows lowered. She looked like a furious goddess. Beautiful beyond imagination. He clenched his hands at his sides to stop himself reaching for her.

Devil take it, he needed to get a grip on reality before his endless hunger for this woman drew him into doing something utterly reckless.

Something that put his family forever beyond his reach.

"I'm not trying to be funny, Erith."

His humor evaporated in an instant. "I know you're not. You're not trying to insult me either, even if that's the end result. I know what the bloody gossips say. Can't you make up your own mind?"

She ignored his last question. "I asked Perry about you before I accepted your suit."

"And of course Lord Peregrine is an expert on my life and habits," he said tersely.

"He told me what he'd heard."

"A lot of damned poppycock."

"Do you deny you've killed men in duels?"

Old shame clenched his gut. Those men shouldn't have died. "Good God, that was nearly twenty years ago. When I didn't care if I lived into tomorrow. And I didn't care if anyone else did either."

It was the first time he'd admitted that, although he'd known it was true even as he accepted the challenges. Each matter of honor had concerned a woman. He remembered that much even if he couldn't remember the actual women.

The bristling tension drained from her willowy form. "Oh."

"Yes, oh." He paused. "Don't you want to know why I felt like that?"

"No." She took a step back as if he physically threatened her, although he hadn't moved. She bumped into the mahogany chest of drawers behind her.

"No?"

"You're not the only one with eyes in your head, Erith." She cast him an irritated glance under the thick fringe of dark gold lashes. But her voice, when she spoke, was grave. "You loved your wife, and her death left you devastated."

The stark words fell between them like pebbles thrown over a cliff. Each sharp ping as they landed made him wince.

"How did you know?" he asked quietly after the silence had stretched into tension.

"I guessed. And when I did, so much made sense. The man I'd heard about didn't match the man I started to know. You have a reputation as cold and heartless. Yet . . . " She looked toward the curtained window as if seeking inspiration. Then she turned back to him, her lovely face even more somber. "Yet you've been anything but heartless with me."

"My wife was the light of my life." He was surprised how easily the words emerged.

He never spoke of Joanna. To anyone. It was as much a rule as not cheating at cards and keeping his linen clean. She lived on in a candlelit shrine in his heart, where she stayed untouched and beloved. Pure and unsullied by his sins.

More bizarre that he should speak of Joanna to a fallen woman like Olivia Raines. And that he knew she'd understand where nobody else would. Although he didn't fool himself about what his wife would have thought of his current mistress. Joanna would have despised everything about Olivia.

"You still love her." The words weren't a question.

"Yes."

"I admire that." She turned and poured two glasses of

wine from the decanter on the sideboard. "She must have been a remarkable woman. You were lucky."

"Yes, I was."

What a revelation. He'd been blessed with a great love and all he'd done since was run away from the fact that God had granted that gift, even if for too short a time.

He accepted the crystal glass filled with wine the same color as the robe Olivia wore. She settled herself cross-legged at the end of the bed. Too far away to touch, damn it.

Her effortless grace, the way she crossed her legs, modestly folding the satiny material across the enticing paleness of her thighs, reminded him of women of the seraglio. She was endlessly alluring. Endlessly erotic. Endlessly exotic. Wherever she'd been born.

She took a sip of her wine, never shifting her clear scrutiny from his face. "So why did you abandon your children?"

He choked on his wine. "Confound it, Olivia!"

He caught his breath and stared at her in shock. For a moment she'd lulled him into a sentimental dream. He should have known she wouldn't let him linger there.

He found his voice. "Bloody Montjoy has a busy tongue, hasn't he?"

"Perry told me what he knew."

"What he *thought* he knew."

"So he was wrong?"

Damn it, he wanted to lie. Damn it, he wanted to tell her to take her curiosity and her presumptuous self and remove both from his presence until she was prepared to be the mistress he'd bartered for in Montjoy's salon.

Except he didn't want that cool, self-possessed beauty, in spite of her spectacular looks and vulpine cleverness. He wanted the disheveled woman who stared him down over a glass of wine and asked him questions he didn't want to answer.

Hell, he wanted her and as more than a temporary bedmate. He had no idea what he could do about it.

Nothing. That was reality.

So against his will, against his inclination, but at the bidding of his cold, empty heart, he answered her. "I couldn't bear to stay after Joanna died. I couldn't bear the sight of my own children because every time I looked at them, I saw my wife. Even as a baby, Roma looked heartbreakingly like her mother. Then I remembered my wife was dead."

He recollected few concrete details of those first months after Joanna's accident. It was a time he never revisited. Which meant it haunted him like an angry ghost.

Olivia leaned forward and placed one slender hand on his knee, bared by the gap in his robe. He didn't understand it, but the touch made him feel more whole than he'd felt since that tragic, horrific day sixteen years ago when his world had disintegrated.

"I'm sorry, Erith."

Even her voice soothed his pain. How did she do that? And because she did that, how could he live without the balm of her presence? He felt himself sinking deeper and deeper toward inevitable disaster.

Very slowly, as though the gesture had a significance into a future he couldn't imagine, he lifted his free hand and put it over hers. He felt her momentary tension before she relaxed. As if she accepted his touch. As if more existed between them than just a contract between keeper and courtesan.

He curled his fingers around her hand in a light hold and spoke. Against his expectations, the words emerged without difficulty. "It wasn't Roma and William's fault that I felt like I'd died with Joanna. The damnable thing is, it wasn't anyone's fault except my own, unless I blame Joanna's stubbornness."

"What happened?"

He took a fortifying sip of wine, feeling the rich liquid slide down his throat. His hold on Olivia's hand firmed. Her touch was his only lifeline to the present.

* * *

Olivia studied Lord Erith as he struggled to summon words to describe his wife's death. How strange to think that only a few days ago he'd seemed superhuman, almost from a different species compared to other men she'd known. A cold automaton with intelligence that cut and wounded.

Attractive, certainly. A challenge. A bait to her curiosity. A fillip to her reputation for eternal irresistibility. Nothing more.

The man before her was tired and sad and had known too much loss and pain. Most of the time, his vigor and his brilliant mind meant his age was hard to guess. Now he looked older than he really was.

She'd fought stalwartly against admitting that he touched her heart. It was a fight she'd finally lost in a rain-sodden grove in Hyde Park. Even if a heart was a luxury no courtesan could afford.

His voice was different, flat, grim. "We quarreled. She wanted to go riding just after she told me she carried our third child. Joanna was a punishing rider. I've never seen a woman like her on horseback. If you met her in a drawing room, you'd think her the perfect lady. Put her in the saddle and she was an Amazon. But she'd had two hard deliveries. I worried about her health and tried to coddle her."

Self-loathing and savage sorrow vibrated in his voice. The heart she refused to acknowledge ached for him. She should have guessed something like this from the first. His guilt about his wife was too close to the surface for him not to blame himself. Inwardly Olivia cringed with shame to remember Perry's cavalier recounting of Lady Erith's death and how she'd accepted the bald facts so easily, so thoughtlessly.

But of course, she'd been a different woman then.

She made herself speak calmly. "Of course she rebelled and took the horse out."

"She marched off in a fury and had her favorite mare saddled and . . . " The hand that held hers tightened. Not to the point of pain but with a firmness she felt to her bones.

She saw him swallow. The gray eyes were bleaker than the North Sea on an overcast winter's day. "Stupidly, I gave her half an hour's start so she could collect her temper. Then I set out after her. She had a customary path through the park, so I knew where she'd be." He paused again, and his baritone voice was low and unsteady when he went on. "Or I thought I knew."

"Erith . . . " she whispered. His pain reached out and grabbed her by the throat so she couldn't breathe. She twined her fingers around his in silent empathy.

He leaned across and placed his wine on the table beside the bed. His hand trembled so badly that liquid sloshed over the edge of the glass. She wanted to cry as she witnessed this strong man shaking with grief and remorse.

How he must have adored his wife.

She'd seen so much fault and folly. She'd never believed love like this existed. The purity of emotion in his strained face cut right to her soul.

And hurt more deeply than anything since her brother's betrayal so many years ago.

Nobody would love her like that. Ever. The glow in Lord Erith's eyes—eyes she'd once thought cold and emotionless—made her want to rage with envy for a dead woman. Olivia's essential, inevitable and eternal isolation stabbed her anew.

"I rode out to fetch her. I came to a bend in the bridle path through the woods and . . . " He snatched a shuddering breath. "The mare must have shied at something. We never found out exactly what happened. The horse was skittish. That's how Joanna liked her mounts, fresh enough to be exciting."

That's how Joanna liked her husband too, Olivia thought. He must have been breathtaking when he was young and madly in love. The idea shot another arc of pain through her.

Hard to imagine him innocent. Not so hard to imagine

him in love—he still worshipped his wife, for all his dallying with the fallen sisterhood. She read that now as an attempt to fill a life left essentially meaningless after the collapse of its central pillar.

His voice seemed to scrape out of his throat. The gray eyes were opaque as a silver mirror as he relived that afternoon so long ago. "I heard the horse screaming. The poor brute had broken its leg and was in agony."

He stopped. His hand flexed in hers, and she knew that whatever horrific visions paraded before his inner eye, he knew exactly where he was and who he was with. He hadn't left her, however powerful the harrowing memories that held him in thrall.

The knowledge meant more to her than it should. Than a woman like her could allow it to mean. "And Joanna?"

He gave an infinitesimal shudder and his eyes were bleaker than ever when they met hers. "I think she was killed instantly when the horse fell on her. I can't be sure. Her face was peaceful, so I've always prayed she didn't suffer before she . . . she died. I can't bear the thought of her calling for me, that I failed her. Just as I can't bear to remember that our last words were spoken in anger."

"She knew she was beloved." At a profound level, Olivia recognized that if this man committed himself, you could trust that commitment to the end of the world.

"Yes," he said dully. "I worshipped the ground she walked on and she knew it."

"Then she was a lucky woman, and the last thing she'd want is for you to destroy yourself with remorse."

His gaze sharpened and the frightening blankness left his expression. He sounded like he woke from a long nightmare. "I've never told anyone about Joanna."

She wondered at the people close to him, that nobody had forced this story out of him before, like lancing an infected wound. Then she realized a proud man like Erith would permit very few people close, probably no one.

Looking down, she contemplated their joined hands, his skin so tanned in comparison to the pale olive of hers. Desperately she sought for words to give him solace, strength.

"It's sad to keep our loved ones trapped in our hearts and never speak of them. We kill them again with our silence."

"For years, how she died has haunted me. I should have been on my knees with gratitude that I knew her at all. She was beautiful and spirited and full of life. Yet I've locked her away in the dark like a prisoner."

"Oh, my dear." The endearment slipped out before she could catch it. Just as she couldn't stop herself from surging forward and taking him in her arms.

She'd only comforted two men in her life. Not men, boys. Perry, years ago when his father tormented him to the edge of madness. Leo as a child.

So why did it feel so natural to draw Lord Erith's head down to her shoulder, to press him against her breast, to try and infuse warmth into his cold, cold sorrow?

She expected him to resist. But he came shaking into her embrace.

Silence reigned. She didn't speak, even when she felt the dampness of his tears against the skin of her neck.

Chapter 16

*E*rith reined his horse in near a stand of oaks in Hyde Park and waited for Roma to catch up. She was several hundred yards back and bouncing about like an ungainly sack of potatoes on her long-suffering mount. Beside her, a groom jogged along with a stoic expression that indicated he'd seen it all before.

His daughter certainly hadn't inherited either of her parents' facility in the saddle. Odd he'd never known that about her. But then she was basically a stranger. The magnitude of the task he'd set himself before he left Vienna struck him yet again.

This visit to London proved a salutary lesson for his conceit. He'd imagined his children would fall upon him in tearful gratitude the moment he showed a spark of interest. He'd imagined any mistress he selected would be the easy conquest women always were.

Laughable how divided his imaginings proved from hard reality.

He'd left Olivia toward dawn. He hadn't made love to her again. Even though he'd been hard and ready, he couldn't bear another unfulfilling encounter.

Or unfulfilling on any level but the basest.

At sunrise he'd walked out, purged of sixteen years of poison. He had so much to thank Olivia for. When they first met, he'd thought she was extraordinary. Little had he known how extraordinary she truly was. Yes, he still missed Joanna. He'd always miss her and mourn the tragic waste of her death. He'd always regret that their last words had been spoken in temper and that he'd failed to save her life.

But over time, that harrowing afternoon had become the sum total of his memory of his wife. Since leaving the house in York Street this morning, a flood of recollections had washed away much of the old rancor.

He remembered the golden weeks of courtship, the sweetness of the first time they made love, their joy at the birth of the children. Afternoons of laughter. Evenings of dancing. Nights of almost innocent pleasure.

He recalled other things too that until now he'd forgotten or had felt too racked with guilt to dwell on. That Joanna had been obstinate and a little too fond of her own way. That at times he'd wished she would catch onto a joke more quickly or read a situation's undercurrents.

Ever since that moment of ineffable sweetness when Olivia took him in her arms, Erith had felt Joanna's dear presence. Her ghost hadn't been vengeful or accusing. Instead, he'd felt bathed in love and forgiveness.

His lighter heart had prompted him to ask Roma, who usually ate breakfast with him in sullen silence, to come riding. She hadn't responded with great enthusiasm. But then she never responded to anything he said with great enthusiasm. She'd greeted him with surly dislike when he arrived from Vienna, and her attitude hadn't warmed since. He'd allowed her to get away with her open resentment because he felt guilty.

He wasn't letting her go unchallenged any longer.

He'd returned to London on a quest to reconcile with his family. A quest he now intended to pursue with his full powers.

He'd been wrong to blame himself all these years for Joanna's death. It had just been a tragic, horrible accident.

But his appalling treatment of his children was his fault. Dear God, perhaps even an unforgivable fault. It was time he remedied his sins. It was time he and his children came to an understanding. Affection was perhaps too much to ask, although he'd sell his soul to establish even an ounce of the respect and love he'd witnessed between Olivia and her son yesterday.

Unfortunately, he suspected things with his daughter would worsen before they improved. *If* they improved. An uneasy, lowering truce had persisted thus far. Would it disintegrate into open warfare before he left for Vienna?

Roma was puffing when she reached him. She was plumper than Joanna had ever been. From what he saw, her activities mainly involved lying on a sofa in her room devouring the latest novels and scoffing bonbons. It was a puzzle how she'd exerted herself to catch a nonpareil like Thomas Renton. Although occasionally Erith had chanced upon her laughing with a friend and glimpsed a different side to her. And she seemed popular enough when he'd escorted her to the endless balls that formed her nightly entertainments.

"Do you remember your mother, Roma?" he asked as she brought her horse alongside his.

He'd deliberately selected a smaller mount than Bey for himself. Even so, he still towered above her. The groom hovered outside earshot but kept a watchful eye on Roma. It suddenly struck Erith that perhaps his daughter had trouble staying in the saddle and the fellow had rescued her before.

The thought should have roused wrenching memories of Joanna's accident. But Roma was such a completely different rider, and one who rarely extended herself beyond a trot, that he found it hard to worry. His pride winced to think a child of his so inept a horsewoman.

She sent him a sulky glare, familiar from weeks of sharing Erith House in fulminating hostility. "Aunt Celia has told me about her. I was only two when she died." She spoke as if she expected him not to know.

"Of course I remember how old you were," he said mildly. "And William was three. If you like, I could tell you about her."

He caught a flash of vulnerability in the blue eyes with their thick dark lashes. Eyes that broke his heart every time he looked into them because they were so like Joanna's. Then the sullen recalcitrance returned, making him wonder if he'd mistaken that brief flare of pain.

"You didn't care about my mother. You don't care about us. You're here for my wedding just for the public show. Then you'll go back to Vienna and your mistresses and your drinking and your gambling and forget all about your family again."

The rancorous tirade startled him. It revealed more spirit than he'd ever seen in her. She urged her horse forward, but she was such an execrable rider that he had no trouble keeping up.

"I loved your mother, Roma. Your mother loved me."

"Well, I'm sorry for her then," the girl said dully. "You're not worth loving."

Joanna hadn't thought so. For Joanna's sake, he had to persist with her daughter. It might be too little too late—it was—but he had to form some relationship with this girl he loved but didn't know at all.

And he'd have to fight the same battle all over again with his son. William dealt with his father's long ago desertion by pretending his father didn't exist. To date, the boy had only come up from Oxford once to see him, and that was clearly under sufferance.

With every day that passed, Erith witnessed what damage

his selfishness had wrought. A heavy weight of discouragement settled in his gut as he recognized that his sins were almost certainly irredeemable.

But God help him, he had to try to fix what he'd done.

"I wish you would go away again," Roma said stubbornly. "I wish you had never come back."

The words might be childish but they stung all the same. "You and William are the most precious things in my life."

Her sarcastic laugh rang of his own sardonic humor. "That's why you left us with Aunt Celia when we were little and never came near us."

This girl broke his heart, but he couldn't pretend not to love her. He'd die for her. Unfortunately, dying for her would be easy. Making up for his grave wrongs against her was much harder.

"I beg your forgiveness," he said in a low voice.

She frowned. "I don't understand."

He pulled his horse to a stop. "Do you want to get down and walk?"

"No, I want to go home." Her sulkiness didn't emerge as naturally as usual.

"Do you really?"

She cast him a look of intense loathing under the shadow of her hat. "If I do, will you let me?"

She asked the question as if it held some significance. He couldn't imagine why that should be, but he answered her seriously. "Yes, of course. I'm not an ogre, Roma."

"No, you're just a man who never gives a thought to anyone's convenience but his own."

"That's not true." He should be angry. But his principal reaction was astonishment. Since he'd returned to London, Roma had rarely brought herself to address him, unless she whined about a bonnet she wanted or a ball that clashed with another engagement.

"Yes, it is. Have you ever once asked William or me what we want? Have you ever given me a choice about anything?"

"You were a baby, sweetheart."

The involuntary endearment was a mistake. She visibly bristled. "I'm eighteen now."

"Do you want to go home?"

She paused. He wondered if she was obstinate enough to insist on her way. Eventually she shook her head. "No." Then with a hint of bitterness, "It's taken me all my life to get this much attention from you. It seems a pity to cut it short."

Oh, yes, she definitely had more backbone than he'd given her credit for. She no longer looked like the girl who slunk around Erith House trying to avoid his notice.

He dismounted and helped her down. Roma was smaller and rounder than Joanna but looked enough like her mother for the resemblance to cut him to the quick every time he looked at her. Now that she was more animated, the resemblance was stronger than ever. He realized with a shock that his daughter was a beauty. A young woman with her own wishes and tastes and ambitions. Of which he knew nothing.

What a bloody criminal mess he'd made of everything.

In silence, they walked, leading the horses. It was a pleasant morning and sunlight dappled the fresh spring growth. In spite of lack of sleep, Erith was keyed up after the astonishing emotional turmoil of the last twenty-four hours. Ending in this fraught confrontation with his daughter.

"Can I tell you why I left you and William with my sister?" he eventually asked. Roma didn't vibrate with belligerence anymore, but he wasn't sure how long the current détente would last. How ironic. He was renowned for his skills as a diplomat but had no idea how to placate one angry, hurt young girl. "It wasn't because I didn't love you."

"Why are you being so nice?" Roma's voice was laden with suspicion.

He smiled. Her wariness inevitably reminded him of Olivia. "Because I'm your father and I want you to feel that you're my beloved daughter."

"It's too late."

The quiet words made his heart slam against his chest in grief. Dear God, if she was right, his life had come to ashes.

How appalling that she believed that. He knew his behavior had given her the impression he didn't care. When the tragic truth was that he'd cared too much.

"Is it?"

She cast him another glare as she removed her hat. Her brown hair was untidy and flat, and strands had come loose to frame cheeks that still hadn't lost the roundness of childhood. "You've never wanted to talk to me before."

"I hoped you'd let me at least explain."

"Why bother? You'll just go away again. Anyway, I'm about to be married. I have my own life."

"Aren't you at least a little curious about your father?"

"I used to be. But I'm a woman now. I have other things to worry about. You aren't important to me."

That was so obviously a lie, he suspected they both recognized it as such. Color rose in her clear white skin.

"Well, pray grant me a woman's patience and hear what I say."

He waited for her to snipe about patience being something he'd demanded for too long. But she studied him with her heartbreaking blue eyes and nodded. "As you wish." Then couldn't resist adding, "Although I can't see what good it will do."

He gave a grunt of sour amusement. "Confession is good for the soul. Perhaps it will help me even if it doesn't help you."

She didn't smile but he knew she listened as they strolled along the shady path. The muffled clop of the horses' hooves on the leaf litter, the soft jangle of bits, and the distant birdsong calmed the storm in his blood.

"You're very like your mother, you know," he said softly. "She had your eyes and your hair and sometimes I catch an expression on your face that's Joanna come to life."

"I know. Aunt Celia is always telling me. Anyway, I've seen the marriage portrait."

Of course she had. He'd forgotten sending the large Raeburn across to his sister's home before he left for his first diplomatic posting. Obscurely, through the blind haze of grief, he'd imagined his children would feel some connection to the absent parents in the picture.

In retrospect, his painted likeness seemed a vilely poor substitute for a real father's presence. Almost cruel, in fact.

He wondered why he'd never seen this so clearly. He wasn't a stupid man. But learning about Olivia's past yesterday had made him think about so many things differently, including how he'd treated his children.

He'd been a bad father. He'd let himself down. He'd let Joanna down. Worst of all, he'd let William and Roma down. He wondered again if anything he did could make amends when the sin was so heinous. But dear Lord, he had to try.

"From the first moment I saw your mother at Almack's, she owned my heart. She was younger than you are now. Seventeen. And I was only eighteen. But the match pleased our families and there was no barrier of rank or fortune. We were young, we were frighteningly innocent, and we were madly in love. Nobody saw any reason why we shouldn't marry as soon as decorum allowed." He and Joanna had been so hungry for each other in that first rapturous flight of love.

Roma eyed him with cautious curiosity. "I can't imagine you ever being the same age as I am."

He laughed shortly. "Believe me, I was."

She sounded doubtful, which amused him, in spite of the moment's seriousness. He remembered feeling the same about his elders. He'd even said as much to his father when he pushed for a quick marriage to the woman he already knew was the love of his life. He might have been young, but he'd known his heart. Better than he'd known it any time since.

"We lived together for almost four years and had two children we both adored."

Roma must have jerked on the reins because her horse snorted in protest and tossed its head. He waited for her to argue his choice of words but she didn't speak. He had her complete attention. But what she felt, he couldn't have said. It struck him again that his daughter was a stranger.

"When your mother died, I wanted to die with her. In many ways, I did die with her. Your aunt offered to look after you and William. Everyone told me it was the best thing."

"And you wanted to run away."

"Yes, I wanted to run away." How could he explain to a girl of her age what that grief had been like? How crippling. How selfish. How all-encompassing. He couldn't bear to be in the same room as his children because they were alive and his beloved was dead. He realized he owed Roma the full shameful truth. "I was a coward."

She studied him with a steady gaze that he couldn't entirely read. There was certainly condemnation in her eyes. Which God help him, he'd earned. There was also something that could be the birth of understanding. "You were only twenty-two. That's just four years older than I am now."

"I was young. That doesn't excuse the wrong I did."

"No, but it makes everything a little easier to comprehend."

She was far from offering him forgiveness. His sins of weakness and neglect against her were so great, he wondered if he deserved forgiveness.

He'd been wrong to abandon his children. A broken-hearted boy might evade his responsibilities. To be fair to Celia, he'd been in such a fit of sorrow after Joanna's death, he hadn't been capable of caring for his son and daughter. But he flinched to think that so many years had passed and he'd never returned to shoulder his family duties.

That was where his real crime lay.

Overwhelming guilt left a rusty taste in his mouth. He'd give his soul for a chance to change the past, to fix his multitude of mistakes, but it was too late. All he could do was blindly stumble forward in hope that the future might allow him some bond with his children.

"I'm glad we had this talk," she said softly as they came out into the sunlight.

Her small, almost grudging admission made him feel like a king. Those few words signified a massive concession. Choking gratitude ambushed him and he had to struggle for words. "So am I."

He couldn't pretend he'd won the battle for Roma's love and respect. That would take time and perception and every ounce of love he could find. But perhaps this morning he'd made a small step toward what he wanted. With patience and, heaven granting, goodwill on both sides, perhaps that small step would be followed by another and another.

Olivia, you've taught me so much.

They entered a busier section of the park. The time for confidences had passed. He turned to his daughter. Odd what a difference an hour could make. "Let me help you into the saddle. It's getting late. Aunt Celia will think we're lost."

Surprisingly, she giggled. He realized with a pang that it was the first time she'd shared a moment of genuine amusement with him. "She'll think I've fallen off and you've had to chase my horse all over the park. It's happened before."

"I'll give you riding lessons if you like."

The lovely openness left her expression and familiar wariness returned. "I'm no good with horses. I never have been. There's no point trying to change me."

"I wasn't—" he began impatiently, then realized that if this was a test, he was about to fail. "The decision is yours, Roma. I ride every morning. If you'd like to come, you're welcome."

Her eyes filled with amazement that lasted even while he lifted her into the saddle. It was torture not telling her to straighten her back and relax her stiff arms but somehow he managed it.

Calling an order to the groom who had fallen into a doze on his bay pony, Erith strode across to his horse and mounted. He wheeled his horse around and found his attention riveted on a woman riding a spirited chestnut thoroughbred.

Olivia.

She was well across the clearing but he recognized her immediately. Even though her back was to him. Even though she wore the black riding habit that was any serious horse-woman's uniform. Even though she'd bundled her distinctive hair under a stylish and rather mannish hat.

Her horse curvetted restlessly but she quieted it with a casual movement of one graceful hand. Joanna had been a magnificent rider. But Olivia surpassed her the way the sun outshone a candle. She and the horse looked like one being. Her seat was perfect, her posture graceful, her supreme confidence clear. And that ebony habit followed every sinuous line of her body so closely that he guessed she'd been sewn into it. It was a courtesan's trick he'd seen before, but never to such glorious advantage.

The horse was an eye-catching beast. Fresh, all long sensitive lines and delicate legs and curving neck. But the woman atop his back was more striking still.

Erith's breath stopped in his throat at the superb sight.

Beside him, Roma had trouble getting her placid mount under control. He was vaguely aware of his daughter's fumblings, even as his gaze remained glued to Olivia.

His mistress chatted to two young bucks. One looked familiar. Erith supposed he must have been at Lord Peregrine's. The other was a stranger. Handsome, blond like a Norse god, young, obviously rich, riding a roan almost as fine as Olivia's chestnut.

Was she using her morning ride to select a new lover from among the young men who frequented the park at this hour? The thought ate at him like acid and his hands clenched, so his mount danced under the unexpected tug at the bit.

He tried to stifle his wild and immediate jealousy. Unreasoning, unacceptable, unprecedented jealousy.

What was wrong with him? He'd recognized the reality of his liaison with Olivia from the first. She was a courtesan. This was her livelihood. Of course she'd tout for her next keeper. Erith only stayed until July.

Did he expect her to enter a damned convent then and lament his absence for the rest of her life like some spineless heroine from an opera?

She had a career. As did he. And the two would soon put them a continent apart.

None of these undisputed facts quieted the anger and denial twisting like adders in his gut.

Olivia guided her mount to face him. Even across the distance, he knew she recognized him, even if she gave no overt acknowledgment.

That was how it must be too, blast it all to Hades.

"I don't see what all the fuss is," Roma said flatly from beside him.

"What did you say?" he asked, wondering what she was talking about.

She tipped her head, now covered with its hat, toward Olivia. "That woman. Your doxy. I don't see what all the fuss is about."

That was startling enough to capture Erith's wandering attention. "What in blazes—" He sucked in a deep breath and struggled to control the furious shock rocketing through him. "I beg your pardon, Roma."

Her lower lip protruded in a way that was regrettably familiar. "You'll tell me I shouldn't know about such things. But of course I do. I'm not stupid, nor am I deaf. Your flagrant affair with that harlot is the talk of the ton. It was bad enough for the family when you kept your mistresses on the other side of the Channel."

"This isn't something I can discuss," he said gently, cursing blue murder inside. How the hell had she found out so much?

"Well, I think it's disgusting," she snapped, and kicked her horse into a canter.

The groom perforce pursued her, his expression concerned. Obviously the speed was unusual for Lady Roma and he worried about her tumbling off. Erith watched the retreat and echoed his feeling. Roma bounced around with no sense of the horse's rhythm. The poor beast must feel like it had a bag of wheat bumping about on its back.

He looked up and noticed Olivia studying him. She must guess something of what had happened. And a woman on the fringes of society would have a good idea that the young girl in his company was his daughter.

A message passed between them as if she wordlessly sent him strength. Although nothing changed in that beautiful, strong-boned face.

No observer would have an inkling of the silent communication they'd just shared.

Then she turned back to her companions and treated Erith as a complete stranger. Somehow that dismissal was the worst part of the whole damnable situation. Not that his frail truce with his daughter had shattered. Not that he still had to approach his hostile son. Not that he needed to chase after Roma and make sure she didn't land on her aristocratic rump. Not even that Olivia flirted with another man.

No, the worst part of the whole hellish, bloody morning was that Olivia wasn't at his side, openly acknowledged as the lover he was proud to own.

$\mathcal{T}$he footman let Olivia into the house. She'd been out since her ride in Hyde Park that morning. Now it was past seven o'clock. Perry had wanted more help than she'd expected with the final arrangements for his thirtieth birthday ball, then he'd wanted her to stay for a nice long coze.

He felt neglected. She could understand that. Even so, his insistence on detaining her seemed deliberate, as if he plotted to keep her away from Erith.

Of course he did. His animosity toward the earl was as marked as ever. Stronger.

Now she felt tired and edgy. All afternoon, impatience had eaten at her. Pleasurable expectation focused on a lover was so outside her experience that it shocked her more than all the wanton acts she'd committed. But what else could the lightness in her step signal but happiness at the prospect of seeing him?

Thank goodness Erith left London in July, or she might make an utter fool of herself.

Her racing heart steadied, took up a fatalistic beat. The prospect of Erith's departure didn't give her spirits the boost she'd hoped for.

In a pensive mood, she removed her bonnet and passed it to the butler. "I'll have a bath and a light meal, Latham. Tea. Not wine."

"His lordship is here, madam. In the salon on the first floor."

Surprised, she paused in pulling off her gloves. After spending so long in her company yesterday, she'd assumed he would have family commitments today. "Has he been waiting long?"

"Since four, madam."

Four? That seemed unusually early. "Thank you, Latham. You'd better wait to order my bath."

"Very good, madam." The butler bowed and left.

Even though Erith had been cooling his heels for more than three hours, she paused before going up. After the dangerous emotional storms of yesterday, she wanted to be sure of her composure when she saw him again.

In the hallway mirror, she met her troubled light brown gaze. The woman in the reflection wasn't the self-possessed queen of the courtesans. The woman in the reflection was vulnerable and unsure and afraid that she'd already given away too much of herself.

Where could she and Erith go after yesterday?

With him, she'd experienced something she had never felt with a man. A strange, electric intimacy. More than friendship. Different from the bonds of familial love.

When he'd wept in her arms, she would have offered all of herself to save him shedding one of those difficult tears. It hadn't been only the worldly demimondaine who suffered for him, but the lost girl who skulked inside her. And Leo's yearning mother. And the free woman she hoped to become when she abandoned this decadent life forever.

She didn't understand the feeling. But she recognized its power. And its appalling perils.

She'd never felt connected to any of her lovers before. But from the beginning, Lord Erith had set out to foster a link between them that she now had no power to break.

Curse him for luring her into this quicksand. He must know that any genuine emotion between them was doomed to end in heartbreak and loss.

He was an aristocrat at the summit of society. He had a family to whom he owed duty and care. She was a whore.

For both of them, the affair could only be a brief interlude.

Slowly, she made her way up the stairs, doggedly rebuilding her defenses with every tread. She was strong. No man could do her lasting damage. She would survive anything.

Still, as she opened the salon door, knowing Erith waited, she was trembling as she'd trembled when he kissed her in the rain.

Erith sat in a large leather armchair turned away from the fire. He had a book on his lap and his hair was ruffled as if he'd repeatedly raked his fingers through it. In his black silk robe, he presented a picture of perfect relaxation, with one hand holding his book steady and the other curled around a half-full glass of claret.

She tried to stem the wild fountain of pleasure that the sight of him set flowing. But it was like trying to stop a thunderstorm or a tidal wave.

He looked up at her entrance and gave her a sweet, lopsided smile.

She'd seen him rakish. She'd seen him sardonically amused. She'd seen him laugh.

But this smile was so exquisitely tender, it made her heart turn over in her breast. And sent any chance of her playing the cold cyprian flying to the winds.

Stop it, Olivia. He's a man. All he can offer is pain, slavery, and destruction.

Too late for warnings. Under that smile, her icy, barren soul expanded as though it basked in the sun's warmth after endless winter.

Would she freeze again or was this feeling a portent of summer?

"Good evening, Olivia." Even his voice sounded tender.

"Good evening, Lord Erith." Devil take her shaky response. She closed the door after her and took a few steps into the room.

"So formal?" He placed his wine on the mahogany side table.

Her eyes followed the movement. A bundle of colored silk rested on the polished surface near his glass.

Ribbons? She dismissed the small puzzle as she found herself drawn back to studying his face.

"Erith."

"Julian."

She didn't know why, but using his Christian name denoted surrender. Nonetheless, she nodded. "Julian."

The smile deepened. "Thank you." He spoke as if she'd granted him the greatest reward.

She sank into the chair opposite, never taking her eyes from him. She couldn't read his mood. What she did recognize was that he hadn't retreated from yesterday's intimacy.

After seeing him in the park, she'd wondered if when they met again he'd pretend they had never shared difficult confidences in the quiet watches of a rainy night. It would be simpler if he chose that path. But then he never did choose the simple option.

He hadn't yet touched her, although his state of undress was a message in itself. Even so, his physical reality captured her so strongly that he might as well have grabbed her up against him.

His eyes were a soft, misty gray. Hard to remember a time when she'd considered that steady gaze steely and unemotional.

Gray, God help her, was quickly becoming her favorite color.

"You've waited all afternoon." An inane remark, curse her for a bedazzled fool.

He bent his head in agreement. "Yes."

"I was with Perry."

Another inane remark. Anyway, she didn't owe Erith explanations of her whereabouts. That was the bargain they'd made.

But she was despairingly aware that what hovered between them had nothing to do with that cold bargain and everything to do with a dangerous, world-shaking emotion she could never acknowledge. Even to herself.

Yesterday had changed so much. If only he hadn't followed her to Kent. She might have some faint hope of dousing this wildfire inside her if he'd stayed a stranger.

The smile still teased his mouth and he hadn't taken his eyes off her. In all her years as an object of desire, no man had ever regarded her with quite that degree of attention. It was unnerving.

Except she couldn't look anywhere but at Erith either.

"No matter. I needed time to think."

She avoided the obvious question. She wasn't sure she wanted to hear the answer. "Have you eaten?"

"Later. Have you?"

She'd had cakes and sandwiches with Perry mid-afternoon and had felt mildly hungry when she returned to the house. Enough to seek some fortification before her night with the earl. But this strange encounter sent any thought of food to oblivion.

"I'm fine, thank you."

He laid his book on the table with the wineglass and the pile of ribbons. "Good."

She leaned forward in her chair. "Erith, I hate to admit this, but you're making me nervous."

He smiled again, or rather the curve of his lips stretched

into something closer to real amusement. "You have nothing to worry about."

The hands she braced on the arms of her chair curled into fists. "Now I'm really worried."

"Would you like wine?"

"Why?" she asked suspiciously. "Am I going to need it?"

He laughed softly and the deep sound trickled down her spine like warm honey. "You may. I want to play a game."

Her gaze returned to the seemingly innocent pile of ribbons. Except they weren't exactly ribbons. More like silk cords in an assortment of jewel colors.

"You want to tie me up," she said flatly.

He had grown tired of coaxing and persuasion and patience. Now he meant to try and force a response.

If asked, she'd guess he had more imagination than this. She'd overestimated him. Clearly his imagination followed the same tired rut as every other man's.

She supposed she should be flattered he took this trouble to gain her participation. In an obscure way, this new strategy made him both more dear and more disappointing.

Muffling a sigh, she sat back and felt the tremulous tension flow out of her. At last she was on familiar, if banal ground.

He watched her steadily. "You have no objection?"

She began to unbutton her spencer. Of course he'd want her naked. The other men who wanted her arrayed as a captive certainly had. "No. I have no objection."

Except it would leave her feeling sick and unsatisfied again. And Erith with that hurt, puzzled, sad look on his face.

She could do this, but heaven help her, she didn't want to.

"Good. We'll try that next time, then."

Her fingers stilled on the third button. She rose to her feet, wondering if her unsteady legs would support her. "What did you say?"

Erith picked up the cords and began to play with them. Her eyes focused on the hypnotic shifts of those powerful tanned hands. The endless movement was vaguely unsettling, definitely suggestive.

"I said we'll try it next time," he said peacefully.

The mundane certainties of a few seconds ago scuttled out of the light like crabs disturbed under a rock.

"So what do you want now?" She forced the words past the constriction in her throat.

He stood and moved within touching distance. As always, he towered over her, the only man she knew who made her feel small and feminine. Suddenly, the idea of him tying her down and trying to seduce her into pleasure tugged at her curiosity in a way she wouldn't have thought possible a week ago.

A minute ago.

He still held the bunched cords. "I want you to tie me up."

She retreated a step. She hadn't read Erith as a man who liked to be beaten into submission. One of her previous lovers had needed pain to reach satisfaction and she'd quickly ended the affair. It nauseated her to subject anyone else to a travesty of her first keeper's violence.

"No."

Erith gently let the cords slide down his fingers back to the table. "As you wish."

Her gaze focused on the tangled, vibrant silks cascading onto the rich dark mahogany. Even to a woman dead to allure, there was something undeniably sensual about the slow drift of those delicate strands of color through his elegant fingers.

A strange feeling rippled through her, and she gave a tiny shiver, as if those long fingers touched her bare skin. Then she realized what he'd said.

"You don't want me to beat you?" she echoed, bewildered.

Shock crossed his face and he looked directly at her. "Do you *want* to beat me?"

"No." She frowned. With every moment, she slipped further from understanding what was going on. "Wasn't that what you asked?"

The smile teased his lips again and he took her hand. As she tried to pull away, he resisted. The warmth of his touch seeped up her arm and melted more of the ice inside her.

Soon no ice would remain at all. Then heaven help her, what would be left?

"You saw me with my daughter this morning."

"Yes."

"She made me realize my greatest sin against her wasn't my desertion, bad as that was. It's that I've never given her any choice in what happened to her." He paused, and she recognized the ghost of last night's sadness. "I lost Joanna because I tried to impose my will on her."

She tilted her head and arched her eyebrows. "You're a man. You like to push people around."

"Not tonight. Not you." He released her hand and straightened. His expression was as somber as she'd ever seen it. "I've been doing some hard thinking, Olivia. Thinking that shines an unforgiving mirror on my behavior toward you. Toward all the women in my life."

She linked her hands together, trying not to miss his touch. "You've behaved well toward me. And I've hardly endeared myself to you."

He reached out to touch her cheek briefly. The contact was fleeting and soft as the brush of a swallow's wing. But its tenderness flowed all the way to her toes. "Don't be a fool, Olivia. Endearing yourself is exactly what you've done."

She blinked away that annoying mist that appeared before her eyes when he said things like that. She wished he wouldn't. Because one day very soon, he wouldn't be here to say them. Even if he was here, he might lose the urge to say them.

Every time he spoke such words, she was like an opium

eater getting her daily dose of poison. And like any poor devil caught in the drug's coils, she only wanted more.

"I haven't proven much of a mistress," she said huskily.

"We're not done yet, my love."

Astonishment poured through her in a great wave. He didn't seem aware he'd used the endearment.

Perry called her his love now and again in a careless way. But those two words didn't sound at all casual from Lord Erith.

She berated herself for a sentimental idiot. But nothing stopped her soul from unfurling like a sail in the wind.

"I can't give you what you want." She had to make him see he wasted these sweet, poignant caresses.

"Give me what you can."

She licked dry lips and straightened her shoulders. "That's nothing."

"Not true, Olivia. You've already given me so much."

The tender smile returned. Oh, dear God, how she wished he wouldn't look at her like that. Every time he did, he pierced her heart with a flaming spear. He pushed her to her limits, forced her to acknowledge her failings, threatened the shell of indifference that held her safe.

He was an unmitigated disaster.

And she wouldn't have missed knowing him at any price. If at this moment he fell on his knees and offered her the world in exchange for his departure, she'd deny him.

Utterly terrifying.

She started to shake and her heart raced like a wild horse set free. "What have I given you?" she asked belligerently.

"Don't you know you've given me back my soul?"

His stark words cut through her prickly anger like a knife through butter.

With difficulty, she forced astringent words out. "Perhaps you'll think me worth the money, then."

He didn't react with anger. She should have known he

wouldn't. Instead he looked unutterably sad. Which left her feeling more crushed than anger ever could.

"Olivia, don't."

Just two soft words and the coiling, raging beasts of shame and truculence and defiant loneliness lay down as peacefully as a child tired after a long day in the sun.

"I want to give you back your soul too." He spoke so softly that she leaned forward to hear. Drifts of his musky scent made her dizzy with longing.

Longing? She never longed for a man. Even if she did, what use would she be to him? With her body dead to touch and her heart dead to feeling.

Although astoundingly, her heart now was too constricted with painful emotion for that to ring even partially true.

"You're talking about sexual pleasure," she said dully.

What was the point of all this? He must know it would get them nowhere, whoever tied whom down. Last night was the closest she'd ever come to wanting a man. What a miserable failure that had been.

"It was an unforgivable crime that your capacity for pleasure was stolen from you."

"I've survived."

"Survived but not lived."

She blinked away hot moisture. Just as she could no longer lie about wishing she was the woman he wanted her to be, she could no longer pretend he didn't move her to tears. And what he said was so true and so tragic.

"It's too late."

He shook his head. "No."

She felt he looked at her more deeply than anyone ever had. She dreaded to imagine what he saw.

"Do you trust me?" he asked.

She glanced at him uncertainly. "I don't trust anyone."

"I know." He paused. "Could you trust me tonight? I'm not asking for forever."

"People like us don't do forever," she said sadly.

"Yes, we do." His voice was deep and sure. "At least give me the privilege of your honesty."

She summoned the tattered remnants of resistance. How she wished she could diminish him, make him like every other pathetic man she'd ever had in her bed. "I'm a whore. Honesty is a luxury."

"Do you feel like a whore when you're with me?"

How could she answer that? "What do you want, Erith?" she asked desperately, as she'd asked before.

"I want what you want."

"That's nonsensical."

"Unprecedented, perhaps."

"No man has ever said that to me."

"I know." His eyes filled with such compassion that she almost reached out to touch him. But she stopped herself.

If she yielded the last of her defenses and he betrayed her—and as a man, betrayal was his essential nature—it would break her.

She ignored the tiny whisper that any barriers against him had fallen long, long ago.

Without looking, he stretched down to pick up the cords and extend them toward her. "Tie me up. Then do whatever you want."

Astonishment kept her silent. And automatic, vehement rejection of what he asked.

Something essential in her resisted the idea of placing him so overtly in her power. An alarming admission when power over men was what she'd lived for since she was fourteen.

Old cynicism surged up, defiance from the Olivia she'd created over so many turbulent, unhappy years. "Can't I trust you unless I bind you?"

"Of course you can." Again that smile. Heavens, she wished he'd stop. "But if you tie me up, you'll *know* I'm in your power."

She didn't bother to rein in her sarcasm. "And I'll give you pleasure. Goodness, what a sacrifice."

"Do whatever you please."

"Beat you?" Although she never would.

"If you like."

"Ignore you?"

"Yes."

"Leave you?"

A muscle flickered in his lean cheek, and she realized that in spite of his outward calmness, he was far from indifferent to her decision. "If you must."

"Why are you doing this?"

He shrugged again. His voice was impossibly grave. "We have to break the impasse between us. Or we'll end up destroying one another."

"The easiest solution is to part."

"Do you want easy?"

She didn't dare answer that. "So I tie you up and do exactly what I want?"

"Yes."

She put out her hand. To her astonishment, it was completely steady. "Give me the cords."

Chapter 18

$\mathcal{H}$oping to hell he knew what he was doing, hoping to hell he'd survive whatever came next, Erith passed the silk bindings to Olivia.

Once she realized what he intended, she'd become surprisingly calm. When she first came in, she was visibly uncertain, bewildered. Then she tried to draw the protective shell of the courtesan about her. Without succeeding, he was encouraged to note.

Surely that meant something.

Now what did she feel? Was she angry, reluctant, resigned, triumphant? *Repelled?*

Devil take it, he had no idea. Not for the first time, he doubted the reckless strategy he'd devised after his troubled conversation with Roma. In theory, it offered a way out of an impossible dilemma. In practice, he felt like he put his head inside the mouth of a hungry tiger.

And Olivia hadn't even tied him up yet.

But it was far too late to back down.

Imperious as any queen, Olivia gestured in his direction. "Take off the robe."

He'd sworn to do her bidding. And by God, that's what he'd do. No matter how hard it was for a man of his overweening pride to submit to a woman's command.

Without comment, he shucked the black silk garment and let it slip to his bare feet.

Nor did he speak as she contemplated his nakedness for what felt like an eon. Her eyes glided over his shoulders and chest and homed in on his cock. Which predictably rose to the unspoken challenge.

He'd have to be dead not to want her. But he didn't feel comfortable standing before her like this. She studied him like an object. Like a marble statue in a gallery.

Slowly, she circled him, considering him with the cool gaze of an art connoisseur. Her arms were folded in front of her as if she didn't find the work on offer worthy of particular appreciation.

Worst of all was when she passed behind him. She seemed to stare at his bare backside forever. Every muscle tensed along his legs, over his buttocks, and up his back. He had to steel himself to stand where he was and not fumble after the crumpled robe like a nervous virgin on her wedding night.

Damn it, he was an acknowledged rake, a virtuoso in the sensual arts. He'd stood naked before a host of women.

But never had he felt so bloody . . . *naked*.

He abhorred feeling like this. Loathed it to the depths of his being.

And she knew it, the witch.

He braced himself to endure. If he could break through the shell of ice that enclosed her, he'd gladly subject himself to the worst torture she could devise. Somewhere in their liaison, he'd reached a point where releasing her from the prison of her frigidity was more important to him than his next breath.

He could do this for her. *He would do this for her.*

What happened between them then was in the lap of a fate he'd learned to distrust.

How had he got to this point, where her wellbeing outstripped his pride and self-preservation? But he'd passed the stage where he could cavil at the obscure path he'd chosen. Now he was well and truly lost in the woods. He just hoped his instincts about this woman showed him the way home again.

The memory of how Olivia looked when she told him of her past strengthened him, and he set his shoulders. She'd borne her hardships with such courage. This silent subservience was all he could offer as recompense. He hoped to blazes it proved enough.

As if she touched him, he felt her burning eyes trace the line of his spine from his buttocks to his shoulders, which knotted with tension. He waited for the brush of her hand, but she merely shifted around to face him.

"Lie on the bed." Her face was smooth and expressionless as alabaster. And just as cold.

The electric possibility of danger, even physical harm, hovered in the air. Her slanted tiger eyes promised retribution, punishment . . . *pleasure*.

Without protest, he prowled into the bedroom, crossed to the bed and stretched out. The room was so quiet he heard the faint swish of her skirts as she followed. On the way, she picked up his robe, which she tossed across a chair in the bedroom.

His heart raced with a strange mixture of emotions. Excitement, certainly. But trepidation as well. And a stirring of masculine resentment that he couldn't quite stifle.

Even if he had nobody but himself to blame for his predicament.

No woman ordered him around. Especially in the bedroom. He'd always been in charge. Damn it, he liked to be in charge.

This obedience to a woman's whim was new. Unsettling.

But something deep in his gut insisted that humbling his pride was the only way to grant her true freedom. If it cost him a moment of humiliation—he hoped to Hades she didn't plan more than that—then he could withstand it.

If she only once showed him genuine desire, he'd face the fires of hell and smile as the flames roasted him.

The reminder of what was at stake drained his cramping tension. Even so, when she grabbed his wrist and dragged it up toward one bedpost, he started.

Her firm, completely unseductive touch shot a wild jolt of incendiary heat through him. He grit his teeth and fought for control.

She was close enough for him to snatch into his arms. But if he did that, the brittle trust building between them would shatter forever.

"Relax. This won't hurt a bit," she murmured as her clever fingers looped a dark blue cord around his wrist then tied it to the bedpost with an efficient knot.

"Easy for you to say."

He sought reassurance in the fact that she felt safe enough to tease. Perhaps everything would be all right after all. A tendril of uncertain hope uncoiled in his desperate heart.

"Easy for me to do." She looped his other wrist to the second bedpost with more of that impressive dispatch.

"You've done this before."

"On my father's estate, we learned to tie stray animals up securely or we'd be out looking for them."

Her father's estate? Her slip confirmed Erith's earlier guess about her wealthy background. He bit down on another wave of futile anger at what her brother had done.

Still, it was a struggle to keep the light note. "Do you liken me to an animal, Miss Raines?"

"Let's see." Very deliberately, she ran her hand down his naked chest and over the vulnerable plane of his belly. Every muscle of his body clenched as he waited for her to touch him where he wanted her most.

She paused just short of his erection.

He ground his teeth, biting back a strangled plea, waiting in trembling yearning for her to move that final inch. Just one little inch.

Good God, he felt like he'd been hard for a century.

But her cool hand remained flat on his belly. Close. But not close enough.

His hips jerked upward.

The tiniest of smiles twitched her lips, and her feline eyes sparked as she withdrew her hand. Not for the first time, he imagined the velvety mole near her mouth was a witch's mark. She certainly cast a spell on him. She had from the first moment he'd seen her.

"You torment me, she-devil," he gasped.

His heart pumped as though he'd just run up a steep mountain. He'd only started this cycle of torture and already he was in extremis.

How in Hades would he survive?

"Mmm," she almost hummed.

"What do you plan to do with me?" His voice was hoarse with the effort of controlling his titanic hunger.

"I haven't decided yet," she said musingly, moving down the bed and taking one of his ankles in a firm grip. Again the impact of her hand on his skin shuddered through him like a collision with a speeding coach.

"I think you have."

Erith might have gone disastrously wrong with the women in his life. But he knew enough about the sex to recognize her expression. He'd seen exactly the same look on the stable cats at Selden when they had a mouse in their claws. His future unquestionably involved teasing, torment, and eventual destruction.

Even so, he didn't resist as she bound each foot to the posts at the end of the bed. He lay spread-eagled and vulnerable in front of her.

Before buying the silk cords, he'd tested them. For all their satiny smoothness, they were terrifically strong. He wasn't sure he could break them if he had to.

That was the trust he placed in Olivia. Tied up, he truly was defenseless. He did this right or not at all.

As if she read his mind, she spoke. "Try those knots for me."

He noticed since he'd given himself over to her domination, she'd stopped using words like "please" or even addressing him with his title.

"As you wish." He tugged violently at the bindings on his arms. They didn't shift. He tried to kick his legs. Again no movement. Those animals on her mysterious childhood estate had been well and truly tethered.

"Nothing?"

She stood at the base of the bed, her scrutiny more clinical than loverlike as it ran across his body. Even so, every sinew tensed. He tried not to resent her coolness but it was difficult. Especially when he was a raging furnace of need.

"Nothing."

"Good." She trailed one finger up his instep and along his ankle and his shin to his knee. Where she paused . . . and paused . . .

Every drop of moisture in his mouth evaporated.

Higher, higher.

The demand was a fractured scream inside his head. He gritted his teeth until they ached. He'd promised her complete power over him. He'd sworn to accept anything she did.

Even when he'd made his plans, the prospect of achieving what he set himself seemed unlikely. Now that he was actually roped down like a bull for slaughter, he wondered if his goal was impossible.

Without lifting her hand from his leg, she drifted around the side of the bed. Her alluring smoky honey scent combined with his own musk to make him dizzy. Her gaze on his nakedness sent him into a cold sweat. Although that was all that was cold about him. He'd had the fire built up before she returned so the room was warm. But hotter still was the blood pounding through his veins.

She performed a devilish little circle with her forefinger on his knee. His cock jerked as he imagined that finger sliding up to stroke him.

"Olivia," he grated out, knowing his mind followed exactly the path she intended.

"Yes?" she asked in an indifferent tone. "Do you want me to untie you?"

Yes.

"No."

"Good."

As if to reward his answer, she made a foray up his thigh. Still just with one finger. His heart faltered as he waited for her to complete the caress.

Surely she knew where he wanted her. His mouth was parched and his jaw throbbed from clenching his teeth.

Olivia, please . . .

She lifted her hand away and stepped back from the bed. "If you need anything, call. I'm sure the servants will hear you." She paused. "Eventually."

"Where are you going?" He despised the begging note in his voice.

She was almost at the door to the hallway. She stopped and glanced over her shoulder with a derisive little smile. "Good-bye, Erith."

Good-bye? What the Devil was going on?

"Hell, Olivia!" He struggled in earnest against his bonds, fighting with much more force than he'd used testing them. Still they held. "Olivia! What—"

She opened the door and slipped out of the room without another word.

Chapter 19

$\mathcal{E}$rith had fallen into an uneasy, exhausted doze when the door opened again. He lifted heavy eyelids and stared sightlessly into the shadowy room. Through the fog of emotional and physical misery, he dully supposed a servant had arrived to release him at last.

The fire had burned down to embers in the grate and full night had descended. His arms blazed with agony from their unnatural position above his head. He'd been flat on his back so long, his muscles screamed with painful stiffness. He was deathly cold.

After that shocking moment when Olivia left, he'd spent fruitless energy battling like a maniac to break free. But all he'd gained were raw wrists and strained muscles. His frenzied writhing had only tightened the cords. She hadn't exaggerated when she boasted of tethering him like a beast.

Eventually, logic had pierced his insane fury. Struggle was useless.

Hope had taken much longer to die than anger.

At first he couldn't believe she'd gone and left him help-less. His heart had howled incredulous denial as she closed the door behind her.

She'd be back. Of course she'd be back.

She was only teasing him. He'd always known she would torment him before she relented. Hell, he'd as much as in-sisted she torment him when he asked her to do what she willed.

But as grim minutes advanced, turned into hours, and still no Olivia, bleak reality sank in. He saw what he should have seen much earlier.

He'd given her freedom. Like the smart woman she was, she'd taken it.

He could have called for help, as she'd so derisively sug-gested. But some stubborn skerrick of pride kept him silent: pride and, even more pathetic, hope that she might return to find him steadfastly waiting.

What a damned fool he was. Of course Olivia wasn't coming back.

He closed his eyes and felt desolation creep through his veins like a slow river of frost.

"Erith?"

His heart stopped, then began to race in a crazy rhythm. Had he gone mad indeed? God help him, he'd thought never to hear that soft voice again.

His head jerked in her direction and he wrenched upward before he remembered the cords that held him. Through the gloom, his blurred gaze focused disbelievingly on her.

She leaned against the closed door. The fire's low glow turned her red silk robe into gleaming ruby mystery. Her beautiful hair was a loose tumble of bronze around her shoulders.

Lord knew what she meant to do. But she was here. That was all that mattered.

Tense silence stretched between them.

"You came back." His voice emerged as a croak from a

mouth dry as desert sand. A wild mixture of joy and wonder clogged his throat.

"Yes."

"I thought you'd left me," he said rawly.

"I'm sorry."

"No, you're not." His mind, blank with despair only seconds ago, kicked into operation under the invigorating reality that she hadn't deserted him. "It's what you wanted me to think."

"Perhaps." Her voice was enigmatic, and in the poor light, he couldn't read her expression.

Then the greatest revelation of all. Although he should have guessed her game when she agreed to take part in this little contest. "By God, you're testing me."

"Yes." She stepped farther into the room, nearer the fire. He could see her face. It was calm, almost emotionless.

"And I'm failing."

She pursed her full lips briefly in a way that made him want to kiss her.

Would he ever kiss her again? An iron certainty grew that they'd emerge from this night bound as tightly as thread to a bobbin, or else this was the end of everything between them.

"I wouldn't say that." She glided closer to the bed. "You must want to get up."

"I could have called a servant."

"Yes, but you didn't," she said neutrally.

"I would have soon. I can't feel my legs."

That brought her rushing forward in a rustle of silk. She came close enough for him to smell her sweet floral soap and, beneath it, the warm essence of her skin. She must have just left her bath. He'd have thought he was too tired and disconsolate and racked with pain to respond to her. But immediate sexual awareness curled through his belly like a snake.

"I'll release you." Her mood was no longer opaque. She sounded upset and guilty. "I left you here too long."

"Does that mean I've failed?"

She gave a contemptuous snort at his mulishness. "Would you rather stay there till Doomsday?"

"If I have to." Now that he knew she hadn't left, his determination resurfaced that tonight would mark a new beginning or the death of his every hope.

He'd reached this conclusion during the harsh, unrelenting hours of self-reflection before Olivia arrived home from Montjoy's. He thought he'd prepared himself for the risks of his last ditch attempt to shatter the deadlock between them.

He'd had no bloody idea.

"You're an obstinate devil." Did he hear admiration in that low contralto?

He forced out the cruel words that needed to be said. "Has tonight given you any joy? Have you tortured me to your satisfaction? Will anything make up for what happened to you? I know the world owes you recompense. And you're more than welcome to take it out of my hide if that helps. But, Olivia, you must see that nothing can erase the vile injustices of your past."

He heard her startled intake of breath. Then there was a delicious slide of freshly washed hair over his chest as she leaned down and tugged at the knots fastening his left wrist to the bedpost.

"You claim to know so much about me?" He couldn't mistake the fear that lurked under her defiance.

"Know you?" He made a derisive sound deep in his throat. "You're more mysterious than the depths of the Pacific Ocean or the wastes of the Arctic."

"Oh, both horribly cold and wet." As usual when he veered too close to her essential self, she fended him off with humor. "Not sure I approve of your mode of address, Lord Erith."

"The jungles of Peru?"

She still fiddled with the ties. "Dank and . . . Blast! I need more light."

To his regret, she stopped nudging his ribs with her fragrant warmth and went across to the chest of drawers. She moved from lamp to lamp, lighting them so each detail of her beauty came into view like stars winking into life in the night sky.

The lamps lent her thick mane of hair a myriad colors. Bronze. Auburn. Rich brown. Gold. Strands of flaxen blond. It shifted as she moved, rippling and catching the light.

She bent and fed the fire, using the poker until the blaze rose high and flickered gold over her face. Only then did she return to him. "Aren't you going to insist I let you go?"

"You're in charge."

"Even if I untie you?"

He stared steadily up at her. Demons from hell stabbed his body and shoveled red hot coals down his nerve endings. He could bear anything if it meant he achieved his ends. "What do you think?"

She smiled with radiant approval that made his gut twist with yearning. "You've earned your freedom."

She leaned over him again and with a few deft pulls released the cords that held him down.

"Thank you," he said through dry lips. He struggled to bend down, intending to untie his feet, but his muscles had seized up. The blood rushing back into his limbs left him light-headed with pain.

"Oh, Erith," she cried in dismay. "I'm sorry." Quickly, she reached down to release his ankles. "I had no right to do this."

"Yes, you did." He grunted as he struggled to sit. He'd spent the last hours frantic to move. Now that he could move, the agony was indescribable. "I gave you the right."

"This wasn't fair." She frowned in distress as she passed him his robe. Then she began to rub his legs with frantic vigor. "It's obscene to make you pay for other men's sins."

Her sweet concern and care made him feel . . . *loved*.

The thought should have aroused more apprehension than

he was capable of summoning. Love had never been part of the arrangement. But after tonight, things could never be the same again.

Never.

"I've committed my share of sins, Olivia." Clumsily he tugged the robe over his nakedness.

"Not against me." She darted across to the sideboard and he heard the clink of glass. "Here. You must be thirsty."

"Thank you." With a shaking hand, he accepted the glass of water and lifted it to his lips. The cool benediction of the liquid was the sweetest thing he'd ever tasted. If he didn't count Olivia's hard-won and reluctant kisses.

She stood staring at him with an appalled expression. "Erith, I was unforgivably wrong to do this. I don't know what got into me. Suddenly when I had you tied up, I didn't see you, I saw every man who had ever used me." Her hands twined with palpable distress in front of her. "You must think I'm mad."

"I think you're beautiful," he said, grateful that his words no longer scraped across a desiccated throat. "But of course you know that."

She reached out to take the glass and replace it on the sideboard. "You're as mad as I am." She spoke without force.

"Probably."

She shifted close to the bed and placed her shoulder under his arm. "Let me help you up."

He accepted her aid until he was upright. He tottered and she caught him. Her voice was thick with tears and the eyes she raised to him were turbulent with guilt and regret. "You should hate me."

He raised a shaking hand to touch her cheek. With every moment free of those damned cords, he felt stronger, more himself.

"Don't be a nitwit, Olivia." He sucked in a deep breath then winced as the involuntary expansion of his ribs hurt his chest. "I need a moment's privacy."

Surprisingly, his worldly mistress blushed. "Of course."

Very slowly, like an old man, he limped to the dressing room. He retained enough arrogance to abominate appearing before her at such a disadvantage.

As he came back through the door, he staggered. Suddenly Olivia was there, holding him. He drew another deep breath, easier this time, relishing her fresh, warm woman scent. Her strong slender arm encircled his waist and her other hand braced him against her.

Her voice vibrated with concern. "Do you want to lie down again? Or sit up in the chair?"

"I need to get my circulation going," he groaned.

Damn it, he wasn't as young as he used to be.

"I'll help you."

"Thank you."

But he was so clumsy, and she was so extravagantly determined to support him, that balance proved increasingly difficult.

He wavered.

She grabbed at him.

He stumbled.

She held tighter.

He snatched at her. But his numb fingers slid uselessly off the slippery silk that covered her shoulders.

"Hell," he managed to grit out, and in a chaos of flailing limbs fell, taking her with him.

A moment of weightlessness as he went down. A shriek from Olivia, more shock than fear. A grunt from him as his abused sinews protested the sudden movement. She landed on the mattress with a bounce and he landed awkwardly on top of her.

Her eyes, wide, startled, beautiful, clear as whisky, darted up to meet his. Her lips parted. She struggled for air.

His torso crushed her breasts. His hips pressed hard into hers. Both feet touched the floor. His arms framed her head, trapping her luxuriant hair.

"Erith," she said breathlessly.

"Julian," he said with a longing he couldn't hide.

She licked her lips and he nearly groaned. Then in a melting voice he'd never heard before, she sighed his name.

"Julian."

He should move before he crushed her, but he couldn't budge to save his life. Her hands had closed over his back when they fell. Now they slid upward over his shoulders and neck in a frantic caress.

With more emphasis, "Julian."

Her fingers dug into the thick hair on the sides of his head. With rough urgency, she dragged him down until his lips met hers.

Chapter 20

$\mathcal{E}$rith's mouth fastened hot and open upon Olivia's.

Voracious. Hungry. Demanding.

Even though she'd initiated the kiss, he'd seized control. She shut her eyes and waited for the dark waters to close above her head. But the old, sick, suffocated feeling didn't surface.

There was just the astonishing heat and closeness of his body over hers, and the sharp, evocative tang of Erith on her tongue.

This was a universe away from the gentle, teasing kisses in the rain yesterday. Or even the hard kisses he'd forced upon her when they met, alerting her to his intended possession.

These were the kisses of a man struggling to retain the last shreds of sanity.

And she seemed to be kissing him back just as ferociously.

How strange. How unprecedented.

How wonderful.

His free hand held her head, as if she'd disappear unless he kept her there. Foolish man. Surely he knew this searing enchantment bound her too. He turned her wild and wanton and more a woman than she'd ever been before.

He thrust one shaking hand under the robe to cup her breast. Her nipple pebbled against his palm and she rolled her hips restlessly, feeling his burning hardness.

"Oh, yes," he breathed into her mouth.

He pressed her down into the mattress, making her feel his weight and size. And how aroused he was. Only two layers of thin silk separated them, and his scorching heat radiated through the flimsy barrier.

Blood thundered in her ears, making her deaf to everything but clamoring need. Her hands traced an erratic path down his back, scrunching his robe beneath her fingers. She hungered to feel his bare skin against hers.

Instincts she'd never known took over. She sucked his tongue into her mouth, savoring his taste. He had the rich and heady flavor of the finest wine.

Who knew a man could be this delicious?

His tongue slid against hers. Immediately a flare of response ignited in her belly. The sudden, blazing reaction made her shift again. He groaned and deepened the kiss, plunging his tongue into her mouth in a rhythm that was familiar, yet new to her as spring grass to a newborn lamb.

And her heart skipped like a newborn lamb in wayward, unsteady bursts of speed and stillness. Then stopped altogether when he gently squeezed her breast.

She moaned into his kiss and arched to increase the pressure on her breast. She nipped at his lips. Licked at him. Swept her tongue into his mouth in a dance of passion.

With a gasp, he broke free and nuzzled her cheeks and jaw and neck. Dizzy for lack of breath, she opened her eyes.

She didn't want air. She wanted Erith's kisses. She could live on those alone.

"Don't stop," she whispered.

"I won't." Then with an edge of desperation, "God help me, I can't."

Her fingers kneaded his shoulders, testing the heavy muscles, the tight sinews. All this masculine strength should make her feel threatened, defenseless. Instead it excited her. His leashed power was unequivocally hers. He'd proven in the most harrowing circumstances that for her sake, he could rein in his will. No matter what suffering it caused him.

Trust.

Such a small word to transform her world.

"Kiss me." She'd never asked a man for anything. But she'd go on her knees to beg for more of those earth-shaking kisses.

"You're driving me mad," he groaned. He raised himself above her and stared at her with hungry concentration.

"Then go mad," she whispered, barely knowing what she said.

In all her decadent life, she'd never desired a man.

Dear heaven, she desired a man now. She desired Erith.

There was no mistaking the roiling tumult in her belly or the pounding rhythm in her blood. Desire. Visceral, elemental, passionate. It was real. It was thrilling. It was shattering.

The violence of her need shocked her. Could this wild, rapacious creature be Olivia Raines?

His kiss wasn't gentle. The man who had shown such heartbreaking consideration for her vulnerability was gone. Instead he tasted her voluptuously with teeth and tongue and lips. He feasted on her as if he starved and she were the finest banquet.

Once, frightened, crippled Olivia would have shrunk from his passion. Now she reveled in its power.

He drew back onto his knees, his eyes never leaving hers. His impressive muscles bunched as he reached down to grab her hips and slide her across the bed. After being tied down so long, his movements were ungainly. A pang of remorse struck her at what she'd done to him.

She caught his wrist and heard him stifle a groan. She looked more closely. His skin was scored with raw welts where he'd struggled against his bonds.

Another stab of guilt, more painful this time. How wicked she'd been to treat him so. Hot tears rose to her eyes.

"I'm sorry." Her whisper was choked.

"It doesn't matter," he said unsteadily.

"Yes, it does." Very gently, she brought his wrist to her mouth and placed a lingering kiss on the angry red marks. The kiss was a plea for forgiveness, an act of homage.

"Olivia . . . " His voice vibrated with emotion. As if he understood everything she silently tried to tell him with the soft touch of her lips to his torn skin.

She raised her head and looked deep into his eyes. Endless silver. Burning with light. Beautiful.

This time when he pressed his lips to hers, there was passion, but also a reverence that pierced her heart. He made her feel treasured. He made her feel pure.

It was as if his touch created her anew.

For a moment there was a lovely, endearing clumsiness as he fought to continue the kiss and remove his robe at the same time. Their lips slid and clung and parted and clung again. His unsteady breathing and muttered curses rasped in her ears.

No way on earth was she letting him escape. She followed him up as he sat back to discard his clothing. Her hands curled around his neck, tangling in the warm, soft hair at his nape, and she kept kissing him.

"You'll have to let go of me, Olivia," he said breathlessly as his robe slipped away with a soft susurration and he pressed his naked body to hers. He was big and eager and ready. And he smelled glorious, musk and sandalwood and male.

"Never," she said shamelessly, rubbing herself against him like an animal in heat. She *was* an animal in heat. But with the savagery, sweet tenderness lingered, a rich, low note beneath the rising pleasure.

She felt hot and damp and restless and dizzy. She'd never experienced anything like this. She pressed her thighs together to try and temper the increasing pressure but the movement only intensified her craving to have Erith inside her.

"Olivia, I need to get this robe off you. Now." He sounded like a man at the end of his endurance.

"I don't want to let you go," she murmured.

"All right," he said in a gravelly voice. "Remember you damned well asked for this."

"I damned well did," she said, then her smile became a gasp as he roughly stripped the last barrier away. With equal ruthlessness, he grabbed her waist and tipped her back onto the mattress.

The room lurched. She clutched his shoulders as the only solid object in a reeling world. Her heart leaped with anticipation.

"Shocking language, Miss Raines." A wry smile twitched his lips as he knelt between her legs.

She'd never laughed with a lover before. Amazing what piquancy it added. "Your pardon, Lord Erith."

"I told you to call me Julian."

He kissed her hard. Pleasure crackled through her like lightning through a stormy summer sky. The throbbing heat in her loins built to a crescendo.

"You're very masterful all of a sudden." She angled her chin up, hoping he'd kiss her again. For a woman who'd avoided kissing her entire life, she found herself with great zeal for the activity.

Demanding kisses. Soft kisses. Tender kisses. Passionate kisses.

Who knew kissing offered such delicious variety? She'd never tire of Erith's mouth on hers.

"Julian," he prompted, sliding his hands from her waist

until they rested just below her breasts. Tantalizingly close to where she wanted them. Her nipples ached for his touch.

"One might even say pushy," she said in a husky voice, squirming to make him shift his hands upward.

"One might."

She remembered the arcing pleasure when he'd palmed her breast. She wanted that again. She wanted *more*. The peaks tightened with every second he delayed. She made a growl of protest and bent her legs so her inner thighs caressed his hips.

He bent his head and scraped her neck with his strong white teeth. She smothered a tormented whimper. She was so on edge, even the brush of his hair on her skin made her shiver.

"Stop being a stubborn wench," he said hoarsely. "Give in. Call me Julian."

"I've already called you Julian."

"Do it again."

When he bit down gently on the tendon between her shoulder and neck, she shuddered with excitement. It stole her breath to cradle him so close to where she craved his hardness. He was massively aroused. Hunger steamed off him. Something loosened, melted, liquefied inside her. Hot moisture flowed between her thighs.

For the first time she was drenched wet for a man. The strangeness jerked her from her sensual haze.

Trembling, she tried to close her legs, to hide a response that seemed too raw, too revealing. But each wriggle encountered the immovable barrier of Erith's body.

Shamed heat flooded her cheeks. Although she'd lost the right to blush nearly twenty years ago.

He wrenched his head up and stared at her, his gray eyes impossibly brilliant. His nostrils flared as if he tested her arousal with the air.

"Olivia."

Nothing else. Just her name in a voice that only made her shake more violently.

The most beautiful smile she'd ever seen curved his lips. At the sight, something uncoiled in her chest. Something that made her heart somersault with a painful mixture of joy and sorrow. Something she feared would change her life forever.

"You do me too much honor," he whispered, and kissed her right breast just above her puckered nipple.

Her breath caught in her throat. Such a seemingly innocent touch, yet its tender worship made her pulses race.

"Oh, Julian." She was hardly aware she willingly gave him what he'd sought to tease out of her.

Very gently, he plucked at the engorged crests, rolling them in his long fingers. Every touch sent wild sensation rocketing through her.

"Please, oh, please," she cried in a broken voice. "Don't wait. I can't bear it."

Helpless need goaded her. It was like being sucked into a whirlpool. It was like riding an unbroken horse that bolted through a thick forest.

It was like . . . *desire*.

She tilted her hips so her damp cleft brushed his member. The muscles in his back tightened under her hands. Shuddering, he raised himself on his arms. The veins and sinews stood out in stark relief. His back tensed until it was rock hard.

On a great hissing exhalation, he pushed forward. She braced for the usual difficulty and discomfort, but he slid into her with smooth, exquisite heat. Then he held himself completely still.

She'd never known such a moment of perfect closeness.

After a long time, the ocean of tenderness inside her made her shift one hand in a tiny stroking glide down toward his waist. The muscles under her fingers contracted. Infinitesimally he rocked his hips.

In amazement, she stared up into his eyes. It was like looking into polished silver mirrors. She thought he'd gone as deep as he could but the small push settled him more fully, more surely, stretching her anew.

His sheer size was part of the magic. He claimed her in a way no other man had.

He moved again. Astonishingly, he penetrated farther. A moan escaped her, just audible, but enough to snap the golden filament of silence that bound them.

With silence, stillness went too. Slowly, so she felt every sleek inch of withdrawal, he pulled back. After an impossibly long pause, he thrust again.

Deep, deep, as though he touched her heart. As though he took possession of her soul.

He held himself motionless then repeated the movement, even more slowly. She lifted her hips to meet him. The pleasure was so excruciating, it verged on agony.

He dragged back again and surged forward. As relentless as the tide. Ruthless. Hard. Dominating.

Impossibly tender.

At the peak of each thrust, he paused. Balancing her on a moment of perfect eternity. Perfect communication. Perfect stillness.

The connection was electric, powerful, more emotional than physical. Her hands formed claws on the slick skin of his back.

Over and over he used her like this. He didn't touch her breasts. He didn't stroke between her legs where she was so wet. He didn't kiss her.

It was as though the intensity of the joining demanded this simple, primitive, utterly sexual dance. The deliberate rhythm. Her blood beating in time to his. The soft gasps and moans of mating.

She closed her eyes and gave herself wholly into his keeping. She became his creature. For good or ill. He could destroy her with pleasure and she wouldn't utter a word of protest.

In the dark world behind her eyes, everything was Erith.

This world smelled of Erith and tasted of Erith and sounded like Erith. The sun in this world rose and set in time with his deep, deliberate, controlled movements. Each thrust forged another shackle around her heart.

She knew with fatalistic certainty that when he finished, she'd never be free again.

His body's endless rocking set up a strange turbulence in her blood. The turbulence eddied into swirling whirlpools of sensation as he moved back into her.

"Come for me, Olivia," he said in a voice she didn't recognize, it was so deep and rough. His words shuddered through her and made her muscles tense involuntarily around him.

"Oh, yes," he crooned, still in that gravelly tone. "Do that again."

"This?" She clenched, deliberately this time, and felt reaction shudder through him.

"More." He gasped the command as if his breath failed.

He changed the angle of penetration, going in harder and higher. She juddered under the power and shifted her hands to his shoulders, her only anchor in a dissolving world.

What was happening to her? She'd never felt anything like this before. Every thrust of Erith's body took her further toward some unknown, mysterious crest.

He was shaking as he approached his own crisis. The rhythm changed, became faster, more urgent, harder. In. Out. In. Out. She feared the universe would end if he stopped.

The pressure inside her mounted and mounted. Her muscles contracted even as his thrusts became choppy, wild, uncontrolled. Her spine bowed and she pushed up toward him.

He withdrew then drove back in with a thrust firmer, surer, than any before.

She sobbed aloud, abandoned in the open sea. She'd drown before she reached land. She knew it. The icy waters would suck her down to oblivion and she'd be lost forever.

One boundless moment of waiting.

Then the black wave broke and crashed down upon her.

As darkness overwhelmed her, she screamed.

Vaguely through her shattering peak, she heard him groan on a low, drawn-out note. Then she felt a hot liquid sensation deep within as his seed flooded her womb.

The darkness was blinding, frightening, obliterating. She kept her eyes shut as force blasted her, flinging her away from reality.

It was dark, so dark.

Then behind her closed eyes it wasn't dark at all. The midnight sky exploded into a conflagration of a million stars. A million suns that illuminated a new world.

This new world was beautiful. More beautiful than anything she'd ever seen.

For an eternity she hung suspended among those blazing stars. Earth had no meaning. She left mortality behind. Instead she was a being of star fire and passion.

Shaking with reaction, Erith collapsed against her. Slowly the stars winked out and Olivia drifted back from the outer limits of the sky. Sight and hearing gradually returned.

For a long time neither of them moved.

Erith lay spent and exhausted in her arms. He'd given her such joy. Joy beyond anything she'd ever imagined.

Poignant tenderness filled her. Her hands began to play upon his sweat-sheened back.

He made a sound deep in his throat, like a lion's satisfied growl. When he buried his head in her shoulder, his damp hair pleasantly tickled the side of her neck.

With every second she became more aware of a reality that had faded to nothing in her rapture. The room reeked of sweat and sex. Wind rattled the windowpanes. The fire crackled in the grate. Wrapping her arms more tightly around Erith, she drew him hard against her. They were still joined.

He lifted his head. For a long time she stared into his face, cataloguing his features. The straight forehead, the long nose, the slashing black brows.

His beautiful mouth was relaxed and tender. The gray eyes were clear as she'd never seen them. She felt she saw his soul.

He leaned down and placed a lingering kiss on her brow. A kiss shocking in its sweet innocence after what they'd just shared.

Except what they'd just shared had held a trace of innocence too.

His regard was impossibly somber. "What becomes of us now?"

Chapter 21

"Nothing can become of us," she said with a wrenching sadness she couldn't hide.

Her voice sounded scratchy and unused. As if she'd just screamed loud and hard. With blind ecstasy.

Gently, Erith withdrew from her body. His absence brought a pang of loss. He settled on his back with a long, satisfied sigh and angled his head to watch her out of gleaming silver eyes.

"After that?" He gave a grunt of scornful amusement and shook his head. "Good God, woman, what poppycock you talk."

How foolish she was to hear an echo of her own awe at what she'd discovered in his arms. Confronting the bleak reality of their liaison stung when those glorious moments still sang in her blood.

She strove to rebuild her scattered defenses, to be sensible, practical, unemotional. Impossible when she was wet with Erith's seed and slow waves of pleasure continually rolled through her.

"It doesn't change anything," she said in a flat tone.

What a blatant lie. He'd changed her utterly.

Wary, lonely, proud Olivia Raines, glamorous center of the demimonde, was no more. That ice-hard creature had shattered on a peak of sexual ecstasy beyond anything she could have imagined.

In her place, Erith had left a woman whose muscles were slack with repletion and whose heart was tragically open to hurt.

She dreaded the awkward discussion that surely was coming. Erith would want to gloat now that he'd achieved the goal he set on their first night. He had every right to crow about his victory, but after such transcendence, smugness would make her vulnerable soul cringe.

She didn't want to talk about what had just happened between them. What could she say? Words failed her.

As his body had thrust fully into hers, she'd felt complete for the first time in her life. More, she'd felt that together they soared onto a fiery plane beyond the reach of this world.

Illusion?

Perhaps.

But a stubborn illusion that refused to budge from her dazed mind.

Words would only sully the wonder she'd experienced.

But he didn't boast of his ascendancy over her. Instead his face was grave and unguarded as he stared at her through the vibrant silence. His eyes held no trace of triumph. Rather, she read amazement, appreciation, *peace* in the gray depths.

More dangerous illusion.

His lips tilted into a brief smile that made her ache with longing for what she could never have. She wanted to lie beside him like this forever. She wanted to be his without shame or compulsion. She wanted to be the innocent girl who had grown up on her father's estate, dreaming of one day marrying a man like the Earl of Erith. She wanted a life different from the one she'd been forced to lead.

None of her wishes could ever come true. It was too late for her.

She closed her eyes under a weight of crushing regret.

Dear Lord, she must combat this weakness. She had to fight Erith. But first, and much more difficult, she had to fight herself.

"Come here, Olivia." He shifted to draw her into his chest. His voice, soft as thick velvet, wrapped around her like a warm cloak on a snowy day. "Argue with me in the morning."

It had been a long, fraught night brimming with tumultuous, astonishing emotion, and she was tired and terrifyingly defenseless. His sweet care of her just carved a deeper rift inside her soul.

"I don't want to argue," she said almost tearfully.

"Yes, you do." He ignored her stiffness and curved his big, warm body around hers. "But you won't win."

"I will." Even in her ears, her insistence sounded frail and meaningless.

Cowardly relief filled her when he didn't reply. He tucked her head under his chin, his heat and musky scent surrounding her.

She was fatally stupid to feel so safe when he held her. Erith threatened everything she'd built in her life. But still she shut her eyes and imprinted each detail of this moment on her memory for when he was gone.

As she relaxed, he released his breath in a deep sigh. He brushed her tangled hair back from her face and shifted so they lay more naturally against each other. Such small, commonplace gestures, and each one cut through her barriers to leave her open to destruction.

She buried her nose in the curling black hair on his chest and let his evocative essence seep into her bones. Her eyes ─ered shut before she remembered she had something to

's birthday ball tomorrow night."

"Mmm," he said sleepily, nuzzling the hair at her crown.

She tried to tell her sentimental self she was far too sophisticated to find the action's gentle affection moving. But her sentimental self refused to listen.

Oh, she was in huge trouble.

The sluggish contentment weighting her limbs made it impossible to deny the urge to stay where she was. She forced her wayward mind back to what she tried to say. "So I won't be here."

"Neither will I."

"You have a family obligation?"

"No, I'll be at Montjoy's. With you."

The certainty in his drowsy voice filled her with dark pleasure. "Lord Erith, you should curb this urge always to be in charge."

He settled her more closely. Under the hands she folded on his bare chest, his heart thudded steadily. "My name's Julian."

In a last ditch effort to save a fortress that had surrendered, she ignored the request. "We've never been out in public before."

He laughed softly and his breath tickled the top of her head. Her toes curled with unwilling delight. "Ashamed to be seen with me, Olivia?"

"Not if you mind your manners."

"No guarantee of that." His voice fell lower as he slid toward sleep. "And my name is Julian."

What did this small concession matter when tonight she'd made so many much larger concessions? "Julian."

"My love," he whispered into her hair on a breath of sound so quiet, she pretended she didn't hear.

But she had heard. The two soft words battered at her heart until, powerless to resist, she let them in.

Erith stood on the pavement and let Olivia precede him into the brightly lit town house where Lord Peregrine Montjoy celebrated his thirtieth birthday. From inside, he heard distant but strangely discordant music and loud waves of conversation that rose and fell like stray gusts of wind. It was most definitely a crush.

He remembered the last time he'd entered this house. So much had happened since that night when Olivia exhibited herself dressed as a man. He hoped she'd wear men's clothes again for his pleasure. He hoped she'd wear no clothes for his pleasure. And for hers.

Her uninhibited scream as she'd come last night had resounded like music in his heart all day. The pitch of response she'd attained had been unmistakable. He'd remember that sound until the day he died. And never without a smile.

Just as he would smile to recall her slick heat when he'd taken her. And her tight passage closing hard on him as she embraced him from inside.

Olivia was flickering magic in his arms. Lightning. Flame. An opening flower releasing its perfume to the night air. She'd given him explosive joy and coruscating pleasure. She'd made him feel alive as he hadn't felt in sixteen years.

And the greatest satisfaction of all? Her complete and headlong yielding to the attraction that had simmered between them from the first.

He'd guessed that she hid great wells of passion beneath her cool exterior. But the depth and power of the response he'd drawn from her astonished him. Humbled him. Moved him more than anything he could remember. Volcanic, reckless, unfettered passion. *Thank God*.

He dearly wanted to tempt her into his arms again. Soon. Now.

He hoped she didn't plan to stay long at Montjoy's.

As she climbed the steps to the open front door, he watched the sway of her hips under the voluminous midnight blue cloak. Concealed in the enveloping folds, she was a supremely enticing woman. Tall. Willowy. Mysterious.

Erith's eyelids lowered as he relived what it felt like to have her under him, to have those hips rising in desperate need to meet his.

She looked back over her shoulder to find him loitering. "My lord?"

One sizzling glance so she'd know where his thoughts turned. She had the hood of the cape up, covering her hair, and the torchlight only gave him a shadowy view of her remarkable face. But he'd wager a pile of gold she blushed.

He hid a smile. He got her measure. And her measure fitted him perfectly.

He mounted the steps, took her arm and swept her into the crowded foyer. There was a moment of bustling attention while they removed their outer garments. Erith turned away from the footman to look for Olivia.

And stopped dead.

Any words died on his lips. His heart gave a great lurch against his ribs. His hands clenched into tight fists at his sides. The turbulent ocean of festive noise that surrounded them receded to resonant silence.

He couldn't take his eyes off her.

"By God, I never thought you'd wear it." His voice sounded rusty.

"Neither did I."

She nervously lifted her slender hand with its long, aristocratic fingers. To touch the elaborate ruby collar he'd offered as tribute and that she summarily rejected. Because she wore no man's brand of ownership.

Until now.

The message was plain.

His heart began to pound in great deep beats. She was his. And she'd stay his, whatever the world flung at him.

He strode forward and grabbed her up to press a kiss to her lips. It was quick and hard and a mark of possession. He knew when he lifted his head and stared into her startled tawny eyes that she read it as exactly that.

"My lord . . . " she stammered, and his arm around her slender waist tested her unsteadiness.

Good. He wanted to affect her the way she affected him. After last night, they were equals. He wanted to keep that balance. *He wanted to keep her.*

He tucked the shocking idea away for later consideration.

Vaguely, he became aware that an appalled silence had descended upon the room. He forced his gaze away from her beautiful, astonished, astonishing face.

Everyone in the entrance hall stared aghast at him and Olivia. Montjoy's guests weren't made up purely of the highest in society. There were demimondaines and actors and artists and musicians as well as the ton's wilder element.

Briefly he caught Carrington's devastated expression. The man looked as though every dream had shattered.

She was always meant for me.

Erith saw his boyhood friend acknowledge and accept the wordless message. Then he turned back to his spectacular mistress, slender and graceful in his hold.

"You can let me go now." Olivia's whisper held a delicious tinge of laughter. "We've caused enough scandal."

"I only kissed you," he muttered, even as he took in the incredulity, disapproval, and prurient interest surrounding them.

"I don't kiss," she said gently.

Then very deliberately she stretched up and brushed her mouth over his. He jerked when he felt the hot, taunting sweep of her tongue across the seam of his lips.

A blatant invitation to pleasure or his name wasn't Julian Southwood. He fought the wild surge of passion that heated his blood. He was perilously close to snatching her away from this crowded and ostentatious pile to some private place where he could tumble her unhindered.

Wouldn't that make the damned gossips sit up and pay attention?

The taunting kiss was over before he could respond. She

laughed softly and glided across to the foot of the stairs. In a daze, he followed.

By tomorrow all London would know how utterly in thrall the Earl of Erith was to this alluring witch. And the tragic but unavoidable fact was that all London would be right.

He took her arm again, curling his fingers around the long black silk glove that reached almost to her armpit. The material was warm from her flesh. Another wave of desire slammed through him. He needed to claw back some control or the world would talk about him not only as totally besotted but shamelessly flaunting it.

"You approve of my ensemble?" she asked teasingly as they mounted the marble staircase with its gilt railings and wall of smirking plaster cupids.

"How could I not? You are stunning."

Her silk dress was monastic in its simplicity. Black as night with no distracting adornments of lace or ribbon or embroidery. It was slashed low and square over her bosom, leaving a sweep of creamy skin up to her long neck. Where the ruby collar sparkled like some barbaric badge of slavery.

Then he remembered her guttural, unrestrained cry in his arms last night and realized she wore it as celebration of freedom as much as mark of bewitchment.

When he bought the extravagant and unusual bauble, he'd known it would suit her. He'd had no idea how perfectly.

She wore no other jewelry. With her hair swept up in a severe Grecian style, the savage red glitter of the collar captured all attention.

Unless one noticed the woman wearing it, and how could one not? She was breathtaking. She was a burning flame of enticement. She was love in human form. The flashing rubies and diamonds in the collar were no more brilliant than her tiger eyes.

"Olivia. . . " he began, but they'd reached the top of the stairs and Montjoy rushed out of the ballroom to greet her.

When the fop kissed Olivia on the cheek and embraced

her, there were no gasps of surprise or frowns of censure. But then, Erith suspected most people here knew of the man's proclivities.

It was a louche crowd, cynical, sophisticated, jaded. Prepared to witness anything but a display of genuine passion. How amusing that a simple kiss between a man and woman should shock them to the soles of their dancing pumps.

He stood back and let Olivia and Montjoy enjoy their meeting. Now that he knew how Montjoy had supported Olivia through her darkest days, Erith couldn't resent the fellow.

She'd emerged strong and shining from horrors that would destroy most women. The respectable world might consider her below its notice. He knew better.

She was pure gold to the depths of her courageous soul.

"Erith," Montjoy said coldly, when acknowledging Olivia's companion would mean an obvious slight rather than a slight only the two of them noted.

"Montjoy," Erith said with a bow. "Compliments of the occasion."

Montjoy shot him a killing glare from his large coffee brown eyes. Not for the first time, Erith thought what a spectacularly beautiful young man Montjoy was. No wonder he and Olivia had fooled the greater world into believing them lovers. Her lean, angular beauty and warm leonine coloring provided a perfect foil to Montjoy's dark, Italianate good looks.

"Thank you." Montjoy turned back to Olivia. "Of course, you've saved me all the waltzes?"

Olivia, Erith could see, hadn't missed the silent exchange between the two men. "One perhaps, Perry."

Erith lifted her hand and placed it on his forearm in a proprietory gesture. "I'm sorry, old man, but Miss Raines dances with me exclusively."

"Erith, it's his birthday," she protested, but without withdrawing. Another signal that she accepted him tonight in a way she never had before. His heart leaped with fierce pride. And something else much more dangerous.

The primitive possessiveness that had gripped him when he saw her wearing the collar rose. Very deliberately Erith picked up her hand, placed a kiss upon it, then returned it to his arm. "The waltzes are mine."

"Olivia?" Montjoy looked utterly astonished.

As well he might. Erith already had a good idea of how she'd treated her previous lovers. Like lapdogs she petted or ignored at her whim. And dismissed at the end of the liaisons with hardly a backward glance.

He was determined to be different.

"My waltzes appear to be taken." She gave a husky laugh, and Erith caught a soft note of feminine satisfaction in the sound. "Can you bear to stand up in a contredanse, Perry?"

Montjoy's face paled as he glanced from Olivia to Erith and back again. Abundantly clear were his anger, his helpless bewilderment, and his deep and abiding affection for the woman he addressed. "Oh, hell, Olivia. I told you this would be a disaster."

Olivia's teasing smile faded and Erith glimpsed inner turmoil.

After last night they had to talk. But in pleasure's aftermath, he'd been too tired and too elated to introduce the difficult subject of what their future might hold. He'd been busy with his family all day. And she'd kept him at bay in the coach that brought them to Montjoy's, avoiding anything that smacked of seriousness.

Now he wished to God he'd disregarded the no trespassing signs she'd erected around any topic of importance. The uncertainty was clearly preying on her, just as it preyed on him.

"Perry, I'm sorry," she whispered, the social mask slipping for a revealing second. "I couldn't help it."

Clearly, she was far from easy with what had occurred last night. The need for a discussion became paramount, but

Erith couldn't drag her away in the middle of her best friend's birthday ball. Frustration gnawed at him like hungry rats.

"Oh, sweetheart," Montjoy said with devastating compassion.

"Be happy for me." Her voice cracked. She reached out with her free hand and Montjoy grabbed it. Erith was dismayed to notice that her fingers trembled.

"I can't," Montjoy said in a stark, low voice so nobody around them heard. "When it's all over, I'm here to pick up the pieces."

"This isn't a damned Greek tragedy," Erith snapped.

Montjoy's eyes hardened with hatred as they focused on Erith. "No, it's just a tragedy, you bastard. One you'll walk away from with a shrug, no matter the mess you leave behind."

"Perry, don't," Olivia said in quiet distress. "This is meant to be a happy night."

Montjoy lifted his head with a jerk, as if realizing this wasn't the place for a private discussion. But the look on his face promised that he intended to follow this up when he had the chance.

Erith firmly drew Olivia away and returned that challenge with a haughty glare. "Montjoy, this is none of your concern."

"Olivia is my concern," he said with real venom.

"No, Olivia is *my* concern."

"Stop it, both of you," she hissed. "You're acting like schoolboys. I'm not a bone to be fought over by two dogs. I'm a woman with an independent soul who makes her own decisions."

Erith realized he indeed acted like a cranky mastiff guarding his ewe lamb from a hungry wolf. And whatever he and Montjoy felt about each other, at base, they just wanted the best for her.

His voice softened as he turned to her. "You're right, Olivia. I apologize. Tonight is a celebration."

Erith bowed to her. When he lifted his head, he noticed that astonishment had replaced Montjoy's fury.

"My God," he breathed. "I don't believe it."

"What?" Olivia said blankly.

A genuinely sweet smile lightened Montjoy's expression, and he leaned forward to place a tender kiss on her cheek. Not the happy, excited kisses he'd given her when she arrived but something that conveyed a message, although Erith had no idea what it could be.

"Nothing, darling. I'll come and find you for our dance."

"Perry?"

"Go. You worked so hard to arrange the festivities. The least you can do is enjoy them."

Erith needed no further invitation to end the awkward confrontation. He led her into the huge salon where he'd first seen her. It was almost unrecognizable, decorated like a Russian winter palace with sparkling crystal and swaths of white muslin to emulate snow. The striking style and elegance of the decor were so essentially Olivia that he couldn't help smiling.

All the footmen—handsome to a fault, Erith noted—were garbed in Cossack costume. Montjoy was lucky. The night was warm, so loose white shirts and breeches were perfectly suitable. Shivering servants might add a nice touch of Russian authenticity but they wouldn't weave through the crowd with their current aplomb, bearing trays of champagne glasses or caviar.

There was a balalaika orchestra in one corner, although the buzz of conversation drowned their efforts. Erith heard his name mentioned a few times in passing but he ignored attempts to lure him from Olivia's side.

From the next room, he heard the vague scratch of a more conventional ensemble playing a quadrille. On previous visits he hadn't realized that one wall was actually made up of folding doors, open tonight to allow people to flow between ballroom and salon.

"Don't worry about Perry," Olivia said at his side. Her face was bright with interest as she took in her surroundings.

Erith placed his hand over hers where it rested on his black superfine sleeve. "He's just trying to protect you because he loves you. I admire him for it, much as I resent the fellow's demand on your attention."

She stared at him in shock. Apparently it was a night for people to react with wonder to perfectly normal remarks.

"What?" He echoed Olivia's question to Montjoy.

"Nothing," she mumbled and turned away. "Do you like the frost effect? It was frightfully hard to achieve."

"Olivia," he growled. Something told him she'd been about to say something important.

She turned back with a sigh. "You're a stubborn devil, Erith."

"I am. And I told you to call me Julian."

"Not in public."

A smile that was pure seduction curved her full lips. Her paint was subtle but it highlighted her features in a way Erith found remarkably enticing. Darkened brows and lashes. A touch of rouge to the cheeks. The deep red of her lips. Lips that turned that color naturally when he kissed her. Arousal fermented in his veins.

"Then tell me what you meant."

She shrugged. "I'm always astonished when I hear you speak of love so easily. As though it were a fact of life, like, I don't know, a chair or a table or your carriage drawn up outside waiting to take you to your club."

He smiled back at her, wondering how such a clever woman could be so willfully blind. "Don't be a fool, Olivia. Of course it's real." He tightened his hold over her fingers. "Now, unless you want me to shock every roué and bark of frailty in London by whisking you out of this ballroom for a quick tupping, we need to mingle."

"Mingle," she repeated, but the word clearly had no meaning to her. Her gaze clung to his as though she couldn't bear to look away.

He lifted his hand to tap her chin and gently close her mouth, which was agape. "Yes, mingle. I can wait until later to have my wicked way with you. Barely."

He saw her look around and realize that, just as in the anteroom, they were the cynosure of all eyes. She drew herself up with all the grace and dignity of a princess. The flawless mask of her beauty settled over her face.

She was the queen of this particular world. He should let her reign. The power she exercised over him was a private matter.

He reached out and collected two glasses of champagne from a footman. He handed her one and raised his own. "Let me salute the woman who holds me captive."

"Really? Why then do I feel I'm as much a victim as you?"

He smiled and sipped his drink, hoping the wine's coolness would temper the heat inside him. A vain wish, of course. "Never a victim, Olivia."

He recognized the determined light that entered her beautiful topaz eyes. "Actually, Erith, I'm glad you accompanied me tonight. It will wipe the slate clean between us."

He frowned, something in her tone alerting him to a change in her mood. His instincts shrieked that he wouldn't like whatever was coming.

"What in hell are you talking about?"

"Last night. You won our wager." She turned to face the crowd. "My friends, I have an announcement."

Because so many people observed them, not because her voice made itself heard over the din, the noise level dipped. Even those who hadn't been watching turned curiously to see what the famous, the notorious, the gorgeous Olivia Raines planned for their amusement.

Their eyes glittered with ribald expectation. Olivia always

created a crackle of excitement wherever she went. Because tonight was her first public appearance with her latest lover, the atmosphere was especially vibrant.

Suddenly Montjoy appeared at her side, a concerned expression on his face. "What's the matter, Olivia?"

"I made a promise to Lord Erith."

Erith's every muscle tensed with disbelief and denial. "What is this?"

She couldn't mean what he thought she did. She must know they'd moved on since that stupid bet. After last night, surely, surely she knew. He reached forward to grab her arm.

Shaking free, she dismissed him with an imperious flash of her topaz eyes. "You know what I'm doing. Paying my dues."

She passed Montjoy her glass with a grace that made Erith's breath catch, then turned to him. The silence in the room resonated with expectation. Even the Russian band had stopped playing, although the dance orchestra in the next room continued to saw away at their banal tune.

"When I accepted Lord Erith's carte blanche, we made a wager."

Good God, this was bloody madness. She must know he didn't care a tinker's damn about the bet.

But he looked deep into her eyes and realized her self-respect forced her to fulfill what she saw as an obligation. How odd to realize this infamous wanton was the most honorable person he'd ever met. She took his breath away.

Even so, he couldn't under any circumstances let her debase herself. No matter what outlandish notions she had of the demands of honor.

"Olivia, no," he breathed in horror, still trying to stave off a full-scale scandal by keeping his voice soft. "Don't do it."

His efforts went for nothing. She began to sink down. The crowd edged forward, so agog with curiosity that the air bristled.

"A wager is sacrosanct." She spoke calmly, as if this abomination she was about to perpetrate made perfect sense. "Surely you learned that with your mother's milk, Erith."

"Olivia, for God's sake, the collar is enough," he said urgently.

"I promised."

"Devil take you, stop." Recklessly he shoved his champagne at Montjoy, not caring whether the effete lordling caught it or not. He snatched her arms and with brute force alone held her upright. He hissed at her through clenched teeth. "I don't want this. I never wanted this. Even at the start."

Her expression was puzzled. She hung suspended from his hands. "Erith, I lost the wager. You know I lost."

The room burst into a flurry of whispers and shocked gasps. The crowd's avid curiosity was almost a physical force.

"You didn't lose. Nobody lost. Nobody won." He lowered his voice to save them at least some portion of inevitable gossip. "I don't care about the bloody wager. The wager was only a stratagem to make you stay. You were about to leave and it was all I could think of to stop you going."

"I made the bet in good faith. I said I'd go on my knees to you."

Frantically he forced his mind back to that long ago night when he'd been half insane with the need to keep her. He couldn't believe even then, when every word, every gesture, had been a power play, that he'd insisted on her degradation. Her pride was one of the things he'd always admired about her.

He bit out the words, desperate to end this hideous scene. "I said I'd go on my knees to you. You were merely to admit to me that you surrendered. I never intended your public humiliation. Never."

Brief uncertainty crossed her features. "You wanted me to proclaim that you'd mastered me."

"I haven't bloody mastered you. Haven't you worked that out yet? Nobody's mastered anybody. I don't want a slave. I want a lover."

Her jaw took on a stubborn line, but at least she finally stood on her own two feet. She trembled with chagrin. "You wanted me to yield to you."

"Never like this. Any yielding on your part was purely between us."

He looked around and realized the crowd's interest was more virulent than ever. He had to do something to end this confounded embarrassing scene.

He raised his voice. "Miss Raines wishes to let you all know that after July she will no longer be gracing London's ballrooms. She has granted me the incomparable privilege of agreeing to travel as my companion to Vienna when I return to my posting."

Shock whitened her face, leaving her eyes huge and startled. The subtle rouge stood out in two red lines along her cheekbones. He saw similar amazement on the faces around them. Immediately replaced by speculation and puzzlement and in Montjoy's case open distress.

Quicker minds would already question why she needed to make such a dramatic announcement of her intentions and why she'd looked like she was about to fall to her knees. Erith gritted his teeth with futile anger. There wasn't much he could do about it. The Vienna idea had been the only thing that dropped into his mind at the crucial moment.

Montjoy stared at her in consternation. "Olivia? What does this mean? Is it true?"

"N-No, Perry," she stammered without shifting her bewildered focus from Erith's face.

"Yes," he said implacably. "Now dance with me, Olivia. For Christ's sake, this bloody mess has gone far enough."

Almost roughly, he dragged her into his arms. He lowered his voice, trying to shock her from her stasis. He was sick to his stomach at having to conduct his private life in full view.

Within the space of an hour he and Olivia had provided enough grist to keep the gossip mills grinding for weeks.

He wanted to grab her away from this decadent horde. He wanted her to himself. But a sudden departure would only worsen the scandal.

"If you're so keen to go on your knees to me, do it later when I can take advantage of your position," he muttered furiously, at the end of his patience.

At his earthy suggestion, her eyes sparked gold fire and the blood returned to her cheeks. Satisfied he'd brought her back to herself, he whirled her through the heaving crowd and into the ballroom, where a waltz started.

Chapter 22

$\mathcal{L}$ ord Erith ushered Olivia into the candlelit bedroom. He closed the door and leaned back on it, folding his arms over his broad chest. He looked as indestructible as a basalt monolith.

Smothering her nerves under outrage, she whirled to face him. "You meant it when you made that wager."

With jerky, violent movements she stripped off her long black gloves. She tossed them onto her dressing table, not caring if they knocked the porcelain pots of cosmetics to the floor.

She didn't even know why it was so important to fulfill the terms of his wager. Perhaps she needed to remind herself once and for all that the earl was a client and she his whore, paid to do his bidding.

When he prevented her proclaiming his victory, he'd changed the terms between them and left her thwarted and lost and helpless.

Words she hadn't applied to herself since she was fifteen.

Words she refused to apply to herself now.

"I meant I'd do anything to stop you walking out this door." He stared at her under his heavy lids. His gaze revealed only a narrow glint of bright silver between thick lashes. "I still would."

Her emotions snarled in an impossible tangle. Lately she didn't understand herself at all. And it was utterly Erith's fault. With futile vehemence, she wished she'd never met him.

She'd always thought she knew what he wanted. The acknowledgment of her surrender.

If he didn't want that, what did he want?

She could hardly bear to conjure an answer.

Olivia's belly cramped with rage. She was confused. She was frustrated. And beneath rage, confusion, and frustration, fear lurked like a cold whisper of coming winter.

Scowling, she began to pace the room, black silk skirts rustling around her. She was so stirred up, she had to move or she'd explode. "Stop it."

He didn't straighten from his watchful slouch. "Stop what?"

"Saying things like that. Heartless rakes should be . . . heartless rakes."

He didn't answer her. She came to a trembling halt and braced one shoulder against a bedpost, curling her hand around the polished wood. To calm the raging storm inside her, she sucked a deep breath through her teeth.

She'd felt powerful when she put on the magnificent ruby collar. She'd even felt powerful when she chose to kneel to him. After all, the decision was hers, and her obeisance reclaimed who she was. A proud woman wholly separate from this lover who refused to let her follow the tired, safe patterns of her existence.

"Last night—" She stopped. Discussing the glories of last night wasn't the best tactic to shore up her defenses.

For one blazing moment he met her eyes. Turmoil and determination darkened the gray. Then he sighed and studied the richly colored Turkish carpet at his feet as if it held the answer to the world's deepest questions.

Her fingers tightened convulsively around the tall mahogany column. "The arrangement was that I publicly acknowledged you as my master."

"No, it wasn't." He made a slashing gesture with one hand and sent her a quelling glare. For the first time, his voice held a thread of temper. "Dear God, I can't remember the terms of that damned bet. I doubt we even got to specifics. I can't remember and I don't care. I certainly never demanded you on your knees in front of half bloody London. The collar was enough. More than enough."

"You wanted my surrender," she said stubbornly.

All day she'd berated herself for becoming so fatally vulnerable to a man. She knew men in all their selfishness and arrogance and weakness and unthinking cruelty. Erith at base was just the same as any other male.

She had spent every waking hour steeling herself against him.

Then he'd come to collect her for Perry's party. Without a peep of resistance, she'd immediately fallen prey to his attraction.

"Devil take it, stop talking about surrender," Erith said. "This isn't a war between two feudal empires. It's a love affair, for pity's sake. I wanted the woman I desired to desire me. I wanted you to acknowledge the attraction between us. I wanted you to enjoy sex. Private goals, all of them."

She flung away from the bed and resumed her pacing, trying to outrun what he said. "And what's all this nonsense about dragging me to Vienna? Are you mad?"

"It seems the obvious solution." His brief flash of anger had vanished as quickly as it appeared. "Especially after last night."

His calmness only fed her resentment. "Last night means nothing! We had a bargain which you're only too ready to disregard when it doesn't suit you. I'm your mistress until you leave England. That's what we agreed before we embarked on this disaster of a liaison."

"It's not a disaster." He was so still, he could have been made of stone. "It's a miracle."

With an ominous feeling tightening her chest, she came to quivering rest on the opposite side of the room. Her heart galloped with premonitory fear. Cold sweat prickled at her nape.

His expression became even graver. "And everything changed when I fell in love with you."

Erith heard his words crash into the taut, combative silence. Olivia flinched as though he'd struck her. All trace of color fled her face so her remarkable bone structure seemed carved from cold marble.

"No . . . " she breathed in horror. "No, you can't. You don't mean it."

Sharp pain stabbed his gut at her immediate denial. It had been so devilish hard to say the words.

She sidled away as though his love were a contagious disease. Only bumping into the wall behind her broke her retreat. She flattened her palms against the elegant blue and yellow stripes of the wallpaper.

"Of course I mean it." He kept his voice soft. He didn't want to frighten her further.

Because fear was her principal response.

What the hell else had he imagined? That difficult, proud Olivia would throw herself into his arms with joyful abandon and tell him that she loved him back, that she wanted to stay with him forever?

Not in any real world he lived in.

In spite of his earlier avowal, he knew that this was indeed war between them. He'd just fired the first shot over her lines. He couldn't expect her to raise the white flag before any casualties had fallen.

Because he had no doubt she meant to fight him on this, fight as she'd never fought before.

Which didn't prevent her virulent rejection from making him feel like she'd stamped his heart to gory shreds beneath her heel.

Stubbornly, he refused to retract his declaration. He'd acknowledged his feelings unwillingly and painfully. He'd loved her well before he recognized the fact. After so many years running from any hint of powerful emotion, that wasn't surprising.

As he'd sat alone in the salon yesterday, waiting for Olivia to come home, before she tied him up like an animal, he'd reluctantly faced a number of inconvenient realities. Including the stark truth that he was hopelessly in love with his mistress.

Ever since he'd met Olivia, she'd created an unprecedented storm in his life. An agitated melee of reactions he hadn't suffered in years.

Desire. Jealousy. Anguish. Anger. Possessiveness. Tenderness. Passion. Joy.

Only love explained his extreme emotion during his precipitate ride to Kent. And after. When he'd fruitlessly burned to kill her tormenters. When he'd have taken every ounce of her pain on himself if it gave her one moment's ease.

Erith wasn't a stupid man. And he'd been in love before. He knew what this soul-deep level of turmoil signified.

Nothing but love could bring him to a pass where he was willing to surrender his dominance in the bedroom.

Nothing but love could make him open his vulnerable heart to her now.

She'd changed him forever. She'd revived a dead man, shown him the world still held hope and possibility.

He wanted her to become part of his life. Not just until July. Always.

"You love me, you say?" Her lips twisted in a cynical

smile, but the corners of her mouth quivered. "I've heard those words so often. Many men have imagined themselves in love with me."

"That doesn't change how I feel." Any anger at her jeering died when he saw how she trembled. The brilliant rubies and diamonds in the collar flashed and scintillated with the convulsive movement.

Bitter resentment glittered in her eyes. She continued in the same ugly, scoffing tone. "You just love the fact that you made me come when nobody else could. It feeds your unending vanity."

She was no fool, his beloved. And she knew where to stick the knife to inflict the most damage. Every cruel word felt like it sliced another layer of skin off his hide.

His heart beat with a crazy, wayward rhythm. He fought to keep his voice calm while chill anguish coiled in his belly. "You think I see myself as some rescuing knight and you as a helpless victim?"

"Don't you?

With an impatient movement, he tugged his tight black coat off and flung it over her dressing stool. He was so choked with emotion that its constriction was unbearable. "No."

The simple answer seemed to leave her at a loss.

Oh, Olivia, my darling . . .

She hated him for stripping away her defenses. He recognized the safe cocoon numbness provided. Except eventually the heart trapped inside the sealed haven started to perish.

Not a trace of color remained in her lovely face. "I'm not staying," she said through stiff lips.

"Yes, you are." He began to unbutton his waistcoat. From somewhere certainty, slow and sweet as syrup, seeped into his veins. By heaven, he meant to win this battle. "If you really wanted to leave, you'd have done it days ago."

"We had a wager."

"Devil take it, you didn't stay because of a wager. You make a damned good show of caring about the bloody bet. A pity it doesn't convince. I doubt it even convinces you, although you certainly give it a good try."

Her expression tightened at his scornful words. Grimly he waited for her to argue with his conclusions. Instead she raised her chin.

"If not for the wager, why am I here?" Sarcasm added a harsh edge to her voice. "For the sake of your *beaux yeux*?"

"I know why you stay." He shucked the heavy French silk waistcoat off and tossed it after his coat. He breathed in, gathered all his courage. And took the greatest risk of all. *"You stay because you love me."*

She flung her head back and laughed. The sneering sound echoed around the room.

"Your conceit is beyond belief. I don't love men. I take them to my bed, I service them and I despise them." All trace of amusement left her face and she regarded him as if she loathed him. "All of them."

She was so hurt and so brave, and he wished to God he could make this easy for her. But it was impossible. If the way to her salvation meant she cut his heart to ribbons, well, so be it.

He desperately wanted to take her in his arms. But touching her now would be a huge mistake. She was strung so tightly, she might shatter if he pushed her too far.

"You don't despise Perry. You don't despise Leo." He paused, watching uncertainty flicker in her beautiful eyes. "And you don't despise me."

"Yes, I do," she said without conviction.

"Liar." He tugged his shirt over his head and let it drift to the ground.

"That's enough, Lord Erith." She snatched up her skirts with a flourish and marched toward the door. She walked like a queen to the guillotine, proud, straight, defiant.

Lonely.

He caught her arm as she strutted past. He hated the pleading note that crept into his voice, but he couldn't help it. "Don't run away just because you're afraid, Olivia."

"I'm not afraid!" she snapped, even as she quaked under his hand like a newborn foal. The eyes she focused on him were glassy with terror.

"Olivia, I'm afraid too." His pride revolted at the admission. "Don't go."

"No one will ever control me again," she spat, trying to wrench away. "I will never place my fate in a man's hands. I swore that at fifteen, and it's a promise I'll never break."

For a brief, brilliant moment, he'd thought he could find words to convince her to stay. He'd thought he could find words to make her admit what she felt.

But clearly and devastatingly for a man whose words were his currency, she wasn't listening.

Or there were no words.

Sorrow ate at his gut. He released her with a gesture of apology. He knew what freedom meant to her. He couldn't bring himself to curtail it.

Anyway, what would compulsion gain? He didn't want a reluctant lover. "Go, then," he said hoarsely.

She settled a startled gaze on him. "You won't let me."

"Of course I will. You're free."

"Yes, I'm free." She sounded ridiculously uncertain. Again Erith saw a trace of the girl she'd been before a cruel world crushed her innocence.

He stepped away from the door, his every dream crumbling to ruin. How bitter to remember that only seconds ago he'd thought to prevail against her anguish and fear.

Except she hadn't gone yet.

Nor, he realized with a sudden rally of hope, had she denied she loved him.

It took every shred of nerve to test his supposition. He leaned across and opened the door. "Good-bye, Olivia."

"You insist on my complete surrender."

He spoke with a hint of asperity. "Anyone looking at us would know I'm on my knees here, so any triumph is yours."

"So I win if I leave?"

She willfully misunderstood him. Well, two could play at that game. He pushed the door wide. "If you believe that, go."

Her eyes were blank as she stared at the gap in the doorway. Her face was stony. She looked like her soul had fled her body.

She took a step toward the door.

His heart crashed to a shuddering halt. Bloody hell. Bloody, bloody, bloody hell. His rash gamble to keep her hadn't paid off.

Another step. Soon she'd be in the corridor.

Then out of the house. And out of his life.

His hands curled into tight fists at his sides as he battled the urge to drag her back. He couldn't force her to anything. Too many men in her life had done that.

"This is a trick." She sounded like she accused him of murder. "You'll come after me."

"Is that what you want?"

"Of course not," she snapped. "You deceive yourself if you imagine you have some significance. You're just one more keeper."

"Just because you've had a string of men in your bed doesn't mean you're unworthy of love, my darling."

Her bravado vanished in an instant and he saw through to her essential wretchedness. "Yes, it does," she said flatly.

"I've had a string of lovers in my bed as well, Olivia. Does that make me unworthy?"

"Of course it doesn't," she said with an emphasis that lit a spark of hope in his poor battered heart. "You're a man. It's different."

A sardonic smile curled his lips. "Can this be the great Olivia Raines? The brilliant, gorgeous, headstrong woman who's beaten every fellow in the ton at his own game?"

"I've never beaten you."

"No, just as I've never beaten you. Don't you think there's something marvelous in our equality?"

"We're not equal!" she snarled. "You're an earl and I'm a whore."

He could only speak the truth etched on his soul. "I'm a man in love."

"Stop it!" She lifted shaking hands to cover her ears. She closed her eyes as if she couldn't bear to look at him. "Stop it, stop it, stop it!"

He spread his hands in a gesture of helpless longing and spoke from the depths of his aching heart. "Stop what, Olivia? Loving you? I can't. You're in my blood. You may as well tell me to cut off my right arm. You're heaven and earth to me. How could I not love you?"

When she lowered her hands, he was appalled to see tears shimmering in the eyes that met his. "No good can come of this."

The words, and even more, her continuing presence, were an admission of sorts. With a decisive gesture, he tugged the door shut. She wasn't going anywhere tonight.

Chapter 23

*E*rith watched Olivia start at the sharp snick of the door. He waited for some protest, if only for her pride's sake. But she remained silent, her great, wary eyes focused on him.

She still trembled and her pale face and glazed stare told him she teetered on the brink of exhaustion. He knew this peace was a hiatus. But only a man completely lacking compassion would compel further concessions now, beyond the tacit one she made by not marching out.

When he reached for her hand, she didn't resist, but didn't respond either. Gently, he drew her toward the bed. He wanted to cherish her. He just hoped to hell she'd let him.

"Stop fighting, Olivia," he said softly.

"I don't know how." She came with him readily enough, although he knew it was cooperation born in desolation, not joy.

"Trust me." Last night he thought he'd won that battle. He discovered now that he had to fight it all over again. His only

weapons were his sensual skills. He intended to exploit them
to their fullest.

"I'm not coming to Vienna," she said, even as she stood
beside the bed and let him begin on the long row of black,
silk-covered buttons down her back. Weary defiance tempered the bleak numbness of her tone.

"We'll talk about it tomorrow," he said softly. He flicked
open button after button, revealing her white back and shoulders above the black silk shift and corset. Leaning forward,
he kissed the point of a shoulder revealed under the flimsy
strap of her chemise.

"You're the most frustrating man," she said without venom.

He nipped her where he'd kissed her. He heard her breath
catch. She wasn't immune to him physically. Far from it.
At least that part of last night's victory was still his, thank
God.

The shimmering black gown slithered to the ground. Erith
held her hand while she stepped out of the billowing skirts.
For the moment she accepted his touch. This might be a concession purely of weariness, but he was in no mood to argue
with his fortune.

When she angled her neck toward him, he couldn't resist
the invitation. He kissed her hard on the tendon that ran up
from her shoulder. She'd have a mark there tomorrow. He
was heathen enough to delight in the knowledge that she'd
wear his brand.

His campaign against her descended to guerrilla warfare.
She'd refused to accept his love through words. He'd make
her accept it through passion.

He already guessed her strategy. She thought to make him
forget love by transporting him into a paradise of sensuality.
How misguided she was. His overwhelming desire was an
indelible part of his love.

Her haunting scent surrounded him. Soft and smoky with
arousal. He curled his hands around her and cupped her
breasts through the delicate material of her shift. His every

touch told her how he treasured her, should she choose to read his meaning.

She drew a shuddering breath. Her chest rose under his hands, filling his palms with sweet female flesh. He brushed his thumbs across her peaking nipples.

Tonight he planned to linger on her pleasure. Show her there was more than she'd already experienced, sublime as that had been.

She gave a voluptuous shiver. "Mmm."

The deep sound thrummed through him and made him harden.

"I need to undress you," he whispered.

"What's stopping you?" She didn't sound nearly as tired as she had. Nor as disinterested. She raised her arms above her head and twined them around his neck, pushing her breasts up into his hands.

"You are."

"Mmm."

She rubbed her back sensuously against him. He couldn't stop himself pressing forward to rest his erect cock between the cheeks of her buttocks. He tilted his hips, luxuriating in the hard slide against her firm flesh.

Slowly. Slowly.

She pushed back uncertainly, then with greater purpose. The old, familiar dance. Forward, back, forward, back. Delicious friction. Endless torment because clothing prevented ultimate connection.

So gently that it was a caress in itself, she slid her arms down, trailing her hands across his cheeks. The exquisite tenderness made his gut twist, and he buried his face in her hair with a groan. It took him a few lost moments to realize she rucked her chemise higher.

"I want to do this right," he choked out in halfhearted protest.

The wench laughed. At him, the presumptuous baggage.

The sound vibrated through him like a low note from a cello. "Oh, you'll do it right."

No trace remained of the lost, frantic, angry woman who had threatened to desert him. He rejoiced in the return of her spirit. He didn't want to defeat her. He wanted her to come to him as his equal. In everything.

Her throaty voice made hot blood swirl in his veins. Her chemise was above her thighs now although her drawers still formed a filmy barrier between him and where he thirsted to be.

The air was heavy with female musk. She was more than ready for him. With suddenly ruthless hands, he gripped her slender waist and swung her around so she faced the bedpost.

"Hold on hard."

She grabbed the column, anchoring herself. She bent over so her rump tilted at a wanton angle. The transparent black chemise slowly slid back around her hips.

Roughly, he tore at the fastenings of his trousers. His rod sprang free, hard and demanding. With unsteady hands, he shoved her shift aside so he could rip her drawers off. He growled through the sound of shredding silk.

Enchanted, he paused, staring at the taut pale globes of her buttocks. She was beautiful everywhere. He needed an eternity to worship her as she deserved.

He bent to place a fervent kiss in the center of each perfect cheek. This close, her arousal was headier than wine.

"Hurry, Erith." She quivered with need.

He nipped at one buttock and saw how even that much sensation made her quake. She was very close to crisis. If he wanted, he could make her come through touch alone.

But he was too selfish for that. He wanted to be inside her. He wanted to know she was completely his.

He loved her. He needed to prove that to her in the most primal way.

She might refuse to recognize that his every touch was a

declaration of love. But that didn't change the truth of his feelings. His hands were tender as he bent her toward the mattress. The beast within exulted at taking her like lion mating with lioness, or stallion with mare.

"Spread your legs," he said in a raw voice.

To his joy, she opened before him like a rose. She was wet and swollen and ripe for his taking. He clasped her hips and tipped her toward him.

Slowly, almost reverently, he pushed forward. A moment's luscious resistance then the head entered her. Her muscles clenched to draw him deeper. But he fought the alluring pull.

She moaned and pressed back. He inched deeper and she clasped him more tightly. Lightning sizzled through his veins. His heart pounded with furious excitement. Incendiary heat blasted him.

He moved gradually, feeling each tiny adjustment she made to take him. She was so wet and hot that the urge to thrust was nigh unbearable. His fingers flexed on her hips. His head throbbed with the strain of control. His cock felt harder than a brass cudgel.

Still he held himself back. Kept his penetration slow.

"Julian . . . " His name was forced from her throat. Her breath emerged in erratic sobs. She jerked back, taking more of him. "Don't tease me."

He slid one arm around her waist to change the angle of her stance. He surrounded her completely. Above, below, inside.

"Now," he groaned.

"Now." The sound ended on a low keen as he pushed fully into the moist, mysterious depths.

Against his forearm, her belly quivered. Her interior muscles relaxed and tensed in a tantalizing rhythm that set off fiery sparks behind his eyes. He struggled for breath, his lungs heaving.

She ground her hips, taking him even deeper. Another groan escaped him and he leaned over her, pressing his chest to her back, wanting this sublime joining to last forever. He pressed a hard kiss to her shoulder.

"Julian," she sighed. His name fell from her lips as naturally as a thrush sang in the sweet spring.

The sound shattered any restraint. He drew out, relishing the cling of her inner passage, and thrust back to the hilt. She juddered under the force and he tightened his grip. The cheeks of her buttocks were taut against his belly.

"Yes," she whispered, straining back as if she couldn't get enough of him. "Again."

He withdrew and plunged, feeling her brace for his thrust. He felt how he stretched her, shaping her to him. He closed his eyes and let vibrant, velvet darkness flood his mind.

She circled her hips, changing the pressure, the angle, the feeling.

Oh, yes.

He began to work in and out. Filling his ears with her panting sighs and whimpers, giving her no quarter. He knew she wanted none.

Her climax approached on a quivering wave. She trembled on the brink. But she wasn't there yet. He beat back the overwhelming urge to lose himself. The effort set his jaw so hard, it almost cracked.

Last night he'd made her come once. Tonight, he intended to sate her completely.

He pulled out almost completely, luxuriating in her long moan. Then as he jerked forward, he ruthlessly lowered one hand to touch her hard between the legs.

With a guttural cry, she dissolved into ecstasy. Her spasms squeezed him, milked him, possessed him. Her back bowed until her shoulders butted his chest. Battling for restraint, even through the tempestuous heights of her passion, he rode out the clenching contractions.

Demons tortured him with hot pincers, devils gyrated in his gut, but still he held back. He fought with blind stubbornness, tensing his muscles until they ached.

Tonight, he would give her everything.

This was for her. This was the gift of his love.

She seemed to shudder forever. Her husky cries and ragged breathing tortured him, made him frantic to unleash himself. Her body closed hard on his, searing him with desire.

Just before he crossed the line to madness, just before he reached the final limits of will, her quaking fury ebbed.

He felt her body change, soften. She became boneless in his arms, sagging like a silk banner on a windless day. Her breath rattled in her lungs as she fought for air. Her pleasure had been volcanic.

Exhausted, he cradled her against his chest and buried his face in the warm thickness of her hair, which tumbled from its formal style. His hand slid to her waist to hold her through the fading tremors.

"Julian," she said again.

He'd never tire of the sound of her voice saying his name.

"My darling." He brushed aside her hair and placed a tender kiss on her nape.

She was damp with perspiration. He breathed deeply, savoring her satisfaction. The sweetest scent in the world.

Aftershocks still vibrated through her. The clenching teased mercilessly at his control. He beat back the urge to move, to bring himself to completion.

"I never knew," she said on a sobbing gasp.

She stole his heart anew when she reached down to lace her fingers through his where he held her. The touch conveyed a tenderness her unbridled passion hadn't revealed. The touch told him she felt more at this moment than animal satiation.

As did he. By God, he adored her. Words of love choked in his throat. Although before the night was over, he'd make her listen, damn it.

He felt her stir from her daze of replete exhaustion. "Julian, you didn't . . . "

"Come?"

How delightful that she was a little shy. He smiled into the damp tendrils of hair that clung to her neck and tangled in the ruby collar.

"You're smiling." The hand that rested upon his started a gentle stroking that harmonized perfectly with the way her passage caressed his hard length.

"How do you know?"

"I hear it in your voice. It's nice." She sounded sleepy. After that cataclysmic climax, he wasn't surprised.

He adjusted the angle of his hips to settle more deeply. He desperately wanted to move and possess. He would soon. But for the moment, he couldn't bear to shatter this precious intimacy. There had been times tonight when he'd wondered if he would ever hold her again. He intended to savor every instant of this hard-won closeness.

One of her hands still curled around the bedpost. "I like having you inside me."

"I like being inside you." He tensed and thrust very softly. She quivered in helpless response.

He closed his eyes and held her. Basking in her swift, overwhelming reaction. Her sensitivity to every touch astonished him.

"Stand up and I'll undress you."

She shifted without protest. Each movement changed her body's pressure around his. He closed his eyes and prayed for strength. In the darkness behind his eyeballs, wild lights flashed as he struggled against giving himself to her the way she'd just given herself to him.

Before she straightened completely, he withdrew. She smothered a whimper.

Perhaps he'd been too rough. He was a big man. Long and thick. And he hadn't been considerate. He'd been too hungry for her.

He curved his arms around her shoulders and nuzzled the tender flesh below her ear. "Did I hurt you?"

"No." Her breath caught as he scraped his teeth across her skin. Then with more emphasis, "No."

"I wasn't kind."

She reached up and curled her hands around his wrists. "I won't break."

He felt her inhale, and she rubbed her head against his upper arm. The gesture's natural affection made his yearning heart falter.

"Your passion is exciting," she said. "You have no idea how desirable it makes me feel."

"Every man desires you."

"They desire the courtesan. You desire *me*." She shook her head and her hair brushed softly across his forearms.

Reluctantly he drew away, and she gave a soft mew of disappointment. He began to pluck at the strings on her corset, black silk embroidered with trailing red roses. His hands were all thumbs. No wonder. Every drop of blood in his body drained to one organ.

"Damn this infernal garment. Do you care if I tear it?"

"It's very pretty and it cost you a fortune." Her voice bubbled with amusement.

He loved her when she teased him. He loved her when she was serious.

Oh, hell, he just loved her.

"I'll buy you another one." With a sudden savage movement, he grabbed the sides and tore the corset. Her gasp chimed with the rending of the material.

"Stand still," he whispered. The chemise was pretty too, embroidered to match the corset.

"I can just take it off." Her voice was unsteady with a mixture of laughter and shock.

"Why stop when I'm ahead?"

He hooked his hand into the back of the chemise and ripped down hard. The silk was so fine, it split with a whisper, to reveal the smooth line of her back down to her lissome waist.

"Why indeed?" she said with a touch of irony, and shrugged the ruined garment from her body.

"You are indeed a glory to behold," he murmured, running his hands down her spine. Her skin was warm and satiny under his touch.

When he turned her to face him, she placed her palms flat on his chest. He rested his hands on hers, mimicking the way she'd taken his hand when they bent over the bed.

He looked down at her body. The perfect jut of her breasts, the long line of torso, the flat stomach, the sinuous hips. The tawny curls that hid the treasure of her sex.

Between them, his cock rose hard and insistent. She slid one hand down to encircle his engorged organ. Fire blazed through him, blinding him. He shuddered and pressed into her hand.

She kissed him, sucking his lower lip into her mouth and nipping softly. Her hold tightened as she opened her mouth over his. He shook as he fought the excess of pleasure.

He dragged his mouth from hers but only far enough to place a flurry of glancing kisses across cheek and nose and chin. He wanted to devour her. He wanted to make her part of him eternally.

"Get on the bed," he said hoarsely.

"Still giving out orders?" Her fingers continued their devilish dance on his hot flesh.

"You love it." He grabbed her by the waist and swung her onto the sheets. She landed with a bounce that made her breasts jiggle

"I might not mind it." Her voice was breathless with laughter, surprise, and excitement. "Occasionally. Once in a blue moon. Just to keep you quiet."

He laughed and knelt over her. "No, you love it."

You love me.

With every moment, he became surer of that. She might never say the words but each action was eloquent of her feelings.

"You're such a conceited devil."

He nudged his way between her parted legs. She linked her arms around his neck in ready welcome. How could she ever have believed herself cold? She burned like an eternal fire.

He forced words through his pounding arousal. "Next time I do this, I'm going to take my time. Show you why I'm the toast of Vienna."

"I'll believe that when I see it." Her taunt ended on a moan as he slid into her with one powerful thrust.

Lifting himself on his elbows, he stared down into her face. Her head tilted back and her lips parted as she fought for breath. Her eyes fluttered shut and moisture sheened her brow and cheeks.

She was the most beautiful thing he'd ever seen.

He shifted his hips, pressing deep, seeking the sweetest place. She moaned again, lost in a dark world of desire.

He set the rhythm, each time testing the limits. Each time testing her bliss. Her pattern of sighs told him when he found what he wanted.

"Look at me, Olivia," he said gruffly.

She opened her eyes and focused on his face. Her pupils were huge, almost swallowing the rich topaz. Her lashes were damp and tangled with tears. No trace of the teasing coquette remained. Instead he felt like he looked into her soul.

The earth-shattering honesty of what he felt for her shook him to the core. She was his true match. She was meant for him. She would be his forever. His body claimed her eternally.

"Don't hold back this time," she whispered. "I want you completely."

"I wanted to pleasure you all night," he said roughly as he withdrew and returned, withdrew and returned. "I wanted to show you everything."

"Just show me you want me." She lifted her knees to cradle him between her thighs.

"I want you, Olivia," he said on one last mighty thrust. He couldn't dam the surge of his seed. Just as he couldn't dam the fatal words any longer. *"I love you."*

The ragged declaration faded into a deep groan as he released his essence into her womb. White light dazzled him and the thunder in his ears overwhelmed all other sound. The stark truth of what he felt for her flung him beyond time and place.

Her fingernails scored his back as she attained her own peak. Her body tightened, draining him of every last drop of love. Even when he finished, her passage clenched around him as if she couldn't bear the radiant communion to end.

Exhausted, he collapsed, burying his head in her shoulder. Struggling for breath. Struggling to return to a world that had changed utterly in the last seconds.

"I love you, Olivia," he repeated in a shaking voice.

"And I love you, Julian."

Even through the wild tumult in his blood, he couldn't mistake the bitter, despairing defeat in her voice.

Chapter 24

*I*t was early evening when Olivia returned from her weekly visit to Leo. Spring had finally arrived, and she mounted the steps to the York Street house in daylight.

Two weeks had passed since that extraordinary night of anguish, conflict, and ecstasy when she and Julian had confessed their love. Two weeks of reveling in a passion beyond her wildest imaginings. Two weeks of relinquishing her battle to hide what the earl meant to her. Two weeks of fatalistically recognizing she was helpless to stop him breaking her heart.

On a deep river of sexual satisfaction, she floated unresisting to her destruction. A woman like her couldn't fall in love. A woman like her couldn't leave herself vulnerable the way she was vulnerable to Julian. Those were the inescapable lessons of a courtesan's existence.

This brittle happiness would exact its price. But dear God, not yet, not yet.

The very fragility of her poignant rapture only made her

treasure each shining moment more. Every day strengthened a reckless determination to seize what joy she could.

She knew his plan to take her to Vienna hadn't altered. The argument about that was postponed, not forgotten. While she believed he did indeed love her for now, old betrayals made her chary of committing her future so completely to a man. Any man.

Even Julian.

How on earth could she go with him? Her life was here. Leo was here. She didn't want to trail the Earl of Erith around the Continent, her only role that of complacent mistress. She didn't want an existence of waiting for her lover to come home from a world where he belonged but she had no place.

She lifted her chin with a gesture of scornful defiance. The future could go to the Devil. She refused to worry about tomorrow until it howled outside for her blood. She'd rather think about Julian making love to her last night, slowly, tenderly, with breathtaking skill. No wonder the ladies in Vienna and Paris and Constantinople had sighed after him. She was inclined to sigh after him herself.

When she entered the house she'd always think of as her private paradise, the butler approached with a troubled expression. "You have a visitor, madam."

"Who is it, Latham?" She removed her pelisse, gloves, and bonnet and checked her hair in the hallway mirror. The day was blustery and she looked windswept after her long walk across the fields with Leo.

"A young lady. She wouldn't give her name."

Surprise made her pause. Young *ladies* didn't call on a notorious courtesan. She gathered from his serious demeanor that Latham used the word advisedly.

"Where is she?" Olivia tried to smooth the worst of the untidiness but it was a losing battle.

"In the library, madam."

"I should go and change." She was dusty from the journey

and her skirt was stained after brushing against pollen-laden blossom in the hedgerows.

"The young lady has waited over an hour, madam."

Olivia turned away from the mirror and met Latham's grave eyes. Her imperturbable butler desperately wanted this chit out of the house but was too discreet to say so.

"Ah. Thank you. In that case, she'll have to bear my travel dirt. I'll go right in."

He bowed. "I believe that is best, madam."

Foreboding tinged Olivia's curiosity as she went through to the charming ground floor room she rarely used. Her life in this house was mainly confined to the decadent salons of sin upstairs.

At her entrance, a heavily veiled figure in a black gown sprang up from where she sat near the unlit fire. She was small and round. Under all that bombazine, it was hard to tell much else about her.

"I'm Olivia Raines. I believe you wish to see me." Olivia peered beneath the layers of material.

How on earth had Latham worked out this woman shouldn't be here? She could be anyone from the Duchess of Kent to a scrubber woman. Well, perhaps not a scrubber woman. Her overpowering clothing reeked expense.

With an emphatic gesture, the woman raised gloved hands and flung back the veiling.

Olivia's belly clenched with a bilious mixture of horror and shock. Latham was right to be worried.

The girl stood proudly and glared at Olivia with open hatred. "I'm Roma Southwood, Lord Erith's daughter."

Olivia ignored the girl's animosity and dropped into a brief curtsy. It was only to be expected that a virgin of good family should despise a harlot. Those were the rules of the world they lived in. But what in heaven's name was that virgin doing in the harlot's house? And how could Olivia get her home without igniting an almighty scandal?

"I know who you are, my lady," she said calmly.

"Then you'll know why I'm here." The girl vibrated with contempt.

"No. But I know you need to leave. You've been in my house far too long already."

"It's not your house. It's my father's house. You're his whore. On whom he sates his disgusting passions."

In spite of the gravity of the situation, Olivia suppressed a spurt of amusement. Young Lady Roma had an adolescent taste for drama. The funereal thickness of her apparel and the severely pulled back hairstyle made it clear she'd arrived anticipating a scene of operatic proportions.

"Don't you dare laugh at me." The girl's fists clenched at her sides and she took a threatening step toward Olivia. "You're nothing but a . . . a low-born trollop who spreads her legs for any blackguard with coin to pay for the dubious privilege."

"Perfectly true," Olivia said with equanimity, refusing to rise to the theatrical rhetoric.

At Olivia's easy acceptance of the insult, color rose in Lady Roma's cheeks and lent her a genuine beauty. She was pretty in a very English way, with fine features and blue eyes and shining brown hair. Olivia could only imagine Erith's daughter took after Joanna. Julian was dark as a Gypsy.

"I . . ."

Olivia took pity on her. And remembered what was vitally important here. This was Julian's beloved, troubled daughter, who deserved all her care and protection.

"Lady Roma, if anyone discovers you visited your father's mistress, your reputation will be in tatters. You must go. My servants will call a hackney to take you home, and you can leave by the back garden. My advice is to get out a few streets before you reach Erith House so nobody connects you with this address."

The girl's jaw set in a stubborn line. For a fleeting moment she looked like her father in one of his more difficult humors. "I'm not going until I've said my piece."

"Please listen," Olivia said urgently. "Perhaps you haven't considered the risks of coming here. Pardon my frankness, but it was fatally foolish. You have a wonderful marriage awaiting you, you're the darling of society. But you could lose everything if it becomes public knowledge that you've spoken to me. The longer you stay, the more danger you're in."

"I'm doing no harm," the girl said sulkily.

"Your world won't see it the same way. For your own sake, for your father's sake, please go. You can send me a letter. I promise I'll read it."

"I want to tell you face-to-face. I want you to see how you're ruining my life. And my brother's life. And my father's life."

Olivia grimly realized she wasn't going to shift the girl until this distasteful encounter had run its course. All she could do was make sure it ended as quickly as possible and with no negative consequences.

"Won't you sit down?" She gestured to one of the graceful Sheraton chairs near the window.

Lady Roma visibly bristled. "Why?"

Olivia sighed. Once, she might have grown into just such a self-absorbed chit. Her father had been a gentleman and wealthy enough to indulge his only daughter. But what had happened to her since placed an unbridgeable chasm between her and this spoiled, headstrong girl.

She kept her voice level. "Because I've been traveling all day. If a girl young enough to be my daughter plans to lecture me, I'd at least like to be comfortable."

"I prefer to stand."

"Really?" Olivia subsided into the chair. "You'll forgive my rudeness then."

The girl seemed oblivious to any irony in the words.

The door opened and Latham entered bearing a tray. "I took the liberty of arranging refreshments, madam." He bowed to Lady Roma. "My lady."

"I don't want tea, Latham," she snapped, confirming Olivia's suspicion that Latham was well acquainted with her unwelcome caller.

"Thank you, Latham. I do. The carriage ride was long and dusty."

"Very good, madam." He didn't react to Lady Roma's discourtesy. While Roma stood in mutinous silence beside the fireplace, he set out the tea things on a table in front of Olivia.

After Latham left, Olivia poured a cup of tea and looked up at Roma. "Are you sure you don't want some?"

Roma scowled. "I didn't come here to drink tea!"

Olivia smiled again. Had she ever been so young? She didn't think so.

"No, you came for a row."

"I came to ask that you do the honorable thing. Not that a woman like you understands honor."

"I wonder that you know anything about a woman like me," Olivia said calmly. Ignoring Roma's glower, she poured a second cup and held it out. "Do you want lemon?"

Grudgingly, Roma shook her head. "No, thank you. Just a little sugar and milk."

With a pout that Olivia guessed was habitual, Lady Roma accepted the cup and, clearly not noticing what she did, sat on the chair across the tea table. She even tugged off her black gloves and untied and removed her bonnet.

Olivia sipped her tea, dearly wishing it was a brandy. And wouldn't that shock proper Lady Roma? Although probably it would only confirm that her father shared a den of iniquity with his wanton mistress.

"How did you find out about me? A girl of good breeding shouldn't be aware of her father's liaisons. She shouldn't be aware of anyone's liaisons."

"I'm not a fool," Roma said sullenly, and lifted her cup to take a substantial mouthful. "You're notorious. And after that disgraceful performance you and my father put on at

Lord Peregrine Montjoy's ball, your affair has been the tattle of town."

Olivia had known her appearance with Erith would cause a flutter in her own disreputable world. She hadn't realized it might reach the ears of a sheltered virgin of the highest estate.

"I can only apologize." She put down her tea and frowned. "Your father will be distressed to know people are telling tales."

She extended a plate of sandwiches, expecting a rebuff, but Lady Roma took one readily enough. If she'd been waiting more than an hour, she must be famished.

"I wanted to know." Lady Roma devoured her sandwich and took another, then a mouthful of tea. "I've been quizzing the servants."

Olivia stiffened. "That's not suitable behavior."

Roma slammed the delicate china cup down on the tea tray so hard that liquid sloshed into the saucer. "How would you know? You're nothing but a doxy."

"I know a little about manners," Olivia said quietly. This time the rebuke pierced the girl's anger and she had the grace to blush again.

"It's all over London that you're going to Vienna with him."

Olivia sighed. "Lady Roma, forgive me for saying so, but none of this is your concern. If you'll take my advice, you'll go home, prepare for your wedding, and forget we ever met. Certainly you must never come here again."

"Why should you care? You've done nothing but cause trouble ever since my father met you."

"Sadly, I think he'd agree with you." Olivia tried and failed to lighten the atmosphere. She became serious again. "Please tell me what you want, then you really must go. I assume you haven't just come here to chastise me for my sins."

"No. I've come here to . . . " The girl straightened and stared hard at Olivia. Her blue eyes were full of desperate hurt and unhappiness. She took a deep breath then spoke in a rush. "If you retain even a shred of decency, you'll send my father back to his family."

She was so young and vulnerable, Olivia couldn't help but think of Leo. "I haven't taken your father, my dear." She reached forward to touch the girl's hand. She expected Lady Roma to withdraw in horror but the girl just stared at her with a stubborn misery that made Olivia ache with compassion. "He loves you very much."

"No, he doesn't. He loves you. But you can't have him. He came back to make peace with his family. You should leave him to us. What's one man more or less to you? You'll find a new lover quickly enough. But he's the only father I've got."

It was the wail of an overindulged child. But a child whose heart was breaking. "He has a right to his own life, Lady Roma."

"No, he belongs to us. To William and me."

"You're about to be married, to establish your own family."

"I want my children to know their grandfather. Better than I ever knew my father."

"He's going back to Vienna anyway."

"Only because we haven't had a chance to ask him to stay. He's always here with you in this house."

"That's not true. " Although Olivia was guiltily aware that she'd taken over Julian's thoughts the way he'd taken over hers. That's what happened when you loved someone.

"It is true. I hate that my father cares more for his strumpet than he does for his children. I hate that he shares himself with you and not with the family who have longed for his return for so many years. He's here yet he's still absent." She burst into tears.

"Oh, child, don't take on so." With her free hand, Olivia fished in her pocket and passed the distraught girl a creased handkerchief.

Lady Roma's shaking fingers closed around the pollen-stained scrap of lace and she pressed it to her face. Her voice was choked. "I had to see you, to tell you to let him go."

Olivia went down on her knees beside Lady Roma and took the girl's hand. "It will all turn out right, you'll see."

Lady Roma took a shuddering breath and stared at Olivia through reddened eyes. "How can it? He'll go away and never come back. Just like he did when Mamma died."

"My dear, I know how hard it is for you."

Then just as she would if she'd found Leo so distressed, she put her arms around the girl's shaking shoulders and drew her down to rest against her. She had no right to touch this child. But the sheer scale of Lady Roma's sorrow made it impossible to resist extending comfort.

"I just want my father back. That's all I've ever wanted." Lady Roma clung sobbing to Olivia.

"I know, I know, sweetheart," Olivia crooned as she'd crooned to Leo when he'd been a baby.

The girl wept with an extravagance that made Olivia want to cry herself. The poor child had lost her mother when she was far too young, then her father had abandoned her. Julian was aware of his wrongs against his family, but Olivia suspected he had no idea of the depth of unhappiness he'd caused.

How could she blame him for what he'd done? He'd been little more than a child himself when Joanna died and crippled with grief. He'd been in no fit state to take over two infant children. Whereas his sister was already married with a family of her own.

Eventually, Lady Roma's wild storm of emotion subsided. She pulled away and wiped at her eyes with her hands. It was such an intrinsically childish action that Olivia's heart was touched anew.

How could this girl contemplate marriage in a few weeks? She barely seemed mature enough to be out of the school-room.

Olivia reached behind her and picked up the now cold tea. "Here, have a sip. It will help. I'll call for more in a moment."

Any fight had drained from the girl. And thank goodness, with it, the urge to insult the woman she saw as competition for her father's attention.

Lady Roma nodded and took the cup, lifting it to her lips. Her hand shook so badly, Olivia reached out to support it.

The girl took a gulp and choked. Olivia rose and put her arm around her shoulders through the brief fit of coughing. "Slowly. I have a feeling you're an impetuous creature, my lady."

The girl's muffled giggle was still thick with tears. "You sound like Aunt Celia. I'm always in trouble for leaping before I look." She sobered and studied Olivia with grave blue eyes. "You're not what I expected."

Olivia smiled and sat back. "A painted harpy with a cockney accent and a dress cut down to her knees?"

Lady Roma gave another choked giggle. "I've never met a wicked woman before. Well, not one acknowledged by everyone as wicked. Of course, I know about affairs within the ton."

Olivia tried to frown but failed. "You listen to too much gossip, my lady."

"I like to know what's going on." She put her cup down on its saucer and lifted her chin. "Thank you. You've been kinder than I deserve. I treated you with ill grace."

"You were upset. With some justice. But I can't—"

"Good God, Roma! What the hell are you doing here?"

Chapter 25

$\mathcal{J}$ ulian filled the doorway, his high-top beaver hat in one hand, his cane in the other. An expression of unspeakable horror darkened his handsome face.

Olivia's heart rose to clog her throat. She felt like a child caught in some forbidden act. But his incendiary rage swiftly banished the harmless image.

He looked like he wanted to kill someone.

"Papa . . . " Lady Roma bounded to her feet with an ungainly movement that briefly reminded Olivia of the way she sat a horse. As she lurched up, she knocked the tea table and the tray went flying.

Olivia leaped aside as tea, milk, lemon, and the drying remains of food shot everywhere. With a resounding crash, china smashed against furniture and the floor.

"Oh, heavens!" The girl wrung her hands as she surveyed the disaster. She glanced in panic at her father, then back to the shattered remnants of their tea.

"It doesn't matter." Olivia rushed across to put her arm

around Lady Roma. She glared at the tall, furious man who hadn't shifted from the door. "Lord Erith, you're terrifying the child. For heaven's sake, come in and sit down."

"Terrifying her?" The deep voice that could be as warm and caressing as sable was icy with barely contained temper. "I'd like to take her over my knee and spank her like the irresponsible devil spawn she is."

"Papa, please . . . " Lady Roma's eyes filled with tears and she huddled closer to Olivia.

"And will that help?" Olivia forced a note of command and tightened her protective hold. "Leave the girl until you calm down."

"Calm down?" His nostrils flared with an aristocratic disdain that cut her like a razor. He took a few emphatic strides into the room. "I find my daughter in cozy conversation with my mistress, the most infamous jade in London, a lightskirt whose exploits are the toast of every tavern in the land, and you expect me to like it? Damn it all, Olivia, this is outside of enough."

She flinched back a step away from the trembling girl. He was in a rage and prone to say things he didn't mean. Nonetheless savage hurt arced through her.

He spoke to her like he'd speak to a whore. A whore he despised.

She strove for balance, for reason. He had a perfect right to his outrage. She was a notorious demimondaine. She'd done shameful and wicked things. His daughter shouldn't have come within a thousand miles of her.

That didn't mean she appreciated hearing him say so aloud. And in front of an audience.

She forced a rebuke through numb lips. "Roaring like an angry bear isn't going to improve matters."

"How the Devil did she even get here?" He shot Olivia a killing look. "*Blast you, did you ask her to come?*"

Olivia felt the blood seep from under her skin. She fumbled for the back of a chair. Her legs alone wouldn't support her. The room receded as shocked distress left her dizzy and lost.

He didn't know her at all.

How could he claim to love her yet have such a poor opinion of her discretion or good sense? How could he imagine she'd endanger his daughter's reputation? How could he claim to love her yet address her with such flaying contempt?

Her hand curled hard around the chair as she fought for control. Her answer emerged as a croak. "Of course I didn't."

He didn't heed her vehement denial. With suppressed violence, he flung coat and cane to the sofa. "I cannot believe you encouraged my daughter in this featherbrained behavior. You must know the consequences could be calamitous. Or you would if you'd given the matter a moment's reflection. You have a role in my life, madam. But you have no permission to insinuate yourself into private family business."

"Papa, you're being unfair," Roma interjected in an unsteady voice. "I—"

"Roma, you will not defend this woman." He spat the last two words as if they described a creature lower than mud. "You will not ever mention her to me."

"But, Papa—"

"My lady, don't," Olivia said, trying to deflect his anger even as her heart fractured into two bloody halves. The agony was excruciating. "This is between your father and me."

She succeeded too well. She staggered as furious silver eyes incinerated her. His voice seared. "You've exceeded the bounds of propriety, Olivia. You've exceeded the bounds of acceptability, even."

Hard to believe he'd held her tenderly through the night as she sobbed out her misery over her brother's betrayal. Hard to believe he'd been so deep inside her that she thought he'd touched her soul. Hard to believe they'd laughed and shared a bond that could almost have been friendship.

"My lord, listen to me," she said urgently. "I didn't invite Lady Roma here. She came of her own free will. She realizes how foolish she's been. She'll never do it again. Your chastisement serves no purpose."

He arched his eyebrows with dismissive hauteur as if he caught her out in a lie. "So how did she know where to find you?"

He was pale with fury and a muscle jerked spasmodically in his cheek. She knew concern for his daughter underlay his overwhelming anger. But nothing could excuse either his accusations or his attitude.

If this was his love, it was worthless.

She called on the pride that had sustained her for so long and drew herself up to her full height. Her spine was so rigid, she thought it might snap. She relinquished her grip on the chair. She didn't need any support but her own outrage.

"The girl has ears, my lord." Then she added in an acid tone, "Apparently she's used them to listen to a lot of unsuitable gossip."

Julian had reached a pitch of anger where her tone and her use of formal address made no impression. He seemed blind to anything but his own fury. He loomed closer, a menacing, masculine presence, and fixed his fierce gray gaze upon his daughter. "Roma, we're leaving now."

The girl backed away awkwardly. "I don't want to go."

"I don't give a damn what you want. I'm more worried about what you need. From what I see, that's a keeper." He clenched his fists at his sides and spoke in a harsh voice. "Good God, girl, you're getting married in a few weeks. You'll soon have children of your own, yet you act like a child yourself."

Lady Roma abruptly ended her retreat and stiffened her shoulders. She scowled at her father. "You wouldn't know how I acted as a child. You were never there."

"Don't start, Roma," he growled, his brows drawing together in a ferocious scowl. "I'm not in the mood."

"When will you be in the mood?"

Olivia had already witnessed Lady Roma's foolhardy courage when her temper was up. If she didn't quickly halt the escalating argument, father and daughter would destroy any chance for reconciliation.

"Lady Roma, Lord Erith, please sit down," she said in the tone that always quelled Perry's wilder companions.

Julian glowered from under his lowered brows. He bit his response out as if he could hardly bear to speak to her. "I'm taking my daughter home."

"Not in the state she's in right now, you're not," Olivia said with equal firmness. "Lord Erith, you're acting like an ass."

"Curb your tongue, madam. I'm acting as any father would. She's my daughter. Damn it, you have no rights in this matter."

She struggled to contain the acrid nausea that swam in her belly. How could he speak to her so patronizingly, with such loathing? He'd begged her to trust him yet he betrayed her with every poisonous word.

She swallowed and forced an answer out through her tight throat. "No rights, perhaps. But any fool can see you both need to calm down before you face the world."

"Devil take you, I will not treat this lightly," he snapped.

She gestured to the sofa against the wall, away from the chaotic battlefield of the tea table. Her voice hardened as she turned to Julian. "Lord Erith, pray control your temper in my house."

With a heavy heart, she waited for him to insist the house was his, as he paid for it. But even furious as he was, he wasn't as far gone in anger as that.

She watched him fight for composure. If he hadn't trampled her feelings in the dust, she might have felt sorry for him. He only wanted to protect his daughter. That wasn't a sin.

His sin, and it was irredeemable, was that he'd made Olivia believe he respected and loved her, when clearly he did neither.

After a delay, he spoke more evenly. His jaw worked as he fought for control. His anger was still only barely leashed. "Your pardon, Olivia. Of course you didn't invite my daughter here. Roma's thoughtlessness has dragged you into my family troubles. I realize you have no wish to be involved."

He just condemned himself further. Of course she was involved. She loved him. He said he loved her.

She hid her surging pain and sent him the disdainful courtesan's stare that had cowed so many men before him. "Your daughter is welcome to call whenever she wishes."

Roma's mouth fell open in surprise. "I . . . I am?"

"I don't expect you to take up the invitation." Olivia sent her a small reassuring smile then narrowed her eyes at Julian. "I refuse to throw a distraught girl out on the street just because some bully insists I must."

"Some bully?" Indignant color darkened his cheeks. "What the blazes do you mean by that?"

"I mean that if you don't sit down as I've requested, my lord, I will ask my servants to show you the door."

He flinched and the overwhelming, unthinking rage seeped from his face. For the first time since he'd stalked into the room, he really looked at her. She saw the exact moment when he realized what he'd done. Shock and regret seeped into the silver eyes, turning them a flat iron gray.

She kept her expression determinedly neutral, but damn him, he knew her well enough to penetrate any mask. Pray God he wouldn't guess her desolation. She refused to give him the satisfaction of knowing how mortally he'd wounded her.

Dear heaven, why had he been so cruel? Did he have to shred her soul?

He had every reason to be angry. But he must know she'd never do anything to harm him or his. He must know when he treated her as a harlot, he shattered any trust that had ever existed between them.

He slumped as the bristling self-righteousness drained

from his body. "Oh, hell, Olivia, I'm sorry. You don't deserve this. I'm acting like a savage."

He sounded dismayed, upset. He sounded like the wonderful, considerate, passionate lover who turned her nights to incandescence.

Bitterness surged up to choke her. How could he still act like he cared when he was false to the core? He told her he loved her yet it was apparent at the deepest level that he felt nothing but contempt for her.

He ran his hand through his hair, leaving himself charmingly disheveled. But Olivia was a long way from being charmed. She sought the core of steel within her. The core that had helped her survive trials that would destroy most women.

She turned to the girl who watched them with a mixture of trepidation and wild curiosity. "Lady Roma, will you please sit down? I'll arrange for more tea and have the servants clean up this mess."

"The rug is ruined," the girl said blankly.

The rug, the tea set, and undoubtedly her life were ruined, Olivia wanted to say. But she stifled the words. The afternoon had already provided enough histrionics.

"It doesn't matter." Olivia gestured toward the sofa. The girl finally moved across and sat down. Praying for control, Olivia turned back to Julian. "My lord?"

With unconcealed impatience, he went across and threw himself down next to his daughter. Olivia rang the bell and tense silence reigned while her efficient staff—who sadly, she would miss—did a makeshift job of cleaning up broken china and spilled food and drink.

By the time the servants left, Julian had stopped fuming and Lady Roma no longer looked torn between bursting into another storm of weeping or attacking her father with one of the fire irons.

Olivia wished she felt like doing violence to him. As time went on, anger seethed more powerfully. But far sharper than anger was lancing pain.

He'd created something precious then smashed it without thought to consequences.

She wished to heaven she'd never met him.

"Tea, Latham," she said when finally the mess was under control.

"No." Julian stood, his air of command in place once more. He waited for the butler to leave before he continued. Chillingly, his coldness and steely lack of emotion reminded her of the man who had offered her carte blanche at Perry's. She hadn't liked that man. "Olivia, I need to get Roma home. The longer she's here, the more risk of someone talking. The servants are loyal but . . . "

"They're servants," Olivia finished for him. She strove for a veneer of civilization. What point screaming that he'd broken her heart and devastated her life? Her only choice was to pick up the tattered remains of her existence and move on.

Julian turned to his daughter. "Was it just silly curiosity that brought you here? If so, indulging it may cost you more than you'd like to pay."

He didn't sound angry anymore. Instead he sounded disappointed to the bone. A humiliated flush rose in Lady Roma's cheeks, and she sent Olivia an uncomfortable glance. "I wanted to talk to Miss Raines."

Surprise arched Olivia's eyebrows. That a young lady of such standing would refer to her so respectfully astonished her. Especially when Lady Roma had begun the meeting calling her "whore" and "harlot."

Olivia's respect for the girl rose another notch. Yes, she was spoiled and thoughtless, but there was quality in Lady Roma too. She just hoped Julian wouldn't break her spirit before the quality had a chance to shine.

"I can't imagine what about," Julian said shortly.

Olivia hid a wince. Of course a filthy slut and his sweet innocent daughter had nothing in common. Except their love for him. And he wouldn't reckon that in his assessment.

"Leave her alone, my lord," she said coldly. "She knows she shouldn't have come, and she won't do it again." She moved across to stand at Lady Roma's side. "Your father's right, my lady. I'll take you upstairs to wash your face and hands and then you must go."

"Thank you." Lady Roma rose to her feet.

Olivia glanced at Julian. Her voice was frosty but calm. "I suggest smuggling her into the mews then into your carriage, my lord."

He sent her a searching look but didn't take her up on her formality. "Yes. Nobody will look twice at my rig parked at your door."

Olivia led the silent girl out of the library and up the stairs. The acrid regret coiling in her stomach made her feel ill. But she'd have space to dwell on her sorrows once Roma was safely away. God help her, she'd have the rest of her life. "Take your time. A few extra minutes now will make no difference."

"And give Papa time to cool down."

Ironic that Olivia found herself compelled to defend her shallow lover. "He's only upset because he loves you."

Lady Roma looked at her as they reached the spare bedroom. "He's not very good at showing it, is he?"

Olivia gave a low, caustic laugh. "He's a man. Of course he's not. But he'd die to save you an ounce of pain."

"I know. It's the day-to-day stuff he needs to practice." The girl's eyes became grave. "When I came here today, I hated you."

Olivia's wry smile faded. "I'm sorry you even learned of my existence."

A hint of humor entered the blue eyes. Suddenly she looked startlingly like her father. "Oh, I've known about you for years. You're famous. All my friends wish they had half your dash. I'd give anything to sit a horse the way you do. You look like you grew up in the saddle."

"I did." Although that horse-mad child was a million miles away from the world-weary woman she'd become.

"I ride like a sack of potatoes. My father is ashamed to be seen with me."

"Perhaps you could ask him to give you lessons. Sometimes you have to make the first step, even if you're the one who's been wronged."

"I wish I could know you better," Lady Roma said quietly.

"Oh, sweetheart." Olivia bit her lip to stem her foolish tears. Tears never helped anything. She'd learned that long ago. "You don't, really. But I treasure what you said."

She leaned forward and hugged the girl, feeling the desperate fragility under the defiance. For a fleeting moment Lady Roma was stiff under her embrace. Then she surrendered to Olivia's arms and hugged her back with deep emotion.

If life had proceeded as her parents planned when they hired governesses and drawing masters and dancing teachers for their precious daughter, she could have had a child like this. A daughter to guide and to love when she was hurt and bereft as this child so clearly was.

But Olivia was left with nothing. No brilliant marriage. No sweet daughter. No devoted husband. Not even a lover to warm her yearning heart. Just a son she idolized but could never acknowledge and who would only grow more distant as the world beckoned him.

But she would survive. She always survived.

Even if right now she didn't see much point.

She gathered her courage and gently pulled away from the girl's clinging hands. "Come downstairs when you're ready."

"Papa will scold me all the way home."

"He's right about one thing—you shouldn't have come."

"I'm not sorry."

Before Olivia could summon an answer, Lady Roma slipped into the room and closed the door firmly after her.

Olivia straightened her backbone and lifted her chin. For a brief, brilliant interval she'd believed she could escape the hard, heartless courtesan. Now she knew better.

* * *

When Olivia returned to the library, Julian stood staring down into the empty grate with a brooding expression. She paused in the doorway and watched him for a long, silent moment while she tried to quell the chagrin that ripped at her.

How could she have been so deceived in him? After so many years of hating the arrogant scions of the ton, how could she have been so fatally stupid as to fall in love with one?

He raised his head to meet her gaze and his masculine beauty pierced her like a knife. The rich blue of his coat and the startling white of his shirt and neckcloth emphasized the saturnine distinction of his features.

"I regret that Roma has made things difficult for you, Olivia." The silver eyes glinted between their lush fringe of lashes. He rested one long-fingered hand on the mantel.

"She hasn't made things difficult for me, Lord Erith." She moved into the room, making sure to keep her distance. "I just pray nobody finds out about today's escapade. She mustn't suffer more than she already has."

His mouth turned down in a wry line. "I deserve that."

Olivia sank down onto one of the chairs near the saturated rug. "Yes, you do."

"Damn it, I know I spoke out of turn. It was just the sight of Roma . . ." He paused and made a frustrated gesture. "We can't talk about this now. I've got to take Roma home and then there's a blasted family dinner with the Rentons. It was planned weeks ago and it's important. I won't be back here until late."

"Don't hurry on my account, Lord Erith."

His lips twisted in a sardonic smile. "You don't have to keep calling me that. I know you're displeased with me."

"I'm not displeased with you."

He prowled across to array himself upon the sofa, studying her with heavy-lidded concentration. He looked like some eastern potentate considering his nightly selection from the harem. Except his jaw set in a determined line that indicated he wasn't nearly as relaxed as he wished to appear. "You're doing a remarkable impression, if you're not."

"Displeasure indicates I feel something for you," she said steadily.

A faint mocking smile curved his lips. "And clearly you're a monument of indifference."

"Bickering will get us nowhere." She spoke in clipped tones. "When we made this arrangement, I told you I reserved the right to end the liaison. Well, I'm exercising that right."

Anger sparked in his eyes and he made a sound of denial deep in his throat. "And you tell me now, when I'm on my way to an engagement I can't get out of?"

She clutched her hands in her lap and fought for the cold hard certainty that had gripped her when he'd lashed out at her over his daughter. That was truth. Not this subtle play of attraction.

"Whores can't always be particular about their timing."

"I've never treated you like a whore," he said hotly, his face tightening.

"You did today."

His fist curled on the arm of the sofa. "That's not fair. No man wants his daughter to risk her future."

"Yes, your actions as a parent do you credit, in spite of your temper. Your actions as a lover do not."

His eyes darkened to the color of thunderclouds in a summer sky. He made a convulsive move toward her then stopped himself.

"My God, Olivia. I'm sorry." His voice cracked with regret. "I found Roma here and I saw red. I acted like a confounded blockhead. But you must know I didn't mean what I said. Damn it, I hurt you. I give you my word that was never my intention."

"I'm sure it wasn't." Her words dropped from her lips as if

cut from glass. "But a number of things have become clear, including that this liaison has gone as far as it will."

"For God's sake, stop calling it a liaison." Any pretense of detachment disappeared in an instant. He surged across the room to fall to his knees at her side. His hands shook as they grabbed hers. "I love you. You love me."

From the start, she'd known what they had couldn't last. It had to come to this. She'd tried to prepare herself. But nothing could ready her for the shock of parting from Julian. It was like amputating a limb.

A gangrenous limb.

She looked him straight in the eye and wrenched her hands free of his. "I'm glad I made you think so. After all, you handed over a fortune to have every fantasy satisfied. Arousing a frigid woman was clearly what you wanted."

The muscles of his arms bunched and his face went white as parchment. The color even seeped from his lips. For one appalled moment she feared he might hit her. Trembling, she shrank away before pride stopped her retreat.

He placed one shaking hand on the back of the chair near her shoulder. A tiny muscle at the corner of his mouth flickered erratically as he fought for control. "Damn you, you're lying."

"If you like to think so," she said calmly, while feral beasts screamed inside her. "Obviously I lied about something. It's up to you to decide what was true and what wasn't."

"Hell, Olivia. I can't stay and fight this out now." He bent his head and shook it. His eyes were stormy when he looked at her. "Stick me with knives tonight but don't walk out like this."

"I won't change my mind."

"I might change it for you." He lurched to his feet and frowned at her. "I'll get out of this dinner as early as I can but I can't let Roma down. I've let her down too often."

Olivia rose too, with the courtesan's conscious grace. "Good-bye, Lord Erith."

"Blast you, it's not good-bye." He snatched her into his arms and pressed her to his chest. His heart pounded like a mallet wielded by a madman. "Wait until tonight. You owe me that at least."

She made herself as unresponsive as a doll in his hold although the heat of his hands seeped in to threaten the frozen layer around her cold, cold soul. "You have no right to touch me anymore."

"Don't do this."

"It's done." She tried to extricate herself but his grip was too tight.

She wondered if his grip on her heart was too tight for her ever to be free again. She had a doomed feeling it was.

"Like hell." He grabbed her head with both hands and held her still while he covered her mouth with his. The kiss was hard and unforgiving. Almost insulting in its ruthless possession. But she found herself clawing at his shoulders and responding with every ounce of furious passion in her.

For an endless space they continued their argument with teeth and tongues and lips. Neither would admit defeat. Neither could gain victory.

The fierce heat scorched through her, right to the soles of her feet. She kissed him back but didn't surrender an inch of her determination that this affair ended now. She was adamant as rock.

Until the kiss changed.

Gradually, tenderness loosened the taut hands framing her face. The lips ravaging hers became less insistent. They wooed rather than demanded. She tumbled headlong into helpless pleasure as his mouth became an instrument of forbidden delight. Her body softened, her bones loosened, heat pooled between her thighs.

She wanted to pull away, to dismiss him, deride this magic. But she was unable to stop kissing him, every slide of lips or tongue a warning of how dangerous he was.

He tore away from her. His eyes were alight with hunger

and rage and something she didn't want to recognize as anguish. A muscle jerked spasmodically in his lean cheek.

"And you toss this away for the sake of pride?" His question was blistering.

"It's over," she said rawly. Her knees trembled and she could barely stand. The force of his kiss still pounded through her like a hammer on an anvil. Her hands formed fists and she beat at his chest. "For God's sake, leave me in peace."

He caught her flailing hands. "You'll never be at peace until you come to terms with your love for me."

"I don't love you," she snarled, straining to escape his hold.

"Then why are you so upset?"

"Because you won't let me go."

"You don't want me to let you go."

"Yes, I do."

Temper lit his handsome face and made his eyes flare brilliant silver. His hands tightened on hers, although he didn't hurt her. She wished he would. She'd dearly love some reason to hate Lord Erith aside from the irrefutable fact that she could never be a fit consort for him.

"To hell with you, Olivia. You know I've got to go."

"Then go," she said stubbornly.

"I go and you mightn't be here when I come back." He hooked one hand behind her neck and forced her head up so she met his burning gaze. "If you have an ounce of feeling for me, stay."

"There's nothing to say."

"Well, give me a chance to say nothing, then. I owe Roma tonight. It's my fault she took this stupid risk. She's acted like a ninnyhammer but she's my daughter and I can't abandon her."

"Julian . . . " she started, then stopped, unsure how to continue.

"I'm ready, Papa." Lady Roma hovered at the door.

Olivia expected Erith to jump away from her in embarrassment. After all, his daughter caught him clutching his mistress in a torrid embrace.

"The carriage is at the back gate." He didn't shift his intense stare from Olivia and he only slowly lifted his hands from her. In spite of everything, she mourned that he let her go. He would never touch her again, and his touch had become so very precious to her. For one brief deceptive moment he'd made her feel cherished, alive, clean. "I'm sure Miss Raines will lend you a veil and a bonnet."

"I brought one." Roma went across to the chair where she'd left her coverings. She seemed remarkably unfazed by her father's flagrant flouting of convention.

"Good-bye, Lady Roma," Olivia said with a regret that surprised her.

The girl glanced up and, astonishingly, sent her a smile of surpassing sweetness. "Good-bye, Miss Raines. I'm grateful for your kindness."

"I wish you every joy in your marriage." Her voice was choked and she avoided Lady Roma's curious stare.

"Roma, come along," Erith said impatiently. He turned as he ushered his daughter ahead of him out the door. He sent Olivia a stern look. "Don't you dare think of going anywhere. We're not finished."

"Oh, yes, we are," she bit out, raising her chin and directing a glare at him that in any just world would leave him bleeding on the floor.

"Not in this lifetime."

He wheeled on his heel before she could argue and left with the fast, decisive walk that was his alone. She heard the door close sharply behind him.

He was gone.

Chapter 26

*E*rith returned to the house on York Street, earlier than he should, later than he needed to. Ostensibly nothing was different. His heart racing with foreboding, he dashed up the staircase to the decadent bedroom. He flung open the heavy oak door to the empty room.

The scarlet silk robe Olivia had appropriated from him was still draped across the bed. Her cosmetics were arrayed on the dressing table. He knew without checking that the armoire bulged with the opulent wardrobe he'd spent a fortune buying for her.

Just as he was certain she'd left him. After threatening so often, at last she'd gone. He had pushed her too far. The fact that she left her belongings meant nothing. She'd abandoned him to a life as barren as a desert.

Confound his blasted impetuous temper to Hades.

Regret turned his blood to ice. He'd had hours to rue the damage he'd done with his furious reaction to discovering Roma here. He'd give his right arm to take back the accusations he'd flung at Olivia. He understood the delicate balance of pride and sensitivity that sustained her. He also knew what courage she'd needed to overcome both and admit her love. His thoughtless words were a callous attack on everything she was.

After what he'd said, he could hardly blame her for running. God help him, he had no excuse for his tirade. In his heart, he'd always known she wouldn't encourage Roma to visit.

With no life in the dead garden of his heart, he wandered through to the salon. Of course, she wasn't there either. He felt hollow, numb, bereft.

He trudged back to the bedroom. The room that had witnessed desperate emotions, transcendent moments, a connection beyond anything he'd ever known.

The bed. The door. The floor. The walls. Every inch imprinted with the memory of Olivia shuddering her release in his arms.

After all those women during all those wild, empty years, only these few weeks with Olivia had marked his soul. Indelibly.

She'd still left him in the end. Damn it all to hell.

He snatched up her robe from the bed as if it could tell him where she'd gone. The garment released a drift of her evocative, haunting scent. Under the robe, the extravagant ruby collar lay in glittering splendor on the bedspread.

The message was unmistakable.

She wanted nothing more to do with him.

His bleak numbness snapped in an instant. With a strangled groan, he buried his face in the slippery red material. Closing his eyes, he breathed deeply and tried to convince himself Olivia would return to him.

He looked up to find Latham watching with very unbutlerlike compassion from the door. Without embarrassment, Erith lowered the robe. "Where is she?"

"Madam didn't say, but she left about an hour after your lordship."

Sudden hope surged. "Did she take her carriage?"

He could question the coachman when he returned. Perhaps discover some clue to her whereabouts.

Latham shook his head. "No, my lord. She left on foot."

On foot? Where could she have gone? Then the solution struck him. It would be laughably obvious if he hadn't been so close to shattering.

With a smothered curse, he flung the robe aside and strode out of the room.

Erith forced his way past Peregrine Montjoy's butler into the candlelit salon where he'd made his heartless bargain with Olivia. He'd been a different man then. He hoped she'd been a different woman.

She'd told him she loved him. However unwillingly. He'd bet his life that hadn't been a lie, even if she'd tried to wound him today by denying it. And if she loved him, he'd undoubtedly win her back. He had a weapon she couldn't fight against.

Damn it, he just had to find her first.

At Erith's brusque entrance, Montjoy looked up in shock, but only slowly withdrew the arm he'd draped around the willowy boy at his side. Erith immediately saw that the small circle playing piquet near the fire didn't include a gorgeous tawny-haired siren.

"Lord Erith," Montjoy said, clearly at a loss. He rose to his feet and flung his cards onto the table. Like his three companions, he was in shirtsleeves. He obviously hadn't expected visitors at such an hour. "To what do I owe the pleasure?"

"Where is she?" Erith asked urgently, not caring that his wild chase after his mistress would be the talk of London tomorrow. More scandal for Roma to eavesdrop on from behind closed doors.

"She?"

"Don't play bloody games with me, man."

Montjoy frowned. "Olivia?"

"Of course Olivia. I need to see her."

Montjoy spoke to his friends as he moved away from the card table. "I'll be back in a moment. Freddie, don't peek at my hand."

"Don't interrupt your cards." Erith's fists closed and opened convulsively at his sides. He was only an inch away from choking Olivia's whereabouts out of her elegant friend. "Just tell me where she is."

"My lord, we can't have this conversation here." Montjoy ignored Erith's impatient huff and air of incipient violence and gestured him out into the dimly lit hallway.

Once they were alone, Erith turned on Montjoy and spoke in a rush. If he didn't find her soon, she could slip through his fingers completely. She had money and resources. She could go anywhere. "Is she upstairs? I swear I only want to talk to her. You must know I won't hurt her."

Even in the poor light, Montjoy's troubled look was visible as he shut the door to the salon. "Of course you won't hurt her. You're in love with her."

Erith stiffened with horrified shock, hating the sudden vulnerability that assailed him. He felt mortified color flood his face. Damn it, had she relayed their pillow talk to Montjoy?

"Good God, did she tell you that?"

"No, of course not." A faint smile curved Montjoy's full lips. "But only love could bring an earl famed for his arrogance to apologize without hesitation to a notorious cyprian."

Erith's bristling hostility subsided. Montjoy was right. Anyway, what point denying how he felt? "I'm not the only man who has loved her."

Montjoy's smile became reflective. "Yes, but you're the only man she's loved back."

Montjoy understood her better than anyone. Any niggling doubts that had plagued Erith about her feelings retreated.

He spoke more normally. "I know about your father and how you and Olivia united against him."

Montjoy's face, handsome enough to be called beautiful, paled with shock. "She's never told anyone that. You realize I'm not her paramour, then."

Erith shrugged. This wasn't getting anywhere. "I guessed long ago." He saw by Montjoy's face that the man understood what else he'd guessed as well. He didn't care about the fellow's sexual tastes. All he cared about was finding his beloved. "For pity's sake, man, stop tormenting me."

"And now she's left you." Montjoy didn't sound triumphant. He sounded worried.

"Temporarily." He hoped to heaven that wasn't just overweening optimism.

Montjoy shook his head with grim finality. "When she leaves a keeper, he tends to stay left."

"I have an advantage—she loves me. I honor that you've protected her so long and faithfully. I know you don't like me, but I beg of you—and I beg favors from no man—send for her. It's my turn to look after her now."

Montjoy regarded him with thoughtful eyes before he gave a brief nod. "I believe you really do love her. But I don't know what the hell you can do about it."

"Let me talk to her." Erith caught sight of his face in one of the mirrors lining the hallway. He looked wild, frantic, half mad.

"I would, my lord. I'm as sentimental as the next fellow. The prospect of a woman bringing the all-conquering Earl of Erith to his knees touches my heart." He paused. "But she's not here."

"So where is she?"

"I have no idea." Montjoy's frown deepened. "I hope she's all right."

Erith's temper, barely held in check since she'd deserted him, snapped. He grabbed Montjoy by the shirtfront and lifted him to his toes. "Tell me where she's gone."

"Believe me, old man, I would. But she didn't confide in me." Montjoy appeared unconcerned to be suspended from Erith's clenched hands. "She's been remarkably close-mouthed about your affair. I should have realized earlier that meant trouble."

"If you're lying, *old man*, I swear I'll kill you."

"Beat me to a pulp, Erith. It won't get you any closer to what you want." Montjoy still sounded unruffled. "She's gone to ground somewhere. She's done it before. You won't find her unless she wants to be found. I suspect in this case, she most emphatically doesn't want to be found."

Erith realized he made an utter fool of himself. With an apologetic gesture, he released Montjoy. "I'm acting like a blockhead."

"I find it rather reassuring." Montjoy straightened his clothing with admirable sangfroid. "The man I met in my salon a few weeks ago was a dashed cold fish."

"Would she have gone to Leo?"

"Good Lord, you really have found out a lot, haven't you? She doesn't tell anyone about Leo. Leo is the last bastion."

"No, her heart is the last bastion," Erith muttered, then flushed as he realized what he'd said.

"Yes. And it's a fortress that has never fallen. *Bonne chance, mon ami.*" Montjoy bowed his head as if acknowledging a point in a fencing match. He spoke more seriously. "She might go to him. I would have thought she'd come to me before Leo, if only to avoid a scandal. Perhaps she thinks I'd try and talk her into returning to you and fighting for what she wants."

"That would be outstandingly generous," Erith said, astounded.

Montjoy shrugged. "She deserves to be loved. If your reckless air is any indication, you definitely love her. Go with my blessing. She's been alone too long. Do you know where to find Leo?"

"Yes." Erith started to go then stopped. He turned to face

Montjoy. "Thank you." He extended his hand to the decorative young man.

Montjoy frowned. "You know what I am yet still you're willing to give me your hand?"

"Of course."

Montjoy accepted his hand in a brief clasp whose strength surprised Erith. The man might look like a damned poodle, but there was character there. And unmistakable love for the woman Erith adored above all others.

Erith strode out of the overdecorated mansion. Now it seemed charmingly eccentric instead of oppressive. He truly had changed from the man who marched in here weeks ago with no objective but to claim London's most prestigious bit of muslin as his prize.

On such seemingly unimportant decisions, a life could change forever.

A fine dawn broke as Erith rode up to the stone rectory that sheltered Olivia's cousin and her husband and the child his beloved could never acknowledge. Erith knew how that ate at her. She'd had to endure so much in her life. And she'd done it with grace and courage and style.

He hoped to Hades he could get her to embrace a future with him in similar spirit.

He reined in his tired and dusty horse, Bey, the same animal Leo had admired so extravagantly, and leaped to the ground. Dear God, let him find her here. Let this be the happy end to his precipitate chase.

He tied Bey to a hitching post outside the kitchen. He heard clattering inside. The servants must be up.

"Sir?"

A young girl carrying a pitcher stared nervously at him. He couldn't blame her. He imagined this secluded house had never before witnessed a wild-eyed and travel-worn earl at the door just as the sun crept above the horizon.

At least he was no longer in his evening wear. After leaving

Montjoy, he'd rushed home to change into clothing more suitable for a long ride through the night.

Some faint spark of discretion stopped him from peremptorily demanding to see Olivia. "Is Mrs. Wentworth up yet?"

"Aye, sir."

"Perhaps she'd do me the honor of an interview. Would you please tell her the Earl of Erith is here?"

The girl paled and dropped into an awkward curtsy, clutching the rough white pitcher before her like a shield. "Aye, my lord. Right away, my lord. Perhaps you'd like to come inside and wait, my lord."

"Thank you." Erith followed the girl into the kitchen then cooled his heels by the fire while she ran to fetch her mistress. At a worn deal table, a heavyset older woman kneaded bread for the household. She didn't spare him a word, though she poured him a tankard of ale and passed it across without comment.

He appreciated the gesture. He'd only picked at his hurried dinner the night before and he hadn't stopped for refreshment since he'd discovered Olivia was missing.

He struggled to master his impatience. The urge to rampage through this quiet household in search of his mistress was nigh overwhelming.

He heard someone come in and looked up, expecting to see Olivia's cousin. But instead he met the deep brown eyes of Leonidas Wentworth. Deep brown, perceptive, and bright with hostile suspicion.

"Lord Erith," he said flatly with a brief bow. He was dressed in a plain white shirt and buff breeches, and his long, elegant fingers were ink-stained.

"Leo." Erith leaped to his feet and shoved the empty tankard onto the table. "I hoped to see Mrs. Wentworth."

"She's not dressed yet. She asked me to find out what you wanted. I was up studying."

"Ah, Oxford."

"Yes." There was a pause, then the boy stood aside and gestured toward the door he'd just come through. "Step into the parlor. You won't want to talk in the kitchen."

What Erith really wanted was to shake the boy until he handed over his mother. His real mother, not the woman who bore that title. Blood pounding with the frenzied need to find Olivia, Erith followed the lad through to a small but neat room that was dark and cold at that hour.

Once inside, he whirled to face Leo. "Where is she?"

The boy didn't show any surprise or puzzlement. "I assume you refer to my godmother, Miss Raines?"

"Of course I do. She's not with Montjoy. Is she here?"

"No."

Erith made a slashing gesture of dismissal. "I don't believe you."

"You're welcome to search the house, my lord." After weeks with Olivia, the irony was familiar. "It's not as if we can stop you."

Erith realized he hectored the boy. It wasn't Leo's fault that Olivia had scarpered. He sucked in a deep breath and fought to seize hold of his rising temper. "I'm not here to bully you."

"Odd. That was exactly what I thought you intended, my lord."

"Do you know where she is?"

"No. She was here yesterday but hasn't been back." Realization dawned in Leo's eyes. "She's left you."

Erith ran a hand through his hair. It had been a long day leading into a long night, and he was exhausted and keyed up. Disappointment left a foul taste in his mouth. He knew Leo didn't lie. Olivia hadn't sought refuge with her cousin. He should have realized she wouldn't. The possibility of tarring Leo's reputation would be too great.

"Yes." His pride revolted at the bald admission.

"Good."

Something in that stark response struck Erith as significant. He raised his head and looked searchingly at Leo. "You know, don't you?"

Leo moved across to lean against the mantel. With the curtains drawn and no fire, the room was too shadowy for Erith to read his expression with certainty. Nonetheless, something told him his guess was right.

"That Miss Raines is my real mother? Of course I know."

"She thinks it's a secret. When did you find out?"

The boy shrugged. "I've always known. My resemblance to Lord Peregrine is marked. And why else would such a man express interest in my welfare?"

Erith didn't correct the boy's misconception about his parentage. It wasn't his secret to share, and Leo was better off believing Montjoy his sire than the vile debaucher of children who actually had fathered him. "You don't mind?"

"No. I love them both." Erith sourly noted that Leo spoke of love with an ease he certainly hadn't inherited from Olivia. "They've done their best for me. And my adopted parents brought me up with affection and generosity."

"You're proud of her," Erith said with dawning recognition.

Leo straightened to his full gangly height, and Erith felt his glare through the gloom. "Of course I'm proud of her. She's a remarkable woman, whatever the world cares to say."

"Yes, she is. And she loves me."

"So you say."

"She's told me."

Leo took a step closer and Erith at last saw his face. He looked unhappy. And shocked. "God help her."

"I want to take her to Vienna."

"Like a souvenir of your London trip?"

The boy truly did have an acid tongue. Even if he hadn't known Leo's parentage, he'd have guessed after this interview.

"You're an insolent whelp," he said without heat.

"Are you going to challenge me?"

"No. And don't be so quick to offer a duel. It will break your mother's heart if anything happens to you."

"Damn you, I think you're going to break her heart."

"Not if I can help it." He said it as a vow. "Can you tell me where she is?"

"I can't. She left here yesterday, and I have no idea of her life in London aside from what little gossip filters down to this backwater." The boy smiled with gloating satisfaction. "It looks like she's escaped you, my lord."

"Never," Erith said with complete confidence, straightening as new determination bolstered him, beating back weariness and discouragement. "I'll find her if it takes forever."

"Lord Erith? What brings you here at this hour?"

Mary Wentworth had dressed with such haste that her hair looked likely to fall about her shoulders in a mass of graying brown. She bobbed a curtsy. Hard to believe this plain little sparrow was the glorious Olivia Raines's cousin. Or had played a mother's role convincingly to the handsome young man who stepped to her side to protect her from the big bad earl.

"A mistake, Mrs. Wentworth," he said with a bow. "I'd hoped to see Miss Raines."

"Olivia?" She appeared at a total loss. "She lives in London."

"So I gather." His quarry, he bitterly suspected after his long and fruitless journey, was still in London. Although where? The urgent need to return to the capital and continue the search without delay built inside him. "I apologize for disturbing you."

"But why would you think she's here?" The woman didn't look like she meant to let it go.

Leo put his hand on her arm. "Mother, it's all right. Just a misunderstanding on his lordship's part."

"But to come at such a time to look for my cousin . . . " Mrs. Wentworth frowned. "My husband is away from home or else I don't know what he'd think."

Erith could already imagine the difficulties his wife's relationship with London's most notorious courtesan had caused the vicar. Although in his opinion, the man's generosity in raising Leo as his own was the finest example of Christian charity he'd ever encountered.

"I can only beg your forgiveness again and take my leave, madam." He bowed once more and turned. His mind worked furiously on where Olivia could be. Montjoy was right. She'd gone to ground, Devil take it.

"I'll show you out." It was Leo.

"Thank you."

In unexpectedly companionable silence, they walked out to where Bey drank deeply from a bucket of water someone had given him.

"He's a magnificent beast," Leo said, moving forward and stroking Bey's powerful neck, not as glossy as usual after the dust of the road. His face was full of naked longing.

"You can have him if you tell me where your mother is." He'd gladly hand over his entire stable if it meant finding Olivia.

Leo snatched his hand away. "I haven't lied to you, Lord Erith. I don't know where she is. And I wouldn't tell you if I did."

The boy was extraordinarily brave. Few men would dare to speak to him so frankly. Leo was smart enough to recognize the earl was a powerful man, yet he defied Erith for his mother's sake. Erith's admiration for Olivia's son grew. She was right to be so proud of him.

"I mean her no harm." Erith gathered Bey's reins in one hand and lifted himself into the saddle

Leo looked up at him with a grave expression that for once held no wariness or animosity. "Are you going to tell her I know she's my mother?"

Erith shook his head, automatically quieting Bey, who started to dance now he had a rider in the saddle. "It's not for me to do that."

"But you think I should."

"She suffers from hiding the truth, and she does it for your sake." Erith leaned forward to pat the restive horse's neck. "Good day, Mr. Wentworth."

With a clatter of hooves, he wheeled Bey around and galloped out of the yard. He headed back to London, but where he looked for Olivia next, he had no bloody idea.

Chapter 27

*E*rith slammed the brass lion-headed knocker down on the immaculate black door of the huge mansion in Grosvenor Square. It was late. Too late for unannounced calls on people he barely knew.

He ached with weariness and his heart was heavy with a bitter premonition of defeat. Inevitably the vile, helpless feeling in his gut reminded him of those gray, lost days after Joanna's death.

He'd loved two women in his life. Was fate cruel enough to steal both of them away?

No, he damn well wouldn't accept that.

He'd had a hellish day, chasing Olivia across London. After all his frantic searching, he was no closer to finding her than he'd been at the start.

For a woman of such spectacular beauty and widespread notoriety, his mistress disappeared with impressive effectiveness. Nobody had seen her. Nobody had any idea where she was or even where she might have gone.

Everybody now knew she'd deserted the Earl of Erith and that he was frantic to get her back.

He had seen the pity in men's eyes when they learned that the notorious courtesan had abandoned yet another lover. Most of them assured him he had no chance now that she'd moved on. Once Olivia Raines said good-bye, she never looked back. It was part of her mystique.

Erith had treated such ill-founded opinions with the scorn they deserved. Or he had. Until the uniformity of response started to chip away even his powerful self-confidence.

Olivia had built a legendary and longstanding reputation out of deceiving her keepers. Her lack of sexual response was real, he knew, but her pretense at pleasure had fooled many men before him. As the day spiraled into an ordeal of sheer obstinacy and endurance, the disturbing possibility loomed that he'd been equally fooled.

He loved her. She said she loved him.

Devil take her, had she lied?

As he asked without success at shops, at her friends' houses, at any event he could barge his way into, it became increasingly difficult for him to maintain his optimism. He'd even sent his servants to check hotels and inns. Fruitlessly.

She'd vanished as completely as a drift of smoke on a windy day.

If Olivia set out to make him suffer for his arrogance and vanity, she succeeded mightily. His legendary pride shriveled to nothing.

It was the middle of the night now. The dark hour when hope seemed out of reach. He'd run through every one of his sources and hadn't found her. He had no blasted clue where to turn next.

Except here.

With furious demand, he banged the knocker again and heard the imperious sound echo inside.

The door cracked open to a butler who had clearly dressed in a hurry. The man's mouth gaped with shock to find a peer of the realm on the spotless front steps so late. "My lord?"

After a day devoted to frantic searching, Erith's clothes were rumpled and soiled and he badly needed a shave. If he'd thought about it, he would have stopped to tidy himself before he landed here. But he'd been so bloody desperate, even a moment's delay had been torture.

"Tell his grace the Earl of Erith wishes to see him." He shouldered his way past the man, uncaring that he acted like a boor. After a moment's resistance, the butler staggered back and allowed him into the shadowy hallway.

"Who is it, Gaveston?"

Erith glanced up to where a woman holding a candle stood on the curved staircase. Even in the half dark, even in his overwrought state, even with her heavily pregnant, she stole his breath. Her beauty was so perfect, it was almost unearthly.

He struggled to regain some trace of address. Almost impossible when his life disintegrated to ruins around him.

"Your grace, I beg your indulgence for calling without warning."

Verity Kinmurrie, Duchess of Kylemore, once the famous courtesan Soraya, must have been preparing for bed. She was wrapped in a dark blue Chinese silk robe that did nothing to conceal her protruding belly. Her thick black hair was confined in a plait that curled across one shoulder.

He'd only seen her once, years ago in Paris, when she was mistress to an elderly English baronet. He'd never forgotten her. No man ever did. The only woman who compared was the one he desperately hoped sought refuge in this house.

"Who the hell is calling at this hour?" In his shirtsleeves and with his dark hair disheveled, the Duke of Kylemore stalked from the back of the house. Ink stains on his fingers indicated he'd been working.

The marriage of these two a year ago had ignited a scandal that reached as far as Vienna. Hell, as far as Moscow, he'd guess. The Kylemores' recent arrival in London for the duchess's lying in fueled gossip that had hardly died down since their wedding.

Most men in the ton were sick with envy that Kylemore had the gorgeous Soraya as a bedmate. Although none would face the world's condemnation to marry their mistress and turn illicit passion into official matrimony.

"I have no right to break in on you like this, your grace," Erith said. Behind him, the butler closed the door and stood waiting for instructions.

Kylemore loomed closer. "It's Lord Erith, isn't it?"

"Yes."

Erith turned to the duchess, who had descended to the black and white tiles of the hall. Up close she was even more exquisite, with perfect white skin and rain-clear gray eyes. "Your grace, we haven't been introduced. I'm Julian Southwood, the Earl of Erith."

"My lord." Her voice was low and husky and she spoke with the clipped tones of the upper classes. Just as Olivia did.

"Verity, there's no reason for you to be up. I'll see his lordship in the library." Kylemore moved to his wife's side, and Erith recognized the love that underlay his impatience.

Then he recognized something else more significant.

Neither was surprised to see him. Although they had never spoken to him before. Although it was well past midnight. Although he arrived unannounced and uninvited on their doorstep and forced his way into their house without permission.

Blind certainty surged up. Every instinct went on animal alert. Olivia was near. He could almost smell her.

"She's here, isn't she?" he said flatly.

Her grace shot her husband a frantic glance that was a betrayal in itself, then looked at Erith. "I don't—"

"You know who I'm talking about," Erith said, not caring if his tone was unsuitable for addressing a duke and his duchess. "I just want to talk to her."

"Verity, go upstairs to bed. The doctors say you need rest. My lord, the library, if you please."

Kylemore directed a cold look down his haughty nose. Unfortunately for him, Erith was at least an inch taller and in no mood to bow to ducal authority.

"If I have to, I'll tear this house apart to find her," Erith said grimly.

"Come back when you've learned some manners, man." With a threatening movement, Kylemore stepped toward Erith.

"Stop it, both of you."

Erith's head jerked up and he focused on the woman who hovered in the shadows at the top of the staircase. The other two people with him became as nothing.

"Olivia?" All his love and longing and anger invested the single word, turning it into a symphony of anguished yearning.

"Yes."

The terse answer told him nothing, and he couldn't see her face in the gloom. But as she slowly made her way downstairs, her reluctance was visible.

She was dressed in a soft blue gown he hadn't seen before. Her hair hung in a tawny curtain around her shoulders. As she came into the light, she looked pale and young and vulnerable. Although her jaw was set in a familiar stubborn line.

Erith's hands curled at his sides as he fought the impulse to grab her and take her back where she belonged. This was all wrong. She shouldn't be here. She should be safe in his arms. She was his, damn it.

Vaguely, Erith was aware of Kylemore speaking to the butler. "That will be all, Gaveston."

As the man melted away into the darkness, Erith moved in a daze across to the base of the stairs. Olivia was still a couple of steps above him but close enough for him to see tearstains marking her cheeks. She looked wan and unhappy. His gut clenched with regret and guilt.

"Come home, my love." He needed every shred of eloquence at his command. But with his heart overflowing, he couldn't dredge up anything more than a simple plea.

She stiffened at the endearment. Her grasp on the banister tightened until her knuckles were bloodless. She shook her head, her mane of hair drifting around her like a cloud. "No."

"Please." He stretched his hand toward her.

She flinched as if he offered a vial of poison. Dear God, she wasn't afraid of him, was she? He couldn't bear to think so.

She forced her chin up with a shaky gesture of defiance that broke his heart. "Erith, it's over."

"Never." He let his hand drop, so hurt that he hardly cared two strangers witnessed his humiliation. The only person who mattered to him was the woman in front of him. And she couldn't bring herself to touch him, it seemed.

"Come through to the library," the duchess said softly. "This isn't a discussion for the front hallway."

Olivia sent her a desperate look. "There's nothing to say."

"Oh, yes, there is," Erith said with grim determination. Demons from hell couldn't rip him from her side now he'd finally found her. "We say it here or somewhere else. Your choice, Olivia."

"No woman departs my house without her consent," Kylemore said sharply.

"Thank you, your grace," Olivia said quietly.

"Verity, go to bed." The duke still sounded impatient as he glanced at the duchess. "I'll make sure nothing happens."

His wife threw him a disbelieving look. "Don't be ridiculous, Justin. This is the most excitement I've had in weeks."

Kylemore thrust a hand through his hair. "You don't want excitement. You're about to have a baby."

"And I'm as strong as a horse. Don't fuss."

Erith waited for the autocratic duke to reprimand his wife, but the fellow merely flattened his mouth and gestured in the direction from which he'd come.

Olivia hesitated before descending the last steps. Erith wondered if she meant to flee back upstairs. If she thought he had too much pride to pursue her through the house, she was sadly mistaken. He was within seconds of seizing her, and her powerful friends be damned, when she came down and followed the Kylemores. She deliberately didn't look at Erith and she steered a wide course around him.

She treated him like a mongrel cur. No woman had ever made him feel so low. He loathed feeling like this, blast her to Hades. He stalked after her almost blindly, seething and desperate and yearning.

Like the rest of the cavernous house, the library was dimly lit. Kylemore wandered across to a side table. "Brandy, Erith?"

"Lord Erith isn't staying," Olivia said, her tone fraying.

"Well, you throw the blackguard out, Miss Raines. If I brawl with him in here, it will upset my wife." Kylemore raised the half-full decanter toward Erith. "My lord?"

Erith had been on the move all day. The prospect of a drink was enormously appealing. He also appreciated that Kylemore seemed determined to dispel the heightened atmosphere. "Yes, thank you."

"Good."

"Sit by me, Olivia," the duchess said as she subsided onto the sofa near the desk.

Olivia let the duchess draw her down beside her. Light from one of the lamps slanted across her tawny hair, making it shine with mysterious bronze and gold. Perhaps because he wasn't sure he'd ever see her again, her beauty made the breath catch anew in Erith's throat. Just as it had the first time he'd seen her, when she so coolly chose a lover from the throng at Montjoy's.

"My lord." Kylemore's deep voice was almost gentle as the duke stood before him with a glass in his hand. Difficult heat seeped under Erith's cheeks as he realized that he mooned after his mistress like a stripling ogling the dairymaids.

"Thank you." He accepted the brandy and took a quick mouthful to control his rioting emotions. The liquor hit his empty stomach like an explosion.

He sat down on a leather chair that faced the sofa. He'd reached a pitch of exhaustion where each detail of the room was crystal clear. The soft light. The tall duke. The beautiful duchess. His dear, gorgeous, damaged Olivia, who regarded him as though he were a frightening stranger.

"I shouldn't have come here," Olivia said softly, bending her head and studying the trembling hands she folded in her lap.

"Of course you should." Soraya—for that was how Erith thought of the duchess—raised her head and glared at Erith like an enemy. "I'm not ashamed of what I was."

"But I've made trouble for you."

"Have you? I don't think so. Lord Erith just wants to talk, then he'll go." The duchess's remarkable gray eyes sharpened on him. "Isn't that right, my lord?"

He bowed briefly. "Your grace." It wasn't agreement but it acknowledged her right to make the demand. "I'd like to speak to Olivia alone."

Soraya turned to Olivia. Seeing the two women together, it was easy to understand how they'd brought London to its knees. Even tired and pregnant and dressed for bed, not visitors, Soraya's pale, perfect beauty was like a pearl. Whereas Olivia sparkled with life and vitality. She was tense and upset, but Erith still felt he could hold out his hands and warm them in her life force. He wanted that vivid heat with him always. The prospect of returning to his cold isolation felt like encroaching death.

"What do you want, Olivia?" Soraya asked. "You're our guest. Your wishes are paramount."

Olivia stared across the room at Erith. Her tawny eyes were guarded. For two weeks they had shared such intimacy, yet tonight he had no idea of her thoughts.

Eventually she gave a quick nod. "I'll speak to him. I've

imposed upon your kindness enough. I can handle this myself."

Kylemore held his hand out to his wife. Sourly, Erith watched the naturalness with which Soraya accepted her husband's touch. It inevitably made him remember how Olivia spurned his hand in the hallway.

"I stand as your protector, Miss Raines," Kylemore said gravely.

"She needs no protector," Erith snapped. He was bitterly aware of the word's double meaning.

Kylemore sent him a stern look. "Nevertheless, I consider any insult to Miss Raines an insult to me."

Soraya laughed softly and tugged at her husband's hand. "Come, my love. This isn't getting us anywhere." She turned to Olivia. "We're only going to the morning room."

"Thank you, your grace." She managed a shaky smile.

Erith resented her air of a Christian martyr about to face the lions. Good God, she'd been a willing, even enthusiastic occupant of his bed for several weeks. She'd shared things with him she hadn't shared with anyone else.

She might deny she loved him, but now he saw her, doubts fled. She loved him, all right. It terrified the life out of her.

He was so busy studying his darling that he hardly noticed the spectacular duchess and her overbearing lout of a husband leave. His attention focused on the woman who remained alone on the sofa, chin up, eyes defiant, and cheeks shiny with drying tears.

Thoughtfully, he rubbed his hand over his jaw, feeling the scrape of his beard. Good God, he must look like the worst ruffian. It made him feel even more at a disadvantage.

How the Devil was he to proceed? The rest of his life hung upon this moment.

"You've been crying," he said softly when they were alone.

She flushed with chagrin and looked away. "It means nothing."

He rose with a sudden restless movement and shifted across to sit next to her. He reached to take her hand then remembered what had happened in the hallway and halted the gesture halfway.

Hell, what was wrong with him? He never felt uncertain, particularly with women.

But it had been such a long time since any one woman had mattered more than another.

And this one woman mattered more than his life.

He kept his voice low, unthreatening. "It means you're unhappy. I hate to think I've made you so, my love."

She recoiled against the rich gold upholstery. "Don't call me that."

"Whether I call you my love or not doesn't alter the truth, Olivia."

Her hand formed a fist and she punched her thigh through her filmy blue skirts. "I don't want to be your love."

Oh, yes, he believed that. Just as he believed she didn't want to love him. Although she did. With every second, he was more certain.

Desperately he sought for words to convince her to return to him. Even more important, to stay. "Don't make me live without you. I want you to be my lover. I want you to come to Vienna."

Her lips pursed as though she tasted something sour. "And live as your mistress."

It surprised him that she needed to spell out the arrangement.

"Of course. My precious mistress." He had a sudden insight into what must worry her. "Are you concerned I'll stray? Surely you see those women were just an attempt to fill my empty life after Joanna died. It sounds coldhearted. It *was* coldhearted. But they didn't suffer for knowing me, and we always parted friends. I was faithful to Joanna. I'll be faithful to you. You have nothing to fear from other women."

"I'm a harlot."

His brows drew together. He couldn't see the point of this. He once believed that she suffered no guilt over what she'd done. Now he knew her well enough to realize her feelings about her profession were tangled and ambiguous.

"You were forced into this life." His sincerity came from the depths of his soul. "Do you expect me to berate you for what you are? How can I? My own behavior hasn't been admirable."

The hands twined in her lap tightened. She looked down at them from under her thick fringe of gold-tipped lashes. "Yet you believe without question that I'm not fit to associate with your daughter." Her voice was very low and very sad.

He should have been prepared for the attack. The idea that a few sweet words and a promise of lifelong devotion on the Continent would win his case now seemed fatuous. A sinking feeling in the region of his gut told him that unless he was very careful, this was an argument he'd lose.

With disastrous consequences.

He fought to keep his voice quiet, reasonable, when what he wanted to do was snatch her up and kiss her senseless. But she was strong and clever, and unless he had her willing, he couldn't have her. He knew that in his bones.

"Olivia, you know as well as I how the world works. Probably better because you've suffered more from society's censure. I must put my daughter's welfare first. Perhaps because I've been such a selfish blackguard. Surely you can't expect anything else."

The eyes she focused on him were dull with misery. He'd wished her anger gone, but this was worse.

"No, of course I don't *expect* anything else."

He was seriously worried now. "What does that mean?"

She didn't answer immediately. Instead she stared into a shadowy corner. Her lush mouth was taut with distress.

He watched her so closely, he noticed her slender throat move as she swallowed. Her body vibrated tension. "My father was Sir Gerald Raines, a baronet with an estate outside Newbury."

Her quiet words took a moment to sink in.

Shock at what she told him, lacerating pity at what she'd endured, jolted him. "My God. I knew you came from a good family. I had no idea you came from . . . "

"Your own class?" Her lips twisted in an acerbic smile that held no humor. "If my brother hadn't sold me, I'd indeed be a fit companion for your daughter."

He frowned. "In my eyes, you are a fit companion for my daughter. Never confuse what I think with how society regards you."

"You looked utterly sick when you saw me with Roma."

"You know why."

"Yes, sadly, I do."

He raked his fingers through his hair in frustration. Why did he feel he tried to conduct a conversation in a language he couldn't speak?

"Olivia, what are you trying to say? You know your background—even if more elevated than I suspected—has nothing to do with how I feel about you."

"If my brother hadn't sold me to Lord Farnsworth after he'd offloaded every other scrap of his inheritance to feed his gambling, you and I would have known each other in a completely different context."

He couldn't help it, whatever the risk. He reached out and untangled her twisting hands, taking one and holding it tight between both of his.

"It's too late for regrets, Olivia," he said urgently. "You can't turn back the clock. By God, I'd call your brother out if he was still alive and put a bullet in his worthless carcass. But even if I did that, you couldn't reclaim the life you should have led. It's gone forever. Look toward a new life. With me."

He thought she'd pull away, but she let her trembling hand rest in his. He felt the fine tremors run through her. A frantic pulse fluttered at the base of her pale throat.

"I know," she said with such grief, his heart clenched. "But when I was a girl, I was the victim of a great injustice."

"Yes, you were." He curled his fingers around hers. He tried to infuse his warmth into her chilled flesh.

"Once, I could have looked as high as the Earl of Erith for a marriage partner."

"But your life didn't . . . " All his words disintegrated to dust. He suddenly realized where this odd, difficult discussion led and a shard of ice pierced him. "Ah."

"You keep telling me I'm magnificent and I'm wonderful and that you don't care what I've done. You say how you spoke to me yesterday means nothing and you respect and honor me as a woman." The topaz eyes she leveled on him burned like fire. "Show me."

"By marrying you." The three stark words emerged as a death knell to his dearest hopes.

She didn't blink at the shocking suggestion, proving right his horrified guess about her completely unrealistic plan. "Yes."

He sprang to his feet and looked at her with incredulous horror. "You're testing me. Just as you tested me when you tied me to your bed."

"Perhaps."

"You know this is impossible." An inexorable chill crept over him.

"Is it?" With her free hand, she gestured around the library. "The Duke of Kylemore married Soraya."

Kylemore was a damned fool.

Erith didn't say it aloud. She was tragically serious about this crackpot idea. He couldn't chance driving her away by dismissing it with the derision it deserved.

"Olivia, my darling, choose some other way for me to demonstrate my faith."

She shook her head with a regretful moue of her lips. "There is no other way."

In a burst of irritation, he swung away to face the book-lined wall. "You know I can't marry you. You've finally gone too far."

His sudden emotion left her unmoved. Instead she spoke very evenly and with a conviction he couldn't doubt. "Then there can be nothing further between us."

Chapter 28

"*Y*ou're not being reasonable." Julian whirled to face Olivia. His eyes blazed with rage and determination. And heaven help her, hurt bewilderment. It was the bewilderment that pierced her to the quick. "You ask too much."

"I know." She raised her chin and stared him down while misery howled inside her.

Of course he couldn't marry her.

He was the Earl of Erith and she was a notorious whore. The only future their world allowed them was the one he offered. Good Lord, Soraya was a duchess and society didn't accept her.

"If you know, why pursue this nonsensical course?" Julian still glared at her as if she'd gone mad. Perhaps she had.

She sucked in a shaky breath and sought words to explain. Knowing nothing would make him understand. "In every way except one, I'm an appropriate spouse for you. Even my barrenness isn't a problem, as you already have two healthy children."

"I have two healthy children who don't need their father to create an almighty scandal by marrying his mistress."

He was right, but that didn't stop his response scraping across nerves raw with grief. She blinked back bitter tears. During the long unhappy watches of the night, when she'd lain awake in the huge bedroom upstairs, she'd realized what she wanted. And she'd known what she wanted couldn't come to fruition. What she wanted never did, not since that black day when her contemptible brother had sold her.

She was unjust to demand such extravagant concessions from Julian. Her intelligence hadn't completely deserted her. But her torn, keening heart didn't heed logic or the demands of propriety. Her torn, keening heart would accept nothing less than marriage as unequivocal proof of what she meant to him. Yesterday, in her stung reaction to his cruel words, she'd thought he didn't love her. But calmer reflection today had brought the realization that of course he did. The question was whether he loved her enough.

Erith killed the dragons that ravaged her life and gave her a fairy-tale ending. Or else his love was as cheap and brittle as a china trinket won at a traveling fair.

"Fuck, Olivia," he said under his breath, running his hand through his hair again. The profanity signaled how close he was to losing control. "Don't do this to me."

"I have to." As a girl, she'd been worthy to marry him. In her soul, she still was. Unless he recognized that fact without shame or demurral, they had nothing. "What my brother and Lord Farnsworth did to me was heinously wrong. In my way, I've sought revenge on men ever since. Then I met you. The first man I respected. The first man who matched me. You're as strong as I. Stronger."

"No. Not stronger." He stared at the floor and a muscle in his cheek flickered. His voice was muffled and his fists opened and closed at his sides as if he fought the urge to shake sense into her.

"You're the first lover I don't despise."

"I am the first lover who made you feel anything." He looked up, and she couldn't mistake the bone-deep wretchedness in his face. Nauseating remorse made her stomach churn. She wounded him and she hated it.

"Yes." She admitted so much with that single word.

His voice was strained. "So you lied yesterday."

"You'd hurt me. I wanted to hurt you back. It sounds childish." She bit her lip then forced the necessary apology out. "I'm sorry."

"And you love me."

It was a statement, not a question.

"Yes."

"Isn't that enough? I love you, you love me." He cut the air with one hand as if canceling all her objections. "What does a damned piece of paper matter? There's nothing to stop us loving each other for the rest of our lives. You're throwing away paradise for want of a grand gesture you must know I can never make."

"But perhaps the gesture's very grandeur is all that will convince me we truly have paradise," she whispered in despair.

Guilt lashed her like a scourge. She loathed hurting him. But nothing, not even his visible agony, could shake her adamantine determination. Only this extravagant act would show her he believed she was worthy to stand at his side.

He dropped onto the sofa and seized her trembling hands, pressing them to his chest. Under her palms, his heart pounded with frenetic speed.

"Olivia, if it were just me, I'd do it. I'd do it tomorrow. But there's Roma and William." His grip tightened almost to the point of pain. "And there's Joanna."

She gave a low cry and tried to wrench free but he wouldn't let her go. "You think marrying me would sully her memory."

"The world would see it so." His flushed face was vivid with uncomprehending anger.

"Do you care so much for the world? You say you don't think of me as a whore, but every time you open your mouth, it's clear that's what you believe."

"Just because I won't ruin my family by marrying you?" His body was rigid with resistance to what she said. "You wouldn't exact such a price. Not you. Not the woman who protected Leo all these years and loved Perry, knowing what he is. Not the woman who tried so hard to save Roma from scandal yesterday."

"But I need to believe you think I'm worth the price," she choked out. "Unless you're willing to give up the world for me, I don't want you."

She flinched as his brows lowered in a furious scowl. "You're asking more than any man can give."

Through tight lips, she forced out the difficult truth she knew he didn't want to hear. "Kylemore did it for Soraya."

He made a frustrated sound deep in his throat. "All due respect to his grace, but we have to live in this world you're so eager to abandon. Or at least I do. I have work in Vienna."

"Which you've grown tired of. I saw your face when we drove through those fields the other day, Julian. You were brought up a countryman. You're still a countryman at heart."

"Perhaps. But that doesn't mean I can humiliate my children. Good God, Roma's about to make the most brilliant match of the season. How will her new family react if her father marries the queen of the demimonde?"

Of course she cared about his children and his reputation. *Above all, she cared about him.* The price of her demand—for him, for her, for those he loved—ripped at her anew. But still her heart refused to relinquish its stubborn crusade.

Blinking away tears no longer worked. One overflowed and trailed down her cheek. "And what about me, Julian?"

"Come to Vienna." His grip on her hands softened, became a caress. "You'll be my wife in all but name, loved and safe and protected under the law. I'll have contracts drawn up. Property. An annuity. You'll never want for anything."

"Except for what I really want," she said with arid desolation. "A man who tells me, tells the world, that I'm worthy of his love."

"Don't smash what we have because you can't have everything." His voice lowered and the deep timbre seeped into her bones. She adored his voice. How could she live without hearing it? "I'll love you to the end of my days but I can't change the past."

She realized she leaned toward that honeyed baritone like a starving bird craning for a crumb from the hunter's hand. She jerked back, and this time he released her without protest.

She dashed the torrent of tears from her face, but more just fell to take the others' place. Damn Julian. Before she met him, she couldn't remember the last time she'd cried.

"I want my birthright," she said doggedly, even while her traitorous heart whispered to accept the love he offered so freely. Accept, and forget that he failed her in this ultimate trial.

"At the cost of my children's happiness? I can't believe that of you, Olivia. I can't. I know you better than that."

Every word he spoke flung her dreams further out of reach yet only made her blindly, unreasonably determined to hold her ground. She refused to settle for second best, now that she'd discovered a real, enduring love. If she let Julian treat her as second best, that's what she'd stay forever. In his mind and in hers. Living with that knowledge day after day would crush her. More, it would crush what they felt for each other.

"I don't want to cost anyone their happiness," she said through numb lips. Why, dear Lord, did this have to be so hard? It was like flaying herself alive. "I only know I can't live in the shadows. I deserve better. Our love deserves better. Either you're proud to own me for the entire world to see, or you don't own me at all."

"I won't respond to threats," he snapped, stiffening with renewed rage.

"It's not a threat," she said sadly. "If you can't offer me marriage as a mark of the honor with which you regard me, I won't stay with you."

His eyes narrowed. "Damn you, Olivia, you know I can't do this."

His biting anger didn't cow her. When she spoke again, her words rang with conviction. "I know you're the man I love and you can do anything. I know how clever you are, how resolute, how strong." Her voice roughened with urgency. "If you want it enough, you can achieve this, Julian. Make it so your children don't suffer. Make it so we're happy. Make it so we're together."

He shook his head with horrified disbelief. "You ask the impossible."

"If you love me, you'll make it true." She already knew her words fell on deaf ears. As they'd always been bound to. "I ask you to do the honorable thing."

He stared at her as if he hated her. "By making me dishonor everything else in my life."

She looked away in swift shame. She wasn't a fool. Nothing could restore her innocence or social standing. But if Julian married her, against sense, self-interest, inclination even, she could trust him forever. She swallowed and spoke with difficulty. "If you feel like that, there's nothing more to be said."

"So that's it?" he asked bleakly.

"Yes."

In quivering misery, she waited for him to get up and leave, but instead he grabbed her arms and forced her to face him. Challenge sparked in his eyes.

"What about this?" he asked fiercely.

He wrenched her up and kissed her with unabashed hunger and anguish. She couldn't hide her swift and eager response.

It was the last time he'd touch her like this. She knew that in her soul.

His lips ground down on hers. He'd never kissed her so violently, not even at the heights of passion. She started to cry once more, helpless against the sorrow that held her in its talons.

"Oh, my love," she moaned as he pushed her against the arm of the couch and clumsily shoved the blue dress up.

"Yes," he breathed into her mouth.

Tragic to think how rare kisses had been in her life until she met him. Tragic to think how she'd miss his mouth on hers.

She didn't resist as he parted her legs and stroked her sex. Moisture bloomed and her belly clenched in swift response. How quickly he stirred her excitement. But every moment of pleasure shredded her heart. Until Erith, she'd never known this joy. After Erith, this joy would be forever denied to her.

His eyes were nearly black with desire and overmastering emotion. He trembled with desperate passion and a fierce need to persuade her with his body now words had failed. She knew why he did this. But as her own desire spiraled upward like flame, she couldn't summon the will to resist.

This was the last time.

His stare was unwavering. With deliberate slowness, he lifted his slick fingers and sucked them, savoring her with voluptuous pleasure. The sight of him tasting her so blatantly shocked her, made every muscle tighten, heated the blood in her veins to lava.

His silver eyes glinted with knowledge and unbearable need. He silently told her that both of them were prisoners to desire and she attempted escape at her peril.

"No," she whimpered, even as she arched toward him in frenzied eagerness.

"Yes," he said implacably. His hands were equally impla-

cable as he hitched her hips high and dipped his head between her legs. He'd done this before, in those wild nights
when she'd surrendered herself to love.

But something about his unhurried determination, the
graceful lowering of his dark head, the hard purpose of his
mouth at her core, made her shudder with new passion.

His tongue probed her sleek heat and then he took her in
his mouth and sucked hard. Her body spasmed with dazzled
delight and she shoved a shaking hand between her teeth to
muffle her hoarse scream. She gave herself up to the blinding light. She wanted this one true love to explode to its end
among the stars. When she closed her eyes, she saw radiant suns. Spinning. Dancing. Combusting. Sizzling pleasure
struck her like summer lightning.

She still quaked when he began to lick her again. She was
so sensitive that the faintest brush of his tongue built another
climax.

This one hit hard enough to stop her heart. Without knowing what she did, her shaking hands buried themselves in
his thick hair. Tears poured down her face and she bit down
hard on her lower lip to stifle sobs of sorrow, cries of pleasure. A rhythmic growling sound emerged from her throat.
Too soft to be heard outside the library but enough to inspire
Julian to work his mouth in time with her moans.

Hold, release, hold, release.

Her hips moved toward him and back as they did when his
member was buried deep in her. He gripped her thighs more
firmly, parting them to give him greater access. His tongue
penetrated her and her intimate muscles contracted to keep
him there. Female musk surrounded them in a sensual cloud.

The climb to ecstasy started again. Before the quivering
aftershocks from her previous climax subsided, his fiendishly adept mouth flung her back into a fiery sky.

"Julian!" Her voice cracked as she reached her shuddering
peak. "Oh, Julian!"

She bowed up. Somewhere beyond the brilliant blaze of

sensation, like a shadow behind the sun, lurked the cruel knowledge that after the ecstasy came devastation.

This was the last time.

For an endless space, she clung to that burning height, unaware of where she was. Although she was always aware of who she was with.

Her love. Her only love. Her lost love.

Vaguely she felt him move, shift, reposition himself. Then glorious pressure as he pushed into her swollen, creamy tissues.

"Open your eyes, Olivia." His demand emerged in breathless gasps. He sounded angry. He sounded fierce. He sounded as though love drove him to the edge of madness.

Silently, she obeyed him.

His face was haggard. His lips drew back against his teeth as if he were in excruciating torment. His skin seemed too tight for the bones of his face.

Determination firmed his jaw as he met her stare. "I want you to look at me while I take you," he insisted gruffly. He edged his way farther into her body. "I want you to feel every inch. Then I want you to try and tell me you're leaving me."

He leaned over her, his powerful chest and shoulders dwarfing her. He supported himself on taut arms, and his savagely glittering gray eyes didn't shift from hers. With ruthless purpose he angled his hips and seated himself completely.

She had a dazed second to adjust to how he filled her. Then he began to move, hard, arrogant, commanding.

Every stroke irrefutably claimed her as his.

She clutched at his back as each powerful thrust bumped her against the arm of the sofa. Her hands bunched in the fine wool of his coat. She bent her knees to give him greater access, her thighs chafing against his trousers.

A barrage of sensations attacked her. The vigorous virility of his body in hers. The sharp tang of sweat and desire. Her own flooding, uncontrollable response. His breath rasping as he moved, owning, branding, marking.

She rose to meet him and moaned as he went deeper. He'd taken her so often, but never before had her body become an extension of his.

All the time, those gray eyes bored into hers. Charting the rise of her pleasure.

While part of her resented how easily he subdued her, her greedy soul snatched what pleasure it could. She'd never feel this with anyone else. Every second was precious, perfect, irreplaceable.

Relentlessly he pushed her higher and higher.

After what he'd done to her with his mouth, she couldn't believe she had anything left to give him. But she did.

She reached helplessly into the void. Still, final pleasure eluded her grasp. The pressure built and built until she thought she must shatter.

She gave a choked sob. Her fingernails drove into his back. If he'd been naked, she would have drawn blood. She closed her eyes and arched, blindly seeking that ultimate, transcendent connection.

He withdrew to the limits of her body. She braced for him to plunge back.

Nothing.

She opened her eyes. "Julian?"

"Look at me, damn you." His voice was harsh and shook with the superhuman control he exerted.

"I am looking at you," she said breathlessly, frenzied with the need to have him inside her. She surged up, her hands fisting in his coat.

"And you love me."

"I love you." It was a frantic cry. "Don't stop."

"Never." He drove down hard and everything around her erupted into a coruscating burst of white.

She cried out and clutched at his back as her body convulsed in a pleasure higher, purer, brighter than any she'd ever known.

Through the conflagration, she heard him groan, then she felt him shudder over and over again as he spilled into her. The perfect rightness of the moment held her suspended in joy and anguish as her tight passage milked him of his essence.

She opened tear-filled eyes to see him poised above her, his head flung back, his hair damp with sweat, his face taut. She carved the sight on her memory forever, even while her body gripped him as if she never wanted him to leave her.

She didn't.

She still quivered with helpless reaction and astonished rapture when he pulled out. With a long groan, he collapsed against the back of the sofa. She sprawled where he'd left her. Every bone had dissolved into hot honey. Her face was sticky with tears and stung from the abrasion of his shadow beard.

She ached. He hadn't been gentle. But how could she regret what had happened? The throbbing peak had been unbelievable. Exquisite. Heartbreaking.

His chest heaved as he struggled for air and his pulse beat wildly at the open neck of his shirt. Somewhere in her passion she'd ripped at his neckcloth. She couldn't remember when.

His black hair was disheveled and a lock fell over his forehead. His clothes were crushed and damp with sweat. His trousers gaped, revealing the tangled black curls of his pubic hair.

Neither spoke for a long time. He'd pushed her to her limits. She wasn't sure she'd ever move again.

He looked across to where she lay with her legs splayed and her blue gown twisted around her body. "You look utterly ravished."

He sounded lazy and pleased. He sounded like the exciting lover who had taught her the meaning of pleasure.

"I feel utterly ravished," she said in a husky voice. "I think we've ruined the couch."

"Kylemore can afford a new one." Julian's gorgeous mouth twitched into a sensual smile. "Anyway, after that, I'll gladly buy him a hundred couches." He paused and the smile slowly faded, to be replaced by an intent stare. "Are you coming to Vienna?"

Poisonous reality doused her pleasure like a cold wave washing over footprints on a beach. Her lips were tight as she forced out the question she had to ask. "As your mistress or as your wife?"

He frowned. "You know the answer to that. It's the only answer I can give you. Surely after what we just shared, you can't mean to send me away."

Gracelessly she straightened her legs and sat up. Grief was a leaden weight in her belly, and her heart beat out a grim rhythm of farewell. She had the answer to her question. He loved her but he didn't love her enough. The inevitable moment had come. Passion had staved it off but couldn't change the outcome.

She felt like she poised trembling on the edge of a chasm. She drew in a scraping breath and stepped off the edge. "Yes, I can." Her voice was low but steady. "Good-bye, Julian."

His jaw set in an angry line and he hurtled to his feet, fastening his trousers with violent movements. "Damn you, Olivia. I'm bloody sick of pleading. I'm sick of lying down in the dirt in front of you just so you can kick me."

Aghast, she stared at him. He sounded as if she'd gashed a hole in his heart. How could she stay adamant against his suffering? Was anything worth his crippling agony? She stretched one trembling hand in his direction. "Julian . . ."

He didn't seem to heed her. "Let me know when you change your mind. As you will change your mind. But be warned, my lady—don't expect me to wait forever."

It hurt to swallow the hard lump of anguish in her throat. "I don't expect you to wait at all." Although the idea of him with another woman made her want to yowl and scratch at him like a maddened tigress. "I told you before you gave me that most memorable farewell—it's over."

He sent her a freezing glare. How could eyes that had been

so warm only seconds ago turn so frosty? His voice was cold, hard, superior. "I've begged you repeatedly. I won't beg again. You're doing this out of stupid pride, Olivia. I hope you and your pride are damned happy together."

He turned on his heel and marched toward the door. Her hand dropped disconsolately to her side. He reached for the door handle then paused. And paused.

He kept his back to her but she didn't need to see his face to know he waited for her to call him. Impetuous offers of compromise rose in her throat but she closed her mouth against them. Iron will shackled her and refused to offer the concessions her breaking heart longed to make. She choked on the harrowing desolation.

After another second of charged silence, he turned the door knob and stalked out into the hallway. She heard murmured voices outside. It sounded as if Kylemore had indeed waited for them.

Acrid shame overwhelmed her. For all her brave words, she'd acted like a whore. For all her brave defiance, she was alone and lonely and desperately wanted Erith's arms around her to keep the cold away.

His arms would never hold her again.

Soraya appeared in the doorway and her face convulsed with compassion. "Oh, my dear."

"The earl has gone?"

"Yes."

She forced the pathetic lie to her lips even as a jagged rift opened inside her. "I'm glad."

"Oh, Olivia. You don't need to pretend." Soraya rushed to her side.

A strangled sob caught in Olivia's throat. "Yes, I do."

The sob escaped and she began to cry in deep, ugly gasps. The world shrank to a wilderness of overwhelming pain. She hardly felt Soraya take her in her arms or heard her whisper meaningless comfort.

Chapter 29

$\mathcal{O}$livia hefted the heavy pail through the kitchen door and flung the dirty water on the pink rosebush that climbed up the side of her neat whitewashed cottage. This fine August evening, the flowers' sweet scent drifted on the air like a benediction.

She straightened with a tired grunt and glanced vaguely down toward the estate's imposing wrought-iron gates. A man on a large gray horse cantered up the lime tree-lined drive. The long rays of the lowering sun lit the rider and his mount to gold.

Her heart launched into a veering race. Her hand tightened on the pail's handle until the knuckles shone white. The breath jammed in her taut throat. Quivering with a wild mixture of nerves and excitement and dismay, she waited.

"Lord Erith," she said with artificial calmness when he was within hailing distance.

Because of course it was Julian. The confident easy seat on the horse, the height in the saddle, the rakish angle at which he wore his hat identified him, even before she saw his face.

She knew he'd look for her after that unequivocal demonstration of mutual passion and a good-bye he wouldn't accept as final. When she first sought refuge here, she spent every minute on tenterhooks, expecting him to gallop up like the hero of a poem and fling her across his saddle. But days had turned into weeks and he hadn't found her.

Well, he'd found her now, God help her.

Without smiling, he swept off his hat and bowed as if to a fine lady. "Olivia."

Her heart clenched as she remembered the last time they were together. When he transported her to heights of rapture she'd never imagined. And then abandoned her to unrelenting devastation.

For a fraught moment the memory of that fiery encounter in the Duke of Kylemore's library rose between them, honed and shining like a new blade.

Deliberately, she broke the connection, clutching the empty wooden bucket before her as a barrier.

What did he see when he looked at her? These days, very little remained of elegant, decadent Olivia Raines, glittering cynosure of the demimonde. After hours making preserves, she was humiliatingly aware that her faded linen frock and apron were stained and wrinkled. Her feet were shoved into rough work shoes. Her hands were callused from physical labor. Days in the garden had brought out the freckles she'd spent years trying to vanquish. Her mouth was sticky from tasting the jam.

How she wished she didn't give a fig what he thought. But before she could stop herself, she self-consciously raised a hand to smooth her disheveled hair. It was piled untidily away from her face and up from her neck. With the summer heat, stray strands clung to her damp throat and tickled her cheeks.

She looked like a complete slattern, whereas he, as usual,

was kitted out in the height of fashion. The dark blue coat and tan breeches fit to perfection. Even after the hot and dusty ride from London, his high boots gleamed and his neckcloth was crisp and snowy.

The contrast between them couldn't have been harsher. He was probably wondering what in heaven's name he'd ever seen in her.

She raised her chin and tried to summon defiance. But it was difficult when her heart pounded like a hammer and desperate uncertainty prickled at her skin.

"What do you want?" she asked with a hint of hostility, although there was only one reason he could be here. To lure her back to his bed. Under his concentrated gaze, she shifted like a nervous filly. She fought an impulse to wipe her fruit-stained mouth like a street urchin.

"You've led me a devil of a dance," he said without heat.

He looked relaxed, the hand holding his hat draped loosely over his thigh. The breeze played with his thick black hair. Beneath the sensual heaviness of his eyelids, his eyes gleamed bright silver.

Tingling life returned to her veins. It was so unfair that he turned up without warning to shred the peace she'd fought to achieve. Except if she were honest, she'd admit she'd never found peace. Instead, she'd felt as if someone had ripped her heart from her chest and stamped on it over and over then flung it into an icy river.

Damn Julian for finding her. The long, painful battle to forget him would only start again. A battle she'd been spectacularly losing, no matter how she tried. "Did the Kyle-mores tell you where I was?"

She lived on the Duke of Kylemore's Kent estate, inherited last year through an obscure cousin. After Erith had stormed out of their library, Soraya and her daunting husband offered her sanctuary here. Gratefully, she'd accepted the chance to hide away until she was ready to grapple with the world again. She couldn't bear the idea of staying in London and running into Erith everywhere she went. Or worse, him besieging her with declarations of love that couldn't heal the breach in her soul.

His mouth flattened. "Eventually. But only after I'd worked it out for myself."

The smooth baritone vibrated right to her toes. For one lost moment she closed her eyes and remembered that voice whispering words of love.

When she opened them again, his gaze held a knowing glint, as if he guessed the tenor of her thoughts.

Of course he guessed. He'd known her so well, even if their affair had ended after a few short weeks.

He went on as though that strange moment of shared perception had never existed. "I should have realized you'd be near Leo. I'm sure he's told you I've gone to Wood End searching for you."

"No, he hasn't said anything." Leo had been a regular visitor to her cottage all summer. "He knows I'm his mother."

The gray gaze didn't flicker. "I didn't tell him."

"He said he's always known." She couldn't help smiling. Now she didn't have to lie, her relationship with her son held new depth and intimacy.

"He's a clever lad."

"You didn't come here to talk about Leo." She straightened and sent Erith a hard glare.

She'd forgotten stern looks never got her far. He merely cocked one mocking eyebrow at her. "I'm happy to talk about Leo. I'm in no hurry." The glint in his eyes grew more pronounced. "Although it's a long dusty ride from London. Aren't you going to ask me in? Offer me a drink?"

"You usually don't wait to be invited," she said sourly.

She so wanted to be angry, to hate him. But it was impossible when he sat upon his horse with that wicked gleam in his eyes. He looked like the answer to every desperate prayer she'd whispered through so many wretched, sleepless nights.

"Perhaps I've learned some manners in the long, dismal days since you left."

He didn't sound like the days had been long and dismal. He sounded like he merely made social chat with a distant acquaintance. Then she looked at the dirt and sweat on the horse's coat and remembered how far it was to London.

"When did you find out where I was?" Although she already guessed.

"This afternoon."

He must have galloped most of the way. It gave the lie to his casual act. He was used to hiding his feelings. So was she. For a brief brilliant moment they'd been honest with each other. But that moment had vanished forever.

"Your horse must need a drink." To hide the sharpness of her regret, she turned toward the pump and shoved her bucket under the spout with unnecessary violence.

"By all means, care for the animal first," he said with a trace of irony. She glanced up and noticed a tautness to his mouth that indicated he wasn't quite as self-possessed as he wanted to appear. "Why didn't Kylemore put you up in the manor?"

She began to pump and a satisfying gush of water splashed into the bucket. "He wanted to but I didn't feel that was right."

"My, you're such a humble soul, aren't you, Miss Raines?"

She sent him a quelling look. "If you want more than your horse to receive refreshment, I'd guard your tongue."

"Or use it for something more enjoyable," he murmured.

She pretended not to hear, but a telltale flush rose at the reminder of what he'd done the last time they were alone. As they were alone now. Her maid had gone home for the day, and this house was isolated from the village.

Ungraciously, she plunked the bucket under the horse's nose. As the animal drank with noisy enthusiasm, she glowered up at Erith. "You may as well come in. It's not as though I can keep you out."

"It's not, is it?" He seemed completely unaffected by her prickly humor. Even the brief uncertainty she thought she'd marked had disappeared. With powerful grace that sent her heart into a careening sprint, he swung himself out of the saddle and slid down to stand next to her.

She realized she poised stock-still, drawing his wonderful scent deep into her lungs. He smelled of horses and dust and fresh sweat and himself.

He seemed in no rush to shift either. And still he stared at her. She started as though waking from a deep sleep. If she wasn't careful, he'd know how appallingly vulnerable she was to him.

Fool, of course he knows. That's why he's here.

She'd had no idea how cruel love could be until Julian was lost to her forever. What painful joy it was to see him. Because nothing had changed. The air had a special charge and the light was brighter and she felt alive for the first time in months.

How utterly tragic, how completely aggravating, that a *man* made her feel like this.

"Come in." She spoke in a stony tone. "There's ale in the larder. And I suppose you're hungry."

He sent her a soulful look from those devilish gray eyes as he pulled off his leather gloves. "It's a long ride . . . "

"From London. I know, you told me." With a twitch of her skirts and a huffy sway of her hips, she marched toward the kitchen. "Then you can go on your way."

A single glance over her shoulder told her he hadn't followed. He just stood near the horse, slapping his gloves idly on the side of his breeches. He formed a perfect picture of masculinity, God rot him.

"Go where?" he asked gently.

She paused on the doorstep and shot him a derisive glare. "Back to town. To Maidstone. To Dover. To Hades, for all I care."

"But it's going to be dark soon. And Bey is tired. So am I. A kindhearted person would offer me a bed."

Her lips tightened with impatience. With him and with herself. How she wished she could remain immune to his humor. But she'd always been hopelessly susceptible to his teasing. "You're too old for boyish charm to work, Erith."

"You used to call me Julian."

"Many things have changed since then. Are you coming in?"

"With pleasure."

He drew the final word out, and she couldn't block the reluctant anticipation that trickled down her spine. He'd said those very words the first night he came to York Street.

Good Lord, she needed to put a cap on the insidious enchantment of memory or he'd have her flat on her back before she crossed the threshold. Not that she was averse to one last night of pleasure with the earl. But what would it achieve? She'd only be left lonely and longing again when he departed.

She stepped through into the cool dimness of the flag-stoned kitchen. He followed her inside, and her perfectly adequate kitchen suddenly seemed cramped. Not just because he was a big man, tall and powerful. But because of the contained energy he exuded.

"This is nice." He sat without invitation on the window seat and looked around with unconcealed curiosity. The room was in chaos after her inept attempts at making jam. The air was sickly sweet with the smells of hot sugar and fruit. She tried not to mind but her pride revolted at the mess.

She carried the jug of ale out of the larder and poured him a mug. She passed it to him, careful not to brush his fingers. "You think it's shabby and mean."

"Thank you." He accepted the drink and took a deep draft.

She tried not to watch as his head bent back and his throat worked to swallow. He was such an overwhelmingly male presence. Alien in her feminine world. She tried to resent his invasion of her home. But her heart was too busy dancing with elation at having him so near.

Poor, stupid heart.

Poor, stupid Olivia.

He lowered the mug and sent her a sharp look. "No, I don't. I think it's charming. But it's not exactly how I imagined you living."

"You imagined I'd take another rich lover," she said bitterly, although to be fair, what else would he think? It was the obvious route for London's most notorious cyprian.

His lips twisted in a smile that wasn't a smile at all. "I know you better than that."

She slammed her hand hard down on the berry-strewn kitchen table, suddenly sick of this fencing. "You don't know me at all, my lord. Please state your business and leave."

"I wanted to see you." He slid the empty mug onto the table she'd just thumped. "I've sought you high and low since April."

She swung away and stared blindly into the hallway that led through the rest of the downstairs section. "There's no point to this. I won't come to Vienna as your mistress."

"Wait until you're asked," he said softly.

She turned on him with a flash of temper. "Don't pretend you're not here to get me back. You flaunt a fine uncaring air but I can smell the desire on you."

He definitely wasn't smiling now. "Of course I want you."

"It isn't . . . " She paused. "You said you were going back to Vienna after Roma's wedding in June."

"She didn't marry Renton after all." He raised one booted leg and linked his fingers around his knee. He might admit unrelenting hunger for her but his demeanor conveyed pure assurance. "I thought you'd have heard."

"Gossip doesn't reach down here. And none of my London friends know where I am. Except Perry of course."

"Lying hound told me he didn't know."

"I made him promise not to tell anyone. Especially you."

"Do you know the Duchess of Kylemore was safely delivered of a daughter in May?"

"This is Kylemore's estate. That sort of news doesn't count as town tattle. Tell me about Roma." Then a horrible thought briefly banished her barbed resentment. "The Rentons didn't find out about her meeting me, did they? I swear I never intended her harm, Julian." The name escaped before she could stop herself.

If he said anything smug about her slip, she'd hit him with one of the large copper pans hanging above the range. But he didn't seem to notice. Although she knew that of course he had. Those acute eyes and the even sharper brain behind them didn't miss anything.

"No. Roma's visit to you remains secret, thank God. Although she'll have a reputation as a jilt."

"She broke the engagement?" Olivia frowned in puzzlement. "You don't sound very upset."

He shrugged. "The boy always struck me as a prig and a bore."

"Compared to you, he probably is," she couldn't help saying.

He gave a short laugh. "A low blow, my love." He ignored the killing scowl she shot him and continued. "She's still so young. And immature even for her years. It was a brilliant alliance, but I'd rather she made a match with someone of similar spirit and intelligence. The more I got to know her and the more I saw of the stuffed shirt she attached herself to, it seemed an unequal pairing."

"I think she looked for someone to replace you. Someone to give her the family she felt you'd stolen from her."

How she'd missed talking to him like this. How she'd missed the vital reality of his physical presence. How she'd missed everything about him. Frantically, she threw up a barricade against the softness creeping into her heart. She had no future with this man. She had to remember that.

A shadow of regret crossed his striking features. "Perhaps you're right. She and I have become much better friends. Although she still rides like a bloody loaf of bread. Imagine a daughter of mine so inept in the saddle."

"The scandal of her rejecting Renton must have been awful. Is she all right?" Olivia hated to think of the girl suffering society's disapproval.

"All right?" A wry smile curved his lips. "She's in the pink. And sporting a completely new wardrobe, all based on what you wore this season. You've become a rather powerful influence."

She sought and failed to find resentment in his voice. "You must hate that."

"Only because it reminds me you ran off. But then, I hardly need reminding of that."

"Julian . . . " she began in warning, backing toward the unlit stone hearth, although he made no overt move to touch her.

He spoke before she could complete the reprimand. "I must say I prefer this new dashing Roma to the sulky chit I came home to. She's set on becoming an original. I'm sure she'll find some fellow to take her in hand before she goes too far. Now if only she learned to ride the way you do, I'd be a proud father."

There was a fondness in his voice that hadn't been there when he'd mentioned his daughter before. Olivia smiled. She didn't wish him ill, even if she couldn't be with him. And she knew how the estrangement with his family had gnawed at his happiness.

"I'm glad. And your son?"

"William's getting there, especially now he's lost his ally against me in Roma. At least he's willing to spare me a word these days. Turns out he didn't like Renton either."

"So you achieved what you wanted with your return to London."

"You could say that." His words were slow and considered.

He still stared at her. It should make her uncomfortable. After all, she looked like a peasant, and he came to ask for what she couldn't give. Yet it seemed perfectly natural that his eyes followed her so closely. Just as it seemed perfectly natural to share what troubled him and rejoice that at least one of his sorrows had found relief.

"Is that why you delayed your return to Vienna?"

"I'm not going back to Vienna. I've resigned my post." He paused and drew a deep breath. "I've bought a chateau in France where I'll breed horses."

"France?" The question emerged almost inaudibly. Shock stiffened every muscle. "I thought you wanted to stay in England."

"My plans have evolved."

"What about your estates?"

She tried to tell herself that none of this concerned her. She'd left him and had no intention of returning. England. France. Timbuctoo. He was equally lost to her wherever he settled. She had no reason to feel her life ruptured just because he meant to live in another country. For goodness sake, she'd assumed he was already back in Vienna.

"William takes over once he finishes at Oxford."

"Wouldn't one of your houses here be more convenient for you, for your family?"

He picked up the tankard and turned it in his hands, watching the fading light gleam on the pewter. "After all the years on the Continent, England is too hidebound for me. I had a romantic dream of my homeland and I'll always love it, but, no, France will suit me better. The property is in Normandy. Close enough for regular visits. From either side. All my arrangements have my children's full approval."

"I find that hard to believe."

A wry smile twisted his mouth. "I didn't say immediate approval. But after much discussion, I've brought them around to my point of view."

To hide her unreasoning distress, she injected a note of derision into her question. "So the dazzling, notorious rake, the Earl of Erith, sets up as a mere farmer?"

"I'm looking forward to it. And I'm going to travel. My bride has a yen to see foreign lands." When he looked up, his eyes were clear and brilliant with unalloyed happiness. "Olivia, I'm getting married."

Chapter 30

*W*ith a broken cry, Olivia recoiled. Her head rang as if someone had cuffed her. Julian's words echoed in her ears.

Married? Of course he wanted to marry. He just didn't want to marry her.

Shaking, blind, she fumbled for the back of one of the sturdy rush-seated chairs. She couldn't fall. She couldn't. It would be too humiliating. But her knees felt like string, and the mist that blocked her sight thickened to the same deep gray as Julian's eyes. The workaday room faded from view. She tumbled down a long tunnel toward a dark abyss.

Dimly, through her suffocating distress, she heard a clang as Julian dropped the tankard. Then a resounding clatter as the chair she lurched after overturned onto the stone floor.

He was going to marry another woman. How could she bear it?

Four months ago she'd set him free. He must have devoted the time since to finding a suitable wife. An exemplary creature to become the new Countess of Erith. A woman to live with him and establish his home and be a mother to his children and—oh, God, she felt sick—give him babies as Olivia never could.

She swayed. Why on earth couldn't she breathe? She had to breathe. Her lungs seized up. And she was cold. Deathly cold.

"Olivia? Olivia, my darling, it's all right."

Through an unseeing blur, she felt strong arms encircle her. Then further disorientation as he swept her high in his arms and carried her through to the hallway.

He would marry someone else.

She shivered so hard that nothing could keep her from clinging to his familiar warmth. Not even the devastating news of him taking another woman as his wife.

"Put me down," she croaked through lips that felt like they were made of cotton.

He ignored her. Perhaps didn't even hear her. "You must have a damned parlor. I refuse to talk to you in the bloody kitchen any longer."

He would marry someone else.

Over and over the poisonous words pounded in her brain. Still she couldn't comprehend them.

He shouldn't carry her as if she belonged in his arms. He shouldn't call her his darling. He shouldn't even talk to her alone. He should be in London courting his bride.

He cradled her as if she were the rarest treasure. Conscience prompted her to protest at how he held her. But she'd never been a hypocrite, and she wouldn't start now. She curved her arm around his neck and rubbed her cheek against his chest. Under her ear, his heart thudded slow and steady.

Life and awareness seeped back. She studied his strong profile. His cheekbones seemed more pronounced, as though he'd lost weight. And his expression conveyed a bleakness that indicated he hadn't smiled much since she left him.

Fantasy, all of it. He hadn't been pining for her. He'd been wooing another woman.

"I'm too heavy." Her voice sounded raw and cracked.

He gave the short laugh she loved, as though he were amused despite himself. "You're perfect."

He swung her through the narrow doorway to the parlor and ducked his head under the low lintel. "This is more like it."

"I can stand," she said without great conviction.

"No. You'll only faint on me again." He sank down into the armchair before the fireplace and settled her in his lap.

"I didn't faint." Her legs had gone rubbery, her vision had faded, and she'd felt like she was about to collapse, but she hadn't fainted. Olivia Raines never fainted.

"If you say so. For God's sake, woman, stop wriggling."

Oh, what was the use? She subsided with a despairing sigh. Her frantically beating heart immediately quieted. She was fatally weak but she couldn't bring herself to end the exquisite moment. The wonderful scents of sandalwood and Julian surrounded her, promised pleasure, bypassed anger and shock.

"That's better," he said softly, burying his face in her hair.

She shut her eyes and let his presence wash over her. The joy was fragile, deceptive, wrong, but she couldn't pull away. This was the nearest she'd come to happiness in all the endless, dour weeks since they'd parted.

"Julian, don't torment me," she begged in a broken voice. "It's too cruel."

"Cruel? That's damned rich. Woman, you've given me four months of complete hell," he said raggedly into her hair. His arms tightened with a convulsive movement that told her more than words just how much he'd missed her.

She couldn't fathom what he wanted. He said he'd found a wife. He informed her he left for France. Yet he held her so close and so tenderly, as if he never meant to let her go.

She hooked her fingers in his shirt and leaned her head on his shoulder. His arms firmed, keeping her safe.

Foolish illusion.

Some thread of reason insisted she stand up, be brave, send him away. He wasn't for her. He'd never be for her. He must return to his bride. Then perhaps she had a chance of gleaning some contentment from the dank, colorless years ahead.

He must go.

But not yet. Dear God, not yet.

Hard to believe he belonged to someone else. The bond that had united them during those long passionate nights in York Street seemed as strong as ever. Stronger now that it had been tested in separation and anguish.

She might be the world's greatest fool but she believed he still loved her.

Even if that was true, what good would it do? Her price for staying with him hadn't changed. Although it would break her heart anew to spurn him a second time.

He raised his head and looked at her with a gleam in his eyes. "You smell like strawberries."

"I've been making jam."

"Ah." He tilted her chin up. "Let me see."

Her heart kicked into a gallop and she waited in trembling anticipation for what surely must come next. A better woman than she would tell him she didn't want his kisses. But she'd missed him so much. What could one kiss matter? Surely fate owed her just that small measure of joy before it flung her into frozen misery once more.

Slowly, giving her time to deny him, his head lowered. The gray eyes were radiant, his lips parted on a soft breath. When he gently pressed his mouth to hers, the heavenly sweetness made her melt.

Softly, he tasted her. A honeyed flick of his tongue. The lingering touch of his lips. A kiss unlike any he'd given her before. Almost . . . *innocent.*

Too soon he lifted his head. Trembling in a fever of unwilling need, she waited for him to return, to push sweetness
to passion. He'd enlisted passion before to convince her to
stay with him.

"Mmm, delicious." His lips curved into a smile that held
the same gentleness as the kiss. Her wayward heart paused
in its headlong race, dipped and skittered to a stop.

"Julian . . . " she whispered in a choked voice.

She struggled to remember his engagement, but he was
here and the woman, whoever she might be, was shadowy
and indistinct. Closing her eyes, she fought back a surge of
tears.

As if he realized how close she was to breaking, he
wrapped his arms around her again and pressed her face
into his chest. Her heart began to beat in time with his. She
still tasted his fleeting kiss, headier than any wine, on her
lips. For so long she'd yearned for his touch. Now she rested
in his arms and let the stolen minutes tick by.

"I brought you a present," he said eventually. His voice
sounded grave, the way it had when he told her he loved
her.

Bitter disappointment surged up, slicing through her brief
ease. Did he mean to bribe her, as he'd once tried to bribe her
with rubies? "More jewelry?"

"No. But I'll buy you every diamond in London if you
want me to."

"I don't."

She knew what she wanted. It wasn't the glittering baubles
she'd flaunted as badges of triumph over a despised sex.

"I'll still buy you every diamond in London," he murmured, nuzzling her ear. A thrill ran through her and she
shivered even as she tried to stifle the response.

"I'll throw them away," she said hoarsely.

He angled his head so he could see her face. "Reach into
my inside pocket and take out the paper."

"If it's the title to a house, I don't want that either."

A glint of amusement lit his eyes. "That's a relief. It's not the title to a house."

Nobody else teased her. Why did she have to fall in love with the one man in Creation who did? "Julian Southwood, you're the most annoying man I've ever met," she said grumpily.

"Undoubtedly," he said with another of those odd little grunts of laughter. "Inside pocket, Olivia."

She slid her hand under his coat and fiddled until paper rustled under her fingers. She felt his breath catch then accelerate as she touched him through his shirt.

Her fingers closed around the document. Slowly, taunting him with her lingering touch, she drew it out.

"What is it?"

He stared down at her with an intent and unfamiliar light in his eyes.

She'd mocked him when she said he was too old for boyish charm, but right now he seemed young, unsure. *Shy.* A word she'd never thought to connect with the urbane Earl of Erith.

His eyes shone with a tenderness that sliced right to her aching heart. His expressive mouth was soft and hovered on the brink of one of his marvelous smiles. She caught herself from leaning forward to kiss him, although everything in her ached for the taste of his lips.

He tilted his head toward the paper. "Well, read it."

Reluctantly, she unfolded the document. He obviously made some extravagant gesture to compensate for his forthcoming marriage, or to convince her to return as his mistress.

The day faded but the late summer twilight offered enough light for her to decipher the spidery writing that covered the sheet.

Even so, she had to read it three times before she realized what she held in her shaking hands.

When she looked up at him in shock, his embrace tightened as if he were afraid she'd flee now she knew why he was here.

"It's a special license," she said blankly.

"Yes." The blaze in his eyes almost blinded her. Or perhaps the helpless tears that dimmed her vision made it hard to see.

His Adam's apple bobbed as he swallowed. With a pang, she realized this supremely confident man was nervous about her response. The thought was wrenchingly touching.

And lent her a calm certainty she'd never before experienced.

She reached out and stroked his lean cheek. "Ask me, Julian," she whispered.

He cleared his throat once. Again.

But his voice when it emerged was deep and sure and full of truth. "Beautiful, clever, wise, wonderful Olivia, love of my heart, will you marry me?"

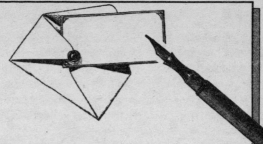

Dearest Reader,

You are in for a treat!

In the coming months we'll read about two sexy devils, one wicked Scotsman, and a little black gown in these four irresistible Avon Romances—all sweeping, sensuous historical romances by four bestselling authors at the top of their game.

Turn the pages
for a sneak peek and be the first
to fall in love with
Avon Books's latest and greatest!

Coming January 2009

Tempt the Devil

Anna Campbell

Olivia Raines has ruled London's demimonde with an iron will and a fiery spirit. Sought after by London's most eligible men, she has never had cause to question her power until she meets the notorious Julian Southwood, Earl of Erith. From the moment he first saw her, Julian knew he must possess her. So when he discovers a secret that could destroy her livelihood, Olivia has no choice than to bargain with the devil.

London
April 1826

Across the packed, noisy salon, Julian Southwood, Earl of Erith, studied the notorious strumpet who would become his next mistress.

He was in the middle of Mayfair on a fine spring afternoon. Yet the reek of sex for sale was as pungent as in the slave markets of Marrakesh or Constantinople.

The crowd was mostly male, although a few provocatively dressed women mingled in the throng. Nobody paid them the slightest attention. Just as nobody but Erith seemed to notice the startling and realistically detailed frescoes of rampant Zeus seizing swooning Ganymede.

From a corner dais a pianist and violinist doggedly plowed through a Mozart sonata. The music came from a different world, a cleaner, purer world untainted by animal carnality.

A world the Earl of Erith would never again inhabit.

Erith shook off the bleak self-reflection and turned to the man beside him. "Introduce me, Carrington."

"Shall do, old chap."

Carrington didn't ask the object of Erith's interest. Why would he? Every man here, including his companion, focused on the slender woman reclining with studied nonchalance upon the chaise longue.

Without being told, Erith knew she'd deliberately chosen her setting in front of the tall west-facing windows. Late afternoon sun flooded her in soft gold and played across her loosely bound tumble of tawny hair. In the clear light, her vivid red dress was like a sudden flame. The effect was worthy of the Theatre Royal.

Even he, familiar to ennui with courtesans' tricks, had felt the breath catch in his throat at first sight of her. One glance and the blood in his veins hummed a deep, dark song of desire, and his skin prickled with the compulsion to make her his.

And she achieved this remarkable effect from half a room away.

Of course, this was no ordinary courtesan.

If she were, he wouldn't be here. The Earl of Erith only bought the best. The best tailoring. The best horses. The best women.

Even by his exacting standards, this particular cyprian was a prime article.

Two extraordinary women had set London on its

ear in the last ten years. One, Soraya, cool, dark, mysterious as moonlight, had recently married the Duke of Kylemore, igniting the scandal of the decade. The other, radiant sun to Soraya's moon, arrayed herself now before Erith like a spectacular jewel.

He assessed her as closely as he'd contemplate an addition to his stables.

Lord, but she was a long Meg. A sheath of crimson velvet displayed her lean body to dramatic advantage. She'd fit his tall frame to perfection, even if his taste usually ran to plumper, more voluptuous bedmates. His memory filled pleasantly with the fleshy blond charms of Gretchen, the mistress he'd left in Vienna a month ago.

Gretchen couldn't contrast more strongly with the jade before him. Where the Tyrolean beauty offered soft, yielding curves, this woman was all spare elegance. The bosom under her gown's low neckline wasn't generous, and her waist was long and supple. He guessed the narrow skirt hid legs as graceful and elongated as a thoroughbred's.

Gretchen had been dewy with youth. This woman must verge on thirty. By that age, most bits of muslin frayed at the edges. But this bird of paradise continued her unchallenged reign over the male half of the ton. Her longevity as the most sought-after courtesan in London made her yet more intriguing.

His gaze slid up to her face. Like her body, it was unexpected. After the rhapsodies he'd heard in the clubs, he'd imagined less subtle attractions. The unmistakable greed he'd heard in her admirers' voices had led him to imagine a brassier, more overtly available bawd.

Her jaw was square, almost masculine. Her nose was a trifle too long, her cheekbones too high. From where he stood in the gilt-framed doorway, it was impossible to tell the color of her eyes, but they were large and brilliant and set at a slant.

Cat's eyes. Tiger's eyes.

Her mouth . . .

Her mouth perhaps explained what he'd heard about her preternatural allure. It might be too large. But who would complain? No man could look at those succulent lips without wanting them on his body. Erith's groin tightened at the decadent pictures rocketing through his mind.

Undoubtedly, she had . . . *something.*

She wasn't a great beauty. She was well past first youth. Nor did she flaunt her charms like tawdry trinkets on a fairground stall. If he'd encountered her at a respectable gathering rather than this louche brouhaha, he'd almost believe she belonged to his own class.

Almost.

After the hubbub, all this was surprising. Disappointing.

But even as he dismissed the wench's heralded charms, his eyes gravitated back to that spare, strangely aristocratic face. To that sin of a mouth. To that luxuriant hair. To that long, graceful body curved in complete relaxation upon her couch while men eddied around her in an endless whirlpool of fascination.

She was the most powerful figure in the room. Even at the distance, he felt the sexual energy sizzling around her.

She swept the room with a contemptuous glance. The raised angle of her chin and the irony that teased the corners of her mouth indicated defiance, courage, challenge.

He tried to deny the sensual pull she exerted. While

his reckless heart kicked into the emphatic rhythm of a drum beating an army into battle.

No, she wasn't what he'd expected, but he didn't fool himself into believing she was anything less than quality.

She lifted her head and smiled at something the effete fellow standing at her elbow said. The lazy curve of those lush red lips shot another jolt of lava-hot arousal through Erith. That smile spoke of knowledge and sharp intelligence, and a sexual confidence he'd never encountered in a woman. Never, even though he'd dealt with the fallen sisterhood for the last sixteen years. Every drop of moisture dried from his mouth, and his interest, wearied through playing this game too long, engaged with an intensity that astonished him. The covetous buzz in his blood notched up a degree.

Oh, yes, she was going to be his.

Not just because she was the elite of London's courtesans and his prestige would accept nothing less as his *chère amie*. But because he wanted her.

More than he'd wanted anything in a long, long time.

Devil of the Highlands

Lynsay Sands

*They call him the Devil, the most notorious laird in all of
Scotland. But Cullen, the new Laird of Donnachaidh, pays
them no heed. He cares only about the survival of his clan,
and for that, he needs a wife. He wants someone stout to bear
him sons. He wants a pliable woman who wouldn't question
his dictates. He wants a passionate woman to warm his bed.
Then he meets Evelinde . . . one out of three isna bad.*

Cullen was the first to see her. The sight made him rein
in so sharply, his horse reared in response. He tightened his thighs around his mount to help keep his seat,
moving automatically to calm the animal, but he didn't
take his eyes off the woman in the glen.

"God's teeth. What is she doing?" Fergus asked as
he halted beside him.

Cullen didn't even glance to the tall, burly redhead
who was his first. He merely shook his head silently,
transfixed by the sight. The woman was riding back
and forth across the clearing, sending her horse charg-
ing first one way, then the other and back. That in itself
was odd, but what had put the hush in Fergus's voice
and completely captured Cullen's tongue was the fact

she was doing so in nothing but a transparent chemise while holding the reins of her mount in her teeth. Her hands were otherwise occupied. They were upraised and holding what appeared to be a cape in the air so it billowed out behind her above her streams of golden hair as she rode back and forth . . . back and forth . . . back and forth.

"Who do you think she is?" Rory's question was the only way Cullen knew the other men had caught up as well.

"I doona ken, but I could watch the lass all day," Tavis said, his voice sounding hungry. "Though there are other things I'd rather be doing to her all day."

Cullen found himself irritated by that remark. Tavis was his cousin and the charmer among his men; fair-haired, handsome, and with a winning smile, it took little effort for him to woo women to his bed of a night. And the man took full advantage of the ability, charming his way under women's skirts at every opportunity. Were titles awarded by such an ability, Tavis would have been the king of Scotland.

"I'd first be wanting to ken why she's doing what she is," Fergus said slowly. "I've no desire to bed a wench who isna right in the head."

"It isna her head I'd be taking to me bed." Tavis laughed.

"Aye," Gillie said, his voice sounding almost dreamy.

Cullen turned a hard glare on his men. "Ride on. I'll catch up to ye."

There was a moment of silence as eyebrows rose and glances were exchanged, then all five men took up their reins.

"Ride around the meadow," Cullen instructed, when they started to move forward.

There was another exchange of glances, but the men followed the tree line around the meadow.

Cullen waited until they had disappeared from sight, then turned back to the woman. His eyes followed her back and forth several times before he urged his mount forward.

It hadn't appeared so from the edge of the meadow, but the woman was actually moving at high speed on her beast, slowing only to make the turn before spurring her horse into a dead run toward the other side. The mare didn't seem to mind. If anything, the animal seemed to think it was some sort of game and threw herself into each run with an impressive burst of speed.

Cullen rode up beside the mare, but the woman didn't immediately notice him. Her attention was shifting between the path ahead and the cloth in her upraised hands. When she finally did glimpse him out of the corner of her eye, he wasn't at all prepared for her reaction.

The lass's eyes widened, and her head jerked back with a start, unintentionally yanking on the reins she clenched in her teeth. The mare suddenly jerked to a halt and reared. The lass immediately dropped her hands to grab for the reins and the cloth she'd been holding swung around and slapped—heavy and wet— across Cullen's face. It both stung and briefly blinded him, making him jerk on his own reins in surprise, and suddenly his own mount was turning away and rearing as well.

Cullen found himself tumbling to the ground, tangled in a length of wet cloth that did nothing to cushion his landing. Pain slammed through his back, knocking the wind out of him, but it positively exploded through his head, a jagged blade of agony that actually made him briefly lose consciousness.

A tugging sensation woke him. Blinking his eyes open, he thought for one moment the blow to his head had blinded him, but then felt another tug and realized there was something over his face. The damp cloth, he recalled with relief. He wasn't blind. At least, he didn't think he was. He wouldn't know for sure until he got the cloth off.

Another tug came, but this was accompanied by a grunt and a good deal more strength. Enough that his head was actually jerked off the ground, bending his neck at an uncomfortable angle. Afraid that, at this rate, he'd end up with a broken neck *after* the fall, Cullen decided he'd best help with the effort to untangle himself from the cloth and lifted his hands toward his head, intending to grab for the clinging material. However, it seemed his tormentor was leaning over him, because he found himself grabbing at something else entirely. Two somethings . . . that were covered with a soft, damp cloth, were roundish in shape, soft yet firm at the same time, and had little pebble-like bumps in the center, he discovered, his fingers shifting about blindly. Absorbed as he was in sorting out all these details, he didn't at first hear the horrified gasps that were coming from beyond the cloth over his head.

"Sorry," Cullen muttered as he realized he was groping a woman's breasts. Forcing his hands away, he shifted them to the cloth on his head and immediately began tugging recklessly at the stuff, eager to get it off.

"Hold! Wait, sir, you will rip—" The warning ended on a groan as a rending sound cut through the air.

Cullen paused briefly, but then continued to tug at the material, this time without apologizing. He'd never been one to enjoy enclosed spaces and felt like he would surely smother to death if he did not get it off at once.

"Let me—I can—If you would just—"

The words barely registered with Cullen. They sounded like nothing more than witless chirping. He ignored them and continued battling the cloth, until—with another tearing sound—it fell away, and he could breathe again. Cullen closed his eyes and sucked in a deep breath with relief.

"Oh dear."

That soft, barely breathed moan made his eyes open and slip to the woman kneeling beside him. She was shifting the cloth through her hands, examining the damaged material with wide, dismayed eyes.

Cullen debated offering yet another apology, but he'd already given one, and it was more than he normally offered in a year. Before he'd made up his mind, the blonde from the horse stopped examining the cloth and turned alarmed eyes his way.

"You are bleeding!"

"What?" he asked with surprise.

"There is blood on my gown. You must have cut your head when you fell," she explained, leaning over him to examine his scalp. The position put her upper body inches above his face, and Cullen started getting that closed-in feeling again until he was distracted by the breasts jiggling before his eyes.

The chemise she wore was very thin and presently wet, he noted, which was no doubt what made it transparent. Cullen found himself staring at the beautiful, round orbs with fascination, shifting his eyes left and right and continuing to do so when she turned his head from side to side to search out the source of the blood.

Apparently finding no injury that could have blood-ied her gown, she muttered, "It must be the back of your head," and suddenly lifted his head, pulling it up off the ground, presumably so she could examine the back of his skull. At least that was what he thought she must be doing when he found his face buried in those breasts he'd been watching with such interest.

"Aye, 'tis here. You must have hit your head on a rock or something when you fell," she announced with a combination of success and worry.

Cullen merely sighed and nuzzled into the breasts presently cuddling him. Really, damp though they were, they were quite lovely, and if a man had to be smothered to death, this was not a bad way to go. He felt something hard nudging his right cheek beside his mouth and realized her nipples had grown hard. She also suddenly stilled like prey sensing danger. Not wishing to send her running with fear, he opened his mouth and tried to turn his head to speak a word or two of reassurance to calm her.

"Calm yerself," was what he said. Cullen didn't be-lieve in wasting words. However, it was doubtful if she understood what he said since his words came out muffled by the nipple suddenly filling his open mouth. Despite his intentions not to scare her, when he real-ized it was a nipple in his mouth, he couldn't resist closing his lips around it and flicking his tongue over the linen-covered bud.

In the next moment, he found pain shooting through his head once more as he was dropped back to the ground.

Coming March 2009

Bride of a Wicked Scotsman

Samantha James

The Earl of McDonough is determined to reclaim, at any cost, the Circle of Light, which the Druids many centuries ago declared would keep the Clan McDonough prosperous, so long as they were the guardians of the mystical silver bands. But the Circle was stolen, and the Clan began to wither, and no one knew the identity of the thief or his descendants until now. For in Lady Maura O'Donnell lies the key to the clan's salvation . . . and to McDonough's heart.

Alec watched as she downed the remainder of her wine. "Why have I not seen you before today? Are you a guest of the baron's?" Lord above, he'd have remembered those emerald eyes. He'd never seen such brilliant green . . . as green as the landscape of this rocky isle.

"Only for tonight."

"Then perhaps introductions are in order." He wanted to know who she was, by God. "I am—"

"Wait!" She held up a hand. "No, no! Do not say. This is a masquerade, is it not? A night to disguise our true selves. What say we dispense with names?" That tiny smile evolved into seduction itself.

Alec laughed. She was sheer delight. And an accomplished flirt. "As you wish, Irish."

"That *is* my wish, Scotsman."

Alec settled down to enjoy the thrust-and-parry. "May I get you something? A plate perhaps? The desserts are quite exquisite." God help him, the dessert he had in mind was *her*.

"I am quite satisfied just as I am."

He was not, thought Alec with unabashed lust. "Well, then, Irish, perhaps you would care to dance?"

Alec didn't. But manners dictate he ask. Beneath her eye mask, her cheekbones were high, the line of her jaw daintily carved. He longed to tear it away, to see the whole of her face, to appreciate every last feature.

Their eyes met. Alec moved so that their sleeves touched. Her smell drifted to his nostrils. Warm, sweet flesh and the merest hint of perfume.

He wanted her. He was not a rogue. Not a man for whom lust struck quickly and blindly. He was not a man to trespass where he should not. He was discreet in his relationships. He was not a man to take a tumble simply for the sake of slaking passion.

Never had he experienced a wash of such passion so quickly. He'd wanted women before, but not like this. Never like this. Never had Alec desired a woman the way he desired this one. What he felt was immediate. Intoxicating. A little overwhelming, even. Not that he shouldn't desire her. She was, after all, a woman who would turn any man's eye. It was simply that the strength of his desire caught him by surprise.

Perhaps it was this masquerade. Her suggestion that they remain anonymous.

He cupped his palm beneath her elbow. "There are too many people. The air grows stale. Shall we walk?"

Laughing green eyes turned up to his. "I thought you should never ask."

A stone terrace ran the length of the house. They passed a few other couples, strolling arm in arm. All at once, she stumbled. Quite deliberately, Alec knew. Not that he was disinclined to play the rescuer.

He caught her by the waist and brought her around to face him. "Careful, Irish."

"Thank you, Scotsman." She gazed up at him, her fingertips poised on his chest, moist lips raised to his.

Alec's gut tightened. She was so tempting. Too tempting to resist. Too tempting to even *try*.

A smile played about his lips. Behind her mask, invitation glimmered in her eyes. "Is it a kiss you're wanting, Irish?" He knew very well that she did.

"Are you asking permission, Scotsman?"

The smoldering inside him deepened. "No, but I have a confession to make." He lowered his head so that their lips almost touched. "I've never kissed an Irish lass before."

"And I've never kissed a Scotsman before."

"So once again it seems we are evenly matched, are we not?"

"Mmmm . . ."

Alec could stand no more. That was as far as she got. His mouth trapped hers. He felt a jolt go through her the instant their lips touched. It was the same for him, and he knew then just how much she returned his passion. His mouth opened over hers. He'd wanted women before. But not like he wanted this one. It was as if she'd cast a spell over him.

And he kissed her the way he'd desired all evening,

with a heady thoroughness, delving into the far corners of her mouth with the heat of his tongue. Tasting the promise inside her. Harder, until he was almost mindless with need.

She tore her mouth away. She was panting softly. "Scotsman!" she whispered.

Alec's eyes opened. His breathing was labored. It took a moment for him to focus, for her words to penetrate his consciousness.

"I . . . what if we should be seen?"

So his Irish lady-pirate was willing—and he was quite wanting. Oh yes, definitely wanting.

"I agree, Irish. I quite agree." He tugged at her hand and started to lead her toward the next set of double doors.

"Where are you taking me?"

He stopped short. "What! I thought you knew, Irish."

"Tell me."

He slid his hand beneath her hair and turned her face up to his. "Why, I'm about to kidnap you, Irish." He smiled against her lips. "I fear it is the pirate in me."

Coming April 2009

Confessions of a Little Black Gown

Elizabeth Boyle

When Thalia Langley spies a handsome stranger in the shadows of her brother-in-law's study, she knows in an instant she's found the dangerous, rakish sort of man she's always dreamt of. But Tally suspects there is more to Lord Larken than meets the eye, and she has the perfect weapon to help tempt the truth from him: a little black gown she's found mysteriously in a trunk.

"Oh, Thatcher, there you are," Tally said, coming to a stop in the middle of her brother-in-law's study, having not even bothered to knock. She supposed if he were any other duke, not the man who'd once been their footman, she'd have to view him as the toplofty and unapproachable Duke of Hollindrake as everyone else did.

Thankfully, Thatcher never expected *her* to stand on formality.

"One of the maids said she saw a carriage arrive, some wretchedly poor contraption that couldn't be one of Felicity's guests and I thought it might be my missing . . ."

Her voice trailed off as Brutus came trotting up behind her, having stopped on the way down the stairs to give a footman's boot a bit of a chew. Her ever-present companion had paused for only a second before he let out a little growl, then launched himself toward a spot in a shadowed corner, as if he'd spied a rat.

No, make that a very ill-looking pair of boots.

Oh, dear! She didn't know Thatcher had company. She tamped down the blush that started to rise on her cheeks, remembering that she'd just insulted this unknown visitor's carriage.

Oh, dash it all! What had she called it?

Some wretchedly poor contraption . . .

Tally shot a glance at Thatcher, who nodded toward the shadows, even as a man rose up from the chair, coming to life like one of the Greek sculptures Lord Hamilton had been forever collecting in Naples.

Yet this one lived and breathed.

Thatcher's study was a dark room, sitting on the northeast side of the house, and with the sun now on the far side, the room was all but dark, except for the slanting bit of light coming in from the narrow casement. But darkness aside, Tally didn't really need to see the man, whose boot Brutus had attached himself to, to *know* him.

A shiver ran down her spine, like a forebear of something momentous. She couldn't breath, she couldn't move, and she knew, just knew, her entire life was about to change.

It made no sense, but then again, Tally had never put much stock in sense, common or otherwise.

Perhaps it was because her heart thudded to a halt just by the way he stood, so tall and erect, even with a devilish little affenpinscher affixed to his boot.

Heavens! With Brutus thus, how could this man ever move forward?

"Oh, dear! Brutus, you rag-mannered mutt, come away from there," she said, pasting her best smile on her face and wishing that she wasn't wearing one of Felicity's old hand-me-down gowns. And blast Felicity's tiresome meddling, for if she'd just left well enough alone and not insisted the trunks be changed around, her own trunk wouldn't have become lost.

"You wretched little dog, are you listening to me? Come here!" She snapped her fingers, and after one last, great growling chew, Brutus let go of his prize and returned to his usual place, at the hem of her gown, his black eyes fixed on the man, or rather his boots, as if waiting for any sign that he could return for another good bite.

"I am so sorry, sir," Tally began. "I fear his manners are terrible, but I assure you his pedigree is impeccable. His grandsire belonged to Marie Antoinette." She snapped her lips shut even as she realized she was rambling like a fool. Going on about Brutus's royal connections like the worst sort of pandering mushroom.

"No offense taken, miss," he said.

Oh, yes. His simple apology swept over her in rich, masculine tones.

Then to her delight, he came closer, moving toward Thatcher's desk with a cat-like grace, making her think of the men she'd imagined in her plays: prowling pirates and secretive spies. It was almost as if he was used to moving through shadows, aloof and confident in his own power.

Tally tamped down another shiver and leaned over to pick up Brutus, holding him tightly as if he could be the anchor she suddenly felt she needed.

Whatever was it about this man that had her feeling as if she were about to be swept away? That he was capable of catching her up in his arms and stealing her away to some secluded room where he'd lock them both away? Then he'd toss her atop the bed and he'd strip away his jacket, his shirt, his . . .

Tally gulped back her shock.

What the devil is wrong with me? She hadn't even seen the man yet, and here she was imagining him nearly in his altogether.

Oh, dear heavens, she prayed silently, *please say he is here for the house party. Please . . .*

"I daresay we have met," she continued on, trying to lure him forward, force him to speak again, "but you'll have to excuse me, I'm a terrible widgeon when it comes to remembering names."

The man stepped closer, but stopped his progress when the door opened and Staines arrived, a brace of candles in hand, and making a *tsk, tsk* sound over the lack of light in the room. The butler shot the duke a withering glance that seemed to say, *You are supposed to ring for more light.*

Poor Thatcher, Tally thought. He still had yet to find his footing as the Duke of Hollindrake and all that it entailed.

"Have we met?" she asked, and to further her cause, she shifted Brutus to one hip and stuck out her hand, which must compel the man, if he was a gentleman, to take it.

"No, I don't believe we have ever met, Miss—"

Oh, heavens, his voice was as smooth as the French brandy she and Felicity used to steal from their teacher's wine cabinet. And it would be even better if he were whispering into her ear.

Tally, my love, what is it you desire most . . . ?

Oh, now you are being a complete widgeon, she chided herself, closing her eyes, for she couldn't believe she was having such thoughts over a perfect stranger. A man she'd never seen. She only hoped this ridiculous tumult he was causing on her insides wasn't showing on her face.

Taking a deep breath, she unshuttered her lashes and, much to her horror, found herself staring at a complete stranger.

Certainly not the man she'd imagined.

Whoever was this ordinary, rather dowdy-looking fellow blinking owlishly at her from behind a pair of dirty spectacles, his shoulders stooped over as if he'd carried the burden of the world upon them?

Where had he come from? She leaned over to peer past him, searching for any sign of the man she'd expected, but there was no one there.

Tally swayed a bit. Heavens, she was seeing things. If she didn't know better, she'd say she was as jug-bitten as their London housekeeper, Mrs. Hutchinson.

But no, all the evidence was before her, for instead of some rakish character in a Weston jacket and perfectly polished boots, stood a gentleman (well, she hoped he was at least a gentleman) in a coat that could best be described as lumpy, cut of some poorly dyed wool, with sleeves too short for his arms. Far too short, for his cuffs stuck out a good six inches. Then to her horror, she glanced at his cravat, or rather where his cravat should be.

For in its place sat a vicar's collar.

A vicar?